Praise for the Brie H

D1087050

"*Picked Off*, the second entry in th⸱⸱⸱ ⸱⸱⸱⸱⸱⸱⸱⸱ ⸱s a delightful mystery filled with ⸱ ⸱⸱⸱⸱ ⸱⸱ memorable and fun characters."

— Robin Burcell,
New York Times Bestselling Author of *The Gray Ghost*

"A ripe, juicy mystery just waiting to be devoured...If you're looking for a fresh cozy, this one's worth a gander."

— Diane Vallere,
National Bestselling Author of the Madison Night Mystery Series

"There's such a lot to enjoy in Linda Lovely's third Brie Hooker mystery...And what kept me flicking the pages fast enough to cause a draft? The twisty, knotty, killer plot underneath all that charm."

— Catriona McPherson,
Multi-Award-Winning Author of the Last Ditch Mysteries.

"A fringe religious cult, a Supreme Court nominee, and goat yoga combine together in a tale mystery fans won't want to miss."

— Sherry Harris,
Agatha Award Nominee and Author of the Garage Sale mysteries.

"Lovely offers up a charming setting that's so real you can almost smell the hay, a story that's laugh-out-loud funny, and a mystery that will keep you up past your bedtime."

— Annette Dashofy,
USA Today Bestselling Author of the Zoe Chambers Mysteries

"Packed with suspense and action and some spicy romance...I ate up every morsel."

— Dorothy St. James,
Author of the Southern Chocolate Shop Mysteries

"This book is a thrill-a-minute read."

– Cindy Sample,
National Bestselling Author of *Dying for a Donut*

"How vegan Brie Hooker balances cheese loving carnivores, more than one romantic interest, and murder in Linda Lovely's *Bones to Pick* is a humorous delight. A well-crafted series debut."

– Debra H. Goldstein,
Award-Winning Author of *One Taste Too Many*

"You'll find yourself muttering, 'What the feta?' as you follow the action around not one but two murders from the edge of your seat."

– Edith Maxwell,
Author of the Local Foods Mysteries

"An entertaining mystery with a cast of colorful characters, a delightful Southern setting, and plenty of action."

– Wendy Tyson,
Author of *Rooted in Deceit*

"An injured football player, a kidnapping, and a murder investigation. Is there anything Brie Hooker can't handle? *Picked Off* is Linda Lovely's best book yet. Pick it up!"

– Cindy Blackburn,
Author of The Cue Ball Mystery Series

"This twisty fun read is packed full of high suspense and high jinx. Add in a delightful cast of critters and characters and you have a not-to-miss whodunit!"

– Sparkle Abbey,
National Bestselling Author of *Barking with the Stars*

"Udderly charming! Hunky heroes and a spunky heroine will sweep you off your feet in this adorable cozy."

– Larissa Reinhart,
Wall Street Journal Bestselling Author of the Cherry Tucker Series

BAD PICK

The Brie Hooker Mystery Series
by Linda Lovely

BONES TO PICK (#1)
PICKED OFF (#2)
BAD PICK (#3)

BAD PICK

A BRIE HOOKER MYSTERY

LINDA LOVELY

HENERY PRESS

Copyright

BAD PICK
A Brie Hooker Mystery
Part of the Henery Press Mystery Collection

First Edition | April 2019

Henery Press, LLC
www.henerypress.com

Trade Paperback ISBN-13: 978-1-63511-471-3
Digital epub ISBN-13: 978-1-63511-472-0
Kindle ISBN-13: 978-1-63511-473-7
Hardcover ISBN-13: 978-1-63511-474-4

Printed in the United States of America

For Stew and Myrt Hooker
Wish you were here to meet the Ardon County Hookers

ACKNOWLEDGMENTS

Special thanks to subject experts Dr. Denene Lofland and retired Chief G. Robert Campbell. Dr. Lofland's areas of expertise include medical microbiology, bioterrorism, and new drug discovery and development. After I explained what I wanted to happen to a victim, her only question was how quickly I wanted it to happen. From his decades of firefighting experience, Chief Campbell offered insights into the behavior of fires and potential firefighting considerations. Any mistakes in interpreting and using their information are mine alone.

Grateful shout outs are due the Henery Press editorial team, including Maria Edwards and Sarah Billman, who helped improve my manuscript. I also owe thanks to Rowe Carenen of The Book Concierge for her efforts to help Brie Hooker Mysteries reach new audiences. Continuing thanks to Kay Kirkley Barrett, Esq., former City of Clemson Attorney/Prosecutor, who offered background into how my character Iris Hooker, Esq., might spend her workdays.

Major thanks to my long-term critique partners—Donna Campbell, Danielle Dahl, Howard Lewis, and Robin Weaver—for their top-notch suggestions, support, and friendship. I'm grateful, too, for valuable input from Beta readers Cindy Sample, Fara Driver, and Dee Anna Brown.

As always my husband and best friend, Tom Hooker, provided spot-on feedback on early drafts and helped talk me through plot dilemmas. For this series, Tom even lent his surname to the main character, Brie Hooker. I've dedicated this book to Tom's parents. His folks made me feel welcome the moment we met. I wish they could have lived longer so we could have enjoyed their love and laughter for many more years.

ONE

"How many people did you con into trying this goat yoga?" Aunt Eva asked as she slapped two strips of cold bacon in a skillet.

"No conning needed," I answered. "Everyone's looking forward to the class."

"You sure goat yoga's a good idea?"

I laughed. "I'm sure. People love it. Admittedly, a sense of humor's required, but it's caught on all across the country. Why don't you join the fun? Class starts at three. We don't have many Sunday customers this time of year. We'll probably have the farm to ourselves by then. You up for some downward-facing dog?"

"No." Eva harrumphed. "Don't go insulting our noble dogs. Bad enough you'll expose our baby goats to human pretzels. It's bound to confuse the poor kids. Won't know which human end is supposed to be up. They'll think all us two-legged beings are bonkers. So who's coming?"

"Jayla, our yoga instructor, wanted to limit the trial class to four students so it's just Mollye, Fara, Mimi, and me."

I pulled out a bag of frozen blueberries I'd picked at the Happy Berry Farm last summer. While Udderly Kidding Dairy, my home for the past seven months, boasted dozens of blueberry bushes, our four-hundred goats called first dibs on the fruit.

"Oh, and Paint's shooting video to promote the class," I added.

Aunt Eva chuckled as she flipped her sizzling bacon strips. "Not a hardship for Paint, videoing young ladies in nothing but skivvies and tutus."

I glanced heavenward. "We don't wear tutus. Our workout clothes show less skin than you do on the Fourth of July."

Eva cocked an eyebrow. "Could be you're helping Paint select babes for the weeks he's not your designated beau."

I opened the cupboard and grabbed a microwave packet of steel-cut oatmeal. "Paint sees a variety of ladies when we're not dating, and he knows everyone in this class. No behind-the-camera scouting required."

"Maybe, but as far as I know, he hasn't seen any of them with their ankles up around their ears."

"And he won't today."

"If you say so, but I swear my old bones creak just looking at some of those yoga contortions."

Eva cracked two eggs in the hot bacon grease, while I used our microwave—a new kitchen addition—to thaw my frozen berries and heat the oats. My usual February morning fare. At Udderly, we didn't chow down until the morning chores were done. That meant I was starved and in dire need of a caffeine injection.

Eva glanced over. "So how's that boyfriend-for-a-week plan working? Who's ahead in the Brie Hooker heart throb race? Any close calls on the clothing discard clause?"

I smiled. "Paint and Andy try to outdo each other in dreaming up ways to initiate a striptease. Despite their enterprising efforts, the nude-default clause remains unchallenged."

Last November, I'd agreed to this bizarre boyfriend pact with Andy Green, our veterinarian, and David "Paint" Paynter, an entrepreneurial moonshiner. Though strongly attracted to both thirty-four-year-old hunks, I'd sworn I'd date neither. Didn't want to lose them as friends or come between them. They'd been best buds for thirty years, practically since they left diapers.

The boys came up with an alternative. I'd date Paint one week, Andy the next, until either I selected a fulltime beau, one of them opted out, or a ridiculous nudity clause kicked in. If I disrobed on any date, the magician who assisted in making my clothes disappear would win by default. Both men swore the arrangement would not affect their friendship.

Me? I felt like I'd been locked in a chastity belt. Foreplay's a lot less fun when there's no after.

"You know it can't last, don't you?" Aunt Eva asked, giving voice to my own misgivings.

"Yep, I do. But like today's sunny warmth—way too early for mid-February—I'll enjoy it while I can."

TWO

Jayla Johnson, our tall, willowy teacher waved as she walked toward me. Had to admit Paint would get an eyeful watching her stretch every which way. He was male, and Jayla was a stunner. As a shorty—I'm five four—I'd always envied long-legged ladies like Jayla. Somehow those extra inches made them look cool and sophisticated.

Luckily, Jayla wasn't in the running to join Paint's off-week harem. She was happily married to one of Clemson University's football coaches and had a darling three-year-old son.

"Do we have a plan B?" Jayla glanced up at the Carolina blue sky. "It's really warm for February, but the ground's too muddy to put our mats down in a pasture. After five minutes, we'd look like we'd been mud wrestling."

"Agreed. It'd be a shame to get that outfit muddy." Jayla looked like an Oreo cookie, her ebony skin a sharp contrast to her snowy outfit. "I did warn you baby goats aren't potty-trained, didn't I? Accidents can happen."

"Not to worry." Jayla smiled. "My laundry room has one whole shelf devoted to stain removers for husband-son accidents. So where are we setting up?"

"The horse barn. Plenty of room and it will be easier to keep Curly, Moe, and Larry contained."

"Who?"

"Curly, Moe, and Larry are the baby goats—five-day-old triplets. We named the kids after The Three Stooges. Full of energetic hijinks. They're also super cuddly."

We turned as Mollye Camp's psychedelic van crunched down the gravel drive. Her van's midnight blue paint job served as a backdrop for a galaxy of glittering stars, a super-sized harvest moon, and a broom-riding witch. Moll, my best friend since childhood, was a gifted potter who sold her creations along with an eclectic hodgepodge of homeopathic remedies, herbs, and astrological doodads in her Starry Skies shop.

Moll jangled as she hopped down from her ride. She adored jewelry and had more piercings than a rapper. A vibrant purple streak adorned her white-blonde hair. She chose a new neon hue every month.

Mollye hustled over. "Who we waiting for?"

"Mimi and Fara," I answered. "We're keeping the group small for the test run. Paint's shooting video."

Mollye checked the amount of cleavage revealed by her scoop-necked purple top and inspected the seams of her orange leggings as they meandered south of her shorts. "Glad I didn't wear anything too revealing. Don't want folks thinking I'd participate in some racy video."

Mimi and Fara's arrival cut short Jayla's and my eye rolls. Racy might not be Mollye's middle name, but outrageous could be. I loved Mollye and her adventurous spirit though it sometimes landed me in hot water. Okay, in one case, freezing water.

With rolled mats tucked under their arms, the class newcomers looked like an odd couple. Mimi, who'd emigrated from Vietnam at age two, stood four feet nine on tiptoe, while Fara, a busty blonde with long braids, topped out at five ten. Mimi was a pharmacist; Fara grew up in her family's funeral parlor and was now the town's youngest funeral director.

Hard for this class to be more diverse. Paint would enjoy himself.

"Hey, Fara, you boxing anyone up today?" Mollye joked.

"Maybe you after class," the funeral director quipped. "You want the deluxe mahogany coffin or a pine box? I'm thinking you and Brie have used up eight of your nine lives. Better not exert yourselves today."

Jayla clapped her hands. "Now children. Snarky is not the proper frame of mind for yoga. Think serenity. We want to clear our minds, be one with nature."

I chuckled at the good-natured kidding. "Follow me to our classroom. We have the horse barn to ourselves. The smell alone will remind you we're one with nature. I evicted Rita and Hank. They're grazing in the pasture. Figured Lilly's mule and Eva's horse were more inclined to nicker than meditate."

"Where are the goats in this goat yoga?" Fara asked.

"Eva will bring Curly, Moe, and Larry in after we start. We need to leave the barn door open for the light. Jim, our Border collie, will keep the little goat Houdinis from escaping."

The triplets' antics drove Jim nuts. Yesterday Moe pranced on top of a picnic table for five minutes taunting the poor herd dog. Jim ran circles around the table, barking in protest, unable to figure out how to nudge Moe back to her pen.

After we placed our mats, Jayla led us through a series of simple warm-up stretches and breathing exercises. I'd been an avid runner and swimmer for years, but yoga was a new pursuit. I was pleasantly surprised to find its emphasis on breathing and mindfulness and its practiced movements helped me shed stress and fall asleep faster.

Believe me, falling asleep quickly is a prized skill for anyone required to rise before the sun. At Udderly, one of my jobs appeared to be waking the roosters.

Jayla announced the cat pose. I knelt on my mat and set my arms to provide four-point support. Then I arched my back like cats do when threatened. I lowered my head, giving my neck muscles a pleasant stretch.

"Looking good, ladies." With my head down I heard the man's voice before I saw him.

"Don't mind me," the newcomer continued. "I'm gonna wander around and take photos."

The sexy baritone belonged to Paint. It should be outlawed.

"Have fun, kids—human and goat." Eva laughed as she let the baby goats loose in the barn. Moe immediately darted under my arched back, executed a one-eighty, and raced back again as if she were playing a game of London Bridge.

My concentration faltered as Curly discovered she had easy access to one of my earlobes and began to nibble with her lips. It tickled.

Fara broke out laughing as Larry scrambled up her arched back and danced a little jig on his newly discovered perch.

"I've got a miniature geisha doing a four-footed massage." Fara giggled. "Actually feels kind of good, though very strange."

"No talking," Jayla admonished. "Concentrate on your breathing, your muscles. Be one with nature."

Paint hooted. "Nature's winning."

Paint obviously felt he was exempt from Jayla's no-talking reprimand. The instructor began laughing, too. Moe had curled her body around Jayla's legs as she attempted to hold the Big Toe pose.

We were all bent in half, butts in the air, when a loud voice brayed, "Oh dear God, save us. They are bowing to the devil, mocking the Lord Jesus by thrusting their bottoms at heaven above."

THREE

What the feta?

I snapped around to see who was calling us devil worshippers. Was this a joke?

Flipping out of downward dog, I body slammed the mat. A second after hitting the plastic, a furry comedian bounced against my side. Curly shook her head as she attempted an impressive four-legged hop. She'd taken my tumble to the ground as an invitation to play. The little goat butted my side again.

"Lord Jesus, help us keep these devil worshippers from claiming more souls!" the stranger bellowed.

I was flabbergasted. No other word for it. Then my shock morphed into anger. Who did this woman think she was, calling us devil worshippers? Who invited her to our private workout? How did she even find out about it?

The plump leader held a super-sized wooden cross before her as if she were fending off a clutch of vampires. I figured her for mid-fifties. Gray streaks wound through her mousy brown hair. Light glinting off oversized spectacles lent her the look of an alien with round yellow bug eyes.

Two cross-carrying acolytes hovered about a foot behind her.

Were these people serious? I felt the blood rush to my cheeks. My heartbeat raced. Angry? You betcha.

I almost yelled one of my old-time favorite curses. Years back, I cleaned up my salty language for dear old Mom. As a vegan, processed-meat-and-cheese exclamations had become my exclamatory substitutes. But *Cruddy corndogs!* didn't quite express my outrage.

Mollye, closest to the barn door, marched toward the scowling leader. "Susan, what in blazes do you think you're doing?" she growled. "I got a restraining order to keep you and your looney-tune zealots off my property. Now you're following me?"

"I didn't know you'd be here," the intruder raged, "though I'm not surprised. Goat yoga! What blasphemy. At church this morning, one of our faithful told me you were planning this abomination. I prayed on it, and decided we had to stop the spread of this evil in Ardon County."

She waved her cross at us. "In the name of the Father and the Son we demand—"

"You need to leave," Paint spoke through gritted teeth. "The only evil here is you."

Susan closed her eyes and rocked back and forth on her heels. "You are Satan's handmaidens duping people into believing Baphomet goat worship is fun."

Susan's diatribe was accompanied by a murmur of "Amen, Sister, Amen" from her backups. The sidekicks still wore church-go-to-meeting dresses, nylons, and heels. They kept sneaking peeks at the ground. Worried their high heels might sink in goat doo-doo during their barnyard sortie?

One of the acolytes looked to be Susan's age; the other much younger, about my age.

"Knights Templar worshipped Baphomet as a deity." Susan's tone changed. Her words flowed in a singsong chant. "These monsters with their snake eyes are his descendants."

"Are you nuts?" Jayla broke in. "How can you think these adorable babies are evil?"

Susan's rant hadn't cowed my friends.

The harpy wasn't deterred. "Open your eyes. The Satanic goat is a source of evil." Her yellow bug eyes flashed at each of us in turn. "You worship the Devil. We won't allow your sickness to infect the pious people of Ardon County."

Aunt Eva appeared in the barn door carrying two pails of goat milk. "You're trespassing and you're scaring the baby goats."

My aunt's face flamed red.

"We'll leave," Susan said. "But this isn't over. We will fight to the death for the soul of Ardon County. Goat yoga will not corrupt our world."

Curly made a break for it. The tiny kid ran pell-mell toward the barn door, which happened to be a few feet beyond where the intruding trio stood. Susan screeched. Did she really believe the Devil inhabited the itty-bitty creature?

The woman raised her leg to kick Curly.

Eva flung both buckets of goat milk, drenching Susan. The white liquid plastered her beehive hairdo to her scalp and her puffy blouse to her chest.

Oh my, was she really wearing a flaming red teddy under her prim white cotton?

A laugh bubbled up. I laughed so hard I doubled over.

Susan shrieked like a storm-warning siren and ran. Though only a few drops of goat's milk spattered her companions, they caterwauled like they'd been doused with acid as they scurried after their leader.

The entire Udderly Kidding Dairy crew exploded in laughter.

Eva halted her hee-haws long enough to imitate a cackling witch. "You've been baptized with the milk of Baaa-Phooey. Your souls belong to us!"

Susan spun when she reached a shiny Chevy van. "You'll pay for this!" she yelled. "Laugh all you want. You'll see Hell sooner than you thought."

I quit laughing as abruptly as I'd started. It was Susan's tone not her words that gave me the heebie-jeebies. We'd embarrassed the woman. Humiliated her. Perhaps she'd started this protest as some form of ecclesiastical theater, art for show, a way to rally the troops.

Now it was personal. Susan had been scorned.

FOUR

"Hope you got that?" Eva pointed at Paint's camera.

"Sure did." He chuckled. "Even caught Susan's heaving tatas. They were giving that red corset of hers a heavy-duty stress test."

Eva rolled her eyes. "Let's try to forget Susan's undergarment surprise. Help me round up Curly, Moe, and Larry. Need to get these energetic babies back in their pen."

I grabbed Curly, who was so wound up her squirming limbs seemed to fly in every direction. As I carried her toward the pen, I glanced over my shoulder at the departing Chevy. A black cloud trailed the oil-burning van. Maybe Susan thought catalytic converters were evil, too.

Once all three kids were happily scampering in their grassed enclosure, Paint locked the gate. "Well, ladies," he began, "it's not quite four o'clock but I'm tempted to pass around some of the moonshine stashed in my truck. What the heck just happened?"

"A little early for 'shine," Eva said. "The sun's not over the yardarm. But I bet none of you ladies want to do more handstands so refreshments seem in order. Brie baked a cake, and we have cold apple cider and goat-milk smoothies in the fridge."

Jayla chuckled. "I'm all in for cake. Right now, my main breathing exercise is a sigh of relief that the whackos have split."

Inside our cabin, I took beverage orders while Eva dished out my pumpkin-walnut cake. Once everyone was served, I collapsed in the last empty seat and took a long swallow of cold cider. "Okay, who is this Susan?"

Mollye let out a long sigh. "Three years ago Susan Young belonged to my church, First Baptist of Ardon, which helps support a local homeless shelter. Susan got her hackles up when the shelter held a bingo night to raise funds. Since Susan categorizes bingo as a deadly sin, she demanded

First Baptist quit supporting the shelter. When she was voted down, she led a splinter group to join the Temple of True Believers.

"Then, last year she picketed Starry Skies because I sell wands and do palm and Tarot card readings," Mollye added. "I assured her it was all in fun. Susan predicted I'd have fun roasting in hell for eternity."

Jayla shook her head. "Another True Believer visited my yoga studio. Said I'd abandoned Christianity for yoga and it was her mission to bring me back to God. I told her practicing Hatha yoga and being a Christian weren't mutually exclusive. When I added that I taught Sunday school, my visitor went bonkers. She couldn't believe any church would let a yoga-corrupted instructor teach the Bible to innocent children."

I glanced over at Mimi and Fara. "Have you two had any run-ins?"

Mimi smiled as she picked up Cashew, my teensie Teacup Morkie, who'd been scouting the kitchen floor for cake crumbs acting as if she hadn't eaten in days.

"I've been on the True Believers' suspect list since we moved here," Mimi said as she petted my Oscar-worthy pup. "We were still unpacking when a man who described himself as a deacon dropped by to ask us to church. I told him we were Catholic. He frowned and said, 'Oh, I thought you were Christians.' I had no clue how to respond to his level of ignorance."

Fara hid her face in her hands then peeked between her fingers. I figured she was looking at me though it was hard to tell. Her left eye had a tendency to wander, and I wasn't always sure where her split vision was focused.

"Afraid I'm responsible for today's visit," Fara confessed. "One of our cleaning ladies belongs to the True Believers' congregation. When she dusted my office yesterday, I was on the phone prattling on about goat yoga with Mollye."

Eva got up from the table. "Susan Young and her friends are nut jobs. But I'm afraid I may have tipped her further into crazy by dousing her in goat milk. What was I supposed to do? I couldn't let her hurt Curly."

My aunt frowned. "Think they'll be back? Still want to go ahead with these goat yoga classes?"

Jayla laughed. "I'm game. There's more to yoga than meditation. What the goats provide is important—closeness to nature and unbridled joy. All part of being present in the moment."

Her students nodded their agreement.

"Guess it's decided," I said. "We won't let a few ignoramuses spoil the fun. By the way, who were the other members of Susan's raiding party?"

"The young one is Karen Vincent," Fara answered. "She was a couple years behind me in school. Karen was clerking at a convenience store until she snagged a job as church secretary for the True Believers. Maybe she figures these little excursions are required to keep the gig. The older lady is the mother of another classmate. Why can't I remember her name? The daughter writes that popular food blog."

I swallowed hard. Uh, oh.

Paint laughed. "Forget their names. Don't need 'em to plaster their faces on YouTube. I can make a great promo showing how exciting goat yoga classes can be."

Eva wagged her finger at Paint. "Don't you dare go poking a hornet's nest. This might blow over if we ignore them. Next week Susan will likely uncover some other blasphemy to elevate her blood pressure. If not, we'll follow Mollye's example and get a restraining order."

"Agreed," I said. "Guess the next step is putting together a marketing plan—with no mention of gate crashers. When can we all get together again?"

Everyone whipped out their smart phones to coordinate. The consensus: four p.m. Wednesday. Since it would be a planning session, there'd be no invite for Moe, Curly, and Larry. I fervently hoped the True Believers wouldn't invite themselves.

FIVE

Once Jayla, Mimi, and Fara vacated the property, Moll asked if I'd had any feedback on the website I'd created for Summer Place. I hoped to turn the dilapidated Southern mansion into a B&B and had built the website to create a little early buzz.

I shook my head. "Not on the website. But I did receive two ominous 'beware of Harriett' warnings."

"Warnings?" Paint jumped in. "Beware of who?"

"Someone thinks I should rescind the invitation Harriett Quinn's already accepted to attend my luncheon tasting. If only I could. I almost lost it when Fara ID'd one of our religious protestors as the mother of some food blogger. Had to be Harriett's mother."

Aunt Eva looked puzzled. "Harriett's that farm-to-table blogger with the big following, right? Weren't you hoping she'd spread the word about Summer Place catering?"

I shrugged. "That's why I invited her. I should have read more of the woman's blogs. She knows how to pen some scathing personal attacks."

Mollye nodded. "Harriett can be a real snake-in-the-grass to anyone who rubs her the wrong way."

I sighed. "I saw her glowing review of a new Greenville restaurant and fired off an invite." I winked at Mollye. "Should have consulted with my local know-it-alls first."

"I'd have warned you off," my friend agreed. "But you can't rescind your invitation. Harriett would really have fun with that."

"So what did these online warnings say about Harriett?" Paint asked. "Were they signed? It might help to know who sent them."

"My new online friend set up a fake digital ID in order to call her out as a scum-sucking blackmailer," I replied. "Went to a lot of trouble to warn me that Harriett's extorted several businesses and savaged the reputation of ones that failed to pony up. I imagine my online buddy didn't pay tribute, and Harriett ruined him."

Paint nodded. "Bad publicity can doom a start-up. Might be easy to figure out the sender's identity. Just backtrack through Harriett's blogs and see which businesses went down the tubes after bad reviews."

"If I had the time, I'd do some sleuthing," I answered. "But I don't. Anyway, not sure it matters who tried to warn me. The good news is Harriett won't be alone at my tasting. I'm hoping any bad review she might dish up will be countered by at least two good ones."

My stomach churned. Despite my brave words, I was scared to death. I was about to turn thirty-three. I had an MBA and several years of banking experience. But I'd chucked a promising financial career to become a chef—and, to make my decision riskier, my dream was to be a chef who catered to a minority clientele, vegans and vegetarians.

My career gyrations baffled my parents. Mom and Dad knew exactly what they wanted to do from the day they set foot on a college campus.

What if I couldn't make it as a chef? Please, please this tasting had to be a success. I was really afraid my time was running out.

Paint lingered after Mollye left.

"I'm headed to Charleston," he said. "Things are looking good to expand Magic Moonshine in the Lowcountry. I'm meeting potential investors tonight. Why not postpone your tasting? Make some excuse and come with me? I mean it *is* my boyfriend week, and Charleston is one romantic city."

He trailed a finger down my cheek and brushed his lips against mine. "I'm sure Eva could spare you for a couple of days. Claim a nationwide shortage of fruits and nuts has forced a cancellation. Later you could quietly set up a new tasting and leave Harriett off the guest list."

Looking into his mischievous mocha eyes, I was sorely tempted. "Wish I could, but I can't. Ursula Billings, Mom's best friend from law school, arrives tomorrow. She's coming to Tuesday's tasting. I'm convinced she's the only reason some of my luncheon guests accepted. Everyone's seen Judge Ursula presiding over her television courtroom. Folks want to meet her in the flesh. I need to shop tonight, cook up a storm tomorrow."

Paint's hot breath tickled my ears as he whispered. "We'd have much more fun cooking something up together in Charleston."

"Could be." I eased back to put a smidgeon more space between our lips and give my overwrought hormones a breather.

"I can't blow this chance to prove I have more than a snowball's chance in Hades of operating a profitable vegan-vegetarian B&B. While my family's been super, I sense they're just on stand-by to pick up the pieces when I fail."

"I believe in you." Paint's eyes locked on mine. "I get how you feel. My folks weren't amused when I told 'em I was going to follow in Grandad's moonshiner footsteps. Even promising the business would be legal didn't improve their attitude. I stuck to my guns, and it worked for me. It'll work for you."

I snuggled into Paint's arms and gave him a well-deserved goodbye kiss. "I needed that vote of confidence. Thanks. I'll have some influential gourmands at my tasting. Maybe they're only coming to dine with TV's Judge Ursula. Doesn't mean I can't dazzle them with vegan fare."

"You do have a magic touch," Paint whispered.

"What I need is magic cash. Fingers crossed I get some catering gigs and private dinner parties to boost my cash flow. It'll be another year before I can open Summer Place as a B&B."

Paint cocked his head. "Fried green tomatoes still top my list of gussied-up vegetables, and you're not likely to meet a more dedicated meat-eater. But your cooking's begun to win me over. You'll do great. Impress Judge Ursula and you'll have it made. Her fans say she's never blown a verdict. But she can sound pretty mean when she thinks the defendant's an idiot."

I nodded. "Mom says Ursula's much nicer than the judge she portrays on TV. Mom and Ursula were the only women in their law school class, and they became really close friends. But I sense Mom was a bit disappointed that Ursula left 'real' law for TV land."

Paint arched an eyebrow. "Plenty of men tune in just to lay eyes on Ursula. She could make a young fella seriously consider pursuing an older babe. When that tabloid published photos of her in a bikini, I was among the happy gawkers."

I punched Paint's arm. "Maybe I shouldn't introduce you. After the paparazzi snapped those bikini shots, a men's magazine offered the judge a pile of dough to shed her black robes and pose nude. I'm no prude, but I'm glad she didn't cash in."

Paint grinned. "Glad to know you're not philosophically opposed to nudity."

I gave his arm another gentle punch. "Go on. Get out of here. You have moonshine to sell, and I need to put on my chef's hat."

He glanced at his watch. "Wow. I do have to run. Have orders to fill, and weekend traffic's always heavy coming or going from the coast."

His arms tightened around me, pulling me close for a lingering kiss. My lips tingled as did all other parts of my anatomy that came in touch with his bod.

"Be back Thursday. Since I'm not on your boyfriend schedule for Valentine's Day, maybe we should plan an early celebration."

Paint wiggled his eyebrows suggestively. I couldn't help but laugh.

SIX

Once Paint left, I logged on to Udderly's online store, printed new cheese orders, and created shipping labels. I startled when Eva tapped my shoulder. With the printer whirring, I didn't hear her come up behind me. She grinned. "Just wanted to say goodbye."

It was one of the days my aunt served as counselor at a domestic abuse shelter. Having been a victim herself, she was passionate about helping frightened, battered women.

"Won't be home for supper," she added, "but should be back in time for cake."

"Since it's a vegan recipe, I figured you were just being polite eating a slice this afternoon. I won't force more down your throat. "

Eva, a world-class champion of meat, eggs and butter, issued a deep-throated "grrrr". I wasn't quite sure how a human could sound so much like a cranky motor. The salute she gave me didn't engage all of her fingers. I laughed.

"Love you, too." My wave employed all my digits.

By supper time, I'd caught up on Udderly accounting and was indulging a guilty pleasure—reading a good murder mystery—while I noisily slurped my supper. I'd heated a bowl of my favorite homemade tomato basil soup. My manners took a vacation when I was by my lonesome, a condition I relished now that it was such a rarity. While I loved my aunt, living and working with her 24/7 sometimes wore me out.

Once the soup was all gone—okay, I licked the bowl—I cut myself a slice of cake and started a lengthy grocery list for my luncheon tasting. I'd almost finished when Mollye's ringtone sounded.

"Hey, girlfriend, I've been thinking about our True Believer party crashers."

As usual Mollye rushed into our conversation before I could eke out a hello.

"Remember Karen, the church secretary? Back in high school, we were buddies, sat side-by-side in homeroom. Maybe if we had a heart-to-heart Karen could intercede. She didn't look like she was really into the protest. Maybe she could steer Susan toward a different missionary battle, say picketing that quack's office on Lucky Lane. I hear the good doctor spits out a tree's worth of opioid scrips a day."

I took a deep breath and broke in on the rapid-fire monologue. "Not interested, Mollye. I'm with Eva. Susan and her followers will probably move on if we ignore them. Doubt they need our suggestions about alternate evil-doers to torment."

"What could a little house call hurt?" Mollye cajoled. "Show Karen there's no hard feelings. You know over spilt milk. You could take a hunk of your cake as a peace offering. Show her we're normal folks who bake cakes when we're not hoisting our butts in the air."

"Like you've ever baked a cake."

"Hey, just saying, you're the one who's always spouting off about the need for civil discourse," she added, "bemoaning how people shout at each other and never listen."

Mollye had a point. I did tend to yammer on, but talk is cheap. Ringing the doorbell of someone who thinks you're in cahoots with Lucifer calls for a larger personal investment.

I mentally shrugged. Maybe making nice could pay off. "Okay, Moll. Guess there's no harm in attempting a friendly conversation. I'll bring cake. You talk."

Thirty minutes later Mollye and I rendezvoused at Publix where I intended to shop after we delivered our peace offering. We could always beat feet if the church scribe answered the door with pepper spray in hand.

"The apartments are about six months old," Mollye commented as I climbed in her van for the five-minute drive to Karen's. "Still mostly vacant."

The apartment complex consisted of four squat brick buildings, each fronted with a dozen uncovered parking spaces. Dead center in the quadrangle a small grassy square broke up the sea of concrete.

The back of Karen's building butted up against undeveloped property. A sign declared it was earmarked for phase two of the complex. The developer must be convinced the flood of off-campus housing for

Clemson University students would someday bring its high-tide here.

We entered the common hall inside Karen's building. According to the central mail slots, she lived in 1-E, an end unit. She appeared to be the building's sole occupant.

Mollye's index finger was poised an inch above the doorbell when I asked, "Do we know if she has a roommate?"

Moll shook her head as she rang the bell. "She lives alone. Her husband was a real loser boozer. She finally kicked him out a couple months ago. Caught him in bed with some floozy. Good riddance, I say."

I never ceased to marvel at how solidly Moll was plugged into the Ardon County rumor mill. Discovering Karen had recently booted a cheat made me feel a certain kinship with the woman. I recalled how sick I'd felt when I learned my fiancé—my ex-fiancé—was boinking two other women. He was among the reasons I'd been happy to depart Asheville when Aunt Eva asked me to help her manage Udderly Kidding Dairy for a spell. The unexpected death of Aunt Lilly, Eva's twin and dairy partner, made it nigh impossible for her to run the farm alone.

Moll rang the buzzer and waited. No answer. My friend put her ear against the door—well as close as she could get it given her intervening collection of earrings. "I hear the TV. She's got to be home."

Mollye knocked. Waited a moment and knocked again. Then again. Without enough warning for me to stop her, she turned the knob and opened the door. It was unlocked. Risky for a woman living alone in a mostly vacant apartment complex.

"Yoo-hoo," Mollye called as she stepped into the apartment. "Karen, are you home?"

I yanked on Moll's billowy top. "Breaking and entering is illegal."

"We didn't break anything. We just entered."

"Still not a good idea. We weren't exactly invited. We probably shouldn't surprise her."

Mollye shook her head. "I'm worried. Maybe Karen fell down and hit her head or something. We need to make sure she's all right."

"Why not call Danny, you know your deputy sweetie?" I suggested. "We can wait outside till Danny or one of the other sheriff's deputies can check on her."

Naturally I was speaking to Moll's back. While I hovered in the open doorway, she crossed the spartan living room with its blaring TV and disappeared down a hallway. "Karen?" she repeatedly called. "Karen, you here?"

Though reticent, I tiptoed after my friend. While I thought it was dumb to tramp through a stranger's open apartment, I didn't think Mollye should tramp alone. I'd just entered the hall when I heard Mollye gasp, "Oh, no. Lord in heaven, no."

I ran toward Moll's voice. She stood in front of a large bedroom closet, her back to me. "Don't come any closer. Don't touch anything. Karen's dead."

"You sure?" I asked.

"Oh, yeah," Moll answered. "You were right. I shoulda called Danny. Let's go outside. I'll call him now. You don't want to see this."

But, unfortunately, I did see. As Moll turned toward me, Karen's crumpled body came into view, naked except for the long colorful scarf knotted around her neck. Her back sagged against the wall. Her legs splayed out in front of her. I imagined I could still read panic in the dead woman's wide-open eyes.

My breath hitched. The poor woman. I wanted to scream. Instead I stood silently as tears pooled in my eyes. Mollye seized my arm and turned me away.

Sheriff's Deputy Danny McCoy arrived in under five minutes with another Ardon County officer. They found Moll and me sitting in the apartment hallway on opposite sides of the door to 1-E.

Danny'd grilled Moll on the phone as he drove to the crime scene. Having heard all of her answers it didn't take much brainpower to figure out his questions, which pretty much mirrored my own. He'd first asked if we were sure the woman was dead. Next he wanted to know how we got inside, and if we'd touched Karen or anything in her apartment.

"Only the front door," Mollye'd answered. "I know how you feel about people who contaminate a crime scene," she added rather peevishly. "And, no, if anyone else was here, they're long gone."

Was it a crime scene? Danny hadn't asked Mollye her opinion of what caused Karen's death.

After Moll ended her phone call and we began our floor-sitting vigil, I asked, "Murder?" I was no coroner but my guess was she'd been strangled.

"Well, it sure wasn't suicide." Moll answered without pause. "It's been years since Karen and I hung out, but I know she loved her folks. If she'd wanted to hang herself, she'd have done so fully clothed. No way she'd subject her grieving parents to the added humiliation of finding her nude."

I nodded. "So murder?"

"What else?"

Minutes after Danny arrived, he politely told us to scram. "Drop by the Sheriff's Office in the morning to give a formal statement. Nothing more for you here."

I was more than happy to follow his suggestion. Mollye seemed less thrilled about being shooed away. She didn't utter a word on the short drive back to Publix.

"I'm so sorry Karen's dead," I said when we reached the parking lot. "I know you two had gone separate ways, but it's still hard to lose an old friend, especially like this. I might not have seen eye-to-eye with her on religion, but she was way too young to die."

Moll nodded. "Thanks. Right now, I don't feel much like talking. I keep asking why. Maybe I'll drop by Summer Place tomorrow afternoon. See if you need help with your tasting."

SEVEN

I woke late Monday morning.

Last night, I'd left a message on Udderly's answering machine to let my aunt know why I was running late. Then I completed my grocery shopping, put all the ingredients away at Summer Place, and returned to Udderly to find a concerned Eva pacing the floor.

Her concern for my mental health actually earned me two extra hours of sleep. She'd tiptoed into my room when she got up and turned off my alarm. She tackled her chores and mine while I snoozed. Eva's crusty exterior poorly camouflaged her generous heart.

My main morning chore was a visit to the Sheriff's Office to dictate and sign a formal statement regarding the discovery of Karen Vincent's body before heading to my parents' house for our lunch date.

My folks owned a comfortable, two-story brick rancher near the Clemson University campus. My professorial dad, Howard Hooker, heads the Horticultural Department, and Mom—Iris Hooker, Esquire—serves as attorney and prosecutor for the City of Clemson.

Their professional success was one reason I felt my current job tending goats and my future B&B hopes might seem underwhelming.

All members of the Hooker clan were South Carolina transplants from Iowa. I grew up in Ames, Iowa, where Dad taught at Iowa State University. He accepted the Clemson job offer while I was attending Furman University. It gave Dad a chance to live closer to his twin sisters, Eva and Lilly, who'd moved south years before. Mom decided she'd had her fill of snow.

In Ardon County, my folks' twelve-year residence wouldn't have counted for much. Anybody whose mamma's mamma wasn't born here was considered an outsider—a Yankee if the person hailed from up north, a nebulous direction that seemed to include Iowa. Yet given Clemson's rapid turnover as a college town, my parents had become community pillars.

When I pulled into the driveway, Mom and Ursula were relaxing in front-porch rockers enjoying the unseasonably warm weather. Mom's old law school pal had just finished a TV shoot in Buffalo, New York. No wonder she wanted to soak up sun.

Judge Ursula's Citizens' Court was a traveling reality show. I'd seen her adjudicating everything from a sled dog's fate in an Alaskan divorce settlement to a dispute over the color of a Florida van's paint job. On one show, a deceased man's wife, mistress, and step-daughter all argued about who should get his frozen sperm. I wasn't sure any of them should reproduce.

As I climbed onto the front porch, Ursula and Mom both stood—the old friend dwarfing my petite, five foot two mother.

"Heavens, can you really be the same Brie I played hopscotch with?" Ursula asked. "What a beautiful young woman you've become. Come here and give me a hug."

The woman embraced me like we were long lost friends. Though I had no memory of any childhood hopscotch date, I returned the hug.

"I'm so glad you can make the tasting tomorrow," I said.

"Wouldn't miss it. I'm not a vegan, but I try to go meatless one day a week. Maybe you'll inspire me to do even better."

When Ursula released me, Mom gave me a quick hug and checked her watch. "Howard should be by to pick us up any minute. We're going to lunch at the Madren Center."

As if on command, Dad's SUV materialized. He pulled to the curb and hopped out to open doors for his passengers. Mom offered Ursula the front seat, but she waved her off and climbed in the back with me.

Since Mom hadn't quizzed me about Karen's death, I assumed it hadn't made the news. The *Ardon Chronicle* didn't publish on Mondays and, if the local radio station was tuned into the police band on Sunday night, they'd probably only reported a suspicious death. I'd tell my folks about it later. No point ruining everyone's lunch.

I tried not to stare at Ursula, who was every bit as stunning in the flesh as on TV. Since she and Mom were classmates, Ursula had to be late fifties. But she was definitely well preserved. Not that Mom appeared to be growing mold. I couldn't spot a single gray hair in Ursula's shiny black locks and no signs of crow's feet around her startling green eyes. Her pale skin seemed to glow. Heck, I had more wrinkles than she did.

She was definitely better dressed. The silky green dress cinched at her waist by a wide belt emphasized her hour-glass figure. A muted Merino wool shawl caressed her shoulders like a hovering cloud. Unfortunately, the shawl made me flash back to the colorful scarf around Karen's neck. I shuddered.

"How long are you staying in Clemson?" I asked to take my mind in a different direction.

"I'm not sure." A slight frown flitted across her face. "Your mother is helping me with a legal matter and my daughter, Amber, is joining me. We both may be here awhile."

Hmm. Curious. Mom hadn't mentioned Ursula's daughter coming. In fact, Mom had never said boo about her single friend having a daughter.

"Amber's your age," Ursula added. "Bet you'll like her. She's a police detective in Miami. I'm really proud of her."

"I'd love to meet her, though if the two of you are staying with my folks, Dad is sure to monopolize Amber. He's a closet crime novelist, loves reading and writing mysteries."

The opening bars of Madonna's *Material Girl* filled the car. Mollye's ringtone. I'd forgotten to silence my phone. Strapped down in my seat with the contraption in my back pocket there was no graceful way to stop it. "Sorry," I apologized, "I'll put it on vibrate as soon as I can get at it."

Ursula seemed amused by the look Mom gave me. "Your folks are super, but I'm hoping a room opens at a nearby hotel before Amber arrives on Thursday. I'm an obnoxious guest. I keep odd hours and I like my space. Given the conversation I plan to have with Amber, she may want alone time, too."

I nodded. What kind of conversation would make Ursula think her daughter needed alone time? I was dying to ask though it was clearly none of my business.

"Just tell my folks you need some personal space. They'll respect that. I doubt you'll find any hotel vacancies. Clemson's hosting an international high school science fair, and there's a Clemson-Duke basketball game this Saturday."

"So I learned." Ursula shrugged. "Think I'd have an easier time booking a suite in Beverly Hills during Oscar week."

I wondered why Judge Ursula was consulting Mom on a legal matter. Did it involve her daughter? Mom was a firm believer in that old saw— "only a fool acts as his own attorney." But given Ursula's celebrity status, and I assumed fat bank account, she could hire any hotshot lawyer she wanted in NYC or Los Angeles, the two cities where she spent the most time.

My mother's skills and intelligence were mighty impressive, but she didn't practice the type of law a celebrity generally needed. When Mom wasn't acting as the City of Clemson attorney, her private practice focused on real estate transactions and wills. She didn't negotiate entertainment contracts or broker book deals. Then again maybe the daughter was coming to discuss provisions of a will?

I was trying to figure out what I could ask next without overstepping "none of my business" bounds when Dad let us out at the Madren entrance. While Dad parked, we claimed our reserved table, a prime one overlooking a portion of the Walker Golf Course and sparkling Lake Hartwell. The early warm spell had even coaxed a Bradford pear tree into a showy display of white blooms.

My father joined us as the waiter handed out menus. I had my fingers crossed there'd be plenty of veggie sides and appetizers. While most restaurants offered lots of a la carte options, it was sometimes a challenge to order sides that hadn't been baptized in butter or performed a backstroke in cheese sauce.

Madonna's *Material Girl* sounded again. I'd forgotten to switch the phone over. I pulled it from my back pocket to silence it before I forgot again. A glance told me the text was from Mollye. What could be important enough for her to disturb my lunch?

Returning my attention to the menu, I spotted a spinach salad and ordered it minus bacon and cheese with oil and vinegar dressing.

Since my parents and I are curious souls, our dinner guests must sometimes feel they're being interviewed by a *60 Minutes*' tag team. Judge Ursula reversed the roles. As interrogator, she made us Hookers look like amateurs.

Before we finished our entrées, Ursula had quizzed Dad about the poisonous plants he grew for cancer research, grilled Mom about town-college battles over legal jurisdiction, and peppered me with questions on a seemingly endless array of topics. Why did I leave the banking job I took after getting an MBA? How had I become a vegan? How long did I think my boyfriend trial would run before someone was declared a winner? When she asked about the upcoming goat yoga my mind crashed back to that closet and Karen's naked body.

Apparently, my face didn't show my dismay or Ursula would have noticed and asked about it. She didn't seem the least bit shy. Instead, she honed in on my upcoming tasting. "What do you hope to accomplish?"

"Want the short answer or the long one?" I asked.

"Long, of course," Ursula replied.

So I did a conversational rewind to explain how I'd inherited Summer Place. My twin aunts bought the dilapidated Southern mansion after I shared a pipe dream of turning it into a B&B that catered to vegans and vegetarians. They'd planned to start restoration and surprise me with Summer Place on my thirty-fifth birthday.

My phone vibrated my butt, and I couldn't take it anymore. What was so important?

"I'm sorry, but someone really wants me. Do you mind if I look at this text?

"No problem," Ursula said.

I ignored my mother's nonverbal response and read Mollye's text. Just two words: *Erotic asphyxiation.*

What in blazes? I'd heard of erotic asphyxiation but why was Mollye texting me about it? I wouldn't find out until I called my friend back. And that wasn't going to happen during lunch. Not if I wanted Mom to continue speaking to me.

When I looked up, all eyes were on me. "I'm sorry. Just Mollye. Anyway, when Aunt Lilly suddenly died in an auto accident, the plan changed. I inherited the mansion three years early.

"Restoring an old structure requires money," I added. "The sweat equity part is going great thanks to friends and family." I paused to smile at Dad. "But I need to hire pros to tackle essentials like a new roof. I'd like to start catering events and hosting occasional dinners on Summer Place's winterized sunporch to pocket money for repairs. My second goal is to start building a clientele. Fingers crossed tomorrow's tasting will generate some glowing reviews."

"Who's coming?" Ursula's follow-up question helped push Moll's puzzling erotica text further to the back of my mind.

"A restaurant reviewer for the Greenville paper, a popular farm-to-table blogger, and the owner of a company that provides concierge services to people who rent luxury lake properties. Mom also invited Dr. Swihart, a professor who helps decide who caters Clemson faculty events. Honestly, I think they all agreed to come in order to meet you. So thanks."

She waved off my expression of gratitude. "Nonsense," she began, "I—"

Ursula's gaze caught on something or someone across the room. Her mouth hung open a second, then her eyes narrowed and her breathing became audible. I wouldn't have been surprised to see steam erupt from her ears.

I looked to see who or what had riled unflappable Judge Ursula. A lanky gentleman, probably late fifties or early sixties, strode toward our table, right arm outstretched for a handshake. Two women followed in his slipstream. His wife and daughter? He seemed confident they'd docilely follow wherever he led.

Had I met this man? I had a hard time telling some of my dad's male faculty members apart, especially if I'd only been introduced once or twice. They all seemed to shop at the same frameless eyeglass store and wore the "casual" academic uniform—pressed khakis, open collared shirt, and sports jacket. This gentleman was no exception.

His sparse hair, a wishy-washy color between sandy blond and gray, was combed back from a widow's peak on his prominent forehead. I could practically see each comb mark.

Dad rose to shake the man's hand, bolstering my assumption he was a university colleague. "Lawrence, I'd like to introduce my wife, Iris, my daughter, Brie, and our friend, Ursula Billings."

Father's smile matched the stranger's toothy display. "Ladies, this gentleman is Lawrence Toomey. I just learned he's been nominated to be a Justice on the Supreme Court. Congratulations, Lawrence."

Mom gave Dad one of her coded cease-and-desist looks. "Howard, you don't need to introduce Mr. Toomey to Ursula and me. We attended law school together."

Given my mother's uncharacteristically frosty tone I leapt to the conclusion Iris Hooker and Ursula Billings weren't Toomey fans.

Yet the Supreme Court nominee either wasn't a genius at interpreting social signals or was determined to paper over the awkwardness by exposing a full-mouth dental display. "Yes, I've known these lovely ladies a long time. So happy to see you again, Ursula and Iris." He turned his gaze on me. "Pleased to make your acquaintance, Brie."

He finally seemed to remember his female shadows. "Oh, I should introduce my lovely wife, Esther, and my daughter, Ruth," he added.

"Pleased to meet you," Dad said and nodded at the women, who made no move to shake hands. Mom and Ursula remained mute, granting only obligatory nods of acknowledgement. The wife, Esther, was quite attractive though model thin. The fattest thing about the woman was her hair, a throwback bouffant do. The daughter, Ruth, was really pretty, and would have been more so if she'd smiled. Sandy hair, hazel eyes, full lips, and a slightly pointed chin.

Mom interrupted my visual inspection when she pushed her chair back with an almost violent burst of energy and stood. "If you'll excuse us, we were just leaving. Ursula and I want to stop in the ladies' room. Howard, Brie, we'll meet you at the car."

Mom and Ursula made a point not to acknowledge the Supreme Court nominee or his family members as they walked briskly away. I kept my seat. My curiosity whetted. How had this man made enemies of my mother and Ursula?

Dad, looking puzzled, signaled a waiter to bring our bill.

Time for me to take up the interrogation slack. "Congratulations on your nomination," I began. "I hope you'll excuse my ignorance but are you a judge here in South Carolina? Do you live in the area?"

"Yes, on both counts." He smiled. "I serve as a judge for the 13th Circuit Court, located in Greenville. But my family and my wife's folks"— he paused to nod at Esther—"have lived in Ardon County for four generations. We're continuing that tradition, though I keep an apartment in Greenville for convenience during the week. That also lets me keep tabs on Ruth here." Another slight dip of the chin, this one toward his daughter. "She's a nurse practitioner and has her own apartment in Greenville."

Not a word from the women.

"So how are you and Dad acquainted?" The relationship seemed curious. Weird, given my father's friendly attitude and my mother's clear distaste.

"We just met," Toomey answered. "I'm on the University's Board of

Directors and Howard made a wonderful presentation yesterday. He has some great ideas for expanding the school's horticultural curriculum."

Got it. They were strangers, didn't know beans about one another.

Dad put down his pen after adding a tip to the bill. "Guess we'd better be off. Don't want to keep the ladies waiting."

"No, can't have that." Toomey chuckled, though it seemed forced. "Have a good day."

As Dad and I stood, Toomey turned toward his wife and daughter. "Esther, Ruth, come along. I see some more friends I should greet."

I nudged Dad's arm as soon as we spotted Mom and Ursula outside the restaurant. Heads close together, features grim.

"What's the deal with Mom, Ursula, and the Toomey clan?" I asked. "Do you know?"

"Not a clue," he replied. "But I'm pretty sure your mother will set me straight soon enough."

EIGHT

We all scooted into our previously assigned seats in Dad's SUV.

"Ursula and I are discussing a legal matter involving Lawrence Toomey," Mom announced. "It's confidential, so no questions about Mr. Toomey."

"Oh, for heaven's sake, Iris," Ursula broke in. "We can make an exception for your family. However, since that slimeball Toomey's appearance made us bolt before dessert, I vote for having a drink in hand before I tell all."

At the house, Dad dutifully played bartender and I waitressed, delivering glasses of chardonnay to Mom and Ursula. Dad and I opted for cold beers. No one in my family tended to imbibe before sundown. Yet this was the second time in twenty-four hours someone had suggested booze as an appropriate daylight response to a puzzling event.

Seated on the couch beside Mom, Ursula shucked her shoes and curled her long legs beneath her body. After a sip of wine, she took a deep breath.

"Once rumors surfaced that Larry the Lech was being considered for a seat on the high court, I started wrestling with my conscience," she said. "He plays the pious conservative to the hilt, railing against our nation's failure to protect the unborn, our loss of family values. This is the same man who waited until I was drunk and semi-conscious to screw me without protection. Once I discovered I was pregnant, he demanded I get an abortion. Said if I tried to lay the blame on him, he'd paint me as a whore."

What? The look on Dad's face said he was as shocked as I was.

"That's not the capper." Ursula's long finger worried the stem of her wine glass. "At the time, Toomey was married, though none of us in law school knew about his shotgun wedding over Christmas break. When I learned I was pregnant, graduation was just weeks away. I told people I planned a well-deserved vacation, backpacking and enjoying nature before starting my career. I stayed with cousins on a Montana ranch. Gave my baby daughter up for adoption."

Ursula turned to look at me. "Amber's your age, Brie. Iris and I were pregnant at the same time. Of course, so was Toomey's wife, Esther. Iris is the only person I ever confided in back then or since."

"Did you consider bringing rape charges against Toomey?" Howard asked.

Ursula's laugh was dismissive. "We were at a party. I drank way too much and passed out. When I began to come to, I felt a weight on top of me. Toomey had his fun while I was in that twilight zone."

"That's horrible," I said.

"When I sobered up and confronted Toomey, he laughed it off. Said I didn't scream so it had to be consensual. It's different today—well, at least it's slightly better. I was no angel in my twenties, though I was very careful about birth control. But every sexual encounter I'd had would have been exploited to make me look like a harlot. My reputation would have been destroyed before I could begin the career I'd worked my ass off to earn."

I frowned. "I understand why you want to expose this guy's hypocrisy, but it's been decades. Wouldn't your charges be dismissed out of hand? After so many years, there's no way to prove Toomey took advantage of you, is there?"

Ursula smiled. "No there isn't. I came here to talk the situation over with Iris—and Amber. While I can't prove date rape, Amber's date of birth and DNA provide concrete proof that Toomey fathered her while his brand new wife was pregnant."

"How long have you been in touch with Amber?" Dad asked.

"We connected five years ago through an adoption reunion registry. Amber considers her adoptive parents her real parents—as she should. We've built a good relationship but have kept it private. Amber thinks it might hurt her adoptive mother's feelings to know she sought contact with her birth mother. I'd never go public without Amber's permission. I'm not sure I even have the right to ask."

"Does Amber know who her father is?" I wondered out loud.

"Naturally she's asked. I've always declined to answer. Said it didn't matter. I was never in a relationship with the man, and he was unaware she existed. I told her I always loved her. I gave her up for adoption because I thought she'd have a better life."

Judge Ursula's normal steely demeanor vanished. Tears meandered down her cheeks. Mom scooted across the couch to put an arm around her.

"I just don't know what to do. What woman would want to learn she was conceived in a sick version of date rape? Should I tell Amber the truth, let her make the decision about going public? Or will knowing only cause Amber more heartache?"

Mom patted Ursula's hand. "Not a word of this can leave this room. If Ursula tells her story and just says she gave a baby up for adoption—no birth date or DNA evidence to prove when Toomey fathered the child, the man can dismiss it as a politically motivated lie. If Amber's not willing to provide DNA, the charges would be pointless, ugly publicity that is far more likely to damage Ursula than that scumbag."

Dad nodded. "Not enough to stop Toomey's nomination from being approved."

"True," Mom agreed. "We've been wracking our brains trying to come up with a legal maneuver that could keep Amber's identity secret while using her DNA and date of birth. Have yet to come up with a foolproof option."

Ursula wiped the tears from her face, and bolted upright. "Brie, maybe you can help me solve my lodging problem. I love your folks but I really do want a little privacy for Amber and me. Are any rooms in your future B&B ready for occupancy?"

I shook my head. "Sorry, no. I don't even stay inside Summer Place when I sleep over. I camp out in a little ramshackle cottage on the grounds. The previous owners rented it to hard-up students. You wouldn't want to stay there. It's drafty and the roof leaks. The toilet and sink boast matching rust stains, and the shower's so small you need to exit and reenter to rinse your back."

Ursula chuckled. "Who could resist that sales pitch? Sold. It sounds perfect. Private. Out of the way. Nobody will look for me there—or Amber once she arrives."

"Isolated and uncomfortable," I countered. "I threw out the moldy mattress the last students left behind. There's just a blow-up mattress on the bedroom floor, and if it turns cold again as predicted, the wood fireplace is the only source of heat."

"No problem. I'll buy whatever we need. I'm sure Amber won't mind roughing it. She's a tough cookie, guess that comes with being a cop, a detective. Anyway, I'll pay three hundred dollars a night for your cottage. That should give you a leg up on funding your B&B repairs."

Holey Swiss cheese.

I glanced over at my folks. Mom and Dad shrugged. My mind whirled. What a windfall? Three-hundred smackers a night. Even three nights and I'd have a down payment on the three-thousand-dollar low bid for a new roof.

Don't let dollar signs sway you. Not fair to Ursula.

"Three hundred is way too much. You need to actually see this cubbyhole before you decide. I'm making my shack sound better than it is."

Mom smiled. "Before you accept any deal, Brie, let me look over the contract. Don't want Judge Ursula sneaking in loopholes that let her sue for spider bites or exposure to dust mites."

I stood. "I'm heading to Summer Place now to start prepping for tomorrow's tasting. I'll be there all afternoon. Drop by any time for a look-see, Ursula. I won't hold you to a sight-unseen offer. Even if you decide to go ahead, you'll have to wait till tomorrow to move in. I need to move my stuff out, and I haven't a minute to spare before the tasting."

"Fine with me," Ursula agreed as she glanced over at Mom. "I figure the Hookers can put up with me one more night. I really do appreciate the hospitality. Just need my own space when I'm camping anywhere this long, as well as some time alone with Amber."

NINE

"Yoo-hoo, anyone here—a frazzled chef in need of more hands?"

I jumped at the unexpected voice and dropped a glass jar of Blue Agave. The sweet sticky syrup oozed around glass slivers on the kitchen's old plank floors.

I wet a towel and knelt to clean up the mess. "Mollye, you scared me silly." I glanced at my friend in the doorway. "Why aren't you at your shop?"

She smiled. "Told you I might swing by this afternoon. Is interrogation any way to greet a volunteer sous chef? I just finished glazing a batch of pierced vases and put them in the kiln to fire. Not much traffic at Starry Skies so I closed up. One of the perks of owning your own business. I also was more than ready to think about something besides Karen's murder."

"Did Danny confirm it was murder?"

"Heavens, no. He won't tell me squat when he's working a case. But I'm sure someone killed her. I'm just not sure they planned to. What do you think about my idea?"

"What idea?"

"Erotic asphyxiation. Naked. Scarf around her neck." Mollye's voice had gone sultry. "Do you think Karen might have been doing the nasty? Tied to the bed when things went too far?"

"Thanks. There's a mental picture I won't be able to purge. What people do behind closed doors is their business. Even church secretaries who accuse me of devil worship."

"Okay, we'll shelve that for now. I forgot how sensitive you are."

"I'm not sensitive. There are just some things I'd rather not imagine."

Moll closed her eyes and touched her fingers to her temples like she was getting a psychic message from the great beyond. "My powers also tell me you need my wit and sass to keep you from obsessing about tomorrow's luncheon. Figured you could use help with chopping, stirring, and what not."

"I was doing okay until you scared the cottage cheese out of me."

Mollye shrugged. "If you don't want people barging into your kitchen, you need to lock the sunporch door."

"Not sure it's worth the bother," I answered. "Doesn't take a lot of talent to pick that old skeleton key lock. I need to install a new lock, but that's way down my to-do list. Nothing to steal in here except groceries and pots and pans."

The prior owners had sold Summer Place's contents to an auction house. They'd cleaned out everything. Not a stick of furniture, a coffee mug, or even a salt shaker left behind. So theft wasn't a big worry.

Since I didn't live here, vandalism and the possibility of homeless folks seeking shelter and getting injured in the renovation mess did worry me. But thanks to vigilant—okay nosy—across-the-street neighbors, neither were huge concerns.

"You know the Medley sisters noted your arrival time," I added. "If my car wasn't in the drive, they'd have phoned by now to give me an intruder alert. They're better security than a paid service. That reminds me, I'd better tell them I may have folks renting that cottage out back for a week or so."

"Really?" Mollye bustled over to a series of wall pegs and grabbed one of the snowy white aprons I'd bought from a supply service. "Who did you con into renting that falling down hovel?"

I hesitated. It was clear Ursula didn't want her location broadcast. "Ursula Billings may be my new tenant, but please don't spread the word. She wants privacy. A friend may join her, too. There aren't any vacancies in hotels or B&Bs within miles."

"I thought Ursula was staying with your folks. What? Did Iris make her wait in line to use the loo? Can't imagine abandoning a comfy house to sleep in your rat hole. Insult intended."

"Insult deserved." I shrugged. "It appears Ursula's one of those people who gets squirrely if she doesn't have her space. Wants to get up, eat, shower, etc. when she pleases without worrying if it inconveniences her housemates. Guess the friend she's expecting feels the same way."

"Friend?" Mollye arched an eyebrow. "Are we talking a male friend?

Bet the tabloids would pay for that news."

"No," I answered. "A woman. A police detective from Miami. Been friends for years. Perhaps they're consulting on a project."

All true, and I still hadn't given a tip-off about their secret mother-daughter relationship. Mollye and I had been best friends since I was eight. But that didn't excuse me from a promise to keep my lips zipped.

When I was a kid, my aunts sweet-talked my folks into letting me stay part of each summer on their goat farm. Moll boarded ponies at Udderly and we hit it off instantly. No matter how much time passed between visits, our friendship rekindled instantly.

"Now and again, I feel the same way Ursula does about privacy," I said, nudging the conversation in a different direction. "I love Aunt Eva but it's sometimes heavenly to be alone. One of the benefits of having Summer Place as a solitary refuge."

Mollye pretended to pout. "Is this your way of asking me to leave?"

"No, just limit yourself to one apron. Want to make sure I look clean and spiffy for the photos Dad plans to take of me performing vegan magic in the kitchen."

"Not a problem. You know how neat I am."

"Right." Neat was not an adjective normally associated with Mollye.

"I love your Aunt Eva," Moll added "But I couldn't live with her. Especially cooped up in a cabin, year-round. And you two get up so danged early. If I see the sunrise, it's because I'm just getting home. You have any regrets about committing to live at Udderly?"

"Not a one. Even though working at a goat dairy was never on my list of desirable, or even possible, occupations."

I thought back to last March when Aunt Lilly, Eva's twin and partner in managing the dairy, died in a car accident.

"I really enjoy helping Aunt Eva. She'd have had a tough time alone on the farm. Though I loved Asheville, it was time to leave. My life at Udderly makes humdrum sous chef duties seem boring, and I was constantly afraid I'd bump into my cheating ex-fiancé. The move's been a welcome change."

Mollye tied her apron. "So what can I do?"

Since vegan cuisine requires lots of chopping, I pointed Mollye toward a cutting board. "How about getting the celery out of the fridge? It needs to be washed and chopped, really fine. I need two cups."

Mollye grabbed a knife while I dumped water off the raw cashews I'd soaked overnight. Prep for making a big batch of cashew cheese—a building block for several entrées. A rich cashew pot pie with a golden flaky crust was among tomorrow's options.

As we worked side-by-side, I decided to tap into Mollye's knowledge as a native Ardon County resident. If there was any dirt about Lawrence Toomey, I figured my friend would have heard it.

"We had lunch at the Madren Center today," I began. "Lawrence Toomey waltzed over to our table to greet Dad. I was surprised to hear an Ardon County resident had been nominated for the Supreme Court. What do you know about him?"

It didn't take much encouragement to get Mollye to share. Between my pal's mom, her granny, and the cross-section of locals who visited Starry Skies, my friend was a treasure trove of longtime Ardon lore and breaking-news gossip.

Mollye quickly filled me in. Larry Toomey had a wife, Esther, and a daughter, Ruth, an only child. His in-laws were none other than Guy Nickles, the pastor of the Temple of True Believers and his wife, Jeannie. While ultra-conservative appeared to be an apt label for all of Toomey's kin, Mollye said his wife—the former Esther Nickles—and her parents dropped completely off the end of the liberal-conservative spectrum into a black hole of religious bigotry, nationalistic paranoia, and conspiracy theories.

Mollye paused in her genealogy rundown to look down at the first two stalks of celery she'd diced. "Is this fine enough for you, ma'am?"

I nodded.

Moll dumped the chopped celery into a large measuring cup. "I'm fairly certain Susan wouldn't have stormed our goat yoga session yesterday without the approval of Toomey's in-laws, Guy and Jeannie Nickles."

"Wow. Does Toomey share his in-laws' 'goats are devils' baloney? If so, it's hard to imagine he could be confirmed to the high court."

Mollye shook her head. "Oh, I have no doubt he'll be confirmed. Questioning a Protestant about his religious beliefs is unsporting, un-American, and blasphemous. Officially, Toomey and the missus belong to a mainstream Protestant congregation in Greenville. My bet is Toomey picked the church with the wealthiest parishioners.

"Of course, Judge Toomey and his wife are in Ardon County more

Sundays than not. When they're here, they attend the Temple of True Believers. If asked, I'm sure Toomey would claim he goes out of respect for his fruitcake father-in-law."

"What's Toomey's daughter like?" I asked.

"Esther—Toomey's wife—married him when she got knocked up at seventeen." Mollye began to warm to her tale. "A hurry-up wedding, though no one mentions baby Ruth made her seven-pound arrival a short five months after they tied the knot. Ruth was in my grade. Quiet, shy. Went to some religious college. She's some sort of health care practitioner up in Greenville."

Figuring I'd learned as much as I could about Toomey's pedigree and family, I gently steered the conversation back to Susan, the goat hater.

"Do you really think Nickles encouraged his parishioners to harass our goat yoga group?" I asked as I started peeling avocados, a secret ingredient in my chocolate mousse. "I grew up in a Methodist Church with a pastor who preached a loving, forgiving God. I still hold on to that vision. I've attended a variety of religious services over the years—Protestant, Catholic, Jewish—and I can't recall a single sermon on satanic goats or Baphomet. Where does this come from?"

Mollye laughed. "I asked Granny about this goat nonsense. She shook her finger and said, 'Where do you think the term scapegoat comes from?' Granny insists sex is the reason goats have been slandered."

"Huh?"

"You've seen firsthand how billy goats behave during rutting season." Moll giggled. "Even if they don't have horns, they're horny buggers and danged determined to boink any female in the vicinity. According to Granny, folks who believe sex is sinful latched onto randy goats as the embodiment of lust and evil."

I shook my head. "And I thought snakes were the only members of the animal kingdom to get a bad rap. Me, I'd nominate mosquitoes and fire ants as the real devils."

About four o'clock, Ursula arrived to inspect the pig-in-the-poke she'd agreed to rent. I introduced Mom's friend to Mollye before guiding her down the gravel path that linked the ramshackle cottage to the front of the property.

"There's no place to park a car back here," I noted. "I'll be happy to help you move your suitcases in. But, if you stay, you'll have to schlep groceries a fair piece."

Ursula waved off my concern. "I travel light and so does Amber. I'm betting most of our meals will be takeout."

I opened the door to the cottage. It took under three minutes for my prospective renter to do a walk-through. "It's just fine," she said. "I'll move in tomorrow after the tasting."

While I still had trepidations about renting the sorry excuse for a building, who was I to argue with Judge Ursula?

Thanks to Mollye's willingness to serve as sous chef, we quickly finished all the advance prep. I glanced at my watch—5:35 p.m. I was beat. I wanted to kick off my shoes and sit. The only downside of being a chef is the hours spent on your tootsies. Yet the occasional twinge in my lower back was far less painful than sitting at a bank desk staring at rows of numbers.

Moll shucked her previously white apron. It looked like modern art with green and purple swirls blending into tomato-red blotches.

"I know you ate lunch out," my friend began. "But let's go wild and crazy and go out to dinner, too. You're tired and you deserve a meal you don't have to make. Call Eva and see if she wants to join us."

"Eva has plans. It's her Red Hat group night," I answered.

"Oooh, cool," Mollye cooed. "I'm gonna join one of those groups soon as I turn fifty. Love that they wear outrageous red hats and purple tops and have no purpose other than having fun with other ladies."

I smiled. "You wear red and purple together now so the wardrobe requirements won't be a strain. And my answer to dinner out is yes. Let someone else do the cooking. Just give me a sec to check in with Eva and make sure our part-timers and Gerri can handle the evening chores."

Four students in Clemson's Ag school provided our part-time labor force, and we'd recently brought Gerri Woods on full time as a farm hand. On weekends, Tess, a friendly retired school teacher, smiled her way through our retail sales on the two days we invited the general public to visit.

I phoned Aunt Eva on our cabin's landline. She was far more likely to answer it than her seldom-activated cell phone. Eva picked up on the fourth ring. Not one for idle phone chatter, she told me all was well, ordered me to have fun, and hung up.

"Where do you want to eat?" I asked Mollye.

My pal tossed out three suggestions. I accepted her second choice as we walked out to Moll's Starry Skies van parked behind my Prius. I'd collect my car after dinner.

TEN

Since Moll drove, I ordered a Michelob Light at dinner. I was so exhausted the beer made me a tad light headed. The sensation had just begun to pass when Mollye dropped me at Summer Place a few minutes after eight.

"You heading straight back to Udderly?" she asked.

"In about five minutes. Just a quick check in the kitchen to make sure everything's buttoned up. Thanks so much for your help today—and your offer to waitress tomorrow. Fingers crossed everyone will love the food, and Harriett won't add me to her blackmail list. Since I'm next to broke and don't have a going business concern, maybe I'll get a pass."

I hopped out of Moll's van and glanced across the street. My neighbors' downstairs lights were on. Good. I'd phone to let the Medley sisters know I'd soon have tenants. Didn't want them calling the cops in panic if they saw strangers coming and going at night.

I walked around the side of Summer Place to reach the sunporch and kitchen, so far the only fully renovated sections of the old mansion. I unlocked the door and flipped the light switch. Mollye'd set the porch table for six with fine china on loan from my mother. The crystal water goblets and wine glasses sparkled in the light.

Huh? Two place settings seemed slightly out of kilter. Looked like someone had walked too close and snagged the tablecloth. I swore it wasn't like that when I admired the set up before Mollye and I left. Did I do it just now?

No biggie. I was tired. Could have missed it. My big concern had been the size of the round table. Did it offer enough elbow and leg room to comfortably seat six?

I straightened the linens. Then I took out my cell phone. I decided to check voicemail and messages before I called the Medley sisters. The one and only voice message was from Janice Medley, one of the neighbors I was about to call.

"Brie?" The elderly woman's high voice held a bit of a tremor. "Janice here. Wanted you to know someone's been fooling around on your property. Normally wouldn't call to tell you about a visitor when your car's sitting in the drive, but my sister let our dog out to tinkle and saw you climb in that gaudy Starry Skies van. Not five minutes after you left someone pulled into your drive and stayed maybe half an hour. It was getting dark and there was mud on the license plate. So couldn't get a number. Thought you should know. Neighbors need to look out for one another."

I deleted the message. I'd given Ursula a key to the cottage but I couldn't imagine her coming back when I told her she had to wait until tomorrow to move in. But maybe she'd wanted to do a second tour to figure out what she needed to buy to make the place a bit more comfy.

I returned my neighbor's call.

"Miss Medley?" It didn't feel right calling her Janice. "I'm letting two women friends use the cottage behind Summer Place for a while so you might see strange vehicles come and go when I'm not here."

"Oh, that explains the truck," Miss Medley said.

"The truck?" I asked.

"Yes, the truck that pulled in your drive right after you left with your friend tonight."

Goosebumps zoomed up my arms.

No way would Ursula be driving a truck. When she'd dropped by at four o'clock, her ride was a sporty, blue Mercedes Benz. Impossible to mistake it for a truck.

I thanked Miss Medley for watching out for my property. News of renters seemed to reassure her there were no new marauders in the neighborhood.

Me, not so much.

Had someone been in Summer Place? I turned on all the lights to make sure no one lurked in the shadows. Then I checked the refrigerator and counters. Nothing seemed out of place. The only oddity was a wet patch on the counter. I opened the dishwasher to see if I should run it tonight or wait till I finished prep work in the morning. I frowned at what I didn't see. One of the mixing bowls I'd used wasn't there.

I opened the cupboard where I kept my mixing bowls. The large red bowl I could have sworn was dirty sat on the shelf. I took it down. Clean as a whistle. Maybe Mollye'd washed it by hand and put it away. She's the opposite of a neat freak but with Mollye anything was possible.

I tried to laugh off my full-fledged set of the willies. The mystery truck, the place settings, the bowl. I shivered. Maybe the shock of seeing Karen's dead body was making me susceptible to fear. As I locked the door behind me, I debated.

Should I phone the sheriff? No, a parked truck, a clean bowl, and out-of-alignment silverware didn't exactly provide compelling evidence of a break-in. He'd look at me like I was nuts if I suggested someone broke in to wash a bowl for me.

Maybe some teenagers parked in the driveway to neck. No nearby streetlights. Lots of trees. Very private. The driveway was an ideal lover's lane.

Don't start imagining things. You have real problems to worry about.

ELEVEN

Though I hadn't slept well, I muddled through Tuesday morning farm chores as quickly as I could. Aunt Eva was faster. Soon as I walked inside, she handed me a cup of coffee and shooed me toward my room.

"Go get ready for your vegan premiere," she said. "I know how much it means to you. Wish I could afford to help you more fixing up Summer Place. Lilly and I had some grand plans."

I put down my coffee cup and hugged Eva. Unspilled tears made her eyes glisten.

"You and Aunt Lilly bought me my dream. How could I ever ask for more or thank you enough."

My aunts had planned to start Summer Place renovations before they handed me the keys. Lilly's death had dealt her twin a financial as well as an emotional blow. The money crunch was exacerbated last spring when Eva was unjustly arrested as a murder suspect.

Eva's eyes began to tear in earnest and she abruptly spun away. She didn't like anyone to see her cry. She worked hard to maintain a tough-as-nails, cantankerous front for everyone's benefit—even the family who loved her. Dad said his sister's bravado façade was a lingering legacy from her abusive husband. She wanted to make certain no one ever believed they could take advantage of her again.

"Go on, git," Eva said. "Sure you don't want me to come and provide a running commentary on your cuisine? I can give them a heads up that what you call cheese is a bunch of crushed nuts pretending to be dairy."

"Gee, thanks, but I think I'll handle the commentary. Just hope Mollye won't add any of her off-the-cuff comments."

By 11:20, the aroma of sautéed onions filled the air, triggering my own

Pavlov response. I was famished. Too bad I'd have to wait until the guests had come and gone for a taste. Didn't want telltale blobs on my white apron advertising the menu.

That worry wasn't shared by my server. Out of the corner of my eye, I spied Mollye popping a miniature cornmeal muffin in her mouth. At least her choice of snack only left a trail of crumbs, easily brushed away.

"Didn't you tell that bunch of freeloaders to be here at eleven thirty?" Moll asked. "Where is everyone? Think they'd be on time for free eats."

I surveyed the drive from the window wall in my renovated all-weather sunporch. "No one's late, and three cars are pulling in right now. Mom and Ursula are the leaders of the pack."

I took a deep, calming breath. Yoga and meditation had taught me to center myself by focusing on my breathing. I had confidence in my skill as a chef. But I'd spent enough time in commercial kitchens to know how many disasters could lurk between refrigerator, stove, and table. Plus not everyone shared my taste. Heck, I had cousins who claimed the smell of green beans cooking made them nauseous, but they snarfed up fried pork rinds.

Car doors slammed. Instead of walking toward Summer Place, Mom and Ursula did an about-face to greet the other arrivals. Ursula was clearly the star of the welcoming ritual. In a rush to shake hands with Ursula, a roly-poly woman, who emerged from the third car, practically bowled over the second car's slender occupant.

Mollye muttered, "Hope you planned extra helpings. Looks like Harriett—she's Miss Muumuu—elected not to wear anything that could restrict her intake."

I glanced at my friend. "You're going to be nice, right? I can remember when someone called you fat. As I recall, you didn't like it. In fact you punched Jessie in the nose."

"We were eight," Mollye huffed. "And I'm convinced it did him a world of good. Besides, I'm much too classy to call Harriett Quinn a tub of lard to her face."

I considered the quasi-antique chairs I'd put round the table and hoped they were sturdy. Had I left enough room for folks to get in and out without knocking knees?

Moldy Munster, quit worrying. Too late to make changes now.

"I didn't realize Harriett was so heavy," I whispered. "I'd only seen the headshot on her farm-to-table blog."

Mollye chuckled. "Yeah, she shows 'before' photos of the food she eats, no 'after' shots of where the calories pitch camp."

I gave my friend a look.

"Okay, I'll put my snark on pause."

I hadn't met either of the two women now chatting with Mom and Ursula, but they provided quite the contrast. Harriett Quinn's billowing flowered muumuu had more room inside than a pup tent. Two boy scouts and their dog could camp inside. In contrast, the perfectly coiffed slender woman she'd hip-checked in her rush to greet Ursula wore a fitted black pantsuit topped with a red silk scarf fluffed around her neck.

"Is the pantsuit lady Della or Professor Swihart?" I asked.

Mollye had met all the tasting guests.

"The black pantsuit lady is Della Doyle," Mollye answered. "After her husband died a decade ago, she started selling high-end real estate. Then she realized she could make more money if she turned wealthy clients into long-term cash cows. Calls herself a concierge. Whatever. Della's clients are part-time rich folks who need windows washed, bushes pruned, and parties catered, but don't want the bother of dealing with hired help. Della solves their problems. Takes a cut from the worker bees and her clients."

"Well, I hope I'm one of Della's finds for catering those parties," I said.

"Bert Rider, your restaurant critic, just arrived." Mollye pointed at a car across the street with a paint job that advertised it belonged to the *Greenville News*."

Bert hustled to catch up with the other guests. His shoulder-length frizzy blond hair was pulled into a short ponytail. Springy spirals escaped at both temples, making his head appear as round as a melon. He wore faded jeans and a rumpled safari jacket chockablock with pockets.

His attire made me guess he favored stubby pencils and tucked sharpened spares in each of his pockets. Bert joined the clutch of arrivals, making it a fivesome.

"Now the professor's the only one who's tardy," Mollye said. "Why did you invite her anyway—doesn't she study bugs or something?"

"Mom suggested I invite her," I explained. "Dr. Swihart's a vegan and she's on a committee that plans events for faculty. The professor's a toxicologist and teaches graduate courses for doctoral candidates."

Mollye pointed at a Beemer backing into a space across the road. "Bet that's the prof," she said.

Mom insisted I'd met Professor Victoria Swihart. Could have fooled me. Dad occasionally cajoled me into attending faculty functions now and again. He never said so, but I think he hoped I'd hit it off with some bachelor prof.

Okay, I had met Dr. Swihart. The newcomer's steel gray pageboy helmet jogged my memory.

By the time the guests reached the sunporch, they'd already completed round-robin howdys. All I needed to do was welcome them and formally introduce Mollye and myself.

After a round of handshaking, I invited the sextet on a quick tour of my spic-and-span kitchen. Polished again this morning. I also gave the guests a glimpse of the major renovations underway. An archway in the kitchen opened onto Summer Place's massive dining hall. I didn't let anyone step beyond that threshold. Couldn't risk one of them falling in a hole, stepping on a nail, or being conked by a plaster stalactite dangling from the ceiling.

Once the group settled around the table, I passed out menus describing each of the six recipes they'd taste. I was so nervous I suddenly felt like I had to pee. Really?

"Uh, Mollye will take beverage orders. I'll be back in a jiffy with appetizers—caramelized onion and asparagus cups and stuffed mushrooms."

I hot-footed it to the kitchen and splashed cold water on my face. Thank heavens, I hadn't worn makeup. Steaming vegetables have a way of turning mascara into drippy Lone Ranger masks. The urge to pee went away or I got too busy to notice it.

Mollye's voice drifted into the kitchen as she chatted with the guests. She was on her best behavior, sweetly offering a choice of wine, beer, water, or sweet tea.

I picked up the tray of onion and asparagus cups and returned to the porch. "Here's the first appetizer. Bon Appetit!" My voice had to be two octaves higher than usual.

Could I be any lamer?

Everyone had the good grace to ignore my squeaky-voiced idiocy. I hurried back to the kitchen to stir the Spanish garden paella. Once all the ingredients were mixed in, the rice had a tendency to stick. Fortunately my favorite cashew pot pie needed no fussing. It was staying warm in the oven.

After the guests began sampling the paella, I was less of a nervous imbecile. Semi-verbal compliments seemed to accompany every forkful.

"What's in this?" Bert asked.

The question relaxed me. No need to consult a recipe card to answer. I could do this. An endless stream of compliments bolstered my confidence.

"Ummm. Delicious."

"Interesting combination of flavors."

"As pretty as it is tasty."

"Could I have a little more?"

Harriett inquired about preparing the cashew cream that served as the pot pie's gravy. I was even happier when Professor Swihart wanted to know if I could scale up my recipes for groups of fifty to sixty. I hoped the professor's interest was actually tied to a faculty event and not simply curiosity. I figured as a scientist she was all-too-familiar with the potential problems associated with going from small batches to large-scale production.

Though we'd served generous portions of the entrées, the plates Mollye and I returned to the kitchen were totally bare. Another good sign.

"I think Harriett licked her plate when no one was looking," Mollye whispered when we reached the kitchen. "Hard to believe a fork could scrape up every smidgeon of sauce."

I didn't bother to send a give-it-a-rest glare Moll's way. She'd been an enormous help and on good behavior, acting like a server in a five-star restaurant. Ought to have her train my future staff.

For my dessert finale I'd paired a gorgeous nut-crusted fruit pie with a creamy chocolate mousse. Even Aunt Eva admitted the mousse was delicious although she always mumbled dairy would make it even better.

"What should we serve first?" I asked Mollye.

"You can't top chocolate," she answered. "Serve the fruity pie first, then the chocolate."

Moll delivered slender wedges of pie first. Once a round of appreciative "umms" were heard in my now messy kitchen, I delivered the dishes of chocolate mousse.

I was feeling almost giddy. Not a glitch. I returned to the kitchen to retrieve a tray loaded with little gift bags for the guests. Smiling, I stepped onto the sunporch just as Della jumped up.

"Why are you here?" Della yelled at Harriett as the chair toppled sideways and fell to the floor. "What a bloody hypocrite!"

"Chill, will ya?" Harriett replied. "I'd be happy to give you one of my AEP t-shirts, they spell out my philosophy: 'Animals Eaten like Popcorn'."

My stomach knotted. What was happening? Everyone was playing nice so long as they had food on their plates. How had AEP come up?

"I'm a proud member of Animals Entitled to Personhood." Della's voice quivered. She was beyond angry.

I screwed my eyes shut. I feared whatever started this argument could only escalate. I had to do something.

I had no idea Della belonged to AEP. The organization denounced dozens of professions as inhumane. It accused cancer researchers who dissected mice as soulless. Pest exterminators were labeled contract killers. Scorn was heaped on fisherman. Veterinarians who euthanized animals were castigated.

"Please, you are all my guests," I interrupted. "Surely we can agree on one thing—plant-based recipes can be delicious—whether we choose to eat them every day or simply on occasion."

Della nodded at me. "The food was fabulous. Thank you. But I need to leave before the company gives me indigestion."

As she marched out, I looked around the table at the five remaining guests. Harriett's pudgy arms crisscrossed her chest and a Cheshire smile of satisfaction rose above her double chins. Dr. Swihart seemed intent on refolding a napkin. Mom frowned. Ursula looked thoughtful.

Bert started laughing. "Guess I have my lead for tomorrow's restaurant column."

Holy Havarti, this kind of publicity would not help.

Judge Ursula pushed back her chair and stood. She raised her wine glass in preparation for a toast. She appeared as she did on TV—in control, sure of her verdict—all she lacked was her black robe.

"Bert, Harriett, Victoria," she began, "remember why you were invited. How you describe today's luncheon can have unintended consequences. Surely you can be generous enough to disassociate our talented young chef from a disagreement among her guests. Brie's promising Summer Place B&B and restaurant doesn't deserve to be caught up in an animal rights feud in which she plays no part."

Bert quit laughing. Harriett squirmed in her seat. They looked sheepish—like so many chastised claimants in Judge Ursula's TV court. Dr. Swihart looked up from her napkin and nodded her assent. *Thank you, Ursula.*

The judge smiled. "Now let's drink to our talented chef. To Brie Hooker. You deserve much success."

Following Ursula's toast, the guests bid quiet farewells full of compliments. They seemed delighted by the gift goody-bags filled with vegan cookies, recipe cards for the dishes served, and of course, business cards with info on catering and dinner parties.

Mom and Ursula were the last to leave.

"So sorry about that row between Harriett and Della," Mom said. "I could see it going downhill the moment Harriett began boasting that she'd scored five pounds of veal for her freezer. That's when Della's eyes narrowed to slits. I once heard Della go off on big chicken producers. Said they should be jailed like their hens and fed antibiotics and hormones until their breasts grew to the size of watermelons. I totally forgot her AEP fervor when I put her on the guest list."

"It's okay, Mom." I sighed. "Seems like people who hold different opinions only yell at each other these days. Judge Ursula saved the day. With any luck, Harriett's and Bert's reviews of the food won't appear as a footnote to an animal rights war."

Ursula smiled. "I hope so. By the way, I plan to move into your little cottage later today. Didn't get my bags packed in time to bring them with us."

Mollye wagged a finger at me as if I'd been naughty. "You're calling that shack a little cottage? There's still time to escape."

Ursula smiled. "The cottage is perfect. Private and off the beaten path. No one will come looking for me there."

"That's a safe bet." Mollye snorted.

"Would you like help moving in?" I asked. "I'll be here a couple of hours cleaning up."

Ursula brushed aside my offer with an "I travel light" response.

Once Mom and Ursula left, Mollye and I headed into the kitchen to scavenge something to eat. While the desserts were totally gone, there were single servings left of each appetizer and entrée. Mollye put her dibs on the stuffed mushrooms and pot pie. The veggie cups and paella were fine with me. I'd have eaten almost anything. Well, baby carrots but no baby cows.

We chowed down standing at the kitchen counter.

"Thanks so much for helping out," I said.

"Always interesting hanging with you, but the WWW match was an unexpected bonus," Mollye replied. "Wonder if Harriett knew Della belonged to AEP when she started poking her?"

"It wouldn't surprise me. I should have listened to the anonymous friend who warned about giving her a seat at the table."

"Have you ever asked Eva how she feels about AEP?" Mollye asked. "Can't think of anyone who treats her own animals more like family."

"Eva thinks AEP folks go too far. Of course, my aunt also likes a rare ribeye now and again."

Mollye laughed. "You know you owe me. Next time I sign up for a booth at an art fair I expect you to sell my pottery."

"Deal," I replied.

Mollye wandered over to the refrigerator. "Sure there's no more chocolate mousse hiding in here?"

TWELVE

I declined Mollye's offer to help with cleanup.

"Go on," I said. "You have your own business to run and I've tied you up most of the day. Doing dishes will give me a chance to power down. My brain can use some mindless task time to sort out what happened."

I spent almost two hours cleaning the kitchen and tidying up. I hand washed all of the crystal and fine china Mom had lent me. I even tackled tasks that didn't need doing just to keep busy. I put shelf paper in an empty cupboard I wouldn't need for a year. Not till I had money to buy the dishes that would go there.

Once I ran out of busywork chores, I set off for a final walk through of the cottage. I checked to make sure I hadn't left any junk lying about for Ursula to trip over. I even scoured the bathroom sink a fourth time, hoping elbow grease might lighten the disgustingly dark stains. No luck.

As I trudged back to Summer Place, Dad's ringtone sounded on my pocketed cell.

"Hi, Dad, did Mom tell you about the tasting? Everyone loved the food. Not—"

"Brie," Dad cut in. "Are you ill? Do I need to come get you?"

Huh? "What are you talking about?"

"I thought you might be sick, too. Ursula and your mom are very ill. Abdominal pain, vomiting. When Ursula's heart started racing, I drove both of them to the emergency room. The ER doctor diagnosed it as food poisoning, since they both presented symptoms shortly after they'd eaten together."

I stumbled on the cobbled footpath. Mom, Ursula, sick? The hairs on the back of my neck rose and bile climbed my throat. "Oh, no. Will they be okay? What did the doctor say?"

"They'll be fine," Dad replied. "Your mother is on an IV to replace fluids, but the ER doctor said she should be able to come home soon. They want to keep Ursula overnight for observation. They took blood and urine samples. But until they determine if the illness is caused by a virus or bacteria, they're not prescribing antibiotics. Just keeping your mom and Ursula hydrated and quiet."

Once Dad's calm voice reassured me Mom and Ursula would be fine, my mind fastened on the reason they were ill—food poisoning. My food. I was horrified. Was I to blame?

"They're sure it's food poisoning? You know how careful I am about washing vegetables, and I'm fanatic about hygiene. Could Mom and Ursula have eaten a snack before they came to Summer Place? Please, no! It can't be the food at my tasting."

"Calm down, honey," Dad said. "I know this is the last thing you want to do, but you need to contact your other luncheon guests. Make sure they're not ill."

Stinky Limburger. I groaned. "How can I call folks and ask if I made them puke? I'm not sick and I ate what they ate. Mollye did, too. She was fine when she left a little while ago."

"Did you and Mollye eat everything your guests did?" Dad, the logical professor, probed.

"Yes. Everything. Except the desserts." I frowned. "The fruit pie and chocolate mousse were all gone. Harriett Quinn and Bert Rider asked for extras. Polished off both dishes."

I moaned. *Please don't let the two food critics fall ill. What a disaster.*

"Start with those two," Dad urged. "If they ate more of the suspect foods, you need to make certain they're okay."

My mind raced. Could I call them on some other pretext? A thank you? Maybe ask if they left behind a pair of sunglasses?

No, I had to warn them. *Grow up.* What if their symptoms simply took longer to appear? Did they live alone? Shoot, I was pretty sure all of the guests except Mom were single, though I had no idea if they had housemates who could help them if they took ill at home.

"I'll contact Bert and Harriett, then I'll try to catch up with Della," I said. "Professor Swihart said she was meeting a doctoral student this afternoon to discuss his thesis. Can you drop by her office at the university?"

"I'll walk over to her building now," Dad replied. "Then I'll head back to the hospital."

"Call me as soon as you know more." I closed my eyes. "Please tell Mom and Ursula how sorry I am."

By the time the call ended, I'd reached the porch. I slumped in a chair and stared at my phone. I didn't have cell numbers for Harriett or Bert. I'd contacted Bert through his email at the *Greenville News*, and I'd sent a personal message to Harriett via her business Facebook page.

I googled the Greenville paper, called the main number, and listened to a robotic voice offer an endless number of extension options. After what seemed like an hour, I connected with a real, breathing human being.

"Hi, could I speak with Bert Rider, please?" My heart raced as I waited for a response.

"Who's calling?" the woman asked.

Reluctantly, I gave my name. If the poor guy was nauseous would he even take my call?

"Sorry, don't know when he'll be back. Came in for an hour. Then he felt ill and left."

Cheeses. Not a doubt now. Somehow I'd made everyone sick. That thought roiled my own stomach.

"I need to reach him. I'm afraid he might be suffering from food poisoning. He needs to see a doctor."

The woman chuckled. "Don't worry. Hope you're not the cook he was cursing. Said he was going to an Urgent Care facility. Then, as soon as he could safely get five feet away from a toilet, he'd head to his lawyer's. Vowed he'd sue the idiot who'd made him sicker than an eight-year-old sneaking a Marlboro from his daddy's stash."

Wonderful. Bad press *and* a lawsuit.

"Thank you," I hung up.

If Bert had already sought medical help and leapt to the conclusion my cooking was responsible, there was no point hunting him down. Nothing I could do except seek legal counsel.

Good thing Mom was a lawyer. Of course, as the City of Clemson's attorney, her primary focus was prosecution not defense.

Okay, how to reach Harriett? I called up her website. It only allowed for contact via an email form. No phone number. I opened the Contact Me app and filled out the comment section, asking Harriett to call me. I added that a luncheon item might have been contaminated and I wanted to make certain she was symptom free. As soon as I pushed the Send button, I wondered if Bert's lawyers could use my wording as evidence against me.

I had Della Doyle's cell number. She answered on the fourth ring.

"Della, I'm sorry to bother you but Mom and Ursula appear to be suffering from food poisoning, and I want to make sure you're okay."

"I'm feeling a tad nauseous," Della said. "Nothing serious. Made a couple of, um, productive bathroom visits. I'm feeling much better now."

"I'm so sorry," I said. "I can't imagine what happened."

"Don't worry," she said. "You're a marvelous chef, Brie. Unfortunately none of us can control what we buy in stores these days. I once served my late husband a mushroom casserole that made him so sick he looked like a bleached dish rag. Don't blame yourself."

She paused. "And I'm sorry I let Harriett bait me into losing my temper. I didn't mean to ruin what had been a wonderful lunch."

The cordial call made me feel slightly better though still plenty worried. Time to phone Mollye. While I was relatively sure we'd escaped whatever plague had attached itself to one of my desserts, I wanted to make certain my best friend was her kick-ass self.

"Hey, Brie." Mollye's cheerful answer on the second ring told me she was fine. A big sigh of relief.

I shared the horrible news, then asked, "Harriett's phone number's unlisted. Don't suppose you know it?"

"No, but she works out of her house. We can probably catch her there."

Mollye gave me the address in a neighborhood that had sprung up on the edge of the town of Ardon. I paid no heed to the posted speed limits as I raced to Elm Street. Still Moll beat me. Mollye looked the picture of health, tapping her foot impatiently as she stood by her Starry Skies van.

"You didn't tell me helping serve your luncheon could also involve doing CPR on your victims," Mollye grumped. "I'll tell you right now, if Harriett has erupted at either end, I'm not helping with clean-up."

The image made me shudder. I screwed up my courage and marched up the steps to the blogger's front porch. Her house was a cute but tiny Arts and Crafts style knock-off. Mollye tagged along, taking refuge behind me as I rang the bell. Didn't blame her. I wasn't eager to come face to face with someone who wanted to chop my head off. Of course, I'd feel worse if

Harriett was suffering like Ursula and Mom, and she had no one to take her to the ER.

No answer. I rang the bell a second time, then a third. I pounded on the wooden door, just in case she couldn't hear the bell.

"Maybe Harriett didn't come home after the luncheon," I said.

"No, she must be here," Mollye answered. "Her car's in the carport beside the house."

My friend strode across the porch to one of three long windows and cupped her hands around her eyes to peer inside.

"Uh...Better start practicing new cheese and meat curses," Mollye said. "Think you're going to need a lot of vocabulary. Harriett's sprawled on the floor. Must be pretty darn sick if she can't raise up enough to see who's hammering on her door like a carpenter gone plum crazy."

I rushed to Mollye's side and looked through the window. My heart sank. "We have to get help." I dialed 911.

Just as I finished the call, Mollye walked in Harriett's front door. "It isn't locked," she called to me. Goosebumps rippled up my arms. Less than forty-eight hours ago we'd walked inside another unlocked house and found someone dead. Dear Lord, not again.

I forced myself to follow Mollye inside. Despite my friend's earlier snark that she wouldn't offer aid to my victims, she marched straight to where Harriett lay face down on the floor and placed two fingers on her neck.

Moll turned. Eyes wide. Lips quivering. All traces of amusement gone. She shook her head as she jerked her hand away. "Harriett's dead."

THIRTEEN

I froze for an instant, standing in a virtual stranger's house, wondering if something I cooked had killed the woman. Strange what imprints on your brain in moments of stress. Harriett's calf-link muumuu had hiked thigh high when she collapsed, creating a series of folds. The flowers decorating the tent dress had collapsed upon themselves. The muumuu's bright orange blossoms looked wilted and clashed with the violet shade of the patterned rug.

Then the smell registered. She'd been sick. *Hairy hamhocks!* I gagged and swallowed, trying to stymie the bile making a run for it straight up my throat.

Snap out of it. You just took a refresher CPR course. Maybe Harriett's not dead. Maybe you can revive her.

"Help me roll Harriett on her back." I wiped my sweaty palms on my pants before I took hold of the woman's shoulder.

Mollye scooted beside me and grabbed a handful of muumuu by Harriett's hips. We pulled and tugged. Harriett teetered on her side for a moment before plopping on her back.

One look at Harriett's pasty and puffy face, and I felt bile make another attempt to climb my esophagus. Thank heaven the newest CPR guidelines emphasized compression, not mouth-to-mouth resuscitation.

Shame immediately followed my selfish thought. I checked Harriett's mouth for obstructions. My ear grazed her lips as I listened for any hint of breath. Nothing. All I could hear was my own hammering heart.

I placed the heel of my right hand on her chest, cupped my left hand on top, and interlocked my fingers. I pushed hard, and set up a fast rhythm. What was the song the CPR teacher told us to hum? Yes, "Staying Alive!" I tried to synch my actions with the song's rapid beat.

"Holy moly, you're gonna break her ribs," Mollye exclaimed.

Tears streamed down my cheeks. Sweat trickled down my back. *Breathe, Harriett!*

After a minute, I stopped. Forced myself to tilt her chin up. I clamped my lips over hers. Two quick breaths. Back to compression. *One, two, three...Staying Alive!*

I don't know how many times I repeated the protocol. I'd entered some twilight zone. Pretended I inhabited an alternate universe. It was almost as if I'd gone outside myself to observe.

Strong arms lifted me up and away. "We'll take over," a man's voice commanded.

I hadn't even heard the EMS crew arrive. As the first responders went to work, Moll helped me stagger outside. At the side of the house, I fell to my knees, my cheek almost touching a forsythia bush flush with yellow buds.

I left my lunch there. Dry heaves followed. A strange thought chased through my brain. Was I frozen in a downward dog yoga pose?

I felt a cool hand on my forehead. "You gonna be sick some more?" Mollye asked.

"No." I squirmed into a sitting position and pulled a tissue from my pocket to wipe my mouth. My hands shook. I wasn't sure I could stand. My legs felt like disconnected rubber bands. "Sorry even a whiff of a hurl turns me green."

In my heart I knew it wasn't the retching that made me so sick. A young woman, younger than me, not yet thirty, was dead. I was to blame. The guilt made me ill.

I curled my legs under me and shook my head to clear the cobwebs. "Dad hasn't called back. What if Harriett isn't the only one to die?"

I looked pleadingly at Mollye as the horror of the situation made it hard to breathe. "Dear God, I hope Dad found Professor Swihart alive."

Moll raised an eyebrow. "Wonder how Della will feel about screaming at Harriett once she finds out she's no longer among the living?"

I phoned Dad and started jabbering as soon as he picked up. "Harriett's dead. The coroner's on the way to make it official. Please tell me is Dr. Swihart okay?"

"Slow down, honey," Dad pleaded. "I just left Victoria's office. She's fine. Not a single symptom of food poisoning. The puzzle seemed to fascinate her. Wondered why she felt dandy when Ursula and Iris got so sick. Victoria volunteered to run lab tests on the food to try to determine cause. Of course, when she made the offer, she didn't know Harriett was dead. Not sure she'll want to get involved now that there'll be an official investigation."

"What do you mean 'official'?" I had a good idea what official meant but a girl can always hope she's wrong.

Mom was the family attorney, but I counted on Dad to patiently explain criminal investigations. His day job might be teaching horticulture, but his passion was crafting mysteries. He was president of the local Sisters in Crime chapter, and he attended the Writers' Police Academy every year to increase his knowledge of homicide investigations, forensics, and general crime fighting.

Homicide? How did that word worm its way into my head? Though my guilt was a heavy weight, I prayed an accidental food poisoning couldn't be deemed murder. A niggle of wishful thinking snuck into my brain. Maybe Harriett's death was totally unrelated. Yeah, right, just a coincidence that three of her lunch mates had simultaneously turned green at the gills.

"Honey, did you hear what I said?" Dad demanded.

Nope. I'd momentarily tuned him out.

"Sorry. I spaced out for a few secs. Could you repeat that?"

"Harriett's cause of death probably will be ruled 'undetermined' until an autopsy's performed. The medical examiner is certain to request lab screens for toxins. I'm pretty sure investigators will visit your kitchen."

The idea that my sparkling Summer Place kitchen might be viewed as a crime scene made me feel ill all over again. On the other hand, I was desperate to know what happened. How could I have served something that cost Harriett Quinn her life?

Dad and I promised to keep our cell phones on and let each other know instantly about new developments. He was staying by Mom's bed at the hospital until she was released.

My next task was to reach Eva, tell her I wouldn't be home to help with evening chores. No sense trying to phone my aunt. She was certain to be outside on such a sunny day. The odds of Eva carrying a cell phone into the barnyard were slightly lower than her forsaking cheese.

Maybe Andy Green, our handsome veterinarian and my every-other-week beau, was in the neighborhood and could swing by Udderly Kidding

Dairy to let Eva know. He answered on the first ring. I explained the situation.

"Do what you need to do," Andy said. "I'll come find you after I update Eva."

The first screams pierced the air as I ended the call. I staggered around the corner of the house to see what was happening. The EMS crew was wheeling Harriett's now shrouded form into the ambulance as a shrieking woman ran straight at Mollye.

"You murdered my baby," she wailed. Moll covered her head as the mad haranguer pummeled her protecting arms with her fists.

Then the woman spotted me. "You devil worshipper," she yelled and made a beeline in my direction. The large shiny black pocketbook hitched over her shoulder slid down her arm. She seized it with both hands and barreled toward me holding the monster bag over her head.

At first, I didn't place her red, tear-streaked face. She was definitely someone who'd loved Harriett. Knowing why the screamer wanted to batter me with a handbag turned off my fight response. My alternate beat-feet option didn't kick in until the pocketbook slammed into my right shoulder. It felt like I'd been slugged with a five-pound bag of Idaho spuds. Ouch.

"Run!" Mollye yelled.

Her exhortation pretty much matched my inclination. I could definitely outrun a middle-aged lady dressed in nylons and pump heels. Not only was I decked out in running shoes and loose pants, I had the assailant by at least twenty years.

Was this really happening? It felt more like a bizarre nightmare than real life.

A sheriff's cruiser swung in front of me and screeched to a stop. Yep, this was real. Deputy Danny McCoy, Mollye's boyfriend, leapt from the car and swerved into my path. I tried to brake. I bounced against his chest, and he swallowed me in his beefy but solid arms. I teetered for a moment before I rocked to a standstill.

"What in Hades is going on?" Danny swung me around, putting his stocky body between the mad woman and me. She was coming for me as fast as her pantyhose-encased legs permitted. Danny's peace-making efforts were rewarded with a pocketbook right-hook to his noggin.

"Hey, stop that, Mrs. Quinn," Danny yelled as she bonked him again while trying to land one on me. "Stop or I'll arrest you for assaulting an officer. Why are you chasing Brie Hooker?"

"That devil woman killed my baby, my Harriett," she screamed. "She's a murderer. Take her to jail before I kill her myself. She lured my Harriett to some pretend lunch to poison her. Bet she killed Karen, too."

Apparently she hadn't heard the erotic asphyxiation rumor. I'd rather take a beating than tell her.

Mrs. Quinn's head darted around Danny's restraining arms so she could level a hateful glare at me. The woman was Harriett's mother, and one of Susan Young's cross-bearing goat haters. That meant she was a comrade-in-picketing of the late Karen Vincent, whose body Mollye and I had discovered.

Holey Swiss on a shingle.

A knot of curious onlookers formed a circle around Mrs. Quinn, Danny, and me. The neighbors had been coaxed from homes by the siren calls of the ambulance and sheriff's cruiser. A quartet of teens held cell phone cameras high recording the thwarted cat fight for posterity.

Wonderful. The Hooker clan had gained enough notoriety last Halloween after Udderly Kidding Dairy became a major crime scene for the second time. The purpose of my tasting was to grab headlines for my cuisine not for how many people wound up dead in my vicinity.

The *Ardon Chronicle* would have a field day. I predicted a likely headline: "Brie Hooker Tasting Kills Food Blogger" or "Brie Hooker: Food To Die For".

I glanced back at the grieving mother and shame mingled with my guilt. How could I be concerned about my reputation as a chef when this woman had just lost her daughter?

"I'm so very sorry," I said. "You don't know how guilty I feel. Believe me, I tasted everything I cooked. I have no idea what happened."

"Did you hear her?" Mrs. Quinn screeched. "She admitted it. Brie Hooker killed my daughter."

A pair of strong hands clamped onto my shoulders. The hold was too tight for me to turn anything but my head. I looked up into a pair of emerald eyes. Troubled eyes.

"Danny, is it okay if I take Brie out of here?" Andy Green asked. "Maybe you can escort Mrs. Quinn back to her daughter's house?"

The sheriff's deputy nodded. "Yes, but don't you leave yet. Let me get

Mrs. Quinn settled. I'll be right back for a few words with Brie."

Andy relaxed his grip on my shoulders. I pivoted to give his lean strong body a hug. His work shirt smelled of cows and sweat. The odors didn't stop me from hugging him a second time.

Deputy Danny came back in a flash. "I asked the crew of that second ambulance to treat Mrs. Quinn for shock." Danny fumbled in his shirt pocket for a spiral notepad. "Brie, what made you say you felt guilty?"

I gave a brief synopsis of the tasting, providing Danny with the names of all my guests. I added that his very own Mollye helped prepare and serve the lunch. I also provided an update on my guests' current health or lack thereof.

"You know where to find Brie," Andy said. "And Mollye can certainly fill you in on more details. So how about letting us leave? I think Brie's continued presence will just stir up more trouble with Harriett's relatives."

"Go on, get going," Danny said. "What a nightmare. Mrs. Quinn said she's calling Reverend Nickles to come pray with her. Sure hope Sheriff Mason gets here soon."

FOURTEEN

"Thanks, Andy," I whispered as we walked away from the growing crowd.

"Go on and get in my truck. It's parked down the block," he said. "I see Mollye by the ambulance. I'll let her know you're leaving with me. Did you and Mollye drive here together?"

"No. The ambulance is hiding my Prius. I met Mollye here."

"Okay. We'll come back for your car later. Where do you want to go?"

For a second, the serious look on Andy's face lightened. "Your eyebrows are doing that meet-in-the-middle, what-the-heck number. Just a guess, but you have no idea what to do next."

"Right you are. I'm confused. Hey, didn't I just call and ask you to stop by Udderly to see Eva? How did you get here so fast? Udderly's at least half an hour away even if you speed."

"A lucky coincidence. I was at the feed store when you called. Eva walked in a minute after you hung up. Said she'd call one of the temps to help Gerri with evening chores. Ordered me to locate you, and—okay, these are her words—'pull Brie's fanny out of whatever fire is scorching her bottom'."

"Ah, yes, Aunt Eva doesn't pull punches. Unfortunately her analysis is spot on. Harriett's mother's convinced I murdered her daughter, and she suspects I had a hand in Karen Vincent's death, too. She'd like to burn me at the stake."

"Karen wasn't at your luncheon and Mollye told me the two of you discovered her naked body. Why on earth would she think you had anything to do with her death?" Andy asked.

I shrugged. "Maybe she thinks the goats told me to kill Harriett and murder Karen after stealing all her clothes. When we ran Susan Young, Mrs. Quinn, and Karen off Udderly yesterday, they were mighty steamed."

"Say what?" Andy shook his head. "Boy, do I miss out on news when it's not my designated boyfriend week. Who did you run off Udderly? No wait. Tell me all about it after we escape. I'll let Mollye know we're taking off. Should I tell her where we're headed?"

I nodded. "Dad's bringing Mom home from the hospital so I'd like to make my folks' house our first stop. Tell Mollye she's welcome to join us. Not that she ever needs an invite. It would kill her to miss out on the latest news."

A bit unsteady, I walked to Andy's truck and climbed inside the cab. I had no trouble keeping Andy's six-foot-four frame in sight. He was a head taller than most of the crowd. He looked like a nimble giraffe as he loped along the sidewalk, dodging oblivious curiosity seekers. He buttonholed Mollye. She looked my way and put her hands on an imaginary wheel to pantomime driving. Her way of confirming she'd be on our tail.

Ten minutes later we arrived at my parents' house. A slight breeze ruffled the blooming Bradford pear trees and teased their blossoms free, creating a virtual snowstorm of white petals. Dad's SUV sat in the driveway—a good sign he'd brought Mom home.

I gave the front door a "we're coming in" warning knock before rushing inside. The door was unlocked as usual. Oh, no. They needed to start locking their door. Any illusions I had about small-town safety were fast disappearing.

I couldn't wait to see Mom with my own eyes. Despite the advantage provided by his long legs, Andy barely kept up.

My heart seized when I spotted Mom huddled at one end of the living room couch. Her dainty feet encased in pink slippers peeked out from under the blanket tucked around her tiny body. A size two who could shop in the children's section, Mom's petite build served as effective camouflage when unknown opponents faced her in court. They never seemed prepared for her towering intellect or powers of persuasion. Today, however, she looked pale and oh so fragile. Still she managed a welcoming smile.

"I'm so sorry about your tasting, Brie. I know how terrible you must feel."

"You're sorry?" I exclaimed. "Harriett's dead and you, Ursula, and Bert are ill. I'm the one who's sorry. It's all my fault. How's Ursula doing? Can she have company?"

"Ursula's much better," Dad answered as he walked in from the kitchen. "She'll be released from the hospital tomorrow morning. She isn't blaming you, Brie."

"She doesn't have to," I said. "I'm blaming myself. Something I served did in poor Harriett and made everyone else sick."

"Not everyone," Dad interrupted. "Dr. Swihart didn't have a single symptom, and Della's reaction was quite mild. Are you sure Dr. Swihart and Della ate everything you served?"

"Absolutely," Mollye chimed in. She'd barged into the living room out of breath before Andy closed the front door.

"We served the same size helpings to everyone and when I took the plates away they were empty. Since Cashew wasn't around to beg for scraps under the table, Della and the professor must have eaten their desserts."

I nodded. "No other way to make the food disappear. Impossible to stash that much fruit and gooey chocolate under a napkin unnoticed."

I glanced over at Mom as she took a sip of water. She didn't need a crowd in her living room. "You need your rest, Mom. We should leave."

"Don't be silly," she replied. "I'm happy to see you, and Andy and Mollye, too. Sit down. With Harriett dead, there'll be an investigation. Maybe we can help the authorities figure out what ingredient might be tainted. Whatever it is, it needs to come off the shelves before more people get sick. You've narrowed it down to the desserts, right?"

I sat next to Andy on a loveseat, while Mollye settled on the opposite side of the couch from Mom. Dad, as usual, claimed the room's large leather recliner.

"It has to have been in the fruit pie or chocolate mousse," I answered. "Mollye and I ate everything else and neither of us got sick."

Andy cleared his throat. "But, as Howard pointed out, Dr. Swihart didn't get sick either. Maybe the three of you have immune systems that can handle whatever germ, toxin, or bug is at fault."

Dad's eyebrows bunched together. "Good point. Whatever caused the illness appears to affect individuals differently. Maybe Harriett died because she had a compromised immune system. Any possibility she was HIV positive?"

Mollye sputtered. "Man, if she was, Mrs. Quinn will have a conniption fit. According to her church, HIV is God's way of punishing people for sins of the flesh."

"You're talking about the Temple of True Believers?" Mom's

eyebrows shot up.

Mollye nodded. "Yep. Didn't Brie tell you that Mrs. Quinn was a member of the religious vigilante party at Udderly Kidding yesterday? Three idiots spouting nonsense about evil goats."

Mom's and Dad's blank looks provided Mollye with an answer.

Andy rubbed his hands together. "Okay, Brie. What's Mollye talking about? I've been dying to hear the rest of this story. What gives?"

I filled Mom, Dad, and Andy in on the appearance of Susan Young and her posse as well as her vow to prevent us from luring Ardon County residents into goat worship and putting them on a fast track to hell. I also described Aunt Eva's goat-milk, Baa-phooey baptism of Susan.

Andy and Dad howled with laughter. Mom didn't crack a smile.

"The 'true believer' portion of that cult's name should tell you something." Mom scowled. "They truly believe God has anointed them to do whatever they happen to decide is His bidding. The laws of mortal men don't apply. Fanatics of any stripe are downright dangerous. Remember that sex toy store that got torched on Highway 33, killing the cleaning woman trapped inside? Scuttlebutt around the courthouse said the arsonists belonged to that temple's congregation. There simply wasn't enough evidence to bring anyone to trial."

"Was Harriett a member of that church?" I asked.

Andy nodded. "She was. I know the Quinns. Whole family attends the Temple."

"Given the congregation's apparent belief that goats are the devil, or at least his surrogates, why did Harriett accept my luncheon invitation? Maybe she didn't know I was one of the Hookers living at Udderly Kidding Dairy."

Mollye chuckled. "Nah, Harriett knew. What with all the fall media frenzy about you and Rita the Mule playing dodgeball with hired killers, every living soul within five hundred miles of Ardon knows who you are and where you live."

She paused to suck in a breath. "Hey, it's simple. Harriett saw your tasting as a free lunch. Sorry. Mama would wash my mouth out for speaking ill of the dead. But it's true. Harriett used her farm-to-table blog to snag all the freebies she could. Guess she was of a mind to separate church gospel from her pocketbook."

I glanced at Mom. Her eyelids fluttered and her head dropped. She looked exhausted. I walked over and kissed her forehead. It felt cold and clammy.

"We need to leave so you can rest, Mom. I'll make a list of every ingredient in those desserts, and I'll bag samples of every morsel still in my kitchen."

"Good idea, dear." Mom's voice had turned soft and breathy. "That'll show you're conscientious and eager to help determine if there's a continuing threat to community health."

FIFTEEN

Andy drove me to Summer Place; Mollye followed in her car. Though Daylight Savings Time was still a month away, the days were lengthening. It was still light when Andy pulled his truck in the driveway.

As he made the turn, the curtains twitched in my across-the-street neighbors' house. One of the Miss Medleys was on alert, cataloguing the comings and goings at my future B&B. My cell phone beeped right after I switched on the kitchen lights.

"Brie, there are lights on in Summer Place but I don't see your car, just a truck and that flashy van Mollye Camp drives. Since she's there, I assume your visitors have permission. But better safe than sorry."

I assured Miss Medley I was among Summer Place's current occupants and thanked her profusely for keeping tabs on my property.

Andy smiled. "Wow. If she's going to report every vehicle that comes and goes, the woman's going to have her work cut out for her once you open your B&B."

"She's harmless and I'm glad she keeps an eye on Summer Place while it's vacant," I said. "I've worried teens might decide it's a great place for a clandestine hook up. But it's a construction hazard zone. Lots of accidents waiting to happen to anyone sneaking about in the dark."

I frowned as I suddenly recalled Miss Medley's suspected intruder report from last night. An unknown truck had pulled into my driveway after Mollye and I left, and it had lingered for maybe half an hour. Then there'd been the clean bowl. The one I hadn't remembered washing.

Rotten ribeyes! Could a visitor have broken in, used the bowl to add poison to my chocolate mousse, then washed it so I wouldn't notice?

Andy and Mollye looked skeptical as I formulated my theory of a poisoner intruder. I'd settled on the chocolate mousse as the carrier since its dark, rich taste would camouflage any additive stirred into the mix.

Andy rocked back on the porch chair he'd claimed. His crossed arms signaled doubt. "What's the motive? Someone wanted your tasting to be a big failure and didn't care if the little prank cost someone her life?"

Mollye jumped in. "Maybe Brie's not off base. Maybe someone purposely poisoned Harriett because she was blackmailing them. Perhaps the killer researched Harriett's medical condition and knew whatever he added would make her croak. Could be he thought it would only make the others embrace their toilets."

Andy shook his head. "You have such a way with words."

Mollye held up a finger. "Wait. Here's another idea. If there really was an intruder maybe he—or she—only intended to embarrass Brie, and Harriett's death was, oops, a surprise. The goal might have been to make everyone puke, and no one was supposed to kick the bucket."

I shivered. "Geesh, of your two motives, I have to say I prefer Harriett being the intended victim. I'd hate to think someone despises me enough that they're willing to poison innocent bystanders. I've lived in Ardon County less than a year. Hard to imagine I've stirred up that much animosity."

Mollye harrumphed. "You've been pretty quick to inspire both love..." She paused to batt her eyelashes at Andy. "And hate. For the most part, the hate's sort of a side effect of your role in catching murderous scumbags. While said scumbags are now either dead or in jail, they have plenty of relatives in Ardon County."

Andy uncrossed his arms and rocked forward to lean his elbows on the table. His green eyes darkened as he studied my face. "Moll has a point. We should make a list of potential enemies—yours and Harriett's. I'd put Susan Young and Mrs. Quinn of the True Believers on your side of the list, but I can't believe they'd risk harming Harriett, one of their own."

"Harriett posted she'd be at the luncheon, but that doesn't mean the church folk read her blog," I added. "Maybe none of the True Believers knew Harriett was coming."

"How ironic would that be?" Moll asked. "Religious whackos poisoning one of their own. Nope. Doesn't compute. Anyone who tampered with the food had to know Harriett was coming. Her blog was the only way people who weren't invited knew there was a tasting. It wasn't advertised."

I held up a hand. "We're getting ahead of ourselves—and reality.

Time to quit fantasizing and do what we came to do—get samples of all the ingredients in both desserts. Contaminated fruit might be to blame. Avocadoes are what make the mousse so smooth and creamy. Let's make two sets of ingredients. One for Dr. Swihart, one for Sheriff Mason."

I checked the internet to see what steps someone was supposed to take if food poisoning was suspected. South Carolina's Department of Health and Environmental Control—DHEC—offered explicit directions for bagging and labeling foodstuffs.

It took us half an hour to gather the ingredients. The fruit pie's crust was made from dates and nuts, while smashed bananas served as a creamy binder for strawberries, raspberries, and mandarin oranges. We bagged dual samples of everything except the berries. Since I'd used every berry I'd bought, my only recourse was to retrieve packaging from my trash bin to indicate the source. If the berries were contaminated, there'd be other reports.

The chocolate mousse recipe had fewer ingredients: pulverized avocadoes, raw cocoa powder, cashew milk, stevia, and vanilla. I added unpeeled avocados to my inventory and labeled plastic baggies holding tablespoons of the dry ingredients. I poured some of the cashew milk in two small containers and put them in the refrigerator.

"Dr. Swihart's going to analyze one batch of samples, right?" Mollye asked. "Who do you suppose Sheriff Mason will get to test the other set?"

I frowned. "If there's a suspicion of contaminated food, I think it's a special epidemiology team from DHEC but sometimes they call in specialists from the Centers for Disease Control."

Andy looked thoughtful. "They'll screen for things like E. coli, salmonella, listeria, the bacteria commonly introduced during food harvesting or processing. But I'm not sure routine tests would pick up the type of toxins someone might have deliberately introduced to harm folks."

I shivered. "Surely they'll keep testing if the initial ones prove negative. As a toxicologist maybe Dr. Swihart can devise a testing protocol right off the bat to look for more exotic possibilities."

I stashed the samples for the "official" inquiry in Summer Place's commercial size refrigerator. We packed the rest in a cooler for Dr. Swihart.

Moll got up from her chair. "I'm starving. Don't take this personally, but I think I'll pass on any item in your refrigerator. For once, I'd rather raid my own fridge."

I sighed. "I'm afraid that's how everyone will feel once word of Harriett's death circulates. I sure hope the cause doesn't remain a mystery. If it does, I might as well put Summer Place on the market. No one will want to visit a B&B with a to-die-for kitchen."

Andy walked around the table and hugged me.

"Hey, is that allowed?" Mollye tsk-tsked. "Isn't it Paint's week as the boyfriend?"

Andy grinned, his emerald eyes twinkling. "This is a hug from a friend. If it were my week, I'd ask you to leave the room. But I do plan to call Paint tonight. He's goofing off in Charleston when he should be on Brie duty. If he plans to spend more time at the coast, we need to amend our original agreement with an 'alternate' clause—e.g., if boyfriend of the week is absent more than twenty-four hours, the alternate has approved access to Brie Hooker's lips."

Mollye snorted. "What if you're tied up more than twenty-four hours birthing colts or operating on cats?"

"That's different," Andy replied straight-faced. "Brie has the option to tool over and visit me, wipe the sweat from my brow as I bravely coax a breech colt to enter the world."

My nose wrinkled. "Sorry Andy, but given a choice between playing scrub nurse in a barn or buzzing off to Charleston to dine with prospective investors, Paint would have the edge. He did invite me, you know? Now I wish I'd gone instead of staying for this *wonderful* tasting."

"I'm crushed," Andy replied. "Guess it's time to drive my *friend*, Brie, back to pick up her car. Wonder if anyone from the sheriff's department is still at Harriett's house."

I locked the sunporch door as we left. Andy reached behind me and rattled the knob. "Doesn't hurt to double check," he said.

SIXTEEN

We stuck the cooler with Dr. Swihart's samples in the cab of Andy's truck and drove to Harriett's. Sheriff Kyle Mason was climbing inside one of the two cruisers sitting at the curb ready to leave.

I hopped out of Andy's truck to buttonhole Mason. I held on to a slim hope he'd share information that would clear me of even a peripheral role in Harriett's death.

"Hi, Sheriff. Guess you heard Harriett was one of my guests at a tasting today."

Mason nodded, and I hurried on before he could deliver the lines he'd spoken so often last fall: "Can't comment on an ongoing investigation."

"Since some of my other guests have taken ill, a contaminated ingredient in one of my desserts may be to blame. I just left Summer Place where we put together samples of all the ingredients for testing. I'm as eager as anyone to find out what happened."

Mason's eyebrow lifted. "I think Mrs. Quinn may be a little more eager. She's leveled some serious accusations. Namely that you poisoned her daughter to get back at her for protesting—do I have this right?—goat yoga devil worship."

Andy interrupted. "Brie's own mother ate the same food as Harriett. Surely that proves Brie wasn't trying to kill anyone."

The sheriff closed the open cruiser door and leaned against it.

"Mrs. Quinn and Reverend Nickles have an answer for that. They say Brie dusted the other folks' dishes with just a touch of poison to make it look like Harriett's death was accidental. The reverend made sure I knew about Professor Howard Hooker's poison expertise. His theory? Professor Hooker told his daughter exactly how much poison to apply to make people sick versus dead."

My fingernails bit into the palms of my hands. A distraction to control my anger. "We went through this malarkey about Dad's poison plants when another Ardon native ate a fatal brownie. Since that happened before your time, here are the facts: Dad grows poisonous plants for Medical University of South Carolina researchers to test as potential cancer treatments. None of his plants are poisonous enough to kill adults unless they consume humongous quantities in a single sitting or over time. Harriett couldn't have died from any plants in Dad's garden."

Sheriff Mason shrugged. "We've spoken to Mollye Camp and all the other luncheon guests," he added. "Not everyone took sick."

"That's not unusual," Andy interjected. "Bacteria can cause violent reactions in some people and mild or no symptoms in others."

"I'll leave the medical opinions to the professionals," Mason said. "Brie, I want you to meet me at Summer Place at nine a.m. tomorrow. Don't go back inside until I arrive." He rubbed his jaw. "Sure wish you hadn't returned tonight. Now no matter what a lab finds Mrs. Quinn will claim you scurried back to get rid of evidence that could prove it was murder. Members of DHEC's epidemiology team will meet us there."

Andy trailed my car back to Udderly Kidding. Aunt Eva flung the cabin door open while we were walking up the steps.

"'Bout time you got home." Eva's scolding tone said she'd been worried. "Andy, glad to see you escorted our wayward chef. Now what's all this about you making your lunch guests sick and killing Harriett?"

The three of us sat at our cabin's kitchen table, and I walked Eva through the day's high and low spots, ending with my troubling conversation with Sheriff Mason.

"Maybe Mrs. Quinn has a point," Eva said, holding up her hand to halt my sputtering retort. "Could be someone wanted to kill Harriett and spiked all the food to make it look like accidental food poisoning."

"Tell Eva about Miss Medley's sighting," Andy interrupted. "There's a possibility someone slipped into Brie's kitchen the night before the tasting."

I told Eva about the truck loitering in the Summer Place driveway and the clean bowl conundrum. "If someone really did sneak in to poison a dessert, how could he be certain only Harriett would die?"

Andy tapped his spoon against his cup. "Maybe he didn't care if everyone died. Maybe he was willing to chance multiple deaths to kill Harriett."

I slumped in my chair. "All I know is that I dished out the desserts, and Mollye delivered them at random. Mollye and I were the only ones who could have given Harriett a pre-determined portion. Despite Mrs. Quinn's ravings, neither of us had any desire to kill the blogger—or Karen. But she didn't want to hear me."

Eva leaned back in her chair. Her eyes looked unfocused. Then she suddenly leaned forward and slapped the table.

"Sometimes those cobwebs have a way of trapping thoughts for a time," she said. "There is a way to use poison and specifically target one person at a table for six. Talk with your friend Mimi, the pharmacist, about drug interactions. Maybe the killer knew Harriett took a medicine that would interact with whatever he added to your dish."

Andy nodded. "Possible. I constantly read about new drug interactions. They concern veterinarians as well as MDs. Still it isn't a very efficient murder method."

"It leaves a lot to chance," I agreed. "Maybe Harriett passes on tasting the dish that's poisoned. Maybe she quits taking the medicine that interacts with the poison. The killer would have to know Harriett very well to know her medical history."

"Maybe not." Eva rose from the table, retrieved her purse, and pulled out a CVS sales slip like a crackerjack prize. "If I throw this slip away, a would-be killer can sort through my garbage and puzzle out every prescription and over-the-counter med I take. Simple as pie."

"Okay, I'll mention the possibility to Sheriff Mason, though I'm sure he'll blow it off. Just fanciful thinking for someone in dire need of an alibi."

My stomach growled. Despite all the talk of food poisoning, my tummy was reminding me I hadn't eaten supper.

"Andy, Eva, are you willing to eat something I cook?" I walked to our cabin's refrigerator to check on leftovers. "I need to eat something or I'll have a headache."

Eva shook her head. "I didn't wait for you to dawdle home from your escapades. Already had me a nice juicy hamburger covered with lots of melted cheese. Yum."

Andy smiled. "Have to admit that burger sounds good, but I'm a nondenominational kind of eater. I'll pretty much snarf up anything you put in front of me, Brie. I have no fear of eating whatever you cook."

I rummaged through the shelves and found leftovers from a vegetarian enchilada casserole. I dished out servings for Andy and me and nuked them in the microwave. "Choose whichever dish you want," I said. "Think I'll make that offer from now on so folks will think I'm at least willing to play Russian roulette if I've poisoned one of the plates."

We'd just started eating when the cabin phone rang. Eva answered. She muttered "un huh" responses to whoever was on the other end of the line.

"That was Governor Strong," she said. "Nice to have friends in high places. Carol says rumors about Harriett's suspicious death have already found their way to Columbia. Apparently the Reverend Guy Nickles is stirring up the right-wing fringe, backing Mrs. Quinn's contention that Brie Hooker, devil goat worshipper, has murdered one of his congregation's true believers. He's calling for an all-out investigation. Says he and his flock won't let authorities bury the matter."

"Wonderful."

Suddenly the enchilada casserole lost all flavor. I pushed my plate away.

"Don't worry." Andy reached over and squeezed my hand. "Your flock of friends is just as determined. I'll call Paint soon as I get home. We may need to put our every-other-week boyfriend routine on hold so we're both around."

"Thanks, Andy," I said. "I'll keep you and Paint up to date. Maybe the three of us should attend church together Sunday. Usually I go to Methodist services. I've never visited the Temple of True Believers. I'd love to show the reverend he can't intimidate me. I could hand out flyers advertising our goat yoga classes as people leave the sanctuary."

Eva frowned. "Whoa. I know you're angry, and I admire your spunk, Brie. But you'd better not be serious. I'm not known for discretion, but lying low until this nonsense blows over makes a whole lot of sense."

Eva had one thing right. I was angry. The idea that a bunch of lunatics were saying I'd poisoned someone on purpose was totally unfair. These people were murdering my reputation, killing my dream.

SEVENTEEN

After Andy left, I called Dad for a bedtime check on Mom and Ursula. Mom had eaten a little chicken noodle soup before retiring, and Ursula was determined to check out of the hospital come morning.

"I hope Ursula isn't planning to move into the cottage out back of Summer Place when she checks out," I said. "She shouldn't be alone right now, even if she's feeling better."

"She's agreed to stay with us for at least one more night," Dad replied. "However, Ursula still wants to move into your cottage as soon as Amber arrives."

Hmm. Amber was a police detective. Maybe she could help us brainstorm.

Knowing Mom and Ursula were on the mend improved my mood—a touch.

Since I hadn't helped Eva with evening chores, I set my alarm even earlier than usual. I wanted to finish all my tasks well before my nine a.m. meeting with the sheriff.

Just two weeks ago my kitchen had passed the required inspection for preparing food for public consumption. Now it was designated a potential crime scene.

Goosebumps slowly meandered up my arms. I definitely wanted to observe while the authorities snooped. Mom was my usual companion if it appeared I was in any legal jeopardy. But since she was under the weather, Dad had insisted he'd pinch-hit.

I arrived at my folks' house at eight-fifteen. Dad gave me a hug and led me to the kitchen, where the Hooker clan always tended to gravitate. Mom hoisted a coffee cup in my direction as a welcome. Though smiling, Mom looked pale, and she was wearing a bathrobe, unheard of attire for Iris Hooker, Esquire, at this time of day. On most weekdays, Mom would have been at her law office for an hour already. She liked to tidy up paperwork before any private clients or city officials called.

"I think Eva would declare you look a might puny," I said.

Mom smiled. "Yeah, a little weak. I wanted to go to Summer Place with you and your dad, but Howard didn't think it was a good idea."

"Agreed. It's your job to get well fast in case I need a legal defense."

Mom's smile vanished. "Don't worry about the empty threats Bert left on your voicemail. People can't sue for accidents unless there's neglect, and you didn't leave food sitting out or fail to wash anything—lettuce, dishes, or your hands. The Greenville paper never published the review Bert claimed he wrote. Legal counsel probably advised against a personal diatribe loaded with unsubstantiated accusations. Don't worry. Sit, have a cup of coffee with me. You have time."

Dad poured me a cup of his stand-a-spoon-up brew, a close cousin to espresso. Since leaving home, I'd migrated to lighter coffee roasts but given the upcoming ordeal I welcomed the added caffeine to stay alert.

"Have you heard from Ursula this morning?" I asked, happy to change the subject.

"Yes," Dad answered. "I promised we'd pick her up at the hospital as soon as we're finished at Summer Place. Ursula seems confident she can arrange a jail break by then."

We chatted a few minutes before Mom waved her hand at me. "You keep glancing at your watch. I know you want to get over to Summer Place. So go. No need to keep me company. Howard, you're taking a notebook, right? Notes can be helpful if Brie ever has to deal with a nuisance lawsuit."

I wished she hadn't reminded me about a possible legal battle. Mrs. Quinn and the Reverend Nickles, a man I'd yet to have the pleasure of meeting, gave me enough problems to think about.

Dad drove. As we turned into my driveway, I spotted Janice Medley walking her poodle. Since the law officers had yet to show and we couldn't go inside until they arrived, I strolled over to chat with Miss Medley. I hoped a proactive approach would stave off neighborhood alarm and wild rumors.

"Hi, Miss Medley." I knelt, gave her poodle a quick pat, and explained that the officials were searching for a source of accidental food poisoning. "If they can ID the source, they can prevent others in the community from buying the same item and falling ill."

As sharp as she was nosy, Miss Medley quizzed me about the dishes I'd served. She seemed determined to make certain no potential threats hid in her pantry or refrigerator. Her white dentures flashed a big smile once I finished my ingredient list. Our menu choices had zero intersections.

She pulled a plastic bag from her sleeve to pick up the doo-doo her poodle had deposited near the curb. "Do your friends still plan to stay out back at Summer Place?" she asked.

"Yes. But they may not move in for a day or two."

When Sheriff Mason's cruiser arrived, I bid my neighbor goodbye. An unmarked white panel van pulled in right behind him. Good thing I had a long driveway.

As I hustled across the street, Sheriff Mason and Deputy Danny exited the cruiser and walked over to Dad, who'd been leaning against his SUV, browsing on his smart phone. Unlike his sister, Aunt Eva, Dad was a cell phone addict, though he still subscribed to ban-the-phone etiquette at any meal.

Before I reached the group, two men emerged from the panel van carrying what looked like large satchels.

"I have the key," I said. "Ready to go in?"

"Yes." Mason's curt reply made me think he'd had a bad night. Had the True Believers been hassling him? He made no attempt to introduce Dad or me to the techs.

I led the way to the sunporch entrance where the tasting was held. I put my palm on the door as I prepared to slide my skeleton key into the lock on the antique door I'd refinished. The unlatched door swung open.

"Holy Havarti. I locked this door last night."

Then I saw the sunporch's overturned chairs. I started to rush inside, but Sheriff Mason grabbed my arm and pulled me back.

"I'll go first. Danny, follow me. The rest of you wait until we make certain it's safe."

My stomach clenched. Someone had broken in last night. I choked back tears. Were they the same visitors who snuck in before my tasting?

Mason and Danny appeared in the doorway. "You can come in but don't touch anything," the sheriff said. "It's a mess."

My body trembled. Dad slipped an arm around my shoulder and hugged me to him. The kitchen I'd spent so much time renovating was a disaster. I gasped when I saw the gleaming commercial oven I was buying on an installment plan desecrated with red spray paint. In all caps, the graffiti delivered a succinct message: BURN IN HELL.

With a steely squint, Sheriff Mason did a slow 360 to catalogue the mayhem. "You sure you locked up when you left last night?"

"I'm absolutely certain." I fought to keep my voice calm. I wanted to scream. "Ask Andy Green. He and Mollye were with me. Andy even checked the door after I turned the key. He wanted to make certain it was locked."

Mason, unblinking, leveled one of his confess-now stares at me. "Did you come back later? Alone?"

I shook my head so violently I could almost feel my brain sloshing from side to side. "No. After we put the samples together, Andy followed me back to Udderly, where we had a bite to eat. When he left, Aunt Eva and I went to bed. I didn't return to Summer Place until I drove over with Dad a few minutes ago."

The sheriff scanned the kitchen. "Where are those samples?"

Uh, oh. Dread mingled with my anger. I turned toward the counter where we'd lined up our little plastic baggies of dry ingredients. Andy, who had the tidiest printing, had neatly labeled each one. The counter was bare.

Braunshweiger on a bun.

I inclined my head toward the empty stretch of counter. "We put samples of dry ingredients and items like bananas that didn't need refrigeration on that counter." I paused. "They're gone."

Mason slipped on a plastic glove. "Guess we ought to see what's in the refrigerator."

I held my breath as he opened the door, afraid of who knew what—a horse's head...a coiled snake...a bomb?

My breath came out in a large whoosh as I peered inside. Empty.

Well, not totally. They'd missed a shriveled lemon wedged at the back of the refrigerator's middle shelf. Everything else was gone—including plenty of items I hadn't used in preparing the tasting selections. The filched foods even included the baby carrots and hummus I kept to snack on during breaks from renovation tasks like sanding woodwork and peeling faded wallpaper.

I bit my trembling lip. "I don't know what to tell you, Sheriff. That refrigerator had stuff on every shelf when I left last night."

Mason looked over at Deputy Danny McCoy and the unintroduced techs. "Glove up and open the cupboards. Let's see if there's anything left here to test."

Dad clamped me to his side as we stood in the kitchen doorway and watched the men fling open door after door to reveal cupboards empty of any foodstuff.

"This makes absolutely no sense," I whispered to Dad. "Why would someone strip the kitchen of everything? If the burglars were the same people who poisoned the food I served, they had to know which dessert they'd doctored. Why would they make a clean sweep and take stuff like my stash of peanut butter?"

The sheriff spun toward me. Apparently Mason had excellent hearing or my whisper wasn't quite as quiet as I thought. "Good question. That is if there really was a break-in last night."

What? *Limburger and Liverwurst.* Was the sheriff insinuating I'd stolen my own food to hide evidence?

"Surely you're not implying Brie snuck back last night to clean out her own kitchen?" Dad's voice rose in volume with his disbelief.

Mason didn't look a bit cowed by my father's ire.

"I'm sure that will be Mrs. Quinn's theory," he calmly replied.

He turned toward the unnamed techs. "Given there's no food to test is there anything you can do?"

"Not really," the taller tech answered. "We can swab the sink drain but can't imagine how it will help. Maybe after the medical examiner autopsies the deceased we'll have a better idea what to test for."

The vandalism felt like a punch in the gut, and my brain acted like a merry-go-round with the same questions circling around and around. When I finally shook off the daze, I spoke to Mason.

"I can still provide samples for testing. We put together a second set for one of my luncheon guests, Dr. Swihart, a toxicologist. She was intrigued that some folks fell quite ill while she had no symptoms so she volunteered to do some testing of her own."

"Where are those samples?" Mason barked. "Does Dr. Swihart have them?"

I took a deep breath before I answered, knowing full well my reply would move me farther into idiot or suspect territory.

"We put the samples in a cooler and stuck it behind a seat in Andy's truck. I imagine the cooler's still there. My brain was fried by the time we got to Udderly, I forgot all about the cooler."

Deputy Danny spoke up. "Andy's supposed to be at my Cousin Larry's farm this morning vaccinating cows. I'll call." The deputy whipped out a cell phone and punched buttons.

After a brief conversation, Danny moved the phone away from his ear to give a report. "Andy's literally penned in with a half-dozen baby calves and their mamas," he said. "But he gave Larry the go-ahead to get the cooler out of his cab. My cousin's walking to the truck now."

While we waited for Larry to finish his treasure hunt, Mason quizzed the techs about testing items that might have spoiled because they hadn't been refrigerated overnight. The answer? Spoilage probably wouldn't mask a toxin's presence.

After Cousin Larry confirmed the cooler was in Andy's truck, Mason arranged to retrieve it. He also decided Dad and I were no longer needed.

"You two can leave. I'll have my people dust for fingerprints and secure the house as a crime scene. We'll let you know when you can return."

He paused and focused on me. "I'd suggest you get a decent lock for this sunporch door. Any kid with a piece of wire or a hairpin could have jiggered it."

I nodded. The sheriff didn't bother to say he'd have more questions for me or that I wasn't to leave Ardon County without letting him know. The two of us had done this dance before. We both knew all the steps.

I just hoped Mason recalled who the bad actors were the last time we danced. Though a suspect, I wasn't among the villains bound for prison when the music stopped.

EIGHTEEN

Dad maneuvered around the sheriff's cruiser and van to back out. Two wheels strayed off the drive and onto the Summer Place lawn. I didn't object. Maybe the tire tracks would murder some of the crabgrass and weeds I eventually had to exterminate.

"Call Ursula," Dad suggested. "Find out if she's cleared to check out. We should be there in ten minutes or less."

I reached Ursula. She said a doctor was about to give her a get-out-of-hospital free card, but she might be incarcerated fifteen more minutes.

Dad parked in the visitors' lot. As we walked toward the hospital, I spotted Lawrence Toomey, the Supreme Court nominee, chatting with a younger man. Given the younger guy's white coat and the stethoscope around his neck, I assumed he was a doctor.

I tugged Dad's sleeve. "Want to find out what Toomey's doing here?"

With a brief nod, Dad took the lead, walking purposefully toward a man he might have once put on a list of males least likely to be a sexual predator.

Toomey saw us coming, pasted on a smile, and stuck out his hand. "Hello, Howard." He inclined his head to include me. "And it's Brie, isn't it? Have you come to see Ursula?"

"Yes," Dad answered deadpan. "We're hoping to take her home with us. I understand she's much better. Are you visiting a friend or family member who's ill?"

"No, no." Toomey smiled. "I dropped by to congratulate the hospital administration on an excellent rating in Medicare's Hospital Compare analysis. Then I heard Ursula, my old law school classmate, had been admitted."

He put a hand on the doctor's shoulder. "Howard, Brie, have you met Dr. Ridley? He treated Ursula, and says she's doing much, much better."

Toomey flicked a look my way. "I heard it was a bad case of food poisoning. One that also killed Harriett Quinn. Any progress in finding the source?"

I ignored Toomey's question and held out my hand to the physician.

"Hello, Dr. Ridley, I'm Brie Hooker. Dad told me how nice you've been. We're so grateful. Any thoughts about what might have made them sick?"

"Judge Toomey just asked the same thing," Dr. Ridley answered. "We ran screens on blood and urine from both patients to see if any of the usual culprits like listeria were at fault. Afraid we didn't find anything. There are many possibilities, but I have no answer."

Dad tugged my arm. "Gentlemen, if you'll excuse us, Ursula is expecting us. Good to see you."

I wished Dad hadn't pulled me away.

"Why didn't you give me a chance to ask Dr. Ridley more questions?" I asked Dad once we reached the elevators.

"I have questions, too," Dad said. "But I didn't want Toomey listening in on the answers. I wonder if he knows Ursula's considering unmasking him as a miserable, misogynist bastard."

When we entered Ursula's room, her bed was empty. Had she tired of waiting for us and left ahead of schedule?

The door to the room's private bathroom was closed. Dad walked over and knocked. "Ursula, you in there?"

"Give me a moment." The warble in her voice suggested she'd been crying.

Ursula opened the door. Her eyes were red and swollen. Her complexion blotchy. She bore no resemblance to the composed Judge Ursula of TV fame.

"Let's get out of here," she managed. "The paperwork's all done. Just need to call a nurse and submit to the final indignity of being wheeled outside."

She attempted a smile. "Come give me a hug, Brie. I can't tell you how sorry I was to hear Harriett died. Please don't let the bad press or anything else make you feel guilty. This wasn't your fault."

Bad press? Racing through my chores at Udderly before meeting the sheriff, I hadn't listened to any newscasts. We didn't take the paper. Aunt Eva refused to subscribe to the *Ardon Chronicle* and give the owners a single penny.

"I haven't read or heard any news today." Did I want to know? I was more than a little afraid to ask. "What are they saying?"

Ursula shuffled over to a nightstand and handed me a copy of the *Chronicle*. This was the same newspaper Allie Gerome, the former publisher, had used to accuse me, Aunt Eva, and Eva's good friend, Governor Carol Strong, of all manner of evil deeds.

The family newspaper was now operated by Allie's nephew, Nate Gerome. Though less toxic than his predecessor, Nate would relish printing any article that cast the Hooker clan in a bad light.

"You can read the story," Ursula answered. "But first, get me out of here and as far away from that slick monster Lawrence Toomey as humanly possible."

"What?" Dad exploded. "Has he been bothering you?"

"You could say so." Ursula choked back a sob. "I'd dozed off for a few minutes. When I woke, Toomey was at the foot of my bed, studying my medical chart. The door to the hospital room was closed. He walked over and grabbed my left hand so I couldn't reach the nurse call button. He squeezed so hard I thought my fingers might snap."

She looked down at her hand and flexed her fingers.

"Once he had my attention, he leaned in to whisper a threat. Said I'd better not dredge up any ancient accusations about a 'sexual indiscretion'—of course, he didn't utter the word 'rape'."

"What?" I gasped. "He threatened you while you were lying in a hospital bed?"

"He promised any attempt I made to sully his reputation would backfire and result in my own character being ripped to shreds. Claimed he'd chatted with several former classmates, male friends who'd swear on a stack of bibles I was a boozing slut, who'd have a hard time remembering how many men I'd screwed on any given night."

A blotch of red climbed Dad's throat and colored his cheeks. A sure sign he was angry. "Toomey made certain no one overheard him, right? He was just paying a 'get-well' call on an old college friend."

"Naturally," Ursula agreed. "Dr. Ridley came in seconds after Toomey threatened me. Larry the Lech smiled and patted my hand like he was consoling a friend." She shuddered. "I don't want to think about it anymore. Let's go."

*   *   *

I was so incensed by Toomey's threat I forgot all about the *Ardon Chronicle* clutched in my mitt until I scooted into the backseat of Dad's SUV. Ursula was tucked into the front passenger seat. She and Dad were both uncharacteristically quiet. That gave me a chance to scan the article as we drove to my folks' house.

The story was mostly factual although the reporter—or Nate as editor—had carefully selected which facts to exclude. The headline? "Invitation-Only Luncheon Leaves 1 Dead, Others Ill."

Comments from Bert Rider and Mrs. Quinn were pulled out of the body and printed in bold type as graphics. Bert was quoted as saying he'd never felt so sick and planned to sue and demand DHEC revoke Summer Place's certification as a commercial kitchen.

Harriett's mother repeated the accusation that I'd intentionally poisoned her daughter and suggested I did it as revenge towards Mrs. Quinn's participation in a protest of alleged satanic activities at Udderly Kidding Dairy.

Would wonders never cease? Nate hadn't contacted me for comment.

It concluded that Sheriff Mason would look into Mrs. Quinn's allegation I'd intentionally tampered with the food, which, if proven, would make Harriett's death a homicide.

Naturally the newspaper didn't mention I was fully cooperating with the sheriff or that the food poisoning victims included my own mother. It also failed to identify the alleged Udderly satanic activity as a harmless goat yoga class.

"Good grief," I muttered as I tossed the paper on the seat. Too bad I didn't buy the old adage that any publicity was good publicity. I couldn't fathom how Summer Place's new-found association with food poisoning and accusations of satanic activity could in any way be good publicity.

Ursula heard my muttering and turned around. "You still tormenting your aunt and mom with cheese-and-meat substitutes for cuss words? If so, I think you're entitled to blast out your whole blue cheese and baloney vocabulary after reading that paper's slanted coverage."

She frowned. "The reporting made me realize how that rag would react if I denounced Toomey as a sexual predator and hypocrite. Makes me even more determined to expose that slime bucket. Toomey does not deserve a lifetime Supreme Court appointment. The White House and Congress are entitled to appoint someone who shares their Constitutional outlook. That doesn't mean a misogynist, blackmailer, and liar should be awarded that honor. I just hope there's a way to reveal his true character without hurting Amber."

NINETEEN

As Dad parked in my folks' garage, my cell phone vibrated. The display offered a surprise: Aunt Eva. She only called if she needed me to do something pronto. My aunt "didn't cotton" to using telephones for gossip.

I sighed. I'd hoped to stay for lunch. Dad had to leave soon to teach afternoon classes. I wanted to pamper Mom and Ursula, fix them whatever comfort food they fancied. Then again, my former victims might be happier if I didn't prepare another midday meal.

"Get your buns back here, Brie, soon as you can," Aunt Eva blurted. "We have company. A bunch of nutcases from the Temple of True Believers with his holiness Pastor Gooney Guy Nickles leading the crazies."

"How many people are we talking about?" Alarmed, I imagined Eva trying to hold off a mob with a pitchfork and a bucket of goat's milk.

"Fifteen maybe twenty. Chanting and carrying signs."

Signs? "What do the signs say?"

Eva harrumphed. "'Bout what you'd expect. 'Justice for Harriett' is real popular. 'Sinners Repent' and 'To Hell with Goat Yoga' are tied for second place."

Murderous mincemeat. "So who's in the crowd? Mostly women?"

"No. Brought along some menfolk and a handful of kids—youngsters who darn well ought to have their fannies parked at school desks. Probably homeschooling the little snot noses, teaching them Lucifer loves to jump into goat skins for earthly visits. They'll likely get extra school credit for this civic outing. Today's lesson: ways to show hatred toward all who think differently than you."

"Are they actually on Udderly property? Trespassing?"

"Not exactly. They're outside the gate. Probably think they're interfering with business. Idiots must not realize we only open our retail store weekends. But I'm feeling a mite uneasy. Keep remembering how that lunatic Susan Young was ready to kick one of our babies like a soccer ball. Don't want Nickles to get his cult followers so worked up they think they're ordained to hurt our animals. The commotion's already riled our guard dogs something fierce."

I gritted my teeth as I tried to picture the scene. "I'll be right there, and I'll call the sheriff."

"No, don't do that," Eva snapped. "They'd be pleased as punch if we brought the law in. A confrontation would let them showboat for the media. Ignoring them's more likely to get their goat. 'Course if they start messing with our goats, dogs, or even Riley the Rooster, they'll be sorry. My shotgun's primed and loaded."

I hung up and shared Eva's report with Dad and Ursula.

"I'm canceling my afternoon classes," Dad stormed. His face was beet red again and I worried about his blood pressure. "I don't want you and Eva facing down those self-righteous imbeciles alone. I've seen Guy Nickles in action. He brought his followers on campus last year to protest Clemson University admitting Muslim students. He's a bigoted bully."

I reached across the car seat and squeezed Dad's arm. "Aunt Eva's right. If we shrug off their little carnival show and act as if it's no big deal, they'll slink away. If they imagine they're getting to us, they'll redouble their efforts. If you come, it'll make them think they've scared us."

Ursula sided with me. "Howard, don't cancel your classes. These folks may be a nuisance, but, based on what Eva said, there's no reason to think they'll turn violent. And you know your sister." Ursula smiled. "Eva's bluster alone could turn back an armed regiment. And, if that fails, her buckshot should do the trick."

Dad's grim face said he wasn't convinced.

"If things turn uglier, Brie can call you or the sheriff," Ursula added. "From what I hear, your daughter has two admiring young hunks who'll run to her rescue if she whistles."

Reluctantly, Dad acquiesced. He'd return to campus, though he made me promise multiple times to phone immediately if any True Believers set foot on Udderly proper.

Once Dad was out of earshot, Ursula whispered, "Wish I were feeling well enough to come with you. My Judge Ursula alter ego is pretty darn good at intimidation."

*   *   *

I reached Udderly Kidding Dairy in under fifteen minutes. Two hundred feet from the turn-off, I caught my first glimpse of the protestors. Curiously they were facing away from the farm. Why? What were they looking at?

A minute later I solved that mystery. A gaudy magnetic sign—*Ardon Chronicle*—was plastered to the side of a car parked on the verge opposite Udderly's entrance. A middle-aged reporter in tan chinos leaned against the car and scribbled notes as he chatted up a man holding a large "Justice for Harriett" sign. The sign's bright red ink looked like wet blood. I was surprised it didn't include a subhead—"String up Brie." Though the face of the interview subject was blocked, I gathered it was Reverend Guy Nickles.

While the reporter interviewed the leader, other Temple apostles posed for a news photographer in front of the Udderly Kidding Dairy sign. As I motored ahead, a scowling mother leaned over and yanked her little girl's arm. "What did I tell you?" she barked at the scrawny kid, who'd let her sign droop sideways. "Don't slouch. Hold that sign up straight."

The message on the kid's sign? "Do Your Yoga in Hell."

The protestors' bodies were strewn haphazardly across the Udderly Kidding entrance, blocking my car. I tooted out a "shave and a haircut" tune on my horn to warn them my Prius and I were coming through. Nonetheless, I approached slower than molasses to ensure no one could claim injuries if the blockers refused to relocate their derrieres.

The reporter sprinted across the road and banged on my rolled-up car window while his photographer snapped pictures. The man the reporter had been interviewing glared at me over the shoulder of Ardon's wannabe Clark Kent.

I felt certain I'd just had my first glimpse of Pastor Guy Nickles. Irises so dark they blended into his inky pupils. Black as coal hair. Square jaw. Wild eyebrows. Powerfully built but his skin sagged a bit. Signs the muscles below were wasting?

As Nickles turned his head slightly, I noticed he'd let his hair grow. Proud that he'd sprouted nary a gray hair or proud of his dye job?

Despite my revulsion, I smiled at both men and firmly shook my head at the reporter's entreaty to roll down my window and answer questions.

"Sorry, can't stop," I mouthed with a little wave as my Prius inched forward. "Have animals to care for and chores to finish."

Pastor Nickles responded by jumping ahead of the reporter to beat on my car hood and spit on my windshield. He screamed, but I could only decipher a few of the words. He was so worked up I thought he might be speaking in tongues. The words that did filter through included "murderer", "witch", "evil", and "devil worshipper".

After what seemed an hour, my car completed its crawl through the human blockade and on to Udderly soil. I spotted Eva, hoe in hand, supposedly tilling our herb and vegetable garden. Her shotgun rested against a tree less than three feet away. My aunt was monitoring my progress, not even pretending to see what her hoe was striking as she banged it into the earth with impressive force.

I paused long enough to rummage through my glovebox for the clicker that automatically opened and closed the wrought iron gate. I hit the button and nothing happened. Dang. Batteries must be dead. We usually left the gate open.

Figuring Eva had my back, I exited my Prius and walked around it to punch in a code on a gizmo mounted on a pole near the gate. The gate groaned as its two wings slowly stuttered closed. I smiled. Now the protesters would have to make a determined effort to trespass. With the gate secure, I hopped back in the car and drove down the graveled drive to my usual parking spot in front of our cabin.

Eva walked briskly toward me. She'd abandoned her hoe but not her shotgun.

"Saw the *Ardon Chronicle* vulture pestering you for a quote," Eva muttered. "Hope you didn't lambast him with some of your cheesy swearwords. Let's go to the barn where they can't spy on us. Maybe that'll convince them to call it a day. Our guard dogs will let us know if they try anything stupid. Imagine they'll leave soon now that they've gotten the media attention they crave."

"Going inside is a really good idea." I shivered as I rubbed my arms. "It was so pleasant yesterday. The temperature's dropping fast. I watched a few snowflakes melt on my windshield. Maybe the wind chill will send the loonies scurrying. Even that reporter was swiping at a runny nose. Bet he doesn't stay much longer."

"Let's hope word didn't leak out that your yoga buddies are coming over." As Eva led the way to the barn, she didn't loosen the grip on her shotgun. "This is just a gabfest with your friends, right? No actual yoga?"

"Right," I answered. "Just like you weren't doing any *actual* hoeing. Can't say I've ever seen you with a hoe in any of our gardens, let alone pulling a single weed."

"And you aren't likely to see it. The gardens—including your dad's poison patch—were Lilly's bailiwick. Now they're yours. That garden just offered the best vantage point to keep an eye on those pusillanimous polecats while I nonchalantly went about my chores."

I laughed at Eva applying Gabby Hayes' choice description of cowards to Nickles' True Believer troops. I used to love sitting between my aunts and watching the old-timey Westerns they adored. Of course, back then I believed popcorn was the perfect TV-watching treat so long as it was coated with enough butter to leave a salty film of grease on my stubby fingers.

"Not sure you convinced the True Believers you were tilling the garden. Looked more like you were trying to beat a rattlesnake to death."

Eva snorted. "Well, just be glad I don't have pictures of you as a young whippersnapper trying to hoist your chubby behind on a pony. I've seen three-legged varmints that were a sight more graceful."

I smiled. "I think my chubby handicap might've had something to do with you and Lilly letting me eat chocolate sundaes for breakfast."

We entered the barn and collapsed on side-by-side hay bales. My ribbing ended abruptly when I saw how tired Eva looked. My goat yoga brainstorm was adding unintended stress.

The True Believers were targeting Udderly because I'd insisted goat yoga would be a fun farm outreach—and I'd had the bad luck to find two Temple congregants dead—one who'd eaten my killer desserts.

"How long before your yoga buddies arrive?" Eva asked. "Would be nice to get a little work out of you today."

"They'll be here about four o'clock," I answered. "Mimi's pharmacy shift ends at three and she had errands to run afterward. Jayla, Fara, and Mollye had no problems adjusting their schedules to meet then."

"Good," Eva answered. "Plenty of time for you to muck out the stables while I make a batch of cheese. We can meet back at the cabin for a late lunch. With any luck the goons at the gate will be long gone by then."

I needed to trade the preppy "I'm innocent" attire selected for my meeting with the sheriff for work clothes. I snuck out the rear of the barn and trotted down a path that led to our cabin's back porch. The round-about trail couldn't be seen from our front gate.

After a quick change of clothes and a little loving on my pup Cashew, I trudged over to the barn to complete one of my least favorite farm tasks.

By the time I finished, I was famished and couldn't wait to chow down. This time I left the barn via the front entrance. Excellent. Not a single True Believer loitered outside our gate. I slipped my cell phone out of my jeans pocket and checked messages. I opened Paint's text message first.

Leaving C-town. Pick U up 4 dinner at 7. OK?

My reply? An enthusiastic "Yes".

I smelled bacon frying the moment I entered the cabin. BLTs were one of Eva's favorite sandwiches. I decided to join her. I'd just forgo the B and have an LT with Vegenaise slathered on my bread instead of mayo.

I took my first bite. Juicy. Delicious.

"Did you recognize any of the picketers besides Pastor Nickles?" I asked Eva.

"Unfortunately, yes. The missus was with him. Name's Jeannie. You'd probably remember if you caught sight of her. It's a wonder some baking company isn't using her mug to sell cookies. With that fluffy white hair, she looks like a kindly grandmother. Add in rosy cheeks and those brown doe-like eyes and you'd think she'd never tell a fib or intentionally hurt even a mouse. She plays the sweet-old-lady image to the hilt. Never see her in pants. Always wears 1950s' era housedresses with frilly lace collars."

I chuckled. "Didn't notice her. Too preoccupied—make that spooked—by her husband. I saw him staring at me. It felt like he was looking right through me. How old is he? I figured he must be at least as old as you but—"

"I wouldn't finish that sentence if I were you," Eva scolded. "The reverend is actually a few years older than me. I'm guessing sixty-five."

I grinned. "I was going to say you looked much younger than him."

Eva took a drink of goat's milk. "Sure you were. He does look younger than his years. Think it's that pact with the devil thing. By rights, he ought to look ten years older than me given how much time he's spent sucking on cigarettes and guzzling booze. When I arrived in Ardon County as a teen bride, Nickles palled around with my late, unlamented husband.

We're talking forty-plus years ago. Back in the day, the man smoked, drank, whored, stole, and brawled. Then he wrecked his motorcycle and found Jesus."

My aunt took a large bite of her sandwich. She closed her eyes as if she were in ecstasy as she savored her BLT. I was dying to hear the rest of the story and suspected Eva carefully timed her chewing to hype the suspense. Finally, she patted her lips with a paper towel, our customary stand-in for napkins, and continued.

"Rumor has it that motorcycle accident left Nickles more than a little tetched in the head. Not sure how he and Jeannie linked up, but she tended to him after the accident. Before he'd shed all his casts, Jeannie was pregnant with their daughter, Esther. Their girl is now Toomey's wife."

I smirked. "Maybe Nickles just had a splint on some of his parts."

Eva wagged her finger at me, but her lips snuck up in a smile. "Some folks believe Jeannie has the only brains that exist in that marital union. It's no secret she writes his sermons. Claims he dictates them and she just transcribes them. I seriously doubt that. I'm convinced Nickles is the woman's Frankenstein. She pieced his parts back together and the whole kinda looks and acts human but isn't quite. I think Jeannie can wind him up and point him in any direction she wants."

Eva meandered over to the cookie jar for dessert. While my aunt seldom deigns to try my vegan entrées, she doesn't squawk about my baking. Sugar appears to make up for any sins of egg, milk, or butter omission.

"Let's talk about something more pleasant," she said. "Is Paint headed back tonight? Surprised he took off when it meant missing out on boyfriend days."

"Couldn't be helped," I said. "When you're looking for investors, they call the tune and the time. Paint texted a little while ago. He's picking me up at seven for dinner. Hope that's okay. Billy's coming over, right? I'd have said no if I thought you'd be alone. Don't want you to face some torchlight True Believers' vigil by your lonesome."

"Right as rain Billy's coming." Eva grinned. "And he's a much better shot than I am. Could snuff out the flame on a torch at fifty yards." She lifted an eyebrow. "Since Billy and I haven't seen each other in a while, I'd just as soon you and Paint stay out late."

Billy, Udderly's farrier, shoed Hank the horse and Rita the mule. His own shoes found their way under Eva's bed on a regular but unpredictable basis. Neither Eva nor Billy seemed to have any hankering to marry. They clearly loved each other though. The cabin walls were mighty thin so I couldn't help but hear every bed squeak. I slipped on headphones whenever the racket started and told myself they were playing on some form of a trampoline. My mind seemed to rebel at picturing the alternative.

TWENTY

After lunch I worked on Udderly Kidding's accounting books until Mollye's van pulled in. I put away the paperwork and hustled to greet her. I was surprised to see all my fellow yoga buddies tumble out of her van.

"Hi, Brie," Fara said. "Jayla drove by Udderly at lunchtime and saw you had a sizable True Believer delegation. She suggested we meet in the Bi-Lo parking lot and carpool in case the picketers were still on duty."

"Yeah," Mollye waved a hand dismissively at her yoga pals. "These wimps know I'm already on the True Believers' unsaved and unsavory list. No reason for any of them to be singled out for retribution."

"Hey, you know that's not true," Mimi objected. "If we were afraid of them, we wouldn't be here to plan the launch of goat yoga."

I saluted the group. "You're all brave and good friends and probably freezing your buns off. Come on in. Want something hot to drink? Coffee, tea, hot chocolate?"

While I waitressed, Mollye yoo-hooed for Eva.

"Where's Eva?" she asked when my aunt didn't answer. "The True Believers haven't kidnapped her, have they? Do we need to search for a remote cult hideout that specializes in brainwashing?"

"Oh no, you're not talking me into a field trip to some crazies' hangout again. Besides I can't imagine anyone brainwashing Eva," I answered. "The True Believers lost their picketing enthusiasm once the *Ardon Chronicle* reporter vamoosed and snowflakes dusted their cars. Eva's taking advantage of the picketing lull to run errands and drop by to see Mom and Ursula."

I sat down, cupping my hands around my own mug of piping hot green tea. "Between Charleston meetings, Paint found time to edit the goat yoga video. Though my aunt calls us contortionists, I think you all look terrific—agile and graceful. Of course, the baby goats still steal every scene.

When they bounce, they look like furry pogo sticks. Want to see?"

I screened the edited footage for the ladies. No one asked to see the shots Paint left on the digital cutting-room floor—Susan Young's tirade and Eva's goat milk counterattack. Those images would sit tight in my Dropbox folder in case we ever needed to prove what really happened. I had no doubt the extremists would describe the incident quite differently. Everyone applauded Paint's cinematography efforts.

In short order, we decided classes would start late February when we expected Udderly's newborn population to swell. Each class would be limited to fifteen students. A thirty-dollar fee would include yoga instruction, after-class goat cheese snacks and smoothies, and keepsake digital photos for every participant.

Mollye banged a knife against her cup to command the floor. "Udderly Kidding should get half the money," she began. "Brie and Eva are providing the facilities, the kids, the treats, and taking the brunt of the devil-worshipper heat."

Mollye looked over at Jayla. "As our instructor, I recommend you get 29 percent. I mean there wouldn't be any 'yoga' in goat yoga without you. That leaves 21 percent, which splits nicely into thirds for the class helpers—Fara, Mimi, and me."

"I can live with that," Jayla said. "Everyone else think it's fair?"

Nods of approval all around ended the discussion. Goat yoga wouldn't make any of us rich. Eva'd washed her hands of the "hot mess" the minute I suggested it, leaving all related decisions up to me.

"How are we going to get the word out?" Mimi asked. "Social media, radio, the newspaper, advertising?

"I'll set up a Facebook page for Udderly Goat Yoga," Fara volunteered. "Not a biggie. I already set one up for our mortuary."

"I'll expand Udderly's website to include a goat yoga section," I said. "We already accept credit payments for cheese orders. I'll just add the yoga class as another 'product'."

"I'm all for advertising immediately," Mimi said. "Showing those baby goats at play should counteract any evil propaganda the True Believers dish out." She paused. "Is anyone concerned about blowback at work?"

Mollye frowned. "When those crazies first called me a witch, curiosity actually increased Starry Skies traffic and sales. It never dawned on me that their ire might hurt some of you in the pocketbook. D'you suppose the reverend might order his flock to boycott Ardon Mortuary?"

Fara shook her head. "Dad and I talked it over. As long as our goat yoga sessions aren't held inside our mortuary, he saw no problem. Remember, it was one of our cleaning ladies who blabbed about our goat yoga practice. That means Reverend Nickles and the Quinns are well aware I'm an evil goat worshipper. That didn't stop Harriett's folks from asking us to arrange her funeral. Her body will arrive at our mortuary as soon as the autopsy's complete."

"Are you surprised the Quinns chose your funeral home?" I asked.

Fara shrugged. "Not really. Not much local competition. After the law marched Chester Finley off to prison, the older Finleys retired to Florida and sold their mortuary to a Hispanic couple. Many of the True Believers are such white supremacists they're not keen on being touched by anyone who isn't white as a sheet.

"The Fisher Crematorium is the only other local burial option" she added. "That's who's handling Karen's cremation. Karen's folks are Baptists so they haven't been indoctrinated by Nickles' suggestion that intact corpses get preferential treatment at the pearly gates."

I grimaced, thinking about Harriett's post-autopsy remains. If the Quinns subscribed to such nonsense, I feared their daughter's autopsy would cause them additional grief. Did they know the organs were returned to a body after examination?

Mimi, my fellow green tea enthusiast, jumped in with a question for Fara. "Did the Quinns say how long it'll be before Harriett's body's released?"

"Autopsies only take two to four hours," Fara answered. "If there's a multi-day hold up, it's because a bunch of bodies are queued for autopsy. Don't know if the morgue's busy right now, but, if it is, Harriett got bumped to the front of the line. The Quinns were told the autopsy would be completed tomorrow. Harriett should arrive at our facility in the morning."

Fara's answer switched my morbid train of thought onto a new track. "Are the Quinns planning a visitation?"

"Yes, late Friday afternoon. On Saturday we'll deliver the casket to the church for the actual funeral."

I took a deep breath. Good to know what places to avoid Friday and

Saturday. For the foreseeable future it seemed prudent to detour around any place the Quinns and their fellow worshippers might congregate.

Mollye glanced my way. "Time for this gathering of great minds to do a little brainstorming about what—and who—caused Harriett's death. I have my sources." She winked. "Overheard Danny talking with another deputy. The sheriff seems convinced both Karen's and Harriett's deaths were accidental."

"What?" Fara interrupted. "Wasn't Karen strangled?"

"Yes, and she was naked. But now Sheriff Mason suggests it's because Karen got her knots mixed up," Mollye explained. "We're assuming erotic asphyxiation."

"What?" Fara said. "You never told me Karen died having sex."

"We don't know that," I protested. "We just know she was in the closet, naked, with a scarf around her neck."

"Apparently, some folks believe a little choking enhances their climactic pleasure," Mollye's tone had become almost professorial. "If they happen to be flying solo, it's called auto-erotic asphyxiation. As a safeguard, they tie knots in their nooses that loosen automatically if they fall unconscious and let go the end that's looped over something like a closet rod. But if they're bad with knots..."

"Ugh," Fara said. "That doesn't sound like Karen. Do you buy it?"

Mollye shrugged. "Maybe. But it's also a way to kill someone and make it appear an accident. Just like food poisoning."

"That brings us back to Harriett," I said. "Has the sheriff totally dismissed the possibility someone other than the two of us could have doctored the desserts?"

Mollye frowned. "Looks that way. He believes the poisoning is accidental. I don't. Someone killed Harriett on purpose, and it sure wasn't either of us."

Jayla walked over to the coffeepot for a refill. "So you know somebody who wanted Harriett dead?"

"As a matter of fact, yes," Mollye answered. "Actually more than one somebody. During the past six months, Harriett handed out a scathing review to Farmer Fred's Organic Eggs and another stinker of a thumbs-down to Gussies' Grass-Fed Beef. Both businesses have since gone under.

"I worked the merchant rumor mill a bit this morning. Farmer Fred (a.k.a Fred Adams) and Gussie (a.k.a Gertrude Danson) both blame

Harriett's blogs. They say she launched her smear campaigns after they refused to pay blackmail."

My jaw fell open. Mollye'd given me no hint she'd launched her own investigation.

Moll pulled her iPad out of her oversized purse. "Here, I'll show you some of the comments Fred and Gussie made about Harriett on their personal and business Facebook pages. Even with expletives deleted, it's easy to tell they wouldn't have bothered to spit on Harriett if her hair was on fire."

"Okay, I'll buy Harriett had enemies. Who doesn't?" Jayla commented. "But would either of these folks risk killing a room full of people to do Harriett in?"

Mollye shrugged. "Why not? Years back some sicko tampered with bottles of a popular brand of pain pills his intended victim downed like candy. Thought he'd hide his motive by making it appear to be pharma-terrorism. The extra victims were simply collateral damage."

Mimi raised her hand as if she needed permission to add her two cents. "The killer wouldn't have to be a cold-blooded mass murderer. If he knew what medicines Harriett took, he could select something known to cause a fatal interaction. His choice might do little more than make the others sick."

I nodded. "Dad and Andy mentioned the possibility. A drug interaction or medical condition might explain why only Harriett died. Dad noted an HIV-positive person could be more vulnerable to germs or toxins."

Mollye glanced at our resident pharmacist. "Do you happen to know what medications Harriett was taking?"

Mimi shook her head. "She wasn't a customer. But, it doesn't matter. I couldn't tell you even if Harriett had filled her prescriptions at our pharmacy. That information's confidential. The sheriff could subpoena it, but there'd still be a hearing to determine if releasing her records would violate HIPPA confidentiality rules."

"Even if the patient's dead?" Mollye's eyebrows ratcheted up.

"Yep, even if the patient's dead," Mimi answered.

Fara snapped her fingers. "I know. Let's call Harriett's mom and ask what pills she popped. I'm certain she'd be happy to chat with us."

Though Fara was being facetious, she raised an interesting

possibility. Who might know Harriett well enough to answer that question? Did we have any friends in common with Harriett?

"Maybe someone outside her family would know." Mollye somehow channeled my thought. "How about 'frenemies'—one-time friends she screwed with her blog? I can start chatting up that list."

While I could make no such list, I was a whiz at internet research. Did Harriett post about her health on Facebook? Mention her fondness for a pain pill in one of her farm-to-table blogs? I'd check.

Suddenly I recalled a scene in one of Dad's manuscripts where a fictional PI snooped in someone's garbage. When I critiqued the scene, I asked if the PI's actions were legal. Dad said yes. "If the trash can was on public property, there was no expectation of privacy."

Hmm. After trying to revive Harriett, I'd turned green and stumbled into her side yard for fresh air. On my knees in the grass, I noticed her garbage cans sitting in the alley waiting for pickup. Were they full? Might a search turn up an empty pill bottle or a pharmacy sales slip?

Harriett's house was outside Town of Ardon city limits, and the county didn't offer trash pickup. That meant a private service hauled the blogger's trash away. I was fairly sure the alley was public property. Did it matter? Who'd care if I peeked in Harriett's trash? If I found anything, I'd suggest the sheriff pursue a new lead.

A definite long shot. Yet there seemed no downside to taking a look-see.

I grinned, wondering how Paint would feel about helping me rummage through Harriett's garbage cans tonight.

Maybe if I promised dessert.

TWENTY-ONE

Once again, Mollye banged a knife against her mug, snapping me back to our kitchen clutch conversation.

"Enough talk about Brie and killer desserts." Mollye's devilish grin suggested a sharp conversational detour. "Can't believe none of you noticed my new jewelry."

Jayla laughed. "Kinda tough since you usually wear five bracelets, six earrings, a nose stud, and what else am I missing?"

Moll jacked up one eyebrow—how did she do that?—before she thrust her left hand forward and waggled her ring finger. A red stone twinkled in the light.

I smiled. "Very pretty."

"Neat," echoed Mimi. "Is it a ruby?"

Moll snorted. "Guess I have to spell it out for you wankers. Ta da! I'm engaged!"

Shrieks filled the room. "You're what? When?"

Moll laughed. "Deputy Danny popped the question a week ago. I said yes but told him I thought diamond engagement rings were a bore. Instead I wanted a garnet gem. It's my birthstone and ancient Greeks and Romans thought it protected against negativity. Figured that was a pretty good property for an engagement ring. Plus it was easier for Danny to afford."

I rushed around the table to hug Mollye. "I'm so happy for you."

As the group celebration continued, we peppered Moll with questions. "When's the wedding? Is it gonna be a big blow out? You're not gonna elope, are you?"

She cocked her head as if this were the first time she'd contemplated any of her answers. "Let's see. I want to enjoy being engaged, and you all need time for planning an engagement shower and, of course, a bachelorette party. That, of course, means a junket to Atlanta and one of those bars where we can stick our hard-earned cash into nearly neckid men's jock straps.

"You also need plenty of time for serious wedding gift shopping. Danny and I could tie the knot sooner, but I figure my friends need at least six months. And, of course, we won't elope. Y'all would be devastated if you weren't in on the festivities."

Mimi laughed. "So cut to the chase. What's the wedding date? Need to put this on my calendar."

"Patience. I was getting to that. I ruled out summer. Who wants to get married with sweat dripping off your nose? I nixed winter, too. Don't want goosebumps on my bare arms. That's why we picked the twenty-second of September, the autumn equinox. Night and day are in balance, and so are hot and cold."

Jayla laughed. "Of course you want a temperate weather date. Goes with your reserved personality."

"Watch it," Moll said. "Or you'll lose your wedding invite."

Jayla raised her mug in a toast. "Here's to Mollye and Danny and a long happy life together."

Once the echo of amens died away, Mollye grabbed my hand. "And we definitely can't have you go to jail for some culinary crime frame-up. You have to be my maid of honor."

Fara gave me an appraising look with her right eye. I'd discovered it usually stayed on task even when her left eye took off on a look about. "Maybe Brie will surprise us. Could be she'll be a matron of honor by then. Any chance you're hearing wedding bells when you're with Andy or Paint?"

I shook my head. Had I heard a faint tinkle of bells with either man? If not, what was wrong with me? A thousand women would do just about anything—shave their heads bald, offer their savings as dowry, donate a kidney—for a chance to marry either man.

Moll nodded. "The girl does need to make up her mind. And, I don't know about the rest of you, but I'm darned tired of referring to Paint's boyfriend week or Andy's boyfriend week. Can't we come up with better names? How about Paint the Town week or Handy Andy's Turn? Or maybe Andy's Peeks, sort of a play on the mountain peaks of the Andes?"

Mimi giggled. "We can do even better if we choose names related to their professions. Tons of possibilities for Andy, like Wild Kingdom...You

Animal...Animal Whisperer."

"So what would you do for our moonshiner?" Jayla jumped in. "Liquor Lips Week?"

I didn't bother to protest. It wouldn't get them to stop. They were giggle drunk with possibilities. Why even bother with an eye roll?

"I vote for Moon'em for Paint and You Animal for Andy," Fara piped up.

"Nah," Moll said. "Animal Passion is perfect for Andy. How about Brewing Trouble for Paint?"

I tipped my chair back and closed my eyes, waiting for the madcap nonsense to end with a vote. Moll's suggestions carried the day. They usually did. My friend had a way of convincing you her thoughts were your own best ideas.

"It's unanimous, Brie. From now on, we will refer to Animal Passion when you're with Andy, and Brewing Trouble when you're with Paint. While I'm eager for you to decide which fine stud is worthy of your undying devotion, you'd better not upstage me. No getting married before September twenty-second."

She wagged a finger at me. "I can't have any of you ladies distracted by other nuptials, not until after Danny and I walk down the aisle." She giggled. "If it's an aisle."

"Promise," I said. "I won't get married before you do. Even though I have a strong premonition you'll set the wedding celebration bar awfully high. Might make any wedding that follows—even a royal wedding—seem a drab, disappointing affair."

I laughed. I meant what I said. Mollye's wedding would be amazing. Non-traditional and awe-inspiring. Just like her garnet engagement ring, her nuptials would be a colorful, happy surprise.

Everyone left, smiling and laughing. Delighted for Mollye. I was thrilled for her, too. But I couldn't totally ignore the hint of sadness that made a sneak-attack as I watched my friends leave. My friendship with Mollye was unbreakable, but it was bound to change. Both Jayla and Mimi were married. Fara was happily divorced. Once Moll walked down the aisle, I'd be the group's spinster.

Oh, stop it! Thirty-three is not old age. You love Paint, and you love Andy. You'll figure it out. As Aunt Eva would scold, "Don't be a horse's patoot."

TWENTY-TWO

Paint swept me into his arms the minute I answered his knock. He lifted me off my feet as his soft lips found mine. A tingling heat radiated to all flesh points east and west, north and south. Especially south.

He didn't release me until Billy called out. "Let the girl breathe, Paint. You're gonna smother her."

Eva laughed. "Don't you know such displays embarrass your elders?"

The kiss made me dizzy. Too bad I lacked enough oxygen to instantly lob an insult back at my aunt and her beau.

"Billy, since you elderly folks still play in the boudoir, I'm gonna buy Eva one of those buttons that let old folks call for help when they can't get up." Paint had stepped up to the plate with his own verbal jabs. "Sooner or later, Billy, you'll fall asleep on top and Eva won't be able to shove you off. 'Course I wouldn't envy the rescue workers. The sight of your hairy behind might scar them for life."

Eva chuckled as she shook her head. "Git. It's about time you got here, Paint. I do have plans for Billy before he starts snoring. By the way, Brie's girlfriends have come up with a new name for your designated boyfriend week—it's Brewing Trouble Time."

Paint laughed. "I like it, and I keep hoping to brew enough trouble that Brie's clothes fall off. Did they give Andy's week a name, too?"

I nodded. "Yep. It's Animal Passion week."

Paint's mock reaction was one of horror. "Oh, no, I don't think that's right. His week sounds more dangerous than mine. I'm gonna have to come up with alternates."

I grabbed my jacket off a hook by the door. "No comment. Think I'll just say goodbye. See you when we see you. Take that back. I don't plan to *see* anyone when I get home. I'll tiptoe directly to my room. Won't even stop for a glass of water."

My chivalrous beau helped me into the cab of his distinctive truck. If Paint's ride had been the mystery vehicle parked at Summer Place, Miss Medley could have ID'd it in even dim light. Like Mollye's Starry Skies van, the truck served as a business billboard. Artwork on the cab doors featured a barmaid with two frosty mugs and, *ahem*, two prominent jugs. I'd yet to meet the model who lent her charms to the Magic Moonshine brand, but I had a sneaking suspicion Paint was well acquainted with the lass.

Once he joined me in the cab, Paint leaned across the seat. His big hands cupped my face as he looked into my eyes. Then he kissed me again. A tender, lingering kiss.

"You're supposed to stay out of trouble when I'm out of town," he scolded once his lips left mine. "Bad enough I sacrificed two of my allotted Brewing Trouble days for a business trip. The fact you needed to call Andy for help rubbed extra salt in the wound. We need to do some serious necking to salve that hurt."

I gave his chest a gentle nudge. "I don't neck on an empty stomach. Let's eat."

"How does Chinese sound?" he asked. "Chan's okay?"

"Fine," I answered.

Chan's Asian House in Clemson was one of our favorite restaurants. Paint could pig out on General Tso's chicken while I enjoyed steamed vegetables and rice.

Once we were seated at Chan's, I asked Paint how his Charleston visit had gone.

He shook his head. "Un uh. You go first. Andy gave me highlights of your run-ins with the True Believers but no details. What in blazes happened while I was gone? I can't believe Nickles' followers are suggesting you murdered Karen and Harriet."

My detailed recap, prodded by Paint's endless reservoir of questions, carried us all the way from pre-entrée fried noodle munchies to fortune cookies.

"What does your fortune say?" I asked.

Paint wiggled his eyebrows. "It says, 'A naked lover will make all your dreams come true.'"

I grinned back. "Wonder if you've met her yet?"

Paint's innuendoes and sexy banter offered a pleasant break from my guilt about Harriett and my worries the True Believers might be tempted to do more than picket Udderly. To banish those thoughts a little longer, I asked Paint again about his Charleston sojourn while we waited for the check.

He smiled. "Two more investors on board. Now I just have to find the right Lowcountry location and decide how to brand the fine spirits we'll offer. Magic Moonshine is perfect for my 'shine product line, but not quite the image I'm after to market locally-distilled, high-quality whiskies."

Watching Paint's animated face as he talked about his business, I realized how passionate he seemed about everything. I practically hyperventilated wondering how he'd tend to that naked woman in his fortune cookie fantasy. A flush of heat shimmied up my neck. That man and that blasted dimple of his could make me hotter than a jalapeño with just the promise in one of his looks.

By the time we walked out of Chan's, I still hadn't broached the subject of dumpster diving behind Harriet's house. When we were both back in the truck, Paint asked, "What would you like to do now? It's way too early to go back to Udderly and interrupt Eva's and Billy's fun."

Paint lifted an eyebrow and his lips lifted in a grin that clearly communicated what he'd like to do next. "We could pay my house a visit. Lunar would be delighted to see you again. He loves the ladies. Men, not so much."

"Will Lunar be the only wolf I encounter?" I asked.

Paint had adopted the orphaned baby wolf two years ago. The handsome animal seemed to take a shine to me when we were first introduced. Still I wasn't quite sure I trusted Lunar. A piece of the wild never left him. I wasn't quite sure it had left Paint either.

"I can't make that promise, but all of the wolves at my house know how to respond to commands."

"Interesting answer." I chewed on my lip. "Maybe we can swing by your place after we do some dumpster diving?"

Paint's confused and somewhat alarmed expression made me chuckle. To his credit, he didn't roll his eyes when I explained my idea.

"Guess there's no harm in driving by Harriett's house to see if anyone's there and scooting down her alley if it looks like the coast is clear," he answered.

The minute we turned into Harriett's street it was evident the dead woman's house was occupied. Lights blazed from every window, and her driveway hosted a newer model BMW. Paint drove half a block beyond the house before he extinguished the truck's headlights and pulled to the curb for our stakeout. He'd chosen a spot in front of a house with windows as dark as Harriett's were bright.

"What's the plan?" Paint asked. "Wait? Come back? Looks like a poor time to rifle through Harriett's trash."

I chewed on my lip as I thought. "Let's wait a few minutes. My guess is family members are picking up things for the visitation and funeral. Maybe photos to display at the visitation or clothes for Harriett. I doubt they'd be cleaning out the house so soon."

Paint's fingers threaded their way through my curls as he gently nudged my head in his direction. "Meanwhile I'll be happy to keep you warm."

Unfortunately whoever designed the interior of his truck cab hadn't made ease of necking a priority. When our lips met in the seemingly vast neutral territory between the driver and passenger seats, my neck muscles immediately squawked from the awkward angle. However, the steamy kisses provided sufficient pleasure to overrule worries about a mere neck dislocation.

I'd almost forgotten why we were parked when Paint broke our embrace. "Hey. The lights just went out inside Harriett's house. Someone's hauling out big, bulging trash bags and tossing them in the Beemer's trunk."

I strained to see what Paint was seeing. His driver's window and side mirror gave him a panoramic view. I twisted around to stare out the back window.

"It looks like a woman," I said. "She's wearing one of those shapeless house dresses favored by the True Believers. Can you tell if it's Mrs. Quinn?"

"Nope, not enough light," Paint answered. "But she's getting in the Beemer. If she drives past, maybe we can get a better look."

The Beemer's red taillights flared. "She's backing out of the driveway, headed our way," Paint warned.

I sprang away from Paint and ducked my head as low as I could to be out of sight yet able to take a gander at the car's occupant. If the driver was Harriett's mother, I figured she would not take kindly to me choosing her late daughter's street as a place to park and smooch with my boyfriend.

The car crawled by. It took so long I feared whoever was inside planned to stop and beat on Paint's window, demanding an explanation for our presence. Thank heaven, the car kept inching past.

The breath I'd been holding whooshed out when the Beemer and its super bright headlights turned a corner and disappeared onto a side street.

"Did you see who was inside?" I asked.

"Yeah, it wasn't Mrs. Quinn," Paint answered. "I'm pretty sure it was Jeannie Nickles, the pastor's wife."

"Really?" I shook my head. "Why would she be at Harriett's?"

Paint shrugged. "Harriett's entire family attends the Temple of True Believers. Maybe Mrs. Quinn wasn't up to going inside her daughter's house so soon. Maybe she asked the pastor's wife to collect some things for her."

I nodded. "Makes sense, even though Mrs. Quinn certainly didn't seem to have a delicate constitution while screaming I was a murderer and battering me with her outsized pocketbook."

"You have a point. I know the Quinns and the missus is about as sensitive as a bull in a china shop," Paint agreed. "It's also puzzling why the pastor's wife hauled away bags of stuff. Doesn't make sense. Still want to check out the trash cans in the alley? It's pitch black now. No lights on at neighboring houses. Don't think anyone will notice us if we're quiet."

I shrugged. "Why not?"

Ten minutes later our curiosity was partially satisfied. Harriett's trash cans were empty, but the barren bins hadn't been returned to the house.

"Very curious," Paint said. "The guy who offers private trash pickup in this area prides himself on making sure empty cans are hauled back to the house and there's no litter spill. Look at the bottles and cans on the ground."

I picked up one of the cans. It had once held pink salmon and was particularly smelly.

My nose wrinkled. "This can hasn't been sitting here long. It's still quite fragrant. Do you think Jeannie Nickles carried off Harriett's trash? And, if so, why? Who besides me would care what might be hiding in Harriett's garbage cans?"

Paint shook his head. "You got me. Unless Harriett's family feared someone might find evidence of a different sort. Maybe someone in her family knew she was blackmailing people. Could be they searched the house—and took the garbage—to make absolutely certain the sheriff wouldn't find anything incriminating. If it was determined that Harriett's death wasn't accidental, Mason might get a warrant to search for evidence of the killer's motive."

"Possibly. Then again, maybe Mrs. Nickles didn't know Harriett's trash pick-up arrangements and just wanted to neaten up the place for her family."

TWENTY-THREE

Paint reached over, cupped my chin, and kissed me. "Want to visit any other trash receptacles tonight? The packaging in my recycling bins might give you insights into a carnivore's diet. Lots of telltale wrapping confirming my visits to the deli, cheese, and meat sections of grocery stores."

I punched Paint's arm. "Knowing what you order in restaurants, I have a fair idea what you eat at home. No need to paw through your garbage."

"Good," Paint answered. "Then I have much better ideas of how we can spend the next couple of hours at my house. Pawing is a definite option."

"You do remember no clothing can be lost while we engage in said pawing."

Paint grinned. "In high school, I dated girls who stipulated the same rules. You know clothing doesn't have to interfere with close contact of the best kind."

Ninety minutes later, I had to agree with Paint's assessment. *Holy Havarti.* Clothing and hot-and-heavy full-contact recreation weren't mutually exclusive. David a.k.a Paint Paynter knew how to make a girl's senses sing. Mine kept singing a hallelujah chorus as we left Paint's retreat in the woods. Lunar, the orphaned wolf, howled as our truck bumped down the lane. I felt like howling myself.

Back at Udderly, we kissed goodnight at the door. Neither of us wanted to risk waking Aunt Eva and Billy, or worse, interrupting their recreational activities.

Despite the chill in the air, Paint lingered, holding me tightly in his arms. He repeated his promise to nose around and see if any of his contacts knew anything about Harriett's health or had heard any gossip regarding who might have wanted to hurry the farm-to-table blogger's departure from Mother Earth. He promised to call if he unearthed any interesting tidbits.

Then he reminded me only one night remained of his Brewing Trouble week. "I hope you've scheduled plenty of alone time with me tomorrow evening—no Eva, no Mollye, and certainly no Andy."

"How about I make dinner for the two of us at Summer Place. Candles. Wine. Of course, that means you'll risk eating food in the same location where this chef's last guests were poisoned."

"Hey, if it means I have you all to myself, I'll chow down on whatever you serve, wherever you choose. Of course, I may switch plates when you're not looking."

"Very funny," I replied. "It's a date. But dinner will have to be a little late, say seven thirty. I'll have chores to finish before I can leave Udderly for Summer Place."

Paint's arms snaked around me, pulling me tight against his body. His lean, muscular body. His hot breath tickled my neck as he whispered exactly what he hoped to be doing tomorrow night at 7:31. Yowzer.

I tiptoed to my bedroom to avoid waking Eva and Billy. Loud snores confirmed at least one of them was sound asleep. However, Cashew opened her eyes and unwound from her dog bed as soon as I slipped past. My pup always preferred my bed to hers, but only if I was in it.

The cabin interior felt so cold I was surprised I couldn't see my breath. I undressed faster than Paint or Andy could dream and slipped on a full-length flannel nightie. I jumped into bed and pulled up the handmade quilt. Shivering I snaked one arm out to collect my cell phone off the nightstand to check for messages I'd missed. Once Paint and I were alone, I'd switched my phone off. Didn't want a silent but still vibrating phone to interrupt other sensations.

Three text messages waited. The first from Mom. Ursula's daughter would arrive at noon tomorrow, and Mom's friend insisted on moving into the cottage behind Summer Place. Mom wondered if I could drop by late morning to chat with Ursula before the move.

I texted a simple *OK* reply. I didn't add that I might need an extra fifteen minutes to run a True Believers' gauntlet at the Udderly gate.

Surely Nickles' cult-like flock would take a day off from picketing to prepare for the coming visitation and funeral. Protocol called for mountains of food to be prepared for the Quinns' extended family, the visitation, and post funeral mourning. The weather forecast also predicted more snow flurries. Kitchens and even the mortuary would be warmer spots for the True Believers to hang out.

My second text message came from Mollye, who said she'd harvested some gossip about H's enemies as well as folks who bore grudges against my other luncheon guests.

I figured Moll's enemy lists could wait until morning. It was late and I was dog tired. Apparently, though, not more tired than Cashew, who'd promptly fallen back to sleep curled beside me on the quilt.

Fara had left the third message. *FYI, Harriett will be in our care tomorrow. Want to "virtually" attend the Friday visitation for her? I can arrange it. Call me.*

Intrigued I immediately texted Fara. I wasn't too tired to hear this proposition. *Still up? Too late to call?*

A second later Fara's muted ringtone answered my question. Yep, she was up.

"Last year we installed video cameras and speakers in our chapel and visitation rooms," she explained. "It creeps out mourners when funeral directors hang around in plain sight. They seem to think we're gleefully calculating profits or checking which guests look a little sickly. You know like lions watching a herd of gazelles to spot the slow ones. That's why we installed the monitors. Lets us spot any problems and take care of them without seeming to intrude.

"Anyway you can be invisible," she continued. "You can sit in my office and check out the attendees. Maybe even eavesdrop on conversations if the folks talk loud enough. Whisperers not so much. Want to give it a whirl?"

"What time Friday?" I asked. "I'd need to get there way in advance to arrive unseen. Waltzing in the front door while folks are gathering would kinda defeat the purpose."

"Visitation starts at four, and there's an unmarked drive off the street behind us. It leads to the back of our building. That's where employees park and ambulances deliver bodies. Our building sits on a hill and our lower level is where we do the embalming. It's hidden from the street. I could meet you downstairs and lead you up a back staircase to my office. No chance of being spotted by any of our front-door guests."

I shivered at the idea of arriving via the same portal as corpses en route to embalming but I did want to see who might come to bid Harriett farewell. If I was lucky I might even overhear comments about Harriett's health—prior to her death, of course.

Or maybe I could match visitation attendees to Moll's enemy lists. In the movies police often attended funerals and visitations to scout for potential killers. If Harriett was murdered on purpose, might the killer show up to gloat on his success at getting rid of Harriett and making me the fall guy?

"I may regret it, but my curiosity wins. It's a date," I said. "Thanks. See you on Friday."

TWENTY-FOUR

After I finished the morning farm essentials, I hustled to the cabin for a jolt of caffeine and a little alone time to think. Eva had bid Billy goodbye an hour ago. Now she was out with the goats, checking on the soon-to-be mamas.

I hoped our nannies would delay motherhood a few more days. This season I'd promised Eva I'd play nursemaid to newborns—no small commitment. Our kids were separated from their mothers at birth, but the babes never had a chance to be lonely or hungry. Their assigned humans kept them company around the clock for the first two days, bottle feeding them every two hours. Of course, we made sure they were supplied with first milk from new mothers. For a few days after a nanny gives birth, her milk includes colostrum, which transfers immune-boosting factors from mom to kid and strengthens the newborn's natural defenses.

During the next forty-eight hours, the human parents teach the kids to take milk from nipples on communal milk buckets. After they got the hang of it and seemed healthy and well-adjusted, they graduated to our nursery, a fenced-in pen where they frolicked with siblings and cousins. Of course, they were still petted and cooed over by human visitors at least once an hour.

Eva told me she'd enlisted Gerri, our part-timers, and a variety of friends to foster kids in their homes for this human-animal bonding experience. But with the number of spring births expected, she warned I wouldn't get much shut-eye once the baby goat boom began in earnest.

I took advantage of the cabin's current quiet to do my own internet search. First stop was Harriett's farm-to-table blog. I wanted to read everything Harriet had written about Farmer Fred's Organic Eggs and Gussies' Grass-Fed Beef before I searched for more information on these businesses and their owners.

Mollye was right. Harriett's blogs went beyond bad reviews; they viciously attacked the character of the owners. At the tasting, I'd seen a hint of the pleasure Harriett reaped from taunting a victim. I still cringed when I recalled how she'd leapfrogged from veal to a snide assault on Della's pet charity—Animals Entitled to Personhood.

I could sympathize with Fred Adams and Gertrude Danson. They had every right to be angry. If either had sent me the anonymous warnings about Harriett, I felt a thank you might be in order for attempting to do me a service. Of course, if Fred or Gussie took advantage of my failure to uninvite Harriett and spiked my mousse, they owed me an apology. I'd been set up as a killer chef—a label certain to find its way into Ardon County mythology.

Before leaving Harriett's blog, I scanned her posts from the last six months. Her choice of topics ran the gamut—farmer's markets, craft breweries, restaurants, delis, bakeries, and dozens of farmer entrepreneurs who sold direct to the public. These businesses offered everything from beef, pork, poultry, and eggs, to farm-raised catfish and vegetables. During this timeframe, Harriett had savaged two other businesses. But, based on Mollye's research, they'd survived the blogger's forked tongue. Presumably they had less reason than Fred or Gussie to harbor a murderous rage.

I spent another half hour following digital breadcrumbs to get a better overall picture of Fred and Gussie. What kind of people were they? I paid visits to their Facebook pages, websites that hadn't been taken down for their failed businesses, and LinkedIn profiles. I also searched for liens, Better Business Bureau complaints, and court dockets for criminal and civil lawsuits.

My efforts inclined me to cross Gertrude's name off any potential killer list. She was eighty years old, and her Facebook page was filled with pictures of two really cute great grandkids sitting on her lap. Her grin was contagious. On the other hand, Gussie might have figured if she killed Harriett, got caught, and was sentenced to life, she'd have a roof over her head for what was left of her golden years plus three squares a day, and free medical care. Could look like a reward for murdering the woman she blamed for the foreclosure on her farm.

Fred actually looked the part of the villain. If he were an actor, I'd typecast him as such. In his posted photos, he looked shifty and squinty-eyed. In fairness, most of the outdoor shots had the poor man looking directly into the sun. Fred was a family man, too, though he looked a lot less happy about it than Gussie. I guessed his age at forty, maybe forty-five. But while Fred's Organic Eggs had gone under, corporate records revealed Fred owned a dozen other profitable enterprises.

I checked my watch and figured Mollye was probably awake though not necessarily out of bed. I phoned as I poured a third cup of coffee.

"'Bout time you called," Moll said. "When I didn't hear from you last night, I figured Paint kept you out late. Did he retain any articles of clothing as trophies? With Paint and Andy trying their dangdest to win exclusive boyfriend rights, I'm betting you cave sooner rather than later."

"Yes, I was out late, and, no, I arrived home with clothes intact. I admit I was tempted to discard a few pesky items of clothing last night. What am I going to do, Mollye? I feel like a cheating Jezebel when I'm kissing Paint and realize I'll be smooching Andy the next week—or vice versa. I'm a one-man-at-a-time girl. Not experienced at juggling two men. Paint and Andy act as if they're fine with our deal, but sometimes I think I sense the hurt when I'm out with one and we bump into the other. I may explode. I love them both, though not exactly in the same way. Andy's so sweet. He reminds me a lot of my dad. And Paint, well, he makes me think things I have no business thinking."

"Yep, you need to decide—sometime, but you'd better not be thinking about any knot-tying until after September twenty-second. Remember I get exclusive blushing bride billing until then." Moll's tone was exceedingly cheerful. "Lots of women would love to trade places with you, Brie. Who else gets to date two hunks with no worries about a jealous discovery? But let's skip ahead to why I texted you last night. Just a sec, have to find my notes."

I heard paper rustling and a couple of swear words.

"Forget what I said about Fred and Gussie," she said. "I've moved them way down the suspect list. My new number one choice as potential murderer of our farm-to-table blogger is Matt Hill, who owns a popular Greenville eatery famed for its farm-fresh fare. Hill's preparing to franchise, and word on the street is Harriett was threatening some sort of exposé. Maybe she was blackmailing him for a really large chunk of change."

I sighed. So much for my internet research. A waste.

"While I was at it I mined some gossip about Della," Mollye continued. "Why you ask? Maybe our poisoner sat next to her victim. Maybe Della knew about Harriett's views on animal rights before the tasting and just played nice until after dessert was served. Of course, once I started researching Della, I realized she had a clutch of enemies as well."

"What?" I broke in. "Are you now saying Harriett might not have been the target?"

"That's precisely what I'm saying. Who says your other guests weren't equally capable of inspiring hatred? Perhaps the poison was meant to teach Della, Bert, Dr. Swihart, Judge Ursula, or even your Mom a lesson, and the plan went awry."

My chin dropped. Duh. Mollye was right. I'd been so focused on Harriett's foes I hadn't considered my other guests might have their own enemy clubs. Could Harriett have been an unintended casualty?

I was inclined to rule Mom out as someone capable of inspiring sufficient hatred. Then I recalled her telling me that a young man she'd prosecuted had unexpectedly died in city jail. His relatives blamed Mom for the man's death.

Jumping jerky. I'd rather believe my reputation was the target and the poison was just meant to make everyone sick. I shivered. Could someone be after Mom?

I tuned back in as Mollye started dishing dirt on Della. "She's a bona fide fruitcake. I can see her poisoning Harriett for promoting consumption of mammal meat and poultry. She's given thousands of dollars to Animals Entitled to Personhood. She could have slipped something into Harriett's food when no one was looking. She was sitting right beside her. And remember how chipper Della sounded when you phoned her? Sure she told you she'd suffered the runs, but maybe she wasn't sick at all because she didn't eat what she'd added to everyone else's plate."

I took a sip of coffee and thought about Moll nominating Della as someone likely to want Harriet dead. "I don't buy it. Our killer needed opportunity as well as motive. None of our luncheon guests was alone long enough to poison anyone's food. I'm more and more convinced whoever did this snuck into Summer Place while we were out to dinner. Remember, Miss Medley saw a truck parked in the Summer Place driveway for half an hour. Della doesn't own a truck."

"Yeah, but who's to say she didn't rent or borrow one?" Mollye wasn't anxious to give up any of her potential villains.

"It's easier to buy Hill, the blackmailed restauranteur, as a possibility. He'd certainly know how to mask the taste or odor of a poison. He might have read Harriett's blog to keep tabs on her. If so, he'd have known the details of the tasting."

Mollye laughed. "He could have learned about the tasting from her blog or her Twitter account. The woman was a regular Tweety Bird. An hour didn't go by that she didn't breathlessly report something new about her day and her plans. I checked her tweets. She started talking about her special invite to Summer Place three weeks before the luncheon and followed up with details at least twice a day."

I frowned. "So anyone who followed Harriett knew I was having a 'private' tasting. Did she list the other guests?"

"Yep," Mollye replied. "Of course, any of the other tasting guests could have mentioned the invite on social media or in casual conversation. Word gets around."

I sighed. "That means I can't rule out the possibility the poisoning was meant to embarrass me and doom Summer Place."

"True," Moll agreed. "But I'm leaning toward the theory the intended victim was one of your invitees. Haven't looked yet for any secrets in Bert's or Dr. Swihart's closets. Maybe your dad can tap into the university grapevine to see if the toxicologist has deep dark secrets."

"You left Mom and Ursula off your list of people someone might want to harm," I said. "How come?"

A moment of unaccustomed silence fell on Moll's end of the phone line. "Huh. Your mom's such a sweetheart and, pardon the expression, dudess-do-right, I can't imagine her doing anything to inspire hatred. But I forgot she's a prosecutor. Someone she put in jail might want to get even. And I should have included Ursula. I can see her TV persona attracting unhinged stalkers. But how would a stalker from say New York know to follow Harriett's blog or tweets?"

One of Ursula's enemies was well aware she was in town. Toomey had not only sighted his former victim, he'd threatened her anew.

I couldn't share that information with Mollye, but I added Toomey to my list of potential poisoners with Ursula as his intended victim.

"I'll ask Mom if she can think of anyone who might want to harm her or Ursula," I said.

With that sobering promise, Mollye and I wound up our conversation just before Eva returned to the cabin. After I shared my morning plans, Aunt Eva urged me to take the rest of the day off as I'd soon be working round the clock with the new kids.

"You sure?" I asked.

"Yep, I have plenty of help lined up for today. Go have some fun."

I drove to the front gate. We'd warned Gerri, our new full-time employee, as well as Udderly's part-time workers, about possible picketing. Since we were leaving the gate closed, we all had to stop at a squawk box/gate keeper and enter an open-says-me electronic code. One gatekeeper post sat outside the gate; the other inside. While many security systems were rigged so a motion detector opened gates automatically to let vehicles out, that wasn't a good solution at Udderly. Sensors might not distinguish our large nannies from say a VW Beetle. So we'd opted for a code box on both sides.

On those rare occasions we closed the gates, Aunt Eva and I could use clickers to open them, eliminating the need to exit our vehicles and enter a code. The remotes also let us close the gates from a distance if we were in a footrace with a goat we feared might be hit crossing the county road. The gate was a half-hearted security measure. All our friends knew the "secret" electronic code.

As I approached the gate, I tried my remote. Nothing happened. Crud. I'd totally forgotten I needed to replace the batteries.

Pickled pigs feet. I exited the car to punch in the open-says-me code. The gate's two arched halves slowly swung apart allowing me to pass. Outside the gate, I exited my Prius once again to punch the numbers in the squawk box/entry system to relock it. Before I could climb back in my Prius, a car roared down the road and slalomed to a stop in front of me. The driver had trapped my Prius between his kamikaze car and the closed gate. My heart raced as the driver leapt from his car and ran at me like a football tackle.

What in blazes? I braced for an assault, my mind reviewing the self-defense tactics I'd learned when I started working late hours at an Asheville restaurant. The man had no weapon. He skidded to a stop, thrust an envelope in my hand, and grinned like he'd just won the lottery.

"You've been served," he said.

Nice that some folks got their jollies at work.

I studied the white envelope. I was happy the man who'd scared the cottage cheese out of me only had an envelope in his hand and not a knife or a gun. Yet I knew the envelope's contents had to bring bad news. People didn't chase you down to award sweepstakes prizes.

I climbed in my car and locked the doors before I broke the envelope's seal. I'd been served with official notice that a Mr. Bertrand Rider was suing me for medical expenses and damages related to the pain and suffering he'd endured due to my willful disregard of food safety standards.

I closed my eyes and leaned back in the seat. Good thing I was heading to my parents' house. I hoped Mom would feel up to some legal consulting with me as well as with Ursula. I reconciled myself to the knowledge Rider's lawsuit would not be the last. Harriett's heirs were certain to follow.

I had to prove I wasn't to blame. If I couldn't prove my innocence, Summer Place and my dreams of opening a B&B and restaurant were circling the proverbial drain.

I'd put all my savings into Summer Place renovations. My partially paid for Prius and the semi-dilapidated mansion I'd inherited were my sole assets—the only assets someone suing me could seize. Maybe I should be happy this was a civil rather than a criminal lawsuit.

Of course that could change, too, if the True Believers managed to convince authorities to charge me with manslaughter or homicide.

TWENTY-FIVE

Ursula answered the knock at my folks' house.

"Your mom's stirring up something in the kitchen. As you can see, I'm now quite capable of answering doors and resuming everyday activities."

"That's terrific," I said. "Hope that means you won't join Bert Rider in a class action suit."

While the TV star wasn't wearing her legal robes, I recognized her trademark scowl from watching the courtroom reality show. "What in the devil are you talking about?" she demanded.

Yep, I recognized the authoritative voice, too.

Mom entered the room, wiping her hands on a dishtowel, as I flashed the envelope I held in my hand. "Just got served. Bert didn't waste any time filing a civil lawsuit for medical expenses and pain and suffering damages."

"Pish posh." Ursula dismissed the envelope and its nested lawsuit with a broad sweep of her hand. "It's frivolous, a nuisance suit. He's hoping you'll settle to avoid court. If I were the judge, I'd dismiss it in a New York minute. There's no corroborating evidence. Nothing that shows you were negligent or intended to poison your guests."

Mom nodded. "I agree but it's still bad publicity. Wish I knew the outcome of Harriett's autopsy and what if anything DHEC found when it tested the luncheon ingredients. I'm betting on some snafu in the harvesting or food processing chain. Just bad luck that Harriett was more susceptible than the rest of us."

I shook my head. "That's what I thought at first. But I'm leaning more and more to the notion this wasn't any accident. I think someone added something to the mousse after I whipped it up. Unfortunately, I have no way to prove that. All the serving plates and dishes were sterilized in the dishwasher. Evidence destroyed."

Ursula tapped her finger against her lips. A gesture I'd seen often enough on TV as she listened to testimony. "Maybe, maybe not. The hospital took blood and urine samples from Iris and me. The hospital lab screened for the usual food poisoning culprits, things like salmonella, E. coli, and listeria. But maybe if we can get those blood and urine samples to a private lab, they can be tested for more exotic bacteria or bugs."

I glanced at Mom. "How long does the hospital keep blood and urine samples once they've run their battery of tests? Do they discard them immediately after the patient has recovered and left the hospital?"

Mom's brow creased. "Don't know, but I can find out. Excuse me while I make a few calls."

Ursula sat down on Mom's couch and patted the cushion beside her. "Come, have a seat. I hope you'll allow me to ask you some personal questions."

I fidgeted, reluctant to take an interrogation seat. She studied my face and waved her hand. "Don't look so scared. It's just that you and Amber are the same age. I'd like your opinion about my talk with Amber. If you were my daughter, how much would you want to know? Amber has always wanted to know who her father is. But can I tell her the man raped me while I was semi-conscious...that he demanded I have an abortion or he'd ruin my life?"

I felt queasy. I wasn't Amber. Had never met the woman. No way should Ursula base any of her decisions on my uninformed opinions.

Ursula chuckled. "I'm making you uncomfortable. You haven't allowed more than two inches of your bottom to settle on that seat cushion. Ready to bolt at any moment."

I tried to smile and failed. "My opinions aren't worth much. I grew up with two parents who loved me. I wasn't adopted. Mom has the Caesarian scar and hospital pictures to prove it. It's impossible for me to imagine how Amber might feel."

Ursula nodded. "True. But you share your generation's attitudes about women's rights. You know Amber is a detective. Crimes against women are her specialty. She's tough, seen plenty of misery, knows the horrors people can inflict on each other, things far worse than date rape. I wasn't beaten. Don't have flashbacks of a knife at my throat. I was drunk, semi-conscious. It was more like a very bad dream."

She paused. Her gaze left my face to stare at the hands tightly clasped in her lap. "I'm just not sure it's fair to tell her the biological father she's always asked about—perhaps fantasized as a great guy—is a callous liar and hypocrite? Would you want to know his blood was coursing through your veins?"

Uh, no.

I refrained from saying that out loud. But I couldn't stop the thought. The very notion gave me chills. I let the silence hold a minute as I considered how to corral my emotions into words.

"That knowledge would be a blow, a burden." My voice wavered. "But there'd be a balance. I'd appreciate my birth mother's courage." I paused. "I'm not certain. I think I'd want to see justice served. How well do you know your daughter?"

Ursula closed her eyes and leaned back on the sofa. "Since we made contact, we see each other two or three times a year. Often for long weekends in a spot we're unlikely to run into media types. We make it appear we've met by accident and found we enjoyed each other's company. One time we signed up for a white-water-rafting trip and agreed to share a tent. Another year we joined a small sailboat charter tour off the Greek Islands. So far, no one's noticed our accidental meetings are repeats."

"When you've been together has Amber talked a lot about her work?"

Ursula nodded. "Yes, she's very committed to helping women escape abusive relationships. That might make Amber want to out a man who portrays himself as pious yet uses threats and intimidation to hide his true character. But what if the knowledge tears at Amber's self-image? Would it gnaw at her to know she's the daughter of someone so like the men she works to put behind bars?"

Mom bustled back in the room. I was happy for the interruption. I had no clue what more I could say.

"The hospital still has our blood and urine samples," Mom said. "They agreed to provide them for independent testing if we sign a release. I called Dr. Swihart and she's onboard to run a battery of tests. I arranged for a courier to take the samples to her lab. The professor said she's been knocking around several ideas about what might have caused Harriett's death."

The judge's phone pealed a muted version of the *Dragnet* theme. "It's Amber." Ursula walked toward the kitchen for a private conversation with her secret daughter.

Mom looked tired, worried. "Did you give Ursula any advice about what she should tell her daughter?"

I sighed. "Not really. There's no right answer."

"That's all I could tell her." Mom massaged her temples. "I'll stand by whatever she decides. Ursula has carried this burden a long time. I'll do what I can to help her."

Ursula walked back into the room. "Amber called from the air. Her plane took off on time. She should arrive at the Greenville-Spartanburg airport on time. I need to head out. We'll come to the cottage as soon as we leave the airport."

"That's fine. I'll be at Summer Place all afternoon," I said. "It'll probably take two or three hours to scrub the graffiti off the kitchen appliances and wipe off the fingerprint powder covering everything. Since the vandals took every last condiment and foodstuff, I need to do a major restock. Can I grab anything for the cottage fridge while you're picking up Amber?"

My renter was enthusiastic and grateful. Her short grocery list included bottled water, wine, beer, tomatoes, romaine lettuce, grapes, two types of salad dressing, and a pound of thick-sliced turkey. Sounded like salads and plenty of liquids to lubricate tonight's conversation.

My first stop was the Bi-Lo near my folks' house. Later, I'd take a break from my kitchen clean-up and head to a Fresh Market or a Whole Foods to replace harder-to-find vegan staples.

No one looked askance when I purchased a pound of sliced turkey at Bi-Lo's deli counter. Since I grocery shopped for Eva as well as myself, meat, eggs, and dairy were quite at home in my shopping cart.

I schlepped two bags of groceries to the cottage for Ursula and stocked the small fridge. I left a note on the kitchen counter—positioned to cover one of the more disgusting stains—and invited mother and daughter to mosey up the path to the "big house" should they need anything.

Back in the Summer Place kitchen, I stowed my own groceries before tackling the spray-painted epithets on my cupboards and appliances. Most of the scarlet spray paint came off with Mister Magic sponges and lots of elbow grease, though some of the white cupboards acquired a pinkish patina. Or maybe it was just my tired, bloodshot eyes.

I took my first break from the drudgery to prep dinner for Paint and me. We'd start with a strawberry and spinach salad and end with a commercially-prepared nondairy dessert. Even vegan chefs need to cheat when the clock is ticking. Ice cream made with coconut cream is pretty darn good.

Actually I hoped to sweet talk Paint into heading to Greenville for dessert. I'd offer to buy though that wasn't much of an incentive to make a two-hour round trip for a mere slice of cake. I kinda figured Paint had definite ideas of how he'd like to occupy his hands for those hours. Gripping a steering wheel wouldn't be one of them. Most times Paint's preferences and mine would align. But I really wanted to lay eyes on Matt Hill, the suspect atop Mollye's list of would-be murderers.

To get Paint to agree, I'd need to come clean about why I wanted to check out the restaurant and its owner. Paint might even know the guy. He called on Greenville restaurants carrying his moonshine, and he'd begun promoting his soon-to-debut custom-blended whiskies.

I was snacking on hummus and black corn chips when a knock on the sunporch door startled me. The corn chip crumpled in my mitt.

As soon as I spotted my visitors, I smiled and welcomed them. Ursula and her daughter Amber had accepted my invitation to drop by. Amber shared many of her mother's features, including a regal bearing and raven-black hair. They were about the same height, topping out at five six or five seven. Both boasted hourglass figures.

Then I began to notice differences. Amber's eyes were hazel rather than green, her nose smaller and turned up, her ears considerably larger. Amber's deep Florida tan also contrasted with Ursula's ivory complexion. The daughter certainly wasn't a clone of the mother. Yet once you knew the genealogy, it was obvious they were related.

We went through the standard greeting ritual, and I invited them inside for a drink.

"Appreciate it but think we'll take a raincheck," Ursula said. "Just wanted to let you know we were moving in. Is my car blocking you?"

"No." I smiled. "This morning Dad demonstrated how easy it is to exit the drive and kill unwanted crabgrass at the same time. Your car is fine. Let me know if there's anything you need after you unpack."

"Right now, we're just dropping off our suitcases," Ursula answered. "Want to visit the South Carolina Botanical Garden while there's still a little sun to ward off the chill. I've been a big fan ever since your dad introduced me to the garden. Amber and I both want to stretch and get some fresh air."

"Enjoy," I said. "Many of the winter camellias are in full bloom. It'll be beautiful even if it's a bit chilly. Don't worry about parking when you get back. There's enough room to maneuver around."

I watched the duo stroll down the path to the ramshackle cottage. Was Ursula planning to break the news about Amber's conception while they strolled among the winter blooms? It was a weekday and quite cool. They wouldn't have much company. Lots of privacy.

If I hadn't known Amber was a detective, I doubted I'd have intuited her occupation. She was beautiful enough to be a model. I immediately upbraided myself for the stereotype. Why shouldn't a woman detective be gorgeous? Still I wondered if she wore her long hair loose like that on the job. Did detectives need to worry about someone pulling their hair in a tussle?

To make sure my renters had no problems before I took off on a second shopping excursion, I decided to give them ten minutes. They only needed five to give their bags a heave-ho and take off again. I scooped the keys to my Prius off the table as soon as they cleared the drive.

TWENTY-SIX

When I returned to Summer Place with five more bags of cooking staples, my driveway was filled to capacity—Ursula's rental plus two trucks.

Why were Andy and Paint both here? I parked on the street careful to ensure I was more than ten feet from the Medley driveway. I'd witnessed Janice's back-out skills. Though she maneuvered her car at a snail's pace, she still had an uncanny knack for bumping into stationary objects like mailboxes and parked cars.

"Hey, how about some help with the groceries?" I called as I headed to the sunporch toting two of my canvas grocery bags. Andy looked up and grinned. He was busy screwing something into the porch frame near the door.

"Be right there," he said.

"What gives? Are we double-dating tonight?" I asked as he abandoned whatever he was up to and hurried to my car.

"I wish," he answered as he grabbed the remaining three bags and headed toward the porch.

"Paint and I went in together on a little surprise." He beamed. "Follow me inside and all will be revealed."

"Uh, okay." I could see Paint through one of the sunporch's glass panels. He was hunched over, concentrating on a laptop. I wasn't shocked at seeing either Andy or Paint inside a room I'd carefully locked. Since the men helped with renovation chores and hauled supplies in their trucks, they both had keys to the substantial lock on Summer Place's front door as well as skeleton keys for the porch.

"You're too early for dinner," I commented as Paint looked up.

"I heard the early-bird gets the—" he started.

Andy interrupted. "Best not finish. I know you're a worm."

"So what gives?" I repeated.

"Those idiots breaking in to trash your kitchen worried us," Paint said. "So we bought you a real deadbolt lock for this side door and—"

"And a combo doorbell camera and motion sensor," Andy finished. "Now if you're in the kitchen and someone comes to the door, you'll get an alert on your phone."

"Yep, and you can see who's there," Paint added. "The motion sensor activates the camera even if the troublemaker doesn't ring the doorbell."

"Since the place is empty a lot, we'll put an app on your phone—our phones, too. We'll all get alerts," Andy said. "Whoever is closest can check it out."

"So you think you're entitled to know about every Tom and Dick who comes calling?" I tried for a sly smile.

"Yeah, right, like you have secrets," Paint laughed. "Sorry, Brie, your love life's an open book. Between the two of us and Eva, you have about a minute a day that's not accounted for."

"I might surprise you," I quipped.

A loud knock prompted the three of us to turn in unison. We'd been so busy oohing and ahhing over the technology and ribbing each other, we failed to notice the arrival of visitors—and they were in plain view less than six feet away. I opened the door with its new dead bolt and invited Ursula and Amber inside. My "beaus" weren't shy about checking out the curvy young arrival.

"Hope we're not interrupting," Ursula said. "We heard the laughter and saw the trucks. Thought we'd see if we were missing a party."

"Paint and Andy, I'd like you to meet Ursula Billings and Amber..." I paused for a second when I realized I didn't know Amber's last name and couldn't introduce her as Ursula's daughter. "Amber is Ursula's friend from Miami," I added.

"Nice to meet you," Amber and Ursula said in unison. Then Amber looked at her mother and smiled.

"My last name is Royer," Amber said. "Ursula and I aren't just friends, we're related."

Ah ha. Sounded as if that walk in the botanical gardens had resolved at least one issue. While Amber hadn't exactly announced Ursula was her mother, the fact of a genealogical bond was no longer under wraps. Did that mean Amber knew the truth about her father and was weighing the pros and cons of making that information public?

"I noticed the camera doorbell," Amber said. "Is it new? I installed one on my condo door. Cops can't be too careful these days."

"You're a policeman...er police officer?" Paint asked.

Amber nodded. "A detective with the Miami Police. Just here to visit my mom."

Hmm, she finally said it, called Ursula her mom.

"You two are staying in that rundown excuse for a building out back?" Paint asked. "Sorry, Brie, some truths hurt."

Ursula smiled. "I'd describe it as rustic rather than rundown. I had to twist Brie's arm to let us stay."

"I agreed to the rental before someone broke in and trashed my kitchen," I added. "Andy and Paint, can we put that app on Ursula's or Amber's phone? If someone comes prowling around I'd feel better if they got an alert, too. Anyone headed to the cottage would almost have to walk past this door. The overgrown jungle on the other side of the house doesn't offer much room to maneuver. Does the camera have a wide enough angle to see beyond the stoop?"

"Take a look." Paint swiveled his computer screen so I could see.

"That's really clear." I was amazed at the view. "But what would the camera see at night with all the lights out?"

"It has night vision," Amber answered. "I've been surprised how clear the pictures are. I carry a gun, but forewarning is always a good thing." She handed her cell phone to Paint. "Ursula, do you want the app on your phone, too?"

"No way. I don't want one more app on my phone. They're time sinkholes. Make a quick check on the weather and ten minutes later I'm studying drought maps for Timbuktu. Think I'll head back to the cottage and start making our chef's salad. Thanks for the groceries, Brie."

As the mother and daughter walked away, I turned to my supposed boyfriends. "You can haul your tongues back in." I laughed. "You did hear Amber say she carries a gun."

Paint shook his head. "That only makes her more interesting. But you know my heart's taken. Well, until tomorrow, when I'm free to date, and Andy is up to bat for—are you really going to make me say it?—a week of Animal Passion."

Paint hung his head as if in great sorrow. Then he popped up, eyes round. "Say, you wouldn't mind if I asked Amber out tomorrow, would you?"

He laughed as I punched his arm. He was kidding, wasn't he?

"Give me your phone, love," Paint said. "Let's finish getting this set up."

Ten minutes later, I'd tested the app with Andy and Paint making stealth passes to figure the motion detector's range. Impressive.

"Thank you both." I kissed Paint's cheek and shook Andy's hand. "Saving your kiss for tomorrow, Andy."

TWENTY-SEVEN

Since I couldn't use my run-down cottage's postage-stamp shower, I headed to Udderly to get cleaned up. At a minimum, Paint deserved a date who smelled good and wore clean clothes.

Eva hadn't phoned to warn me about barbarians at the gate, so I was dismayed to find our farm entrance blocked again by a ragtag army of picketers. There were about fifteen True Believer demonstrators. Women outnumbered the men two to one. All adults today.

They'd arrived in an eclectic collection of vehicles. A couple of junker cars, a shiny new Cadillac, a Prius twin to my own car, and three trucks. The caravan had once again parked on the verge opposite the gate. That meant only humans blocked the entrance, no large hunks of metal forming a barricade.

As I approached my turn, I noticed the mud-caked license plate of the last truck in the makeshift parking lot. Not a single one of its digits readable. Could it be the big truck Mrs. Medley spotted at Summer Place the night before my tasting? The night I felt certain someone poisoned my chocolate mousse.

I slowed my car even more, gawking in hopes of seeing who owned the rust bucket. Unfortunately, no one loitered near the suspect truck. The picketers formed an amoeba-like mass in front of the gate. Though this crowd was smaller than yesterday's, their faces appeared more hostile. Then again maybe I was projecting. I felt more hostile. Spending hours removing the graffiti in my kitchen and tapping my dwindling bank account to replace foodstuffs hadn't enhanced my mood.

Sour sweetbreads! I forgot to replace the dead batteries in my clicker gizmo again.

Now I'd have to drive up to the squawk box and roll down my window to punch in the code. Just great. Today's spitters would have my arms and face as a target for their loogies. Double yuck.

In theory, our gate keypad—like all drive-up service windows and banking ATMs—provided easy access to the driver of any vehicle. Ha! Maybe, if you were six-feet tall, drove an SUV, and had guerilla-length arms. Me? Most of the time I had to unbuckle my seatbelt, open the car door, and hang outside like I was counterbalancing a heeling catamaran. Even then my fingers sometimes failed to reach the keypad.

I scooted the Prius inch-by-inch toward the gate. A large woman, who looked like she could qualify for a women's wrestling team, made it her mission to block my squeeze play. No way could I maneuver my car close enough to reach the keypad from the relative safety of my vehicle.

I sighed. Show no fear. It'll only encourage them. Spit washes off.

I took a deep breath, flung the car door open, jumped out, and took two giant steps to reach the squawk box.

The wrestler didn't speak. She did sort of grunt as she poked me with a sign that read: "Hell-Bound Hookers." I assumed the message was meant to inform me my evil deeds would cast me into hell for eternity. I thought it had less the sting of a biblical curse and more the ring of a Westward Ho slogan. Hookers, hell-bound for glory! Since the woman's prod was gentle, I resisted the temptation to grab the cardboard and shove it someplace that wrestling holds weren't allowed. I debated contorting my features, sticking out my tongue, and crossing my eyes. But Mom always warned me I'd be sorry if my face froze in that position. Instead I awarded my jiggling nemesis a smile and a queenly wave.

That made her and her cohorts even madder. A clutch of screaming women instantly surrounded the wrestler. Interestingly, the men seemed to tarry at the back. Among the scowling female faces the one I locked onto fit Eva's description of Jeannie Nickles, the pastor's wife and Toomey's mother-in-law. Unlike her companions, she appeared amused, like this was all good fun. Surely there couldn't be another True Believer who looked like she'd hand you a bag of chocolate chip cookies to snack on during your presumed trip to hell.

I sucked in a sharp breath as Jeannie, the sweet old lady imposter, awarded me a sly smile. If I believed in witchcraft, I might nominate this woman for a trial.

My heart galumphed like I was running the last mile of a triathlon. Get me out of here.

A sepulcher groan finally announced the gates had decided to swing open. I jumped back in my car. I would have loved to stamp on the gas and plough through the crowd. Jeannie's rosy cheeks and saccharin smile gave me the willies. I stymied the urge and inched the car forward like an octogenarian sea turtle.

Maybe I'd stay up all night to avoid sleep and possible nightmares featuring Jeannie Nickles, the pleasantly plump grandma drowning newborn kittens. I was pretty sure Paint would be more than happy to keep me company all the way through to dawn.

I spotted Eva and Gerri, Udderly's new full-time employee, laughing and jawboning as I parked.

"Why didn't you warn me?" I grumbled as I exited the car. "If I'd known we still had demonstrators, I might have remembered to put new batteries in my clicker."

Eva and Gerri laughed harder. "Here we thought your exit-the-car routine was pure bravado. You're ruining your image. You certainly riled that crowd. They've been pretty docile all day. Acted like a bunch of placid cows chewing their cud."

The picture Eva painted made me smile, then chuckle. Laughter was always an excellent blow-off-steam option after fear spiked my adrenalin. And Jeannie Nickles and her compatriots had definitely awakened my fight or flight response.

Eva glanced at her watch. "Hey, aren't you entertaining Paint at Summer Place tonight? If so, you'd better head straight to the showers 'cause that's my next stop after Gerri and I finish. And you'd better not use up all the hot water."

She turned to Gerri. "Brie has a talent for getting in hot water with or without any aid from our plumbing."

TWENTY-EIGHT

I lit tapered candles. Since I'd yet to return the crystal and fine china I'd borrowed from Mom for the tasting, I decided to use them one more time. The porch table's sparkling water goblets, wine glasses, and Wedgwood china looked elegant. Thank heavens the kitchen vandals had been satisfied with spray painting appliances and stealing food. Had they taken Mom's china and crystal I'd be heartbroken.

A deep-throated engine made its driveway entrance. Paint had arrived. Well, at least I hoped the engine powered Paint's ride and not the behemoth with a mud-caked license plate I'd noticed across from the Udderly picket line.

"Hello, beautiful," Paint called as the porch door swung open. "You know this lock only protects if you use it..."

Yowzer. Sometimes Paint's good looks sucked the air right out of my lungs. His thick black hair glistened. The laugh lines bracketing his mocha eyes offset the smoldering intensity of his gaze. Then there was that danged dimple. His broad shoulders challenged the seams of his sport jacket, while the pale blue shirt open at the collar revealed an inviting sliver of bronzed chest.

Paint put down the bottle of wine he'd brought and wrapped me in his arms. The kiss wasn't a quick howdy. He might have been passionately welcoming me home from a long, dangerous trip. Paint's kisses always spelled danger.

When the kiss eventually ended, my mind was mush. What had Paint said when he walked in? Ah, yes, something about remembering to lock doors.

"I knew you'd be here any minute. Didn't imagine there'd be much time for bandits to rush in ahead of you. Besides I now have that early warning system you and Andy installed. If I'd been busy in the kitchen, my phone would have alerted me."

"Okay, I'll give you a pass this time. But please keep the danged door locked."

Paint closed his eyes and inhaled. "Smells great! Whatever you've been busy concocting is making my stomach do can't-wait cartwheels. Guess I didn't have to stop for that burger on the way over after all."

I punched Paint's arm. "You didn't really?"

"No, I didn't." He kissed me again. "Didn't stop at the drugstore for poison antidotes either."

"Then I guess we'll both have to live dangerously. Our salad course is ready. I'll serve it while you open the wine. You can even choose which plate you get. I have only one request. Let's focus on cheerful topics over dinner. No mention of Harriett, lawsuits, True Believers, or vandals. Okay?"

"Fine by me." Paint grinned. "You're giving me permission to bore you with whisky distilling small talk and dazzle you with my entrepreneurial skills. Ta da. Just lined up another Lowcountry investor, and I'm about to close on an ideal spot for my Charleston-area distillery."

"Bravo." We clinked glasses. "You are awesome. I have absolute faith in your entrepreneurial wizardry. I'm so happy for you. It's a huge undertaking, expanding your product line and your territory at the same time."

Paint frowned. "There is one downside. It means I'll be spending a lot more time in Charleston, away from the Upstate, and, more specifically, away from you. But I promised we'd only talk about happy things."

A hint of panic made it tough to swallow the wine I'd just sipped. I sensed Paint was picking at the edges of what was really on his mind. Was he planning to end our relationship? Blame it on the cruelty of a geographic divide? Admittedly it would be hard to plan Brewing Trouble weeks if Paint was tied up in Charleston, a four-hour drive from Ardon County.

Don't jump to conclusions.

I leapt up to clear the salad plates and bring in the main course—a Portobello Stack. The vegetable tower had grilled Portobello mushrooms for its structural base. Layered above were candied carrots, sautéed zucchini, caramelized onions, and fried green tomatoes. A rich cashew sauce meandered its way down the sides of the tower.

"It looks too pretty to eat," Paint said. "Well, almost."

As he took his first taste, I purposely shifted the conversation away from Paint's mention of long Lowcountry absences. Sooner or later Paint would return to the topic. He was a master of timing. He'd know when to make his declaration. He'd probably just tossed in a hint about our inevitable separation to start the idea percolating in my mind. I felt certain he'd had ample break-up experience and knew how to deal with discarded girlfriends' sobs. Best to leave the break-up—if that's what it would be—to the shank of the evening.

Fine by me. I was into postponing sobs.

I tried for my cheeriest tone. "Were you shocked to hear Mollye and Danny got engaged?"

Paint tipped his head to the side. "Not a bit. All the signs were there. Danny was a goner months ago. Crazy, stupid in love. And, despite Mollye's outward leanings toward—shall we say the unconventional—I've always known she'd be a bride. Just didn't know if she'd prefer to wear a wedding ring on her finger, in her ear, or through her nose. I've watched Moll coo over Andy's nieces and nephews. She loves the little ones."

My fork was half way to my mouth. It slipped back to my plate. The engagement announcement had floored me. How had Paint seen it coming a mile away?

Sure, he'd grown up in Ardon County. He'd known Danny and Mollye forever. But that didn't totally explain my obliviousness. Moll and I became summer friends at age eight, spending every minute together when I visited my aunts. When I returned to Iowa, we stayed pen pals, sharing secrets only admitted in teenagers' locked diaries.

After I moved to Udderly Kidding Dairy last spring, it was as if we'd never been apart. We talked for hours about our hopes, our dreams. I knew how much she loved children, and hoped to have a passel of kids. I knew she planned to marry someday.

But I had no idea that someday was like *now*.

"The look on your face tells me Mollye's engagement surprised you," Paint said. "Moll talks a good game. Paints herself as a butterfly of love out to taste nectar on a vast field of flowers. But it's all talk. Bet she and Danny don't even make their first anniversary before they're baptizing a baby."

I toyed with my fork. "I knew she wanted marriage and a family. But she made it sound like a distant dream, not a let's subscribe to *Modern*

Bride priority." I laughed. "Of course, I doubt Mollye would seek advice from any bridal magazine on how to plan her wedding."

Paint nodded. "She'll do it up in style. So, in your talks with Mollye, did you admit to any desire for a husband and children?"

I swallowed. Suddenly I longed to switch the conversation back to Harriett and lawsuits. My feelings were more than a little jumbled. I wanted the kind of marriage my parents had. Mom's example proved a woman could have a wonderful career and a terrific marriage. She and Dad might be halves of a couple but they were both whole, unique individuals.

"I'd like to marry someday and have a family." I admitted it quickly, then paused. "But I won't rush into something I might come to regret. Been there, done that. My next fiancé has to share my definition of love. He can't believe affairs are optional. I need someone I can count on. Someone who'll truly commit and yet let me be me."

Paint reached across the table and took my hand. "You can count on me, Brie. I'd ask you to marry me tonight if I thought you'd say yes. But, this time around, you're the one who needs to commit. You have to choose."

His fingers caressed mine as he gently untangled our hands. He smiled. "You will let me know when you're ready, right? All I need is a hint. Maybe tell me you'd like to see me on one knee. I'm quick on the uptake. Till then, I won't make you squirm any longer. I'll put the conversation on pause."

There's an old cliché about feeling your heart in your throat. I know it's ridiculous, but, if my ticker wasn't choking me, some other large obstruction seemed determined to prevent me from speaking, or even sucking in air. I was undone.

I'd been telling myself I loved both Paint and Andy. But was it true? I loved them both as friends. Yet Paint was the magician. His lips, his touch set me on fire. But fire could burn.

I brought the linen napkin to my face, pretending to cover a cough. I tried to be unobtrusive as I quickly dabbed at the tears pooling in my eyes.

"I wasn't expecting—"

Paint cut me off. "We're moving on to another topic, remember. I'd rather you think for a while about what I said. No panicked response." He cleared his throat. "Now when we spoke on the phone earlier, you said you wanted me to do you a favor tonight. What is it?"

I took a calming breath. Paint was letting me wriggle off the hook. Don't blurt out words you'll regret until you corral your feelings.

"It's a pretty big favor. Can we drive to Greenville for dessert? I'll treat. I hear Matt Hill's restaurant has a menu with more dessert choices than entrées. Do you happen to know Matt?"

Paint leaned back, tipping his chair on its back legs. "You want to meet Matt, don't you? Is he somehow tied into your current run of bad luck? You said not to mention Harriett and lawsuits but I suspect you just changed the rules."

"You suspect right." I hesitated. "Mollye believes Matt Hill could be Harriett's killer. The gossip suggests she had something on him that could ruin his franchise plans. As a chef, Matt would know how to hide the taste of any bitter-tasting medicine or poison."

"Matt, a killer?" Paint's lips quirked up, then he started laughing. "Sure let's head to Greenville for dessert. But, I'll give you a hundred-to-one odds, Matt isn't your villain. Just wait till you meet him."

Paint quit laughing, but he couldn't hide the smile or the twinkle in his eyes.

Why did he think the idea of Matt Hill as killer so preposterous?

TWENTY-NINE

Paint circled the parking lot twice before he found a space big enough for his oversized truck. Matt Hill's restaurant was packed. Paint jumped from the cab and circled around the truck's hood to give me a hand down. Big trucks and short women have compatibility issues.

"Time to meet our murder suspect." Paint grinned. "Let's go in the kitchen entrance. That's how I usually enter. I do believe you have some familiarity with commercial kitchens. Most likely that's where we'll find Matt—unless he's doing a magic act for customers. He's an amateur magician."

I awarded Paint a puzzled look. "Sounds like you know Matt pretty well."

He grinned and grabbed my hand, leading me toward the restaurant's back entrance. The door was located between two giant and quite odiferous trash bins. Not how you want first-time diners to enter your restaurant.

Why hadn't I googled the restaurant and its owner? Given the discrepancy between Moll's suggestion that the owner was a prime murder suspect and Paint's dismissive smirk, I had no idea what I'd encounter inside. I didn't even know what type of cuisine the restaurant served. The fact that Matt Hill had lent an All-American name to the establishment suggested meat-and-potato fare with maybe a few nods to French and Italian dishes.

Though we only had to cover about thirty feet to reach the back of the restaurant, the biting February wind made it seem a race against hypothermia. I couldn't stop shivering, even after Paint cracked the door blasting us with a wave of kitchen heat. Felt like I was trading a refrigerator for a furnace.

"¿Matias Colina, tú estás aquí?" Paint called out. "Tu cervecera

*favorita ha llegado. Tengo una hermosa mujer conmigo, pero debes
mantener tus manos alejadas. Ella es mía."*
What the Feta?
Why was Paint suddenly speaking in foreign tongues? Definitely
Spanish. I'd taken four years of high school French. Since Spanish and
French were both Romance languages, many words were close cousins.
Too bad not enough of them were relatives for me to grasp the gist of
Paint's rapid fire Spanish.
Hmmm. I was pretty sure the word *"mujer"* meant woman. Surely
Paint wasn't joking with Matt, telling him he'd brought along a woman
who suspected him of being a murdering psychopath.
The huge kitchen appeared to be in total chaos as most commercial
kitchens do to the uninitiated. Pots clanged. Waiters yelled orders. Lids on
large kettles rattled from rising steam. The heavy metal door of a walk-in
freezer banged shut as a woman in a white apron nudged it with her hip.
She was one of four white-aproned workers scurrying hither and yon.
It was the kind of controlled chaos I understood. I'd learned a few
things as a sous chef.
Somewhere within the pot-banging din, I heard laughter. It almost
sounded like uncontrolled giggles coming from a spot to my left. When I
looked in that direction, all I could see was an empty counter. Had the
giggler bent down to pick something off the floor?
A second later I saw a blur of red and white rush Paint's legs. One
minute Paint was standing, the next he'd executed a controlled tumble and
was writhing on the floor.
"Tu alto saco de caca. ¿Por qué no me dijiste que vendrías?" Paint's
petite wrestling partner laughed. The little man's inflection suggested he
was peppering Paint with questions.
Stunned, I didn't move a muscle, utter a word.
A minute passed and the men ended their floorshow. Paint panted as
he untangled himself from the chuckling little person, who wore a bright
red shirt, black britches, and a white apron. "Brie, I'd like you to meet Matt
Hill."
"Pleased to meet you." Matt struggled to a standing position and
lifted his very short arm for a handshake. Though he'd just spoken rapid
Spanish, only a hint of an accent flavored his English. His sparkling black
eyes quickly checked me out from head to toe. But the roving gaze seemed

inoffensive, like he was admiring his friend's taste in women.

I smiled as I leaned down. "I gather you are well acquainted with Mr. Paynter. Former teammates on a wrestling team perhaps?"

Matt grinned. "Not quite. Known each other since college. Became friends freshman year when we went to El Salvador to help with earthquake recovery. I had cousins there, and, in a way, Paint had relatives, too. He'd spent a summer in San Salvador as part of a high school exchange program."

Aha. That's why Paint's Spanish was so fluent.

Even on tip toes, I figured Paint's college buddy was less than four feet tall. The shiny black hair atop his head didn't quite reach my midriff.

I recalled Paint's initial reaction when he tumbled on to my reason for wanting to meet Matt. Naturally, Paint couldn't conceive of his old friend being a killer. But one didn't need great height to stir some drug into a chocolate mousse. I had to believe little people were as capable of murder as big people.

"I saw a green VW Beetle outside," Paint said. "You still driving that beat-up old cucaracho? Thought by now you'd own something grander than a bug, you know, like my fine truck."

Matt shook his head. "You kidding? It cost a fortune to tailor what you call my bug to my fine body." He put a hand on his head and did a little pirouette. "If I owned a truck, I'd need mountaineering gear every time I climbed in or out. Besides the ladies love my bug."

Paint cast a told-you-so smirk my way. Okay, I got it. Matt couldn't have driven the truck that parked in front of Summer Place the night my mousse was spiked with some poison. Of course, he could have had an accomplice. An accomplice certainly would have made it easier for him to work in my kitchen with its normal height counters.

Huh? How did he manage here? I gave the large kitchen another visual scan.

"You two are gonna stay till closing, right?" Matt asked. "Can't really talk until then. It's winding down but still busy. Ten o'clock brings in the after-theater crowd for drinks and dessert. Couple of employees called in sick—a waiter and our dessert chef."

Matt quirked an eyebrow as he assessed Paint. "Too bad you don't know how to make Bananas Foster. It's tonight's advertised special. We printed the menus before Francine called in sick with the flu. All the other desserts are premade, but I'm going crazy finishing entrées and making batches of Bananas Foster."

I grabbed an apron off a row of hooks on the wall. "Bananas Foster? Easy peasy. Point me in the right direction."

Paint laughed. "Yes, she's a chef."

"You're an angel." Matt kissed my hand.

He then turned to Paint and made another comment I couldn't follow in rapid Spanish. However, I understood Paint's reply. "Yes, she is, and hands off. She's taken."

Matt gave me a quick kitchen tour and showed me where to find the ingredients I needed—bananas, butter, brown sugar, cinnamon, dark rum, and banana liqueur. Of course, the vanilla ice cream was in the freezer.

The restauranteur announced to his kitchen crew that I was the new Francine. "All Bananas Foster orders go to Brie."

When I turned around, Paint had disappeared. I figured he'd taken a load off and was sitting out front at a good table, probably placing a double order for Bananas Foster and flirting with the waitresses.

Five minutes later I discovered how wrong I'd been when Paint burst through the swinging doors separating the kitchen and dining room. He had a pencil tucked behind his ear and an order pad in his hand. "I need one lasagna and one fried chicken-all white meat."

He looked my way, waved, and picked up a tray filled with glasses of ice water. And he was gone, vanishing once more through the swinging doors.

Son of a salami. Paint was waiting tables.

I smiled. Seemed only fair that he'd been put to work, too. When I wasn't whipping up orders of Bananas Foster, I made chocolate and caramel sauce designs to decorate the chilled plates used to serve the premade desserts. Had to admit it was fun to be back in the hurly burly of a commercial kitchen. On a busy night it was a lot like theater. Only in the kitchen, it was orders that were forgotten instead of dialogue and ingredients that disappeared instead of stage props.

To keep customers happy, a great restauranteur knew how to improvise. Matt was a great restauranteur.

I snuck occasional glances at him as he worked, marveling at his ingenuity. While all the kitchen counters were normal height, attached rolling ladders put every work space within Matt's reach. The ladders resembled the wheeled affairs librarians relied on to reach top shelf books. However, Matt's stainless steel numbers snapped out to become stepstools once they were rolled into position. When he finished, the ladder/stepstools folded flat and were neatly tucked back under the counters out of the way of taller kitchen workers.

Just before midnight the barrage of new orders dwindled to a trickle. Matt rolled one of his ladders to a stop beside me. "Let's call it a night. Only a few hangers on. If they order Bananas Foster, I'll have the waitstaff say a monkey absconded with the last bunch of bananas. Can't begin to thank you. Come join me in the dining room for a nightcap. Seems only fair for you to see what the front half of the restaurant looks like."

I untied my apron. "It's a deal."

As Paint swung through the door into the kitchen, Matt took my hand. "Sorry, Paint, I know you said hands off, but she's too perfect. I'm proposing marriage."

Paint laughed. "Get in line. I asked first."

Matt's eyebrows shot up as he searched my face. "So did you say yes? Do I need to open champagne?"

I could feel the blush. How to answer? "Well, Paint's exaggerating—as usual. He didn't actually propose. He implied he might ask if he knew the answer would be yes."

"Ah ha." Matt chuckled. "I knew a lady would eventually steal Paint's heart. I hope you say yes sooner rather than later. That would improve dating possibilities for the rest of us bachelors."

After settling us at a table, Matt went to get our drinks and I toed off my shoes. It was good to sit down.

Matt returned in a flash with Paint's beer and my wine. "Wish I could talk you two into coming to work here," he said. "Paint, you'd make a fair waiter with a little more training, and Brie, you're a marvel in the kitchen. Where are you working as a chef? I'll pay more."

I told him I'd worked as a sous chef in Asheville and planned to open a B&B that catered to vegetarians and vegans. Had to give Matt credit. He didn't scoff or snicker, even though his restaurant's menu was definitely "beefy".

When I mentioned the name of my hoped-for B&B, Summer Place, Matt's eyes went wide. "Oh no, I read about Harriett Quinn's death. The Greenville paper reported a severe case of food poisoning was believed to be the cause. The story also mentioned Bert, the paper's food critique, was among the luncheon guests who took ill. Bert's reviews can be pretty snarky. Hate to have him write one from his sick bed."

Paint interrupted. "We believe someone intentionally poisoned the food to kill Harriett. Apparently she had a bad habit of extorting restaurant owners, farmers, and other businesses. We thought you might know some of the folks who had a grudge."

"Besides me, you mean?" Matt shook his head. "Don't kid a kidder, Paint. You heard I was one of her victims. You heard right. But I wanted her in jail, not dead. I went to the cops. I was cooperating in a sting operation."

Kidney pie with suet crust!

For a little person, Matt could deliver one whopper of a surprise.

I polished off two glasses of chardonnay as Matt told his story. Harriett had learned Matt, born Matias Colina—Colina means hill in Spanish—had been brought into the country illegally as a child.

She assumed Matt Hill's identity was stolen, and he was using fake documents to claim citizenship. The blogger threatened he'd lose his business and be deported if he didn't pay up.

"Harriett didn't know the other half of the story," he said. "My folks brought me to the States because they knew I needed expensive operations, an impossibility in El Salvador. They took me to an Atlanta doctor who specialized in treating dwarfism. The doctor's brother is a dwarf. The doc managed to get me Special Juvenile Immigrant Status, in other words a green card. My folks had to return to El Salvador but I stayed in Atlanta with cousins. I'm not illegal.

"So, no, I had no reason to kill Harriett," he concluded. "But I'm sure there were others who wished her dead. I'm so sorry for the trouble this has brought you, Brie."

THIRTY

Paint stayed on my bumper all the way to Udderly. I'd met him at Summer Place, and he didn't want me driving home without an escort. It was almost two a.m. Even though it was super late and dawn would come early, I didn't bolt for the cabin when Paint cut his engine and climbed down out of his truck.

"Think we're better off saying goodnight in your Prius than my truck," he hinted. I didn't argue. His kisses were too seductive, and I suspected that sooner or later the truck's intervening gear shift was bound to injure one of us.

When I finally pulled away, my clothes were askew but still attached to my body. Like me, they were holding on by a thread. Paint had a knack for making seams want to unravel.

Cashew woke as I tiptoed to my room. Her unblinking gaze accused me of abandonment. I'd been gone for hours, which I assumed had to equate to months in dog years. Never mind that Eva petted Cashew and snuck her extra treats during even my shortest absences. When I climbed in bed, Cashew hopped on the quilt to join me. She never could hold a grudge.

"Sleep fast," I told her. "Dawn's right around the corner."

Which is exactly how it seemed when my alarm trilled at five a.m. Shivering, I rolled out of bed. The Arctic wave that had descended on South Carolina hadn't waved goodbye. I pulled on wool socks, jeans, and a sweatshirt. Barely seemed enough clothes to dart to the bathroom. I'd add a wool cap, gloves, and a heavy jacket before venturing outside.

Eva greeted me as I exited the bathroom. "Figured you could use a cup of coffee before the chores. What time did you get home anyway? I got up to pee at one a.m. and Cashew was still in her doggie bed. Knew you weren't home."

"Thanks for the coffee." An involuntary full-body shiver-quiver gripped me as my fingers wrapped around the steaming hot mug. "Paint and I went to Greenville and visited one of his old college friends. It's a long story. I'll tell you all later."

"You meeting Dr. Swihart today?"

I nodded. "Her office at eleven. No place to park nearby so I'll leave my car at my folks' house and walk. Gives me a chance to check on Mom."

I didn't bother to knock, just yoo-hooed before I turned the knob. Good, my parents had started locking their front door. I fished out my key and walked inside. Dad taught a Friday morning class, and Mom usually left for her office by seven a.m. Though it was now ten thirty, I figured Mom's bout of food poisoning might have encouraged a late departure.

My yoo-hoo was a courtesy. Didn't want to startle her.

"Come in," Mom called. "We're in the kitchen."

We? Was Dad home, too?

The kitchen table hosted Mom, Ursula, and Amber. If I'd noticed Ursula's rental on the street, I'd have made a more polite entry than my here-I-come barge-in.

"Sorry to interrupt. Figured Mom would be home alone. Just popped in to say hi or, if no one was here, leave a note. I parked out front. Impossible to find a spot on campus so I figured I'd leave the car here and hoof it to Dr. Swihart's office."

Amber stood. "Mind if I come along? Call it professional curiosity. Iris told us the professor's trying to pinpoint why one luncheon guest died while the others had moderate or no symptoms."

"Sure, you're welcome to join the party," I replied. "Maybe you'll have some suggestions of your own once we hear what she's discovered. But we need to leave pronto. It'll take at least ten minutes to walk to her office, and I have the impression Dr. Swihart penciled me into a small window between classes."

Mom waved her hand. "Go on. It'll be noon when you get back. I have plenty of options in the refrigerator. You two can fill us in over lunch."

Amber and I set off at a brisk pace. "I am curious about the professor's theories," she began, "but I also wanted a chance for us to talk in private."

She turned toward me, head cocked. Was she looking for my reaction?

"Ursula told you she planned to finally spill the beans and let me know Lawrence Toomey was my biological father, right?"

I nodded. "I figured Ursula broke the news during your garden outing." Why did it feel like I was treading on quicksand?

Amber managed a fleeting smile. "Actually it wasn't news—though I pretended it was. I solved the last half of my parental mystery two months ago. Sent my DNA to a private lab that analyzes it and gives you a genealogical history. You know, 50 percent Irish, 30 percent German, etc. I then entered my DNA in another database that looks for matches with distant—or not-so-distant—relatives who've also signed into the database. That's how I learned Ruth Toomey was my half-sister."

My feet stuttered to a complete stop.

Great Gouda!

My mouth gaped open Amber had blindsided me. "Didn't see that one coming. Did you contact your half-sister?"

"Yes." Amber tugged her sweater jacket a little tighter. "I'm cautious. Guess it's my profession. Didn't want to leave digital crumbs for some hacker to track. I used another officer's computer terminal to do my research on Ruth. Found out pretty quickly that her father—our father— was being considered for the Supreme Court.

"Ruth's a physician's assistant, engaged to a lawyer with grandiose political ambitions. After I managed to track down her cell phone number, I used a burner phone to contact her. We've talked a few times, but I've never met her in person."

"Why all the cloak-and-dagger precautions?" I asked.

"Seemed prudent to be discreet what with Toomey's nomination and her fiancé's ambitions. I wanted to reassure Ruth I had no plans to make our relationship public."

"Was she upset to learn she had a half sister?"

"Didn't appear to be." Amber shrugged. "Said she always wanted siblings. But Ruth begged me to keep our relationship secret. She didn't voice concern about political fallout for her father. She was worried about her mother—Toomey's wife. Ruth described Esther as emotionally fragile. Said she feared her mom would have a nervous breakdown or spiral deeper into a clinical depression if she learned her husband had fathered a bastard while she was pregnant. Ruth and I had both done the math. I was conceived a few months after the Toomey's' shotgun wedding."

We stopped at a crosswalk. I was tongue-tied. Hadn't a clue what to say.

"Which way?" Amber asked.

"Left." We started walking again. "So Ruth believes Ursula and her father had an affair at law school?" I finally asked. "She has no idea it was date rape?"

I stole a glance at Amber. She stared straight ahead. Her stoic profile gave no hint of her emotions.

"I didn't know Toomey took advantage of Ursula—basically raped her—until yesterday," Amber said. "Still trying to wrap my mind around that bombshell. Don't know whether it's good or bad that my job has given me context. Every day I come in contact with bad men who've spawned good children. At least I don't have some hang-up about being a bad seed."

She paused. "Ursula's definitely telling the truth. She confided in your mother right after it happened. I totally get why Ursula wants to prevent Toomey's confirmation. He shouldn't be a Supreme Court Justice. That would be wrong, very wrong. But announcing to the world why he's unfit could ruin the lives of lots of innocent people. Have unintended consequences."

"Would it be painful for you?"

She nodded. "It would hurt my adoptive parents as well as Ruth, her fiancé, and Mrs. Toomey. They'd all suffer even though they did nothing wrong."

"So how did you leave things with Ursula?"

"For the sake of everyone it would impact, I told Ursula I'd prefer to avoid the publicity. But I gave my blessing on trying to use the facts of my birth to bluff Toomey. She hopes to meet him privately with your mother along as legal counsel. They'll lay out irrefutable evidence of his infidelity—my DNA and date of birth. If he agrees to withdraw his name from nomination, Ursula will agree to keep the whole sordid mess secret."

"Isn't that blackmail?" I was shocked my mother was party to the plan. It seemed a close cousin to Harriett's offer of silence in exchange for Matt Hill's money.

Amber frowned. "I guess you could view it that way. Imagine our mothers prefer to see it as a confidentiality agreement, an exchange of items of value. We've heard plenty lately about men asking women to sign confidentiality agreements."

"Does Ursula think he'll cave?"

"She's not sure." Amber placed a hand on my arm. "This morning Ursula and Iris are putting the finishing touches on a legal agreement that says the facts surrounding my conception will never be made public if Toomey withdraws."

"What about Ruth?" I asked. "Would you ever tell her about the date rape?"

"I doubt it. I'd like to meet Ruth in person. Maybe I can convince her to talk to her father. Let him know she's aware of his infidelity. Maybe she can exert some extra pressure on her father to withdraw for the family's sake."

She paused. "I think if I told Ruth all the gory details it might tip her the other way. I can imagine how hard it might be for her to accept Ursula's version of events. That doubt might make her protective of her dad and less likely to help."

Amber reached over and wrapped a hand around my arm. "That's why I wanted a word with you, Brie. I'd like you to act as my go-between and set up an in-person meeting."

I was unable to stifle my nervous laugh.

"Why on earth do you need a go-between? You've been talking to Ruth on the phone. Just call her and tell her you'd like to meet."

Amber shook her head. "Not an option. Ruth doesn't answer her phone any more when I call on the burner, even though she's answered that number before and knows it's me."

"What do you think's changed?"

"I'm not sure. Maybe Ruth told her fiancé or her father about our conversations and they forbade further contact. That's where you come in."

"I'm a poor choice. I met Ruth one time. We nodded. Didn't exchange so much as a hello. Ruth's grandparents—Pastor and Jeannie Nickles—think I'm a goat-loving witch and, oh, yes, a murderer. They're picketing Udderly Kidding Dairy because they believe I killed Harriett Quinn and possibly Karen Vincent, both members of their True Believer flock. I have serious doubts that Ruth would answer a call from me."

"I agree. My bet is she's blocking calls from all unknown numbers.

That's why you need to bump into her in person." Amber grinned. "Maybe you're not the ideal choice, but there's no one else I can ask. Ruth lives in Greenville, not Ardon County or Clemson. You won't have to run a True Believers' gauntlet or knock on Lawrence Toomey's door to arrange an 'accidental' encounter."

She fished in her pocket and pulled out a slip of paper. "I'm giving you Ruth's home and work addresses."

I frowned. "If you know her schedule, why don't you accidentally bump into Ruth? I still can't see why you need me."

"If people are around when I approach, she might suspect I'm pulling something—that a photographer or reporter was about to jump out of the bushes. Then there's the fiancé. If he's the one who demanded Ruth sever contact with me, she might be afraid of being seen together in public. In either case, she's likely to run for the hills before I can explain why I want to talk."

I wasn't convinced. "Don't you think you should tell Ursula and her legal counsel—my mother—that Ruth knows you're half-sisters? Maybe they can suggest a better way to approach her."

Experience had taught me that keeping secrets from loved ones only upped the odds of disaster. Mom was intimately involved in the situation. That made me even more reluctant to go on a secret mission that kept her in the dark.

Amber shook her head. "I promise we'll tell Ursula and your mother as soon as I manage to meet Ruth." She squeezed my hand. "Please. We're only talking a delay of a day or two. I'm not sure Ursula can separate her loathing of Toomey from feelings about his legitimate daughter. Let me appeal to Ruth as a sister. We've both been dumped in the middle of this mess through no fault of our own. It's the right approach. I'm positive."

Negative was the word that best described my feelings. I'd hoped to keep contact with any members of the Toomey-Nickles clan to a zero. This outreach was akin to sticking my hand in a fire ant hill.

"All right, I'll try."

THIRTY-ONE

We didn't speak again until Dr. Swihart answered my knock. "Come in. Door's open." I quickly introduced Detective Amber Royer as a friend of Judge Billings.

Dr. Swihart stayed seated in her office chair, a large swivel number that looked comfy enough for naps. In lieu of handshakes, she motioned us to two chairs across from her desk.

"Sit, sit, both of you. I only have time for a short synopsis of my research into drug overdoses and interactions. While there are hundreds, I narrowed the possibilities to ones that best fit your luncheon scenario.

"First I catalogued the symptoms experienced by non-fatal victims..."

I flinched at her choice of the term "victims" to describe my luncheon guests. The toxicologist must have noticed my reaction. She paused a second before relaunching her dissertation.

Dr. Swihart held up five fingers. "I had no symptoms, and Della's were minimal." She curled two fingers down. "Judge Billings, Bert Rider, and Iris Hooker suffered varying combinations of nausea, abdominal pain, tachycardia and hypophosphatemia." She lowered the remaining three fingers on her hand.

"Tachycardia...hypo whatever? What do those terms mean?" I interrupted.

"Fast heart rate and muscle dysfunction caused by low phosphorous." Dr. Swihart pursed her lips and treated Amber and me to her best professorial glower. "Please hold your questions until I finish. That will save time and allow me to keep my train of thought."

I meekly nodded. Her manner made me regress to lowly undergraduate peon.

"I searched for drugs that might cause these non-fatal symptoms if people overdosed. Then I narrowed that list based on how difficult it would be to lay one's hands on the drugs.

"One likely culprit was theophylline, a drug used to treat respiratory diseases, including COPD and asthma. While it's a prescription drug, it's common and relatively easy to acquire. Someone could steal it from a medicine supply cabinet in almost any nursing home or hospital. Or it could be ordered by mail easily with a fake prescription."

Dr. Swihart's triumphant tone made me wonder if we were supposed to applaud.

She tapped a pencil on the fat leather-bound volume flopped open on her desk. "I then checked to see if an interaction between theophylline and some ordinary drug could prove fatal, the answer was absolutely." She smiled. "Cimetidine is the main ingredient in a popular over-the-counter heartburn remedy. An overdose of theophylline combined with cimetidine can induce seizures and precipitous drops in blood pressure. The combination could easily have caused Harriett's death."

Unable to sit quietly any longer, Amber broke in. "Did you find evidence of theophylline in the urine or blood samples taken from Ursula and Iris?"

Dr. Swihart frowned. "I was getting to that. Theophylline was present in both samples. I've already informed the hospital and the police that I believe this combination is the proximate cause of the Quinn girl's death."

"How much theophylline would it take to kill someone and make the other luncheon guests sick?" I asked.

"Assuming it was stirred into your chocolate mousse, the poisoner would have needed to grind up enough pills to yield six or seven teaspoons. Probably a thirty-day pill supply would be adequate. A sweet dessert would hide the theophylline's somewhat bitter taste."

Amber's teeth worried her lip as she thought. "Wish we knew if Harriett regularly took cimetidine."

Dr. Swihart shifted in her chair. "Without the Quinn girl's autopsy samples to test, I can't prove Harriett ingested either of these drugs. Until independent lab tests are performed on samples from the Quinn girl, all I have is a theory of the crime."

The professor just had to add that phrase—"theory of the crime".

It was fact, not theory that Harriett died because she ate food I prepared. The fact that a combination of medicines may have caused her death didn't take me off the suspect hook. The True Believers would insist

I knew Harriett took an over-the-counter digestive aid. They'd say I intentionally stirred theophylline into the mousse to kill her.

Still the knowledge was helpful. Now if we could only deduce who her killer might be. Who had a burning desire to murder Harriett? How did the poisoner know she took cimetidine, and how had he or she accessed the prescription drug? The murderer also had to be savvy enough to mask the drug's bitter taste. Otherwise Harriett might have taken one taste and put her spoon down.

My mind was whirring when Dr. Swihart stood. Meeting over.

"I can't begin to thank you," I said. "It's a relief knowing Harriet didn't die as a result of how I prepared the food."

The professor raised an eyebrow. "If I were you, I'd look at suspects with some medical knowledge and access. I'm not sure someone without medical training would choose this murder methodology. As one of the luncheon guests I'm happy the killer was content to just make the rest of the people at Harriett's table sick. He—or she—could have used arsenic or curare. That would have killed us all."

As we walked back across campus, Amber proved eager to share her thoughts. "Heartburn isn't exactly an uncommon complaint. And people often mention it when they're out in public, trying to decide if it's worth the risk to order that spicy entrée. I know. I take omeprazole, a proton-pump inhibitor, to control my reflux."

Her admission surprised me. "Doesn't reflux usually bother older folks?"

Amber shrugged. "In my case, it's probably a hazard of the job. Stress, poor diet." She smiled. "You do know us cops eat our weight in donuts."

I looked heavenward. "I'll buy the stress but you can't keep that figure of yours pigging out on donuts."

"I understand Harriett was obese," she added. "That's often a contributor to reflux, but heartburn impacts people of every size, every age. My point is Harriett may not have been your only lunch guest with heartburn or reflux."

"That opens three possibilities. One, the poisoner wanted to kill Harriett. Two, the unsub hoped to make everyone sick, and didn't know Harriett's extraneous pill popping would prove fatal. Or, three, the villain targeted a different guest known to take cimetidine for heartburn, but, for some reason, the intended victim skipped taking it that day."

I took a deep breath. Amber might have something. "I guess the simplest way to rule out the third possibility is to straight-out ask our luncheon survivors if they've been known to take cimetidine."

Amber laughed. "We already know Dr. Swihart's answer. And we can ask two more of your guests after we walk another block."

THIRTY-TWO

Mom retrieved a large tossed salad from the refrigerator along with a variety of fixings. "You can tell us all about Dr. Swihart's ideas while we eat," she said.

I filled my bowl last, adding nuts and grapes and passing on Mom's cheese and grilled chicken extras.

"So tell all," Ursula urged. "Did the good professor solve the luncheon conundrum?"

Amber and I spoke in unison, our answers slightly different. I replied "maybe," and Amber, "in theory."

"Go ahead, Amber," I encouraged. "Bring them up to speed. You're used to giving evidence reports. Since I'm personally involved, I tend to venture off on a few sidetracks, like 'I didn't do it!'"

The vacationing detective smiled. Her succinct summary left nothing out but didn't waste a single word.

"Do either of you suffer from reflux or heartburn and take cimetidine?" Amber asked Mom and Ursula.

Mom shook her head. "Not me. I only get heartburn when I eat cucumbers, so I avoid them. Easy fix."

Ursula frowned. "Until last month, I was one of cimetidine's best customers. I've been plagued with reflux for years. But I just went the over-the-counter route to treat it. In other words, cimetidine and I were pals. At my last physical I mentioned the reflux to my family doc. He prescribed a proton pump inhibitor. Have to say it works much better for me."

Mom lowered the forkful of salad she'd been ready to pop in her mouth. "Does that mean Ursula might have been the target?" She looked first at Amber then focused on me.

Mom wanted my answer. I chewed on my lip as I considered the possibility. Toomey had threatened Ursula. Could he have tried to sideline her? Was his hospital threat a promise of more to come because his initial attempt to kill her failed?

"Ursula as intended victim fits one of Dr. Swihart's possible scenarios," I said. "But that would mean her would-be killer knew about her cimetidine habit before she quit." I turned toward Ursula. "You stopped taking the pills a month ago, right?"

I purposely didn't mention Toomey's candidacy as killer since he'd have needed to check on Ursula's medicines *before* he'd become the president's pick for the high court. She'd stayed quiet for thirty-some years, why would he feel compelled to plan her murder a couple of months ago?

"The poisoner also had to know Ursula would be at the luncheon," Amber added. "That still makes Harriett the most logical target. Based on the warning messages Brie received, Harriett's enemies were aware she'd be stuffing her face at Summer Place. Her foes also seemed to know Harriett quite well. That bumps up the odds they knew about her favorite heartburn remedy."

I nodded. "Good points. But we should still contact Della and Bert to see if they used cimetidine. Of course I kind of doubt Bert will speak to me given his lawsuit."

"I'll call Bert," Ursula offered. "I can pose as a fellow victim. Tell him I suffer from reflux and think that's why whatever Brie served hit me so hard. I'll just mention cimetidine in passing. Bet I can coax information out of that restaurant critic without him having a clue."

"If anyone can do it, you can," Amber said. "This afternoon I'll do some internet research. I have a few thoughts about how a would-be killer or someone out to embarrass Brie might score the prescription drug Dr. Swihart found in those urine samples."

My cell phone vibrated and I looked at the caller ID. "Gotta take this. It's Aunt Eva." I got up from the table and walked into the living room.

"Got an errand for you." Eva started talking as soon as she heard me breathe. My aunt wasn't one to waste time. "Can you meet some Greenville County muckety-muck at Jamieson Gorge tomorrow afternoon? The county's interested in renting a passel of our goats to clear some rugged terrain overgrown with kudzu and poison ivy. Too steep and rocky for machinery. Too expensive to clear by hand."

A month ago Clemson University had rented a dozen Udderly Kidding goats to eat underbrush on some of its overgrown acreage. Since our goats could be seen from a main thoroughfare, the successful experiment got lots of attention.

"Uh, sure, I guess. As far as I know I'm free tomorrow afternoon. What am I supposed to do when I get there?"

"Charm the guy. Take a look at the land. See how hard it would be to keep our goats from roaming off the property. Need to make sure our eat-anything munchers won't be in any danger from electrical wires, coyotes, or cars if there are highways nearby."

Hmm. Maybe I could arrange my "accidental" encounter with Ruth Toomey in Greenville after this meeting. Would be great to take care of Amber's go-between request on the same trip. Save time and gas and, yes, end the heartburn the idea of that meeting was causing me.

"Confirm a time," I replied. "I can do it."

"You coming back to Udderly soon?" Eva asked. "I could use some help putting together special orders. No worries about picketers today. Looks like they're taking the day off for Harriett's visitation."

"Glad to hear it. I'll be there in about fifteen."

I returned to the kitchen to tell Mom and my fellow detectives I couldn't stay much longer. I found Ursula pacing, phone to her ear, as she bamboozled a variety of newspaper gatekeepers to score Bert's private cell number.

"Got it," she crowed as she disconnected. "Now let's see if I can share some heartburn with old Bert."

"I have faith," Mom said. "I'll phone Della from the living room so we don't talk over one another."

It took Ursula under five minutes to wring all the information she wanted from the unsuspecting restaurant reviewer. No, he didn't suffer from heartburn, and the only medicine he took was an occasional aspirin.

"You'd make an excellent interrogator," Amber said.

Ursula laughed. "And that's different from being a judge, how?"

"Guess it isn't." Amber grinned.

Mom, who'd finished her phone conversation even faster than Ursula, gave her report on Della. "Didn't need any subterfuge. Asked her straight out about cimetidine use. Della didn't even know why you'd take it."

Mom reclaimed her kitchen table seat. "Guess if the luncheon really was the scene of a murder attempt, the killer had to have targeted Harriett or Ursula."

I shivered as I tried to read Ursula's face. The look of triumph she'd worn from successfully extracting information from Bert vanished. Wrinkles I hadn't noticed before creased the skin around her eyes. Her jaw tightened.

"Amber, you should head back to Miami," she said. "If there's even a remote chance I'm the target, being around me could put you in danger."

Amber waved her hand like she was chasing away a pesky mosquito. "I'm in way more danger at home. I'm a detective. Danger comes with the territory. And I do carry a gun. I have plenty of vacation time. I'm staying until this mystery's solved. We need to make absolutely certain some nut job isn't planning a new attack on someone who didn't die when they hoped."

Mom nodded. "I'm ashamed to say it, but I hope murdering Harriett was the end goal. Mission accomplished. Then there'd be no further threat to any of you. Of course, if the theophylline was added to sabotage Brie's catering business launch then it's also mission accomplished. The publicity has been plentiful and all of it bad."

Thanks, Mom. Just the cheery reminder I needed.

THIRTY-THREE

I packaged the last of the cheese orders. All were now ready for FedEx pickup. I'd been eyeing the clock for the last half hour while Eva and I worked, trying to decide if I should accept Fara's invitation to spy on Harriett's visitation.

It seemed a tad unethical even though I intended no harm or disrespect to the woman's grieving family. I didn't kid myself that I'd be able to magically ID her killer. I had no illusions of spotting a smug look on the murderer's face as he stood over the casket. But maybe I could pick up a clue, something to explain if Harriett was intended to be the sole luncheon fatality.

My phone beeped. Mollye. "Hey, girlfriend, Fara told me about her visitation invite. You gonna take her up on it? If so, better get hustling. I can meet you in the Walgreens parking lot. Figure we ought to ride over in your car. Even if we sneak in the back way, my Starry Skies van might be noticed."

What a shock. Moll had invited herself along. The girl did like playing spy games.

"I don't know, Mollye. I feel a little queasy about spying. If we're spotted, it'll feed right into the True Believers' paranoia. They'll be certain we're out for revenge on the whole church."

"Don't worry. We'll just look and listen for a little while. Don't you want to see who's paying their respects to the family? Fara's plan is foolproof."

Foolproof?

I never liked to hear Mollye utter that word.

The Ardon Mortuary's back entrance was as discreet as Fara had promised. I slipped my Prius into a shady corner of the parking lot right beside a big shiny hearse. Between the conifer to my left and the hearse to my right, my car was invisible from most vantage points.

Mollye'd phoned Fara when we were a block away. She was waiting at the back door to usher us inside the walk-in basement. Since our funeral director friend had warned us bodies were embalmed in this underground level, I braced myself for unpleasant odors like the formaldehyde that made me gag in high school biology.

The facility's basement had a definite hospital vibe with its gleaming white tile floors and overhead fluorescents. But I was relieved the hallway's only scent reminded me of lemon Pledge.

"Hurry," Fara urged. "All the cleaning ladies were supposed to be gone, but I just spotted that gossip who tattled about our goat yoga session. Don't know why she's still here. Maybe she's paying her respects to the Quinns before heading home. We can't let her see either of you."

"Where are we going?" Moll asked.

"There's an elevator but it's too exposed. We'll use the back stairs. Follow me."

Fara climbed the stairs two at a time. In her hot-footed hurry, she seemed to forget that a three-person tap dance on metal stairs made one heck of a racket. Our ascent echoed like cymbals in an amphitheater. I held my breath as Fara inched open the door to the upstairs hallway and peeked left, then right.

"Coast is clear," she said. "Let's go!"

Luckily we didn't have far to go. Fara's office was a mere six feet away. Mollye's wheezes from our staircase aerobics weren't exactly quiet. Fara pulled the door firmly shut as soon as we were inside.

"Moll, you should start running with me," I said. "Sounds like you need more exercise than goat yoga. Have to get you in shape for your wedding and honeymoon."

My friend made a less than friendly hand gesture.

"Have a seat." Fara motioned Moll and me to comfy visitor chairs opposite her desk. "I'll turn my monitor around so you can both see what's happening in the Gold Room. That's where we're holding the visitation. Harriett's immediate family has already arrived—parents, siblings, and a grandmother. There's just the one camera, and you can't zoom in for close-ups or anything, but you can see the whole room."

"Aren't you going to stay with us?" I asked as Fara headed to the door.

"No. I need to deliver refreshments, I'll check back with you in a bit. Just don't touch anything and, for heaven's sake, don't answer the door if anyone knocks. I'm locking it so that cleaning lady can't snoop and find you. She doesn't have a key to my office."

Mollye giggled when Fara left. "I have the feeling our friend wishes she hadn't invited us. 'Don't touch anything!' Like we'd play with her audio system and broadcast sounds of clanking chains to freak out the mourners."

I gave Mollye the look. "Don't even think about touching anything. I'm creeped out enough as it is, locked up watching Harriett's relatives on the tube. It's like we've been dropped into a reality funeral show."

Mollye pointed at the screen. "Might as well do what we came for. Most likely I can tell you who's who. That man in the black suit with the high-water pants is Harriett's older brother. The dude with the glasses is Mr. Quinn, the father." Mollye cocked an eyebrow. "Of course, you're acquainted with Mrs. Quinn and her sizable pocketbook."

Mourners started to dribble in, and Mollye lived up to her reputation. She knew almost everyone. Unfortunately, I knew a few of the visitors, too, including Nate Gerome, the publisher of the *Ardon Chronicle*. The new owner of the paper was no fonder of the Hooker clan than his now jailed aunt had been.

I wasn't surprised that most drop-ins were members of the True Believers' congregation. While a few of the folks were Harriett's age— somewhat younger than Moll and me—most of the mourners appeared to be sixty and above.

Where were Harriett's friends? Did she have friends outside the church?

Maybe her pals planned to attend Saturday's funeral rather than today's visitation. After all, it was a weekday. Mollye and I might be able to set our own hours, but lots of people our age or younger were nine-to-fivers. They'd either come late or pay their respects Saturday.

As more and more people crowded the room, the volume of voices rose, making it really hard to decipher individual conversations.

Mollye prodded me with her elbow. "Well, lookey who's come to pay their respects. Quite the family tableau. Judge Toomey, and his wife, Esther, just walked in with Toomey's father-in-law and mother-in-law, Pastor Guy Nickles and Jeannie, his puppeteer."

I scooted my chair closer to the screen. I'd shaken hands with the spit-and-polish Judge Toomey and his model-thin wife, and I'd been treated to Pastor Guy Nickles' spit on my windshield as he frothed at the mouth while proclaiming I was a killer. The Elmer Gantry style pastor looked—if possible—even more wild-eyed today.

The monitor also gave me a chance to study Jeannie, the pastor's wife. I found it a little easier to look at her on the screen than I had through my car window. It felt safer to stare. Her poufy white hair hovered around her face like a cloud. Her plump face was unlined. Her complexion flawless. In some ways she looked younger than her daughter, Esther. Studying her reminded me that some of the world's deadliest snakes were quite attractive.

According to Moll's age calculations for Ardon residents—my friend's sole math superpower—Jeannie was at least seventy-five, while her husband, Guy the pastor, was seventy-three. Of course, I knew Judge Toomey was fifty-nine, same age as Mom.

Moll said Toomey's wife, Esther, was nine years his junior, and she did look younger than him despite her gray hair. Esther's black silk dress hung on her skinny frame. She'd inherited the Pastor's dark eyes. Fortunately, they weren't hooded by his bushy eyebrows, and they didn't appear demented.

Jeannie quickly broke off from her family group to work the crowd. Her smile was relentless as she patted shoulders and squeezed hands. A natural-born politician. I glanced back at her husband. The pastor hadn't moved. Only his eyes darted to and fro. I couldn't decide if he looked angry or frightened. Too many wild mushrooms in his pre-clerical diet?

Jeannie pulled Mrs. Quinn out of the informal receiving line, and the twosome moved to a spot near the mortuary's monitoring camera.

I hoped we'd hear at least fragments of their conversation above the background noise. Sensing the opportunity, Moll and I both scooched closer to the monitor. I itched to turn the volume up, but heeded Fara's warning about not messing with the equipment. Knowing my luck, I'd accidentally turn on the PA system and broadcast a *Moldy Munster!* to the world.

Jeannie patted Mrs. Quinn's arm. "Honey, this is...horrible. We'll make...Hooker woman pay. Did Harriett take any medicine? We can't let the authorities latch on to some bogus health excuse."

Since we weren't on a PA system, I mumbled a few cheesy curses. We weren't picking up the entire conversation. Words dropped out of the audio as glasses clinked and feet shuffled, and I was no lip reader.

However, Mrs. Quinn's nonverbal dialogue came through loud and clear. Sobs wracked her body, making me feel a shameful guilt at witnessing her grief.

"What's it matter?" the mother finally blurted. "My little girl's dead...that Hooker girl is free."

"Gotta watch those Hookers." Jeannie's voice rose as she delivered that verdict. Did she want the whole room to hear? "Iris Hooker's a lawyer...she'll try...to bamboozle folks."

"Jumping Jehoshaphat! Did you catch that?" Mollye's eyes grew wide.

"Shhh! I want to hear what Mrs. Quinn says."

The stricken mother pulled a lace hankie from a pocket in her sack-like dress to blot the tears forging shiny rivers through her pancake makeup.

"No way...those sinners...medical gobbledygook...it was Hooker's poison killed my Harriett...healthy as a horse. Heartburn...only bother...off-the-shelf...not a single prescription."

"Good, good." Jeannie patted the woman's arm. "If the sheriff asks, no...don't mention...Just repeat...'Harriett was healthy as a horse.'"

Mrs. Quinn nodded. Jeannie clasped the mother to her bosom in what looked more like a wrestling move than a hug. When she returned to her own family, Jeannie edged next to her daughter, Mrs. Esther Toomey. The kindly grandmother doppelganger nodded toward Mrs. Quinn and whispered in Esther's ear.

Whatever Jeannie said made Esther Toomey smile.

Fara helped arrange the punch, cookies, and cakes on a table across the room from the camera. As people gravitated toward the refreshments, fewer and fewer conversations proved within eavesdropping range. I checked my watch. Five o'clock. The visitation was half over.

So far I'd seen no one who looked like a killer candidate. Everyone looked sad. Several men began to fidget. Their uncomfortable body language said they'd done their duty, said their piece, and eaten cookies. Time to go.

I hadn't spotted a single soul—male or female—who sported a self-satisfied smirk when no one was watching. Mollye had been able to name almost all of the visitors. None of the people Harriett had trashed in her blog or threatened had come to gloat.

"I've seen enough," I said. "I'm going to call Fara to let us out. Tell you the truth I feel a little slimy having spied on these folks. I may not share their religious beliefs, but their loss and grief are real."

Mollye nodded. "You're right. But don't forget someone in that Gold Room may have broken into your kitchen and poisoned your food to end Harriett's life. If we had any doubt about the True Believer zealots trying to pin Harriett's murder on you, Jeannie Nickles erased it. It's crystal clear she plans to do everything in her power to convince the world you killed Harriet. In my book, that more than entitles you to a little harmless Peeping Tom activity."

Less than two minutes after I phoned her, Fara unlocked the door and slipped inside. "I need you to hustle to the basement stairs the minute I tell you to go. I'm praying that cleaning lady finally left. I haven't seen her in a while, but I can't be sure. Pays to be careful."

Fara opened the door a skootch, then cracked it wider to stick her head out. She looked both directions. Satisfied, she motioned us to follow her the six feet to our upstairs exit. Fara held the door to the basement open as I passed her and headed below. I was on the third rung when I heard a surprised, loud "ooph" followed by a metal rattle.

I did a 360 and ran up the steps to see what had happened. The first thing I saw was Mollye's bare right foot. A foot previously attached to a sandal with a broken strap that sat catawampus to her tootsie. Fara was trying to help Mollye get up off the floor. I had my hand on the door knob and was about to jump into the hall to assist in hoisting Mollye, when Fara muttered sotto voice, "Get out of here, Brie. I see her."

I caught a shadowy glimpse of a woman quite a ways down the hall. I skedaddled down the stairs. Seconds later Mollye tumbled into the stairway. The door clicked shut behind her.

"Afraid I mucked things up falling on my keister," Mollye whispered. "Fara's gonna stall the woman while we vamoose."

A smart cookie and always the trooper, Moll stuck her broken sandal in a pocket, and galumphed down the stairs behind me. Grace isn't entirely possible when one leg is five inches shorter than the other.

"You okay?" I asked. "Did that busybody cleaning lady recognize you?

We need to get out of here pronto."

"No argument from me," Mollye whispered back. "Though I'm not happy. Never going to buy another pair of platform sandals. An accident waiting to happen. Maybe I should sue."

We reached the bottom of the stairs and turned down the long hall leading to the back door and our escape.

Uh, oh. Trapped. A body delivery was underway. If we waltzed out now, we'd have two live witnesses—and one dead one—to our escape.

THIRTY-FOUR

Mollye grabbed my arm and pulled me into a room off the hall.

"I know those ambulance attendants," she squeaked. "And they know me. Problem is they're buddies with several of the mourners. The woman attendant used to be friends with Ruth Toomey, and the guy drinks with some of the Temple crowd, including Mr. Quinn."

I nodded. "Okay, we can hide out of sight for a few minutes. I doubt the ambulance attendants saw us. They were busy navigating that rolling stretcher through the door when you yanked me in here."

I glanced around the space we'd entered.

Rotten Roquefort! I had the distinct feeling the dead body being wheeled down the hall was coming straight to us. We were surrounded by stainless steel and, uh, very cold looking metal tables. Of course, I didn't imagine the mortuary patients ever complained.

"We can't stay here. No place to hide," Moll whispered as she jerked me toward another doorway. Heaven knew what lay behind door number two.

And the answer would be?

Coffins. Dozens of them. Not a showroom. More like a mini-warehouse. Emergency inventory in case of disaster or mass murder? Or maybe Fara's dad had taken advantage of a huge casket close-out sale. There appeared to be three categories of single-occupancy boxes: burnished mahogany, plain pine, and ornate bronze.

Moll scooted over to check out another door.

"Where does it lead?" I asked.

Moll's shoulders slumped. "Right back into the hall, which at the moment looks busier than the Town of Ardon's main street. We can't leave until that ambulance duo drops off the stiff and departs."

That's when I heard and recognized voices. One loud enough to—

excuse the expression—wake the dead.

The calm voice belonged to Fara, the screech to Mrs. Quinn.

"Liz is sure she saw Mollye Camp that psychic witch," Mrs. Quinn yelled. "I'm gonna look for myself. You can't stop me. That woman's in league with the devil and she's a friend of that Hooker girl. They're both witches. Bet they've come to desecrate Harriett's body."

Moll and I looked at each other. Her wide eyes and open mouth gave me a mirror on my own abject terror.

Holey Swiss Cheese! I did not want to tangle with the irate Mrs. Quinn.

Where could we hide?

Of course, dozens of answers lay all around us. All we had to do was climb into a couple of coffins, wait till the commotion died down, open the crypts, and stroll away. No one would be the wiser.

Just a couple of teensy problems. I had no knowledge of casket mechanics. Did they work like roach motels—once you checked in, you never checked out? In olden days when people feared being buried alive, caskets were rigged with cords the "undead" could pull to ring an above-ground bell. One way to alert loved ones they'd rushed the funeral. Somehow I doubted these coffins had bells.

How tight were the seals? Would we run out of oxygen if we closed the lids? What if we couldn't get the lids open again once we were inside?

Mollye watched as I hurried over to one of the plain Jane models and lifted the lid. This coffin had the tapered shape of those featured in old-timey horror flicks. Narrow at the foot and head, wide at the shoulders. She shook her head. "Un uh. I'm not getting in that thing. I'm no sardine. I need something roomier. What if I can't get out?"

"Don't worry," I answered. "We've got our cell phones. All we have to do is wait ten minutes till all the hubbub subsides and call Fara. She'll get us out if we have any trouble."

As Mollye shook her head, her big hoop earrings caught my eye. "Give me your earrings. Climb in one of these, and I'll use your hoops to keep the lid from latching. But hurry. I gotta climb in one, too."

Mollye extracted her earrings and handed them over. "Okay, but I'm gonna be comfortable." She chose an ornate metal model sitting on the floor and knelt to crawl in.

I decided not to mention her choice of a steel box might interfere with her cell phone's ability to get a signal. We were running out of time for casket shopping.

She raised the lid. Well, actually there were two lids hinged together. One designed to cover the bottom half of the occupant, one to give loved ones a final view of the deceased's slumbering face. The inside of Mollye's casket looked like pink frosting. She gave the plush pillow a test squeeze and lowered herself inside as she glared at me.

"My earrings had better keep this lid from closing," she whispered. "If this is my final resting place, I promise I'll come back and haunt you."

I carefully inserted the earrings and closed the lid. Then I slipped into my own budget coffin. Having no hoop stoppers, I'd have to use my arms to brace the top open. There was a one-piece lid. No nail holes. No silk either. In fact I worried about slivers as I scooted inside. I figured my box was either intended to transport a body into a furnace for cremation or designed to disintegrate quickly in a green burial.

I lowered the lid to within a hair of closed. The world turned gray, not black. Light filtered through knot holes in the roughhewn box. The pine muted sound but I could still hear voices. Those voices got a lot clearer when Fara and Mrs. Quinn entered the casket room.

"Mrs. Quinn, I know you're upset," Fara said. "But your friend Liz is wrong. She probably mistook Shirley, one of the ambulance attendants for Mollye Camp. The women are about the same size. As you can see, there's no one here. This is where we store caskets."

"That Camp woman was here." Mrs. Quinn's voice shook. "I can feel the evil. I'm going to sit with my Harriett around the clock. I won't leave tonight. I'm not taking a chance they'll sneak back to desecrate her body. Bad enough the law forced me to let them cut her open. Hope the Lord accepts her body in Heaven now that it's sewed back up."

"I'm sure the Lord welcomes all good souls," Fara said.

An excellent answer. I surely hoped my soul was worthy.

THIRTY-FIVE

My arms trembled from bracing the lid. Finally, all sounds of voices and footsteps disappeared. For an added safety margin I counted to one hundred, then pushed the lid open and off to the side. I'd been inside the coffin maybe five minutes; it felt like five years.

I scrambled out and hustled across the room to extract Mollye. When I heaved the lid open, I panicked. She looked waxen, a sheen of sweat on her face. Her eyes were closed. Then she stuck her arms out straight and rose like a zombie coming awake. I swallowed my laugh.

"Cut the comedy act. We need to scram."

I helped Moll wriggle out of the casket. Not a smooth exit.

"They're not as comfy as they look," she quipped. "Hope I'm not fitted for one for a long time. Why did I listen to your nonsense about calling Fara on my cell phone? I was still trying to get the danged thing out of my pocket when you opened the lid. Not a lot of room for my hips in that sardine can."

I checked my watch. Five thirty. Only thirty minutes had elapsed since we'd made our first attempt at a funeral home escape. I phoned Fara. She assured me all mourners, including Mrs. Quinn, were present and accounted for in the Gold Room.

"Go ahead, leave through the back door. No ambulances and no more bodies scheduled for delivery."

I dropped Moll at her van and headed to Udderly. At the gate, I was pleased to see nary a picketer in sight. The wide open gate suggested a peaceful day at the dairy.

"Any excitement since I left?" I asked Eva.

"Yep, I delivered two more sets of twins." My aunt grinned. "But if you're talking protestors, didn't see a one. Don't worry about these newborns. Already have human moms lined up for these babes. But your time is coming. Imagine you'll be busy very soon, which may prompt Andy to protest. Today starts a new Animal Passion week, right?"

"Correct, but I'm sure Andy will be more than happy to help with the kids. He seemed pleased I'd committed to surrogate nanny duty. Andy has a late appointment in Greenville. We're meeting at that Indian restaurant he took me to on our first date. Since his sister Julie has decided she wants to be a stay-at-home mom for a few years, Andy's interviewing vet techs to take her place."

"Have you seen Julie's baby yet?" Eva asked.

"Sure have. A darling little boy, Jacob. Andy's thrilled. Growing up as the lone male with five sisters he's hoping for more gender equality with this generation."

"And is Andy hoping you'll marry him and provide a baby boy?"

I looked heavenward. "Marriage seems to be on everybody's mind since Mollye announced her engagement. I'm just dating. We definitely don't need to jump ahead to babies. Now if you'll excuse me I'm off to the showers. I'm sticky with sweat."

Eva gave me an arched-eyebrow look. "Yeah, actually you stink. What have you been up to? Hard to work up that much of a sweat cooking, and it's dang nippy outside."

I smiled. "Just running around." No mention of trying on a coffin.

"Well, you just missed your dad," she said. "Howard dropped by to make sure we weren't under siege by the True Believers. Asked you to call him when you got a chance."

I was in and out of the shower lickity split. That gave me enough time to detour past the entrance to Jamieson Gorge on my way to meet Andy. I had a vague notion of the park's location but wanted to make sure I didn't get lost tomorrow. This was the first time Eva was sending me solo to meet with a prospective customer. Didn't want to screw it up. While the wilderness sanctuary wasn't far off the beaten track, Jamieson Gorge truly did look like a wild, lonely place. I'd try to come early for a short hike.

I reached Swad a few minutes ahead of the time Andy'd suggested we rendezvous. He beat me anyway. His vet truck was easy to spot. Andy stood and waved as I entered the hole-in-the-wall restaurant. He'd picked a booth facing the front.

Andy hugged me and gave me a quick peck on the cheek before motioning me to slide into his side of the booth. My thigh grazed his. The instant bloom of warmth helped banish the chill I'd felt ever since my brief stop at Jamieson Gorge.

But the welcome warmth wasn't anything like the heat I felt when I came in contact with any part of Paint's body. Geesh. Was I confusing lust with love?

Stop it. You're with Andy tonight. It's Animal Passion week. You shouldn't be thinking about Paint.

But a snarky interior voice refused to shut up. *Isn't choosing between Paint and Andy the whole point of these boyfriend weeks?*

I cleared my throat.

"Do you remember what you liked best the last time we visited Swad?" I asked.

"Yeah," Andy answered. "We did a fair amount of kissing when we strolled around Falls Park after dinner. I don't remember a thing about Swad's menu."

I chuckled. "I do. You turned beet red and needed several quarts of water to return to normal after sampling one of the spicier offerings."

The chef's wife and co-owner bustled over to our table. "So happy to see you again. Would you like us to prepare another sampling? We have a few new items on our menu."

"No, thanks," Andy quickly answered. "I'll let Brie order for us. She knows my taste buds aren't quite as developed or adventurous as hers."

I ordered mild dishes for Andy and spicy ones for myself, accompanied by plenty of Jasmine tea.

As soon as our orders were in and the tea served, Andy launched into an excited rhapsody about his new vet tech.

"I hired Cindy on the spot. What a find. She graduated from the vet tech program at Tri-County, and she's been working with Doc Burns for eight years. She even has large animal practice experience."

Though the Jasmine tea probably hadn't steeped long enough, I poured some into our cups. "Why is Cindy leaving Doc Burns?"

"He's retiring. Sold his practice to a married couple. They're both veterinarians so they don't need a tech. Burns gave Cindy a sterling recommendation. And I loved her sense of humor. She'll be fun to work with."

"Is she cute, too?"

A blush climbed Andy's neck and painted his cheeks a bright red. The blush made his eyes look all the greener. "Some people might say so." Then he hurriedly added. "But she's not as pretty as you."

"Nice recovery." I grinned. "Just messing with you. Sounds like Cindy is a catch. How long before she starts?"

"She's coming to Ardon tomorrow to complete the paperwork and look for a house to rent in town. Told her we had a pretty decent school system. Her little boy is seven."

"Is there a husband?"

"No, they divorced four years ago, and he moved to California. Said she'd been thinking about moving for a while. Thought a new setting might be good for her boy. "

Hmm. Could it be that handsome, eligible Andy was the main reason Cindy snapped up the job offer? Interesting. Months back when I saw Andy and Paint on a double-date with two knockouts, jealousy made me plum crazy. But the thought of Andy and a cute new tech wasn't making me nutso.

What if it had been Paint hiring a new assistant? There I went. Back to thinking about Paint. His off-the-cuff, quasi-marriage proposal had done a real number on my head.

Our entrées came and I took the opportunity to change the subject. "I did a little detour on the way to drive past Jamieson Gorge. Ever been there? The park might rent Udderly goats to munch their way through some poison ivy and kudzu they're not keen to tackle with machines."

He nodded. "I've visited in the spring. Really pretty when the mountain laurel is blooming. Too bad you can't train the goats to eat only noxious weeds."

"Not possible," I said. "They're omnivores. Didn't actually get out of the car at Jamieson Gorge. Tomorrow I'll scout the site. Maybe there's a way to corral them in kudzu land. Say, what happens when goats eat poison ivy? I assume it doesn't bother them or Aunt Eva wouldn't consider the job."

"No, they're immune. Wish I could say the same."

Our dinner conversation relaxed me. Andy was good company. Entertaining and caring. I was looking forward to spending time with him this week. He'd become family.

Family, yes. But more like a brother than a lover?

Suddenly, he grinned. "Hey, Mollye says your friends have assigned names to the weeks when Paint or I get you all to ourselves. I understand mine is called Animal Passion. Much cooler than Brewing Trouble."

He laughed. "See I tried to warn you that Paint's trouble."

"So glad neither you nor Paint are proctologists. My friends had enough fun playing word games with your professions. I can hear them now. We'd have End Dive and Bottoms Up weeks."

After dinner, we returned to Falls Park where we'd first kissed. But the wind was brisk and the night far too chilly for a reenactment.

"How about a nightcap at Summer Place?" I suggested. "Follow me there. I stopped at the ABC store and bought some Kahlua. Eva and Billy won't be around to interrupt us."

THIRTY-SIX

I went in the kitchen to start a pot of coffee for Andy and me. Shoot. I'd bought coffee but only the high-test stuff, no decaffeinated beans. While I waited for the coffeemaker to stop sputtering, I poured generous slugs of Kahlua into the bottom of two mugs. Wanted to make sure I mixed in enough sleep-inducing alcohol to balance the caffeine buzz. Otherwise I'd never get to sleep before dawn and the start of a new farm day.

While I was in the kitchen, the police siren alarm on my phone blared. I jumped a foot.

"It's Amber. You can relax." Andy called from his sunporch chair. "Not a return of the vandals."

"Good," I replied. "I'm going to turn down the volume on this blasted alarm so it doesn't give me a heart attack or hearing loss."

I left the kitchen, drying my hands on a towel. "Hi, Amber. Everything okay? Need something?"

"Is it safe to light a fire in the cottage fireplace? I didn't want to fill the cabin with smoke. I know the chimney's old and I wasn't sure it worked."

"The fireplace is one of the few things that does work. I made sure of it. A wood fire is the only way to keep warm on cold nights like this."

"Great," Amber answered. "Sorry to intrude."

"No problem. Just make sure the fire screen's securely in place before you go to bed. There's a cord of wood just outside the fireplace, and the last tenants cut a trap door so they could pull the wood in without venturing outside. It's like a doggie door only we keep it latched inside to keep out squirrels and other varmints when it's not in use."

Amber left and I fetched the mugs of Kahlua-laced coffee for Andy and me. In addition to a table and chairs, the sunporch had an old-fashioned glider. Just big enough for the two of us. Since we had no fireplace to light, we snuggled, and talked. I'm not sure whether this speaks to our sparkling conversation or our low tolerance for alcohol, but we both drifted off.

I jumped when the wail of a distant police siren woke me.

What?

Andy languidly stretched like a big cat. My head had been resting on his arm and I imagined it was numb. I vaguely wondered why a police car was chasing some speedster a couple of roads over from Summer Place. Maybe a drug bust?

Suddenly Andy found the muted siren considerably more interesting. In fact, he pushed me away as he bounced up. Annoying.

He gripped my shoulders. "Someone or something's outside, out there," he whispered. "We'd better see what triggered your motion detector."

Duh. The siren wasn't a passing cop car at all. It was the alarm for the doorbell motion detector. I'd muted the alarm after Amber set it off.

I'd turned out the lights before Andy and I settled on the glider with our drinks. Summer Place had no shades or curtains. Darkness was the only way to achieve any privacy when the Medley sisters walked their pooch.

I fumbled through the purse I'd left on the floor by the glider. Andy retrieved his phone first. By the time my fingers wrapped around my cell, Andy had called up the image recorded by the camera. He put his arm around me and pulled me close as we stared at the screen together.

A hunched-over shape in a dark hoodie slunk around the side of Summer Place. No question. This intruder hadn't come to sell magazines or solicit charity donations. I sucked in a shocked breath.

"Where's he going?" I whispered though there was no way the prowler could hear me.

"Could be looking for a back entrance to Summer Place?" Andy whispered back.

I shivered despite the protective warmth of Andy's arm. "Or maybe he's headed toward the cottage. We have to warn Ursula."

"Amber should have received the same alert. She has the app on her phone, too. Stay here and call the sheriff."

"What do you mean stay here?" I grabbed Andy's arm as he stood. "Where are you going?"

"Outside. Need to find out what the guy's up to."

I gripped his arm tighter. "Bad idea. You should wait for the sheriff, too. Unlike Eva, I don't have an umbrella stand by the door with a handy shotgun. The prowler could be armed."

"If it makes you feel better, I'll get my shotgun out of the truck. But I'm going to go. We need to know what he's up to. I'll be careful."

I followed Andy to the porch door as I punched 911 into my own cell.

"I have to go," Andy repeated. "He might be looking for a back way into Summer Place. My truck, your Prius, and Ursula's rental are all parked out front. He must know people are inside, even with the lights off. We can't be sitting ducks. Who knows how long it will be before the sheriff gets here?"

I stepped outside to follow Andy's progress. Bent over, he scurried through the sparse grass beside the driveway trying to make himself as small a target as possible. Running on the grass was a lot quieter than footsteps flinging gravel on the drive.

"What's your emergency?" The operator's voice startled me. I'd almost forgotten the phone was in my hand.

"There's an intruder sneaking around my property."

I quickly gave the Summer Place address.

"Did you get a good look at him?" the operator asked. "Can you describe him?"

"He's dressed in a dark hoodie. Couldn't see his face. He was crouched over and kept to the shadows."

"Did you see a weapon?"

I glanced toward the rear of Summer Place hoping to catch sight of the prowler in the distance, provide more information. "I don't—"

Oh, my God. Flames licked at the front of the cottage.

"Heaven help us. He's set fire to the cottage out back! Call the fire department! There are people in there."

I didn't wait to hear the 911 operator's reply. Andy rounded the corner of Summer Place, and I was happy to spot the silhouette of a shotgun in his hand. Not wearing anything with pockets, I tucked my phone in my bra and ran to intercept Andy. Fear churned my stomach like a Cuisinart on high speed.

"The prowler set fire to the cottage," I choked out. "We have to get Ursula and Amber out."

We ran toward the fire in tandem as fingers of red and yellow flames snaked up the face of the old cottage between the stone chimney and front door. I could hear Andy's size thirteens flinging gravel beside me. No attempt to keep quiet now.

The billowing smoke turned the pale moonlight into a foggy haze.

"That masonry chimney's acting like a firestop. It's slowing the fire's spread on the right side of the cottage. But old wood structures like this can flash over in minutes," Andy yelled. "I'm going around back."

As we skirted the cottage, he grabbed my arm and I almost fell over. "Watch out! Whoever set this may be lying in wait, ready to take out anyone who tries to escape. Let me go, you stay back."

Fat chance, even though I was plenty scared.

I hadn't considered our villain might be setting up an ambush. Couldn't think about that. Two of us had a better chance of rescuing Ursula and Amber than Andy on his own. I shuddered as I thought about the age of the cottage and its dry-as-tinder wood. Little chance of stopping the fire from devouring the whole structure.

We heard the screaming twenty feet out.

"Help! I can't get Ursula up." Amber's loud cries came from the back of the cottage. Not a surprise. The only bedroom was at the back. Right where we were headed.

"Don't open the back door," Andy yelled as we neared the cottage. "It'll let oxygen rush in and draw the fire down the hall."

The back door opened on a hallway that bisected the cottage interior, dividing front room from kitchenette and back bedroom from a bath and closet. "Let's hope the bedroom door's closed, too," Andy added.

He pointed toward a bedroom window cracked open a few inches. The sill was only three feet off the ground.

"Amber, can you hear me?" he yelled. "Keep low, out of the smoke. Stay in the bedroom. I'm gonna come through the window and get you two out."

"You can't," Amber's scratchy voice tried for calm. "The window's stuck. It won't budge."

"Let me give it a try." Andy tossed down his shotgun, hooked his hands beneath the window sash, and shoved. The old wood groaned as the tall window grudgingly moved all of two inches upward.

"Let me help." I wiggled in and Andy shuffled left to make room.

Once my hands joined his under the sash, he counted, "One, two, three, go!"

We heaved. Our reward? Three more inches.

"Still not enough for me to squeeze through. I have to break the glass, even if that means more oxygen to draw the fire this way."

"No. Don't risk it!" I shook my head violently then realized he couldn't see my protest in the dim light. "Besides shards from those old panes would turn you into mincemeat. The window's open wide enough for me to slip through."

"No way," Andy said. "Can't let you go inside."

"Yes, you can and you will. You can still break the window if I can't get them out. Don't argue."

I dropped to my knees and stuck my head and arms through the window. I wriggled left, then right to bump one boob at a time over the danged immovable sill.

"Andy, give me a shove."

"Dammit." His hands settled on my thighs, and he pushed.

"I'm almost in," I called to Amber. "Can you see me? Are you near the window?"

The heat punched me in the face. I gasped and swallowed a lungful of smoke. My coughing jag only made it worse. My throat throbbed. It felt like tiny embers were dancing inside me. My efforts had bent me in two, and I was stuck. My head near the floor, my butt wedged in the window by a wad of clothes. The waistband on my pants had snagged on the sill, dragging my slacks down around my hips as I wriggled forward. The bunched material wedged me firmly in place.

"Andy, yank on my slacks, they're caught," I yelled.

Seconds later, I heard a rip and felt cold air on my thighs as Andy shimmied my slacks down. Amber's fingers found my arm and inched up it to get a tight grip near my shoulder. She pulled just as my derriere, free of interfering fabric, squeezed through the window.

I tumbled gracelessly into the hot-as-Hades room. Heat roasted my bare thighs as my slacks slithered away to pool around my shoes. I'd managed a face plant. I toed off my Sketchers and furiously kicked my bare legs to free my feet from their trouser handcuffs.

"Hurry. The smoke's getting worse." Amber coughed. "I rolled Ursula off the air mattress. She's on the floor."

"Brie, you okay?" Andy yelled from outside.

"I'm good," I answered.

"Amber, is the bedroom door shut?" Andy asked.

"Yes," Amber choked out her answer.

"Good, that helps," he said. "Keep low, both of you. Less smoke by the floor. Try and lift Ursula up so I can grab her arms and pull her through. You push. I'll pull."

Thank heavens Andy was a volunteer fireman. He knew more about fires than I ever wanted to know.

My eyes burned. Tears streamed down my cheeks. Squinting, I made out Ursula's sprawled form and crawled toward her on my hands and knees. Amber scooted to Ursula's other side. Together we dragged her to just below the window.

"Ready to lift?" I asked.

"Go on three," Amber answered.

"One, two, three."

My hoarse count used up scarce breath. I gasped and swallowed smoke. My stupidity launched a coughing jag. We hoisted Ursula's torso up to the windowsill. Through the gray haze and my tears, I glimpsed the blurry outline of Andy's arms, shoulders, and head. Unable to wedge his entire body inside, he'd poked enough of himself through to grab Ursula. In seconds, he pulled her free.

"You're next," I told Amber.

"No way," she said. "You first."

"Nope. You've been in here longer, inhaled more smoke. You go."

"Quit arguing!" Andy snapped. "No time, Amber. Brie's as stubborn as Eva's mule. Give me your hands. I'll wring Brie's neck once you're both outside."

As Amber wriggled through the window, I heard sirens. Real ones this time. Police, fire, or both?

Once Amber's feet vanished from view, I raised my hands toward the open window. Yowzer. Andy pulled so hard I thought my arms might leave their sockets. Before I could blink, he was holding me. Unceremoniously he dumped me over his shoulder in a fireman's carry and trotted away from the building. As my head bounced against his body, I caught upside down glimpses of a swarm of firefighters.

"Ursula? Is she...?"

"Unconscious but breathing," he answered. "She's with the EMTs—Amber too."

When Andy hefted me, my pink hipster panties crawled farther down my behind. I tried to reach a hand around to tug the silk undies up. Couldn't manage it.

"Put me down," I complained. "I'm fine."

Suddenly it all seemed too funny. One, my current position had me mooning the unsuspecting firefighters running to the rescue. And, two, I'd willingly participated in the shedding of clothes while on a date with Andy. Not quite nude, but dang close. Would Andy declare he'd won?

Before I could stop, hysterical belly laughs bubbled up and out. The laughs made my scorched throat ache, but I couldn't stop. Probably did little to convince Andy I was of sane mind.

THIRTY-SEVEN

Andy lowered me to my feet a safe distance from the fire. He gripped my shoulders to steady me as I swayed, dizzy from the carry. My teeth started to chatter.

"I'll get a blanket." He loped off toward an ambulance that had parked on the one surviving patch of real grass.

My laughter died almost as soon as it started. I was scared. Make that terrified. I searched for Amber in the confusion. Spotted her standing by an ambulance as the EMTs loaded Ursula inside. Had Amber heard the prowler alert on her phone?

What in the world was happening?

First, Karen's death, then Harriet's. Now arson? Was this another murder attempt? The lights were off at Summer Place. Had the prowler assumed I was in the cottage? With the truck and cars parked out front, he had to know people were inside one of the buildings when he torched the cottage.

The firefighters hooked up portable lights. Sadly their piercing beams offered a clear view of the cottage's charred timbers and sooty chimney stones. A total loss. It hadn't been much—inside or out—before the fire. I couldn't think of a thing worth salvaging out of the blackened hulk, though I did regret losing my Sketchers and the relatively new pair of dress slacks I'd jettisoned on the bedroom floor.

While I had insurance on Summer Place, I'd settled on a high deductible to make it affordable. Worse, I recalled the "outbuilding" was insured for less than my deductible.

I started to hyperventilate. My shocked body spasmed with aftershocks. I put my hands on my knees and bent over to suck in a deep breath. Anything to stop the trembling.

When I opened my eyes, I spotted something gold glittering in the grass at my feet. I picked it up. A miniature gold gavel earring. Ursula must have lost it. Pretty. I'd have to tell her I'd found it. Tomorrow. Hopefully, she'd be well enough to leave the hospital by morning.

As I straightened, I saw Andy, large gray blanket in hand, rapidly closing in. Absent a pants pocket—or pants—I gave the pierced earring a puzzled look as I tried to decide where to put it for safekeeping.

Then, duh, I remembered I had pierced ears. Mollye had given me earrings, a certificate to have my ears pierced, and a jar of Paint's moonshine as a combo Christmas present. I hooked the orphaned earring through my ear lobe just before Andy wrapped me in the scratchy but warm blanket.

"Thanks," I tried unsuccessfully to stifle another quivering aftershock.

Along with the blanket, Andy brought the fire chief.

"Brie, this is Chief MacLeod. He'd like to ask you a few questions about the cottage."

"Chief, thank heavens you arrived so quickly. You put out the fire in time to save Summer Place."

The chief stroked his white moustache. "Sorry we couldn't save the cottage. And I'm sorry to bother you with questions, but we're trying to figure out what happened. Andy tells me you two reported a prowler minutes before the fire broke out. Is that right?"

"Yes, we can even show you video," I said.

Andy pulled out his phone.

"A motion sensor sends a phone alert when someone comes to the side door or passes by," I explained as Andy played the short video.

"Let's see it again," the chief prodded. "Sure looks like he's up to no good. Too bad we can't see his face. The burn pattern suggests the fire started next to the fireplace. If it weren't for your prowler report, I'd suspect an ember escaped the firebox. Your tenant Miss Amber admitted she and Judge Billings lit a fire early evening to ward off the chill. She swore it was out and the screen securely in place before she retired. 'Course we hear a lot of wishful remembering."

"You're certain the fire started inside?" Andy asked.

"Not a doubt." He frowned. "Miss Amber also claims the cottage door was locked. Based on what you and Andy said about timing, I can't imagine how your prowler had time to jimmy a lock, set a fire, relock the door, and escape, all before you came running."

I closed my eyes to picture the fireplace surround. "He didn't have to unlock a door—at least the kind you're picturing. A previous tenant put a trap door next to the fireplace so he could pull wood in from the woodpile. Pretty ingenious. I've used it myself."

The chief arched an eyebrow. "No lock on the trap door?"

"Just a hook and eye latch to keep critters from pushing their way inside," I answered. "It wouldn't be hard to lift the hook from the outside. Almost any scrap of wood slipped through the opening would do it."

The chief nodded. "Hmm, yes. An arsonist could manage that. Flip the hook, shove some burning tinder inside, and run for it." He cleared his throat. "We'll investigate. I'll talk with the sheriff. Meanwhile, don't discuss this with anyone, including the press. Already saw an *Ardon Chronicle* reporter and photographer here. Can't stop 'em from taking pictures, long as they stay behind our barricades. But they'll get a 'no comment' if they pester me."

I smiled. "Won't say a word. My family's not exactly on friendly terms with the paper's owner."

A sly smile lit the chief's somber face. "Yes, I do seem to recall the Hookers are less than chummy with the local press."

MacLeod tipped his hat and turned to Andy. "You can take the little lady home, son. See you at the station Saturday?"

"Yes, sir," Andy answered.

THIRTY-EIGHT

Trying to keep the blanket wrapped around me, my walk to Andy's truck was closer to a shuffle than a stroll. Snail tempo. Unfortunately, that gave the *Ardon Chronicle* photographer who popped out of the bushes, ample opportunity to snap photos of me and Andy. I couldn't even wave him away or cover my face. Needed both hands on the blanket to make sure he didn't post pictures of me in my underwear.

"Auck!" The photographer toppled like an Iowa tipped cow.

Paint's grinning face appeared out of the shadows. "Too bad you stumbled," he told the downed man. "Lots of tree roots around here."

"You tripped me!" the photographer swore. "That was no accident."

"Prove it." Paint laughed as he walked away from his angry victim to join Andy and me.

"What brings you by? Did a radio report go out that I'd stripped down to my unmentionables?"

Paint hooked a finger in the blanket behind my neck and peered down my back. "My, my, so you have. But I have faith Andy wasn't the immediate cause of said stripping. Don't expect a concession speech."

He cleared his throat. "I was engaged in some stripping efforts of my own when that siren alert told me Summer Place might have a prowler. For the record, said stripping involved a cedar bench I'm refinishing not items of female clothing. Heard the news report of a fire while I was *en route*. What happened? Are Ursula and Amber okay?"

"Yep, though Ursula is once again in an ambulance, headed to the ER," I said. "Amber's with her. They both inhaled a lot of smoke. Ursula passed out, but the EMTs revived her. Said they'd both be fine."

"Good," Paint said. "Was it arson?

"How about we tell you all about it at my folks' house?" I suggested. "I called Mom and Dad right away in case they heard about the fire. While

I figured they were likely in bed, asleep, I feared someone might wake them with the news. My folks insisted I come over. I woke Eva, too. Told her I was fine and would give a full report come morning."

We'd reached my date's truck. "You want to follow us over?" Andy asked.

"Sure." Paint winked at me. "Keep that blanket wrapped tight. Andy's seen enough."

My parents' kitchen table was as welcoming as Aunt Eva's. An hour had passed since we arrived. Time enough for Mom to call the hospital and chat with Ursula and Amber, who were now bedded down until morning for observation. Ursula had recovered enough to speak, though Mom said her voice sounded raw. Amber was kicking herself for shutting off her cell phone. Said she knew Ursula was exhausted and didn't want a call to wake her. She'd forgotten all about the security app.

My suitors, my folks, and I all held steaming mugs of coffee. I'd borrowed a pair of Dad's PJ bottoms. No way could I fit in any of Mom's size-two clothes. I'd pulled the tie waist tight on Dad's oversize flannel jammies and rolled the cuffs up two turns. His spare bedroom slippers kept my bare, bruised feet from the indignities of a cold floor. While my tootsies swam in the too-big moccasin slippers, my curled toes kept them from falling off as I shambled to the coffee pot for a refill.

Once Mom satisfied herself that Ursula and Amber were doing fine, she'd joined Dad and Paint in bombarding Andy and me with questions. It had begun to feel akin to an inquisition when Mom voiced her conclusion: "Someone's out to kill Ursula."

I was leaning toward that opinion as well. It would explain why someone set fire to the cottage. The toxic ingredient—most likely ground-up theophylline—added to my chocolate mousse was meant to end Ursula's life. When Harriett died instead, the killer had to make a second try.

The theory held despite some unexplained disconnects, like Karen's death. It seemed too coincidental for two young members of the Temple of True Believers to die in a two-day span. Then there was the Summer Place vandalism. The spray-painted threats in my kitchen were aimed at me, not Ursula. Two different sets of Summer Place intruders? Or was the vandalism just designed to confuse and distract?

My gaze locked on Mom's worried face as I considered her verdict.

"Remember Dr. Swihart's three theories of the crime?" I began. "One, someone wanted to kill Harriett. Two, someone wanted to kill another luncheon guest and failed. Three, someone wanted to destroy my reputation, and Harriett's death was an accident. The fire—"

"If Harriett was the target, the fire makes no sense," Andy interrupted. "She was already dead."

I nodded. "That makes the two theories I like least seem the most logical. Someone is either trying to kill Ursula or has developed a burning hatred for me."

"Wrong." Dad's voice boomed. "You weren't in the cottage, Brie. Ursula and Amber were. And Ursula was a luncheon guest. I agree with your mother, she's the target."

I figured Dad's response was partly wishful thinking. The arsonist could have seen lights in the cottage and assumed I was inside. Dad didn't want to believe some villain out there might be after his daughter. Nonetheless, I didn't argue.

"Why would someone want to kill Ursula?" Paint asked. "Somebody she ruled against in TV court? A stalker? Who?"

Mom shot Dad a look that said, "We shouldn't have opened this can of worms. Now what?" Her teeth worried her lower lip.

She finally broke the silence. "I can't tell you why without Ursula's permission. But it's quite likely that someone's trying to kill Ursula to make sure a secret stays buried."

Andy shook his head. "Mrs. Hooker, I get that you promised to keep some secret for Ursula, but don't you think we all should know what's going on? How else can we keep Brie safe?"

"Gotta say I agree with Andy," Paint added. "Surely you can tell us who you suspect is behind this? Is Brie still in danger now that the fire has effectively evicted Ursula and Amber from the Summer Place cottage?"

Mom huffed and, in turn, fixed Andy and Paint with angry glares. "I *am* Brie's mother. Of course, her life is more important than any secret. But I don't believe Brie's in any danger now. Ursula is leaving town. Tomorrow. And I'm going with her. Amber will head back to Miami."

My mouth dropped open. So did Dad's.

"You're what?" he said.

Mom waved her hand. "Howard, we'll discuss this later. For now the matter is closed. Ursula's secret won't be secret very long. Then this whole nightmare will be over."

No, it won't.

Karen and Harriett will still be dead. And I'll always know Harriett might be alive if I hadn't invited her to lunch.

Mom stood. "Why don't you boys go on home? Brie can sleep here tonight. Either Howard or I will drop her at Udderly tomorrow morning."

All of the table's occupants knew my mother's verdict was final. No further debate from prosecution or defense.

"I'll walk you to the door," I said.

On the porch, I hugged Paint, then Andy. "Thanks, guys. What would I do without you?"

As I watched them saunter down my folks' sidewalk, I asked myself that question one more time. With feeling. Tears slid down my cheeks.

My heart had decided. My mind argued. But I knew it was another verdict that couldn't be appealed.

After Andy and Paint departed, Mom provided Dad and me with a crucial update. Lawrence Toomey had flown to Washington D.C. yesterday morning to prepare for confirmation hearings.

"Clearly Toomey didn't start that cottage fire, but he could have hired someone to do it," she said. "Ursula doesn't want to spend another night in Ardon County and risk putting anyone else in danger. She figures the best way to end this is to confront Toomey immediately. I'll accompany her as legal counsel."

Dad stroked Mom's arm. "Honey. If someone's trying to kill Ursula, being by her side makes you a target, too. If you're determined to go to D.C., I'm going with you. No argument."

But, of course, there would be. An argument that is. Or discussion as my parents preferred to characterize them. I'd witnessed very few rows between my parents, and, from the look Mom tossed my way, I wouldn't be privy to this one either. When my folks had a rare disagreement, it was private, not public. And, once they came to an understanding, there were no pouts, no recriminations.

How did they manage that?

"Brie, the guest room is made up. Do I need to wake you or will the alarm on your phone do the job?" Mom asked.

I'd been dismissed. For a fleeting moment, I considered weighing in. I did have opinions about Mom's—and Dad's—plans. But why bother? I was an adult and my opinion mattered to them. But Mom was nothing if not stubborn. And Dad loved her—in part for her independence and integrity.

I was 99 percent certain she'd go to D.C., and Dad would hold down the fort in Ardon County. Me? I'd hold my tongue and pray.

My agreement to set up a meeting between Amber and Ruth totally disappeared from my mind until the lumpy, too-soft mattress in my folks' guest bedroom practically swallowed me. Would Amber still want to meet Ruth?

Doubtful, was my last thought before I drifted off.

THIRTY-NINE

Shortly after Dad delivered me to Udderly Kidding, a text arrived. If the subject line hadn't read *Fire Destroyed My Cell*, I might not have opened a message from an unknown address. The anonymous texter had to be Amber.

I have no plans to leave Ardon County. Please go ahead and set up meeting.

Wrong on another front. *Will call after AM chores*, I typed. That's when I realized the cottage fire must have burned up all of Amber's belongings, not just her cell phone. *U need clothes? Place to stay?*

Her reply: *No. Bunking w/ Jane Bonnie, Clemson police. Call me by eight.*

I couldn't decide if I admired Amber's pluck and talent for discretion or felt annoyed her texts had the feel of a superior issuing orders to an underling. I shrugged. She'd been through hell. Deserved the benefit of the doubt.

I raced through my morning chores so I could phone Amber by eight a.m.

"Hi, you still at the hospital?" I asked.

"No, I'm at your parents' house. I've already been to Walmart. Bought a burner phone, a toothbrush, and enough clothes to keep me clean and covered for a few days. Your mom loaned me cash. Called my chief to let him know my police ID, badge, gun, and credit cards were toast. He put me in touch with Jane, a police officer he knew in Clemson. She's putting me up for a few days."

I frowned. "Mom told me you were returning to Miami today. What changed your mind?"

"Didn't change my mind. Ursula assumed that if she flew off I would, too. I never agreed though I haven't broken the news to her yet. Can you try to contact Ruth today? She works till three p.m. on Saturdays. Maybe you can snag her as she leaves the clinic. Her apartment's close and she walks to work."

"You're not worried Ruth might be involved in whatever is going on?" I asked. "Maybe she confessed to her dad that she's been in contact with you, her illegitimate half-sister. Maybe that pushed Toomey to try and poison Ursula and, when that failed, hire someone to kill both of you in a fire."

Silence on the other end of the line. "Toomey was in D.C. when the fire was set," she said, "Both murder attempts were staged to make them. appear to be accidents. So, let's say Lawrence Toomey planned them. If he has any smarts—and he must if he's a judge—he has to realize killing me and Ursula now wouldn't do a bit of good."

"How so?" I asked.

"Your mother would tell the authorities about Toomey's motive if anything happened to Ursula or me. For Toomey that accusation would be far worse than if he simply admitted to a one-night stand. Lots of men have skated in similar circumstances. He'd ask forgiveness, characterize what happened as a youthful indiscretion when he was drunk."

Amber's assessment made sense. If she or Ursula died, my folks and I would definitely point an accusing finger at the Toomey clan. Until Amber noted both murder attempts were designed to look like accidents, I hadn't given that aspect much weight.

If it looked as if Ursula and Amber were victims of an accidental fire, it's unlikely that Mom or I would have made it our mission to reveal Toomey's scurvy past. If it weren't for the motion detector alert and the fact that Andy and I were on the scene, the fire might well have been labeled accidental. The deaths a sad tragedy, not a crime.

I shivered.

Mollye arrived on cue as Eva and I sat down for a late eight-fifteen breakfast. She poured herself a cup of coffee before she walked to the table and slapped a copy of the *Ardon Chronicle* in front of me. Moll set her coffee mug down so she could put her hands on her ample hips in her trademark I'm-really-peeved pose.

"Some friend you are. You practically burn to a crisp, and the fire chief says you saved the lives of two people renting your cottage—names not disclosed—and I hear about it in the newspaper. You're pictured with *both* Andy and Paint on the front page, and do you call me? Not a word. Why is it I don't know jumping jack junipers about all the drama?"

Aunt Eva laughed at her tirade. "It kills you, Ardon's queen of gossip, that you weren't first with all the inside details. Take a load off, and enjoy your coffee. Our heroine hasn't shared with me either."

Moll let out an audible, put-upon sigh and took a chair. "So give." She tapped the newspaper. "Cute earrings by the way. Did your mom give them to you?"

I glanced at the newspaper photo taken just before Paint's "tree root" boots tripped the photographer. The cropped, somewhat fuzzy picture caught me in profile as Andy hugged me. The cameraman must have snapped the second photo while sprawled on the ground. It caught me walking away with Andy and Paint. Swaddled in a blanket, I looked like a child between my six-foot-four escorts.

My fingers flew to my earlobe. The orphaned earring. What did I do with it? I sort of remembered it getting caught when I got back to Udderly and pulled off my top. Had I left it on my nightstand?

"Come on, give," Mollye goaded, forgetting all about her jewelry question and jumping ahead. "What the heck happened last night? Was it really arson?"

I filled Eva and Mollye in on most but not all the drama. Neither my best friend nor my aunt knew why Ursula was visiting Mom. Since I'd kept my lips sealed, neither had the slightest clue that Amber was Lawrence Toomey's daughter and Ruth Toomey's half-sister. If Toomey withdrew his name from high court consideration, they'd never know. Once again I asked myself if Ursula's confrontation and demand constituted blackmail. I chose to consider it akin to a plea bargain. Like most folks, my conscience came equipped with exception clauses, especially if the deed in question seemed just.

Eva and Mollye were all ears as I explained how we believed the prowler set the fire.

"Someone really has it in for you, Brie," Mollye said. "First, the poisoning. Then, the vandalism. Now, arson. What will they do next?"

I shrugged. "I don't think it's about me."

While I couldn't tell them why someone might be targeting Ursula, I could share Dr. Swihart's theories, and the consensus opinion that Ursula was the target, not me. I also shared Ursula's plan to leave town today. My intent was to forestall any Mollye-fueled hysteria about a killer gunning down anyone who got in the way.

"Does the discovery of that prescription drug in the urine samples exonerate you as a food poisoner?" Eva asked.

"Not entirely." My fingers traced the smooth curves of my coffee cup. "Only proves theophylline was added to the chocolate mousse. Not a shred of evidence about who added it, when or why. In all likelihood the True Believers will continue to insist I knocked off Karen and Harriett as revenge for the goat yoga protest. Not sure who could swallow that motive. It's awfully thin."

"Oh," Moll put up her fingers to signal she wanted to speak as soon as she finished chewing a hunk of pumpkin bread. "I have news, too. The Temple folks can't blame Karen's death on you any longer. The sheriff and Danny arrested her estranged husband today."

"Eureka," Aunt Eva exclaimed. "Glad they nabbed him. Was he just getting his revenge because Karen kicked him to the curb?"

"Maybe, but he was also after insurance money. Wanted to cash in before she changed the policy. What a creep! Bad enough he killed her, but it was really sick that he tried to make it look like some sexual fetish did her in."

Moll finished off her second piece of pumpkin bread and downed a third cup of coffee.

"All's forgiven by the way." She dusted some crumbs off her ample bosom and stood. "Guess I get why you didn't think to call your best friend last night." She wagged her finger. "But don't let it happen again."

After Moll left, I helped Eva package more out-of-town specialty orders for FedEx. Since it was Saturday, I technically had the day off though I'd agreed to drive to Jamieson Gorge for the afternoon goat rental meeting.

On Saturdays, Tess, a retired school teacher, staffed the retail cabin and our part-timers gave tours to families who came for weekend visits. However, since I'd spent quite a bit of time away from Udderly lately, I felt I owed Eva a little extra. I moved stockpiled bales of hay into the horse barn, and groomed Lilly's mule, Rita, and Eva's horse, Hank. Since Rita and I had come to a meeting of the minds, I'd ceased to fear the mule nipping or kicking me when I invaded her space.

Those sweaty chores mandated a long hot shower and shampoo before I drove to Jamieson Gorge. As I rinsed my hair, I swore it still smelled of smoke. I gave my scalp a second generous scrubbing and rinse. If it were only that easy to get rid of bad memories—and uneasy vibes. It would be a long time before I forgot the fire's heat on my bare skin and the choking smoke in my lungs.

Still dripping from the shower, I phoned Andy. "Mind if we stay in and spend the evening with Eva and Billy? Eva says they're ready for a Hearts revenge match."

"Fine with me," Andy said. "Can I talk you into a game of strip poker after they trundle off to bed?"

"Nice try, but no," I said. "Figure we can use a sedate evening after last night's excitement. We won't light a log in the fireplace, and I'll keep Eva away from the grill and the stove."

FORTY

Exiting Udderly, I gritted my teeth as I approached the gate. Looked like Harriett's Friday visitation had only offered a brief ceasefire. The war would continue, though surely they'd clear out long before the afternoon funeral service.

Four cars squatted across from our entrance. The milling occupants were making last-minute additions to picket signs. Were they waiting for Pastor or Jeannie Nickles to appear and tell them what to do?

I executed a wheelie about face. Had to let Aunt Eva know idiots were massing at Udderly's property line. Maybe I should call our potential Greenville County customer. Ask to reschedule our Jamieson Gorge meeting.

I wanted to stay and make sure the protestors didn't hassle Udderly's visitors. Saturday was a big family day with "city" folk from Greenville, Anderson, and Clemson bringing their kids to see our kids. Parents often mentioned they wanted their children to realize milk, cheese, and eggs didn't originate on refrigerated grocery shelves.

Guilt tinged my anger. Udderly would never have attracted the True Believers' attention if I hadn't suggested goat yoga, and if Harriett, a member of their congregation, hadn't died because I fed her lunch. Sometimes I wondered if my presence at Udderly was making things easier for my aunt or harder.

I called to Eva as soon as I spotted her in the milk barn. "The whackos are back. Don't know how long they'll stay. Should I reschedule my meeting? Want me to call reinforcements—Andy, Paint, Mollye?"

"Slow down. Your machine-gun delivery is giving me a headache." Eva parked herself on a hay bale and motioned for me to sit, too. "I'm not some clueless old ninny, so don't act like it. This is nothing compared to the ruckus my late husband's kin raised when he went missing. Back then I feared they'd show up with a rope to lynch me. Nah, these folks are harmless. Go on. Git."

"What about our Saturday help?" I persisted. "They'll be here soon. Shouldn't we warn them?"

"Don't think they'll upset Gerri none." Eva laughed. "She'll recommend a cold glass of goat's milk to settle them right down, and Tess will lecture them on manners. Besides, Billy's on his way over. He'll do gate duty. Make sure paying customers aren't bothered."

I breathed a sigh of relief knowing Billy would arrive soon. The farrier was a respected local. No doubt he provided valuable services to a number of the True Believers. They'd be reluctant to give Billy a hard time.

"Okay, I'll go," I said. "But call if you need me. Andy and I are planning to stay in tonight. I'll cook something special. I assume Billy's planning an overnight."

I kissed Eva's cheek and returned to my car. However, before I started the Prius, I texted an update to Mollye, Paint, and Andy, suggesting they might drop by Udderly. *But don't let Eva know it was my idea.*

No one near the gate tried to block my car. My windshield didn't even gather a globule of spit as I vacated the premises. I prayed my departure would siphon off protestor enthusiasm. I was the one accused of devil worship and murder. Eva was only guilty of harboring a killer—well, and harboring devil goats.

It was a quarter till eleven when I walked into my folks' living room. I stopped by to say goodbye to Mom and Ursula since they might be gone before I finished my Jamieson Gorge and Ruth Toomey stalking assignments.

My mother shushed me as I entered the room.

"Just a minute, Brie. We want to hear this update. South Carolina has nice clear skies for our evening flight, but airports up north are reporting delays." Mom unconsciously rubbed her chin as she sat glued to the tube.

I sat down and waited for the Weather Channel's on-the-ground meteorologist to make his report. Decked out in a yellow slicker, he swayed as wind gusts tore at his gear. Sheets of rain almost obliterated the man's features.

"This Nor'easter is turning into a monster," he grunted between gusts. "Just got word all flights in and out of airports from D.C. to Boston are canceled. The weather isn't expected to improve for at least twenty-four hours."

Ursula's hands clamped together, her knuckles white from the pressure.

"Not a chance in Hades we'll get out of Greenville till late Sunday," she said. "At least the weather won't stop Amber from heading to Florida."

"I'm not leaving," Amber announced as she walked into the room. "Not yet. I have a few things I want to do first. A Clemson police officer is putting me up. Says she has plenty of room."

"You're what?" Ursula's voice rose. "You could be in danger here, especially since I can't leave town. I want you to go home."

The look Amber gave her mother wasn't exactly loving.

"I'm an adult. I did just fine my first thirty years when I'd never heard of Ursula Billings. I can and do make my own decisions."

Ursula shrunk away as if she'd been slugged in the gut. I suddenly wished I was somewhere else. Nerves had been rubbed raw. I feared Ursula and Amber might both say things they'd regret.

"I don't think Amber's in danger," I butted in. "Toomey's no dummy. By now he has to figure the Hookers know his secret and a tell-all document has been safely tucked away should Ursula and Amber mysteriously die or disappear."

The look on Ursula's face told me I'd guessed right. She'd made sure an untimely death wouldn't bury her story.

I'd pretty much parroted Amber's arguments. They made sense. Nonetheless, my mother's narrowed eyes told me what she thought about my butting in.

I ignored the look. "I have to go to Greenville this afternoon. Should be back to Udderly by five. Andy and Billy are joining Eva and me for dinner. The more the merrier. I started a big batch of vegetarian chili in the crockpot before I left. Since it doesn't look like you'll be leaving town tonight, come join us. Dad, too, of course. Just give me a buzz."

"Brie, can you give me a ride back to Jane's house?" Amber asked.

"Sure."

Amber walked over and kissed Ursula's cheek—a nonverbal peace offering. "I'll call you later today, Ursula. Sorry you're stuck here. I know you want this finished."

"Goodbye," I called as we left the house.

Amber let out a huge sigh as she climbed into my car's passenger seat.

"I respect Ursula, and I do love her. But our relationship's complicated. Sometimes my emotions get the better of me. She's not my mother. I mean I know Ursula's my birth mother, but my real mother is the woman who raised me. My adoptive father is the only dad I'll ever know. This whole Toomey business will break their hearts if it gets ugly."

Amber directed me to Jane's house, an older brick two blocks north of Highway 123, the busy thoroughfare that became clogged with traffic when the university was in session.

"Will you come to Udderly for dinner tonight?" I asked. "You can invite Jane, too."

"Jane's working tonight so I'll be alone. Maybe I'll make it. Call me as soon as you make contact with Ruth. Okay?"

"I'll call. Can't promise I'll even be able to talk with Ruth let alone set up a meeting."

"I understand." She squeezed my hand before she opened the car door. "All I ask is that you try."

FORTY-ONE

I reached Greenville County's Jamieson Gorge Nature Park at 11:55, a few minutes before our scheduled meet-up. Udderly's prospective client was waiting. Picking him out wasn't exactly a head scratcher. For starters, he was leaning against the only car in the lot. His wrinkled suit and the cigarette he puffed suggested he hadn't come to hike. As I walked toward him, I noticed the stunted corpses of three more cigarettes stubbed out at his feet. Okay, given his litterbug carelessness, I doubted he was any kind of park ranger.

"Mr. Stuart? I'm Brie Hooker from Udderly Kidding Dairy. Glad to meet you." I offered my hand in greeting.

He threw down the cigarette he'd been smoking and ground it under his heel. His handshake was firm but hasty. Despite his fingers recent contact with burning tobacco, they felt like flexible icicles.

"John Stuart," he said. "Thanks for meeting me on a Saturday. We had a death in the family and I took a couple of personal days. So I agreed to handle this meeting on the weekend. The park people are in a real hurry to take care of that kudzu."

For a minute, my mind did a backflip. A death in the family. Could it be Harriett? No, don't be an idiot. He wouldn't have arranged our meeting for the day they were burying her.

Stuart looked askance at a path that led into deep woods. "Never been out here before. Not my usual beat. County maintenance turned in a whopper estimate of what it would cost to clear kudzu and poison ivy out of the gorge the park's named for. No way. Can't spend that kind of dough. Only a handful of people tramp around out here. But the park folks say doin' nothing will cost us more long term if the danged kudzu invades the entire acreage."

"How big's the gorge?" I asked.

"About fifteen acres." His nicotine fingers dived into a file folder he'd set on the trunk of his car. "Here are the forms to submit with your bid. Hope you can get us a bid in a week. Want this taken care of in February. Supposedly it gets busier here in March."

Stuart surveyed the forest beyond the parking lot. His grimace suggested he thought the notion this place ever got busy was a big fat fib.

I took the offered forms. "I'll put these in the car. Then we'll look at the problem area so I can get a better handle on what's required."

He backed away from me like I was a lunatic. "Un uh, there's no 'we.' Take as much time as you need to see what you need to see. I have another appointment."

His rapid blinking and furtive glances to the left suggested his appointment was one honker of a lie. This simply wasn't his idea of how to spend a Saturday.

"No folks on duty today," he added. "They rotate among parks during down times when attendance is next to nil. The rangers say you can't miss the gorge. Just follow the main path till it dead ends at a big hole in the earth. When you get there, the path goes in a circle. Take the fork left or right, doesn't matter. You'll end up where you started."

"Is there a path to climb down?"

"No. You don't need to."

"Any other access?"

His impatient look told me he was eager to leave.

"The Smith farm borders the park to the south. The rangers occasionally complain about hunters using the farm to sneak into the park and poach. But hunting season's over."

All righty. I hoped the hunters had consulted the calendars that decreed deer season ended January first. If these folks were flaunting the law to poach, did they really care if the season to shoot game was over?

Thankfully the scarf wrapped around my neck and tucked into my windbreaker jacket was bright red. I pulled the ends free to make it more visible. Hoped that was a good idea and didn't make me a better target.

Aunt Eva would pay. She hadn't told me my errand entailed a solo safari in a nature park frequented by poachers. That news also raised concern for our goats. Would they be safe or might poachers mistake our wethers for deer?

I watched Stuart's car leave. February's return chill had discouraged any fellow explorers. I was totally alone.

I'd googled the nature park earlier. The write-up claimed Jamieson Gorge was teeming with deer and other small mammals, reptiles, and amphibians. Hmm, what classified as a "small" mammal? Bears were smaller than, say, water buffalo.

The mention of reptiles made my skin crawl. I didn't mind Mable, our harmless black barn snake, but the idea of one of her distant cousins dropping on my head from a tree? No thank you. If you scream bloody murder in a forest and no one's there to hear it, did you really make a sound?

Okay, knock it off. You go running by your lonesome all the time. Start walking. Sooner you start, sooner you'll finish.

The dense woods blocked almost all of February's watery sunshine. I could swear the temperature dropped ten degrees by the time I took ten steps into the forest. I wished I had on something more than a knit top, windbreaker, and scarf.

Speed walking I quickly reached the rim of the gorge. Its steep sides—which I studiously avoided—would make mechanical underbrushing tough. Boulders erupted from the ground at weird angles and unpredictable intervals. I wondered what had forged this deep gash in the earth. The pines and hardwoods that fought gravity to survive on the sides of the gorge had a new enemy—the invading kudzu. It was tenaciously scaling the trees.

I followed the rim path. At the south end, I saw the spur trail poachers probably used to enter the park. I walked faster to complete the circuit and come back to my starting point.

Our goats would munch on every leaf they could reach and nibble the roots down to nubs. But the area would be impossible to fence. The goats we rented were wethers—castrated males. We never sent does as they could damage their udders ranging through rugged terrain. Wethers were docile, but they never lost their sense of adventure. We'd need at least two herd dogs and a human to keep the rental goats in check. I wasn't volunteering. I used my cell phone to snap pictures, hoping they'd help Eva calculate how many goats and days would be needed to clear the property.

Assessment complete, I jogged back to my car. I told myself I was hustling to stay warm. The truth? I was spooked. I was happy to see my car remained the parking lot's only occupant. I wasn't eager to encounter a hulking stranger in this desolate spot.

Once I'd jumped in the car and locked the doors, the lot looked less forbidding. The secluded spot was tailor made for a private meeting. Maybe I'd suggest Ruth and Amber could meet here tomorrow—if I found a way to speak to Ruth today.

Safely tucked into my Prius, I googled the urgent care facility where Ruth worked and put its street address in my GPS. A know-it-all voice promptly informed me my destination was twenty-two-and-one-half miles and the expected drive time was forty minutes. Traffic congestion, road work?

Amber had shared what she knew about Ruth's life based on their early conversations. The half-sister had recently become engaged to Jack Ford, a South Carolina State Senator with much higher political ambitions. Ruth lived in a downtown Greenville apartment and walked to and from her job. She worked Tuesday through Friday from eight a.m. to four p.m. Her shift ended at two p.m. on Saturdays.

If my GPS wasn't shining me on and I got lucky finding a downtown parking space, I could reach the medical facility before she left work. Maybe I'd lurk outside and strike up a sidewalk conversation as she left work. I hoped her fiancé wasn't meeting her.

I'd visited Ruth's Facebook page. I'd only seen her once at the Madren Center restaurant, and I'd been focused on her father. Ruth had been little more than background wallpaper. I hadn't even heard her speak. She'd nodded instead of saying hello. Would I even recognize her?

Though I wasn't a Facebook friend, Ruth's social settings let me view all her recent posts—and there were plenty. Photos of her and Jack Ford, her fiancé. Candids with her dad, Lawrence Toomey, and mother, Esther. None of the photos showed anyone hugging, let alone kissing. The photo subjects were too busy engaging in wholesome activities—tennis, hiking, canoeing. Nothing touchy-feely or overly personal.

Her Facebook page included no mention of the Temple of True Believers or her grandparents. Did that mean she'd separated herself from their goat-hating claptrap? Or was the omission part of a studied public persona geared to make her appear to be Jack's perfect mate. I jumped to his Facebook page. Yep, he was busy campaigning as an All-American, apple-pie conservative.

As I studied the photos, I noticed how many features Ruth and Amber shared. Both had heart-shaped faces, widow's peaks, and large ears with oversized lobes. Their voluptuous builds were similar, too, though Ruth tended to opt for loose-fitting clothes that camouflaged her well-endowed chest.

Of course, if I hadn't known they were related, I wouldn't have picked up on the similarities. Amber had raven hair, hazel eyes, and bronzed skin. Ruth's complexion was pale, her hair an uninspired brown.

I closed Facebook and started my car. Time to see if Ruth in the flesh matched her digital persona.

FORTY-TWO

As my Prius glided to a standstill at each stoplight, I entertained second, third, and fourth thoughts about my mission. Why had I agreed to be a go-between for the half-sisters? Heck, Amber was the detective. Couldn't she have figured out a way to discreetly approach Ruth for a tête-à-tête?

I wasn't convinced Ruth would be any happier being ambushed by me—a virtual stranger.

But I'd agreed.

I counted my lucky stars when I found a two-hour parking space a block from the urgent care facility. I checked the time—1:42. I should be able to catch Ruth as she left work. Fingers crossed she hadn't flown the coop early. I also hoped a co-worker wouldn't leave the building at her side.

I found a sunny spot to loiter unobtrusively. I leaned against the warm bricks of a nearby building as I pretended to read the papers in my hand—the empty bid forms for our goat rental gig. While I could run forever, standing for long periods killed my back. I shuffled my feet and stretched.

At 2:04, Ruth walked through the door. Right on time and alone. Her pace was brisk. I followed at a respectable distance, waiting until we were out of sight of her workplace. Didn't want any co-workers jogging to catch up.

"Ruth, hi. We were introduced a few days ago at Clemson's Madren Center. I'm Brie Hooker."

She looked startled. Her gaze darted right and left. Was she searching for an escape route? Looking for witnesses or her fiancé?

Though she had yet to say a word, I rushed ahead, "Your friend Amber has been staying in a cottage I own. She knew I was coming to Greenville and asked me to deliver a message. Can we go somewhere to talk?"

Ruth's eyes narrowed to slits. "My apartment's around the corner." She turned her face away, looked forward, and increased her brisk pace. Any faster and she'd be running. I stayed a skootch behind so we didn't appear to be together. I made no attempt to engage in small talk. She clearly wasn't interested.

The unlocked door to her high-rise apartment building opened on a spacious marble lobby ringed with retail space. Two elevators sat straight ahead. Ruth pulled a key card from her purse. The lift was apparently off-limits to the general public. I followed her inside the elevator.

She kept her silence as we glided upwards. She glanced repeatedly at the ceiling. Was she checking to see if security cameras were recording our interaction as we climbed to the twelfth floor?

Her apartment was two doors past the elevator. After she unlocked it, she stepped to the side so I could enter. My feet had barely cleared the threshold when she gave the door a hard shove. It clicked closed and I braced myself. I kind of expected an attack.

Ruth took a deep breath with her eyes closed. Preparing for battle?

Her sudden smile, so like Amber's, threw me for a loop, especially after her frosty sidewalk dismissal. Miss Jekyll and Nurse Hyde?

"Go on in the living room. Make yourself at home." Ruth kicked off her shoes and bustled into a galley kitchen just off the hallway. "What can I get you to drink? Ice tea? Beer? Coke?"

"Tea sounds perfect." I was drawn to a window wall offering a panoramic view of downtown Greenville. I could even glimpse a portion of the Swamp Rabbit Trail, popular with urban walkers, runners, and bicyclists. The trail stretched from Travelers Rest through downtown Greenville and Reedy Falls Park.

"What a fantastic view," I commented as I accepted the glass of iced tea. The frosty glass made me wish Ruth had offered hot tea. I had yet to shake the chill acquired walking in the thick woods at Jamieson Gorge.

Ruth stared out the window. "The view sold me. It's a small one-bedroom apartment and too expensive, but so convenient. The view's a treat. Even prettier at night."

I made an appreciative nod. When she turned to look at me, her lips tightened. "So tell me what Amber wants."

"She'd like to meet you in person, someplace private. Tomorrow if possible."

"Why? My fiancé found out I was talking to her, and said nothing good could come of it. He's forbidden any contact with Amber. Demanded I break all communication."

I took a sip of tea before I answered. My first thought was, wow, I wouldn't be engaged very long to a fiancé who felt he could forbid me to do anything. But maybe she'd been brought up to believe the man was the master of the house and it was her unquestioned duty to obey.

"You should meet Amber in person. She means you no harm. Listen to what she has to say. Then, if you agree with your fiancé, tell her to her face that you don't want to hear from her again."

When Ruth failed to launch an immediate rebuttal, I continued. "My Aunt Eva owns Udderly Kidding Dairy in Ardon County and sometimes rents goats to underbrush property."

Ruth's wrinkled forehead told me my non-sequitur had her thinking I was nutso. I laughed.

"Sorry I was going 'round the horn to explain why I visited Jamieson Gorge Nature Park today. It might be an ideal spot for a private meeting. When I was scouting the place, there wasn't another car in the parking lot. Not very popular this time of year."

Ruth scooted forward in her seat. "I've heard of that park but never been there." She nodded her head. "Guess it's closer than driving all the way to Ardon County. What time does Amber want to meet? Tomorrow's Sunday so I have to attend morning services with my fiancé. I think he has an afternoon meeting so I should be able to get away for an hour or so."

"Amber says any time that works for you is fine."

She nodded. "Let's make it two o'clock, Jamieson Gorge."

Ruth studied me as she sipped her drink. The friendly light in her eyes appeared to wink out. "I seem to recall your father's a Clemson professor. That's how he was acquainted with my dad. But your name rings a bell for some other reason. I wish I could remember why. How well do you know Amber? You're sure she didn't tell you more about me?"

I lowered my eyes and took a long sip of tea, a delay tactic while I weighed my options. Perhaps if I answered Ruth's question about how I knew Amber I'd distract her from the other, much tougher questions.

I didn't want Ruth to spend too much time pondering why my name sounded familiar. Had her grandparents told her I was a food poisoner, an evil goat worshipper? Real possibilities if Ruth ever shot the breeze with Pastor and Jeannie Nickles, the rulers of the True Believer cult.

"I met Amber two days ago." I smiled. "She's staying with Ursula Billings, a friend of my mother's. They rented a cottage on my Summer Place property. It was a last resort since all the Clemson area hotels and B&Bs were booked solid. Last night a fire in the cottage evicted them. Ursula booked a flight to leave Ardon County today, but Amber didn't want to skip town until she had a chance to meet you."

No need to mention the 100 percent certainty Ursula's flight would be canceled.

Ruth's face morphed again, back to friendly. I ushered in a new subject before she asked anything else I wasn't at liberty to answer.

My gaze caught on a framed photo of Ruth with her fiancé. "What a great picture. Is that your fiancé?" I played ignorant.

"Yes, Jack Ford." Her proprietary tone screamed "hands off, he's mine". I picked up the picture and took a closer look. Her fiancé looked a lot like her dad might have decades earlier—fair hair, blue eyes, lean build.

"Jack's an attorney. He argued a case in front of my father. Dad was so impressed he invited him to our house for dinner after he ruled on the case. That's how we met."

She frowned. "Jack's the only man who's earned my father's stamp of approval. Dad's delighted we're engaged, though he asked us to hold off setting a wedding date until he's confirmed as a Supreme Court judge. He didn't want media frenzy and all the nomination hoopla to take away from Jack's and my wedding announcement."

I felt uncomfortable listening to Ruth talk about her father. I sensed she loved the man even though she had to be aware of his infidelity. I mean, Amber wouldn't exist if Toomey had been faithful to Ruth's mother. Of course, Ruth didn't know all the sordid details.

Suddenly I was eager to escape Ruth's apartment. I had a bad feeling about the private meeting I'd set up. Somehow I couldn't imagine Ruth trying to talk her father into dreaming up some personal excuse to withdraw his name from consideration for the high court.

"Thanks for the iced tea." I carefully centered my almost-full glass on a cork coaster. "But I really must run."

I made an oh-my-goodness face as I checked my watch and leapt from the sofa. "Wow, where does the time go? Don't want to be late to meet my boyfriend."

Ruth walked me to the door. "Thanks for passing along Amber's message."

"My pleasure," I lied.

A sixth sense told me the coming meeting would be a disaster. Given Ruth's connection to her father I couldn't imagine a happy outcome, not one that would please both half-sisters. I feared Amber and Ruth could never be friends, and might become bitter enemies.

I walked briskly toward my car, thinking all the while about my dad, Howard. What if someone gave me irrefutable evidence he'd cheated on Mom and fathered a child out of wedlock? How would I feel?

Like Ruth, I was an only child. Would I want a relationship with a sibling, one whose existence came as a total shock? I'd be curious, but what else would I feel—sad, betrayed, disappointed?

Whatever my emotions might be, I decided they'd be transitory. I couldn't imagine any revelation dissolving my bond with Dad. Thirty-two years of love couldn't easily be set aside.

FORTY-THREE

Since there was time left on my two-hour parking meter, I caved to temptation and made an unplanned stop at a new kitchen store near Falls Park. I escaped with a mere twenty-six-dollar charge on my MasterCard. Subconsciously I think I wanted to postpone phoning Amber as long as possible. The more I thought about Amber and Ruth meeting at Jamieson Gorge the more I got the heebie-jeebies. I waited until I'd climbed in my Prius to call Amber's burner cell.

She picked up immediately. "Brie, what did Ruth say?"

The detective barreled ahead without so much as a "hello".

I described my meet-up with Ruth—well, at least the words she'd spoken. I didn't quite know how to communicate the undertone, the weird vibes. The woman seemed almost schizophrenic, friendly one second, frosty the next.

"Ruth will meet you at two o'clock tomorrow afternoon," I said. "I recommended Jamieson Gorge as a good spot to meet since I'd just been there. It's definitely private, off the beaten path. But I wish I hadn't suggested it, too isolated. Could be Ruth wants to do more than meet you."

Amber barked a laugh. "What are you saying? Think my half-sister will seize the opportunity to bash in my skull? Why would she? It wouldn't solve a thing. Ursula isn't going to be with me. Killing me wouldn't make my DNA disappear unless she has some way to vaporize my body."

I sighed. Amber was mocking me, trying to joke me out of my vague misgivings. "I know it makes no sense. But you didn't see Ruth's face when she spoke about her father, your father. She loves the man. Let's say Lawrence Toomey had a hand in the food poisoning and the arson. What if Ruth confides in him, tells him she's meeting you? She could set things in motion, things you can't control."

"I'm not some helpless innocent, and even my father must realize it's impossible to murder his way out of this mess. New crimes can't erase knowledge of past bad deeds. Too many people are involved. Too many know Toomey's dirty secret now, including you and your parents."

I didn't respond. The total silence on the line seemed ominous.

"So you're determined to forge ahead?" I finally asked.

"I am." Amber followed her two-word answer with a nervous laugh. "Can't believe I'm about to ask another favor given how you feel about the meeting. But I don't have a car. Could you drive me to Jamieson Gorge tomorrow? I won't risk your safety, just drop me at the entrance and take off. I'll call you to pick me up again if and when it's safe to return."

I really, really wanted to refuse, to say no. Why didn't I? Irrational guilt? Possibly. I'd suggested the site, set up the meeting. How would I feel if Amber rented a car and drove there by her lonesome? I'd be worried sick the whole time. And what if she turned up dead? If I played chauffeur, Ruth would know there was a witness. Surely that would deter any rash move.

"Okay, I'll give you a ride."

"I really appreciate it." Amber sounded as if she'd been holding her breath. "Don't worry. I'll bring my brand new gun. Nothing bad's going to happen. Remember, you'll have a law officer riding shotgun."

Amber's mention of a gun only boosted my anxiety. Note to self: work on ability to say no.

"The park's about an hour from Clemson. I'll pick you up a few minutes before one."

"Fine. See you in a couple hours. I did decide to have dinner at Udderly Kidding Dairy with Ursula and your folks. Please keep it zipped about the meeting. Ursula would have a cow. She has no idea Ruth is aware I exist."

I phoned Mom as soon as I ended my conversation with Amber.

"Hi, Mom, what's the head count for dinner?" I played dumb. "I made a big pot of vegetarian chili, but I'm not sure how far it will stretch. I should stop at the grocery and expand the offerings if we have more than six."

"I believe we're up to nine. Ursula, Amber, Howard, and I make four. Then there's Eva, Billy, Andy, and Mollye. And I suppose you might want to eat, too."

"How did Mollye get an invite?" I asked.

Not that I objected. My best friend never needed a formal invitation to join us. I was just curious. Deputy Danny must be working tonight. Otherwise she'd be pestering him to choose between skydiving in Alaska and spelunking in Antarctica for their honeymoon. I felt certain she'd come up with a wing-ding adventure.

My smile slowly crumpled. Moll would drop in a lot less often once Deputy Danny was elevated from fiancé to husband. I'd miss her. I tuned back into Mom as I realized she was answering my question.

"Mollye stopped by Udderly early afternoon and stayed a couple of hours to help Billy usher customers past the True Believer picketers. Once Eva told your friend who all was coming to dinner, she asked to join us."

"Sounds like I'd better figure out what else I can serve."

"No, you're fine. Since Ursula and I couldn't fly out tonight, we spent the afternoon in the kitchen. Cooking kept our minds off the weather. We're bringing a big pot of white chicken chili and dessert. I used your vegan pumpkin brownie recipe so you can enjoy dessert, too. But we're bringing real ice cream for the rest of us to enjoy with the brownies."

"Thanks, Mom. See you soon."

As I approached Udderly's gate, I was delighted to see there was no one picketing. Then I remembered the reason for the absence. I checked my watch. Five o'clock. The funeral started at four. At this very moment, Ardon Mortuary's shiny black hearse might be carrying Harriett from the Temple of True Believers to her grave in Sunset Gardens.

Another surprise awaited me at the cabin. Andy's truck was parked beside Billy's ride. Wow, my favorite veterinarian was more than an hour early for dinner. As I walked in the cabin, my cheery hello was greeted with total silence. It scared me. Had a lynch mob of True Believers skipped Harriett's funeral to seek revenge?

I threw my purse down on the hall table and ran to the milking barn. No one. My heart pounded. I yelled. The only answers were a few woofs from our herding dogs. It was milking time. Why hadn't Eva sent our Border collies to round up the does?

Maybe the trio had gone to the horse barn. "Eva, Billy, Andy," I yelled at the top of my lungs as I ran to the barn door, fearing my late Aunt Lilly's mule or Eva's horse had fallen ill or broken a leg.

"Stop your caterwauling," Eva scolded as I stood panting at the barn's entrance. "You're gonna scare the newest additions to our Udderly Kidding family."

My tense neck muscles loosened. A relief. The three babies looked adorable trying to keep vertical on wobbly kid legs.

Eva jerked her head toward a stall to her right. "Two more in there, and another two at the back of the barn." She laughed. "Did you put something in the water before you left today? Our does seemed to be having a birthing contest. Pumping out kids left and right. Had to call Andy for help. One of Brenda's twins tried to back into the world and got stuck. Hard for me to help three nannies at once."

Andy's head popped up above the right-hand stall's divider. His smile couldn't have been brighter if he'd been the proud papa. Welcoming new animals into the world never seemed to get old for Andy. How wonderful.

"Come over here, Brie," he said. "Want you to meet all the new arrivals, Cindy included."

Cindy? Ah, the new vet tech.

I peered over the stall divider. Cindy was cleaning the afterbirth off the newest kid on the Udderly block. Yuck. Not among my favorite activities.

Cindy, however, didn't appear grossed out. If anything, her smile was broader than Andy's. Had to admit the young woman was attractive. Okay, she was a knockout. Looked like a Doris Day throwback: blonde hair, eyes an innocent wide-eyed blue, a peaches-and-cream complexion made to look all the more wholesome by a dusting of freckles across her nose.

"Brie Hooker, I'd like you to meet Cindy East. She's had quite the first day as my new tech. The three of us have delivered seven kids in the last hour."

"The three of you? Where's Billy?" I asked.

"He escorted Hank and Rita to their new pasture. More excitement than the old horse and mule wanted and we needed room. He should be back any minute."

Cindy stood. She was a head taller than me but still shorter than Andy, maybe five nine. Dang, I couldn't find any fault with her figure. And it was obvious Andy couldn't either. At the moment, his gaze was fastened on her tight little behind as she dusted hay from her snug jeans.

Andy's face was so easy to read. One of the things that made him so attractive. He couldn't hide his emotions, even if he tried. In this case, love at first sight. Andy was smitten. I was sure of it even if Andy hadn't toppled to it yet.

I smiled as I assessed my own feelings. Yes indeedy. I was fine with that. I loved Andy, wished him every happiness, hoped we'd always be close friends. But...yes, there was a but. Though I'd taken my time admitting it, Andy—one of the world's kindest, most loving men—wasn't the love of my life.

Like it or not, my match was far more ornery, a bigger and trickier challenge. That is, if he hadn't been shining me on. I didn't think so but I was skittish. When it came to handsome hunks who swore their playboy days were over, I was in the you-can-only-fool-me-once camp. My lying, cheating scumbag ex-fiancé had left me with considerable scar tissue.

FORTY-FOUR

By seven o'clock, we finished chores delayed by the birth of seven kids. Cindy helped, and we chatted as we worked. I learned she was in Ardon County alone, her mother keeping her little boy in Greenville until the spring recess at his school. I insisted Cindy join us for dinner. That made ten, not nine, mouths to feed.

One more mouth had little impact on our dining logistics. Six sets of elbows and legs maxed out the capacity of our kitchen table for injury-free dining. I set up a card table in our living room next to the loveseat, while Dad, Billy, and Andy each carried in a front porch rocker. Not much space to maneuver once the chairs were in place.

Though it was theoretically Animal Passion week and Andy was my date, I insisted he and Cindy should sit together at the kitchen table. Ursula declared the other four vacancies at the big table should be taken by Eva and Billy and Mom and Dad.

"Amber and I want to hear more about Mollye's Starry Skies shop." Judge Ursula's proclamation meant Amber, Mollye, and I would join the judge as card table outcasts.

Moll quickly put dibs on the loveseat, thinking it would be comfier than the hard pine rockers. Too big to scoot under the table, the rockers created a long-distance, bowl-to-mouth challenge for their occupants. I eyed my light-colored sweater. I'd be running a race with gravity every time I brought a spoon to my lips.

"It's everyone for themselves," I announced. "No waitstaff. Get in line and ladle up your choice of chili. The red one's vegan, the white's Mom's chicken chili. You're welcome to try both. But, unless you want to use Cashew's water dish, you'll have to make do with the same bowl each time you return to the chili pots."

I hung back until the kitchen parade ended. As I dished up my vegan chili, I was pleased to note the level of both soups had dropped. At least some of the meat eaters were willing to sample my version.

At the card table, I established what passed as Udderly Kidding etiquette by tucking my napkin into the neck of my shirt. "Hey, it's a small deterrent to tomato stains," I said. "I like this top." Everyone at the card table followed my lead, even Ursula.

As I could have predicted, Mollye fascinated her tablemates with descriptions of her store's conglomeration of products, ranging from witches' balls to herbal medicines. Her effervescent salesmanship would likely prompt Amber and Ursula to visit Starry Skies before they left town.

I shook off a sudden chill as I recalled what happened the last time Mollye tempted out-of-towners to visit her pottery store. Unconsciously I fingered the small scar left by the bullet.

Without warning, Mollye reached over and flicked my earlobe.

"Ouch, that hurt," I objected. "Why'd you do that?"

"How many pairs of earrings—gorgeous creations fashioned by my own hands—have I given you? Huh? And do you ever remember to wear them?" She paused to share an aggrieved look with Ursula and Amber. "Can you believe it took me years to talk Brie into having her ears pierced, and she still lets her ears go out buck neckid."

I touched my bare earlobe. "Oh, Ursula. I forgot to mention. I found one of your earrings at Summer Place. It was lying in the grass between the big house and cottage. Well, what used to be the cottage. The earring's in my bedroom. I'll go get it."

Ursula's right hand flew up in reflex, checking her right ear, then her left. Both gold hoops were in place. "I haven't lost any earrings," Ursula replied. "What makes you think it belongs to me?"

"It's a gold gavel; you know like a judge uses."

Ursula frowned. "Not mine. I don't own any earrings like that."

Amber shook her head. "Me either. Closest I come to law-and-order jewelry is a pair of earrings shaped like miniature handcuffs."

"I'll be right back." I jumped up, more curious than ever about the orphaned gold gavel. If it wasn't Ursula's, who else could it belong to? Mom was an unlikely possibility. She'd accompanied Ursula to the Summer Place cottage a couple of times. But I'd never seen her wear a pair of dangly earrings. Mom's taste in jewelry was conservative. Usually petite pearl or diamond studs.

I retrieved the lost earring from my bedside table and showed it to all the dinner guests. "Anyone know who might own this?" I asked. "Found it on the ground near Summer Place cottage while the firemen were fighting the blaze that turned the cottage into a blackened heap of rubble. Didn't have a pocket—or pants for that matter—so I wore the earring to keep from losing it."

I turned the finely-crafted gavel in my hand, looking at it from all angles. "The little marking says its eighteen-carat gold. Not cheap."

My ownership question appeared to stump everyone. Negative headshakes all around except for Mollye.

"Hand it over," she ordered. "I remember noticing this earring in the newspaper photo of you. I kept thinking I recently saw a woman wearing ones just like it. Now who was it? I may not be good at recalling people's hair or eye colors, but jewelry I remember. I noticed the earring in another news photo. Let me get out my iPad."

Mollye motioned for us to pull the card table away from the loveseat so she could scoot out. As we started to inch our heavy rockers back, Mollye said, "Oh, forget it. Faster this way." A second later she'd slid under the table, crawled out my side. How she squeezed through I couldn't imagine.

Moll had dumped her large bag in the corner to get it out of the way. She picked it off the floor, pulled out her iPad, and sat down in Eva's recliner. Then she put her feet up and started her laptop search.

"Who wants brownies?" I asked. All hands shot up. "Who wants ice cream with the brownies?"

The split was fifty-fifty. I noticed Cindy wavered on the ice cream until Andy's hand flew into the air.

"I'll clear the bowls and dishes," Eva said as she began carting dirty dishes to the sink. "Everybody else keep your fannies in you seats. It's a one-butt kitchen, but luckily Brie's and my behinds are both small."

Eva cut generous brownie wedges while I scooped ice cream into five bowls. "I'll deliver these," she said. "You dish out the brownie-only requests."

Once everyone but Mollye had a brownie, I delivered a plate to her easy chair. "Any luck?" I asked.

Moll swiveled her screen in my direction. "Just found it. Guess who? You say you picked the earring up in the grass at Summer Place, right?

What in heavens name would she be doing there?"

I stared at the photo of Ruth Toomey. I didn't answer Mollye, though I had some idea about what might have prompted Ruth to visit. Could she be our arsonist? All Andy and I saw was a blurred image of someone sneaking past Summer Place in a dark hoodie. We assumed it was a man. Maybe we were wrong, dead wrong.

Judge Ursula turned in her chair. She'd heard Moll's "found it" line. The folks seated in the kitchen had moved on to other topics of conversation once brownies were served. They weren't paying attention to the living room outcasts.

"Don't keep us in suspense, Brie," Ursula commanded. "Who owns the mystery earring?"

My mouth went dry. I didn't want to say the name. Several of Udderly's dinner guests had no idea there was any link between Ursula, Amber, and Ruth. They were certain to ask the same question as Mollye: What would Ruth Toomey be doing at Summer Place?

While I pondered what to say, Mollye blurted, "It's Ruth Toomey. Back when the White House made her father's Supreme Court nomination official, Toomey posed with his wife and daughter for a photo op. Ruth's wearing these gavel earrings. I'll bet her dad gave 'em to her in honor of his nomination."

The surprise revelation literally jolted Ursula and Amber out of their seats. Both lost their cool. Jumping up, they knocked the card table askew, sending two plates of brownies and one brownie-and-ice cream bowl crashing to the heart pine floor.

That got everyone's attention.

"What the heck is going on in there?" Eva demanded.

"Mollye just identified an excellent arson suspect." Ursula balled her fists. Her breath came in fast pants. "It appears Ruth Toomey lost an earring while making her escape after setting fire to the cottage. Setting a fire that almost killed Amber and Ursula."

Amber put a hand on her mother's sleeve. "Ursula, you're jumping to conclusions. There's no real evidence against Ruth. For all we know, dozens of people may have those gavel earrings. Or if the earring is hers, she could have lost it before the fire or loaned it to someone else. We'll tell the sheriff about the earring. Let him investigate."

Mollye held up a hand. "Hate to tell you but Sheriff Mason's out of town for his niece's wedding. Lucky for us my fiancé's working tonight. I'll call him."

She pulled her cell from her pocket before anyone could object. "Danny, honey, need you to come to Udderly Kidding Dairy right away."

The room went silent as Mollye listened to the deputy's response. "No, no. No trouble with the True Believers, at least not at the moment. We've uncovered new evidence about the arson at Summer Place."

As soon as she hung up, Mollye scanned the room. "Am I the only one who hasn't a clue why any Toomey would want to torch Brie's cottage? Sure Pastor and Jeannie Nickles are Ruth's grandparents, and they're saying Brie murdered Harriett. But I can't see how that gives Ruth a motive to set the cottage on fire. Come on, what's the story?"

Moll arched her eyebrow as she lasered her tell-all glare at me.

Nope, wasn't going to work. I refused to say a peep. Not my place.

Everyone had abandoned their seats, sensing the electricity in the air. For most, however, the source remained a mystery.

Amber awarded Ursula a sad smile. "Would you let me explain?"

Ursula's chin dipped forward in a small nod.

The police detective offered a sanitized, partial version of the facts for those members of the Udderly assembly who didn't know the background. She explained that Toomey impregnated Ursula while his new wife was pregnant with Ruth. Amber added that Toomey threatened Ursula with dire consequences if she made Amber's parentage public.

"So," the detective summed up, "if Ruth believed knowledge of a bastard child might imperil her father's nomination, she had a credible motive to remove the threat. If the fire killed Ursula and me, problem solved."

Amber provided her recitation in a monotone. Her eyes held the only hint of pain. I knew she'd hoped to become Ruth's friend even if they kept their half-sister relationship secret. It had to cost Amber, accepting the possibility Ruth might have tried to kill her.

The detective's report left out key details—namely, the date-rape aspect of her conception and Toomey's demand that Ursula get an abortion. Amber also gave no hint as to how Ruth might have discovered her father's infidelity.

Why? Did Amber still hope to contain the more salacious aspects of the story? Did she fear she'd damage her relationship with Ursula if she confessed she'd been in touch with Ruth?

Only one thing seemed certain. Amber's strategy—the reason she gave for wanting to meet Ruth in person—couldn't work. Even if Ruth were innocent and wanted to cooperate with Amber, she'd never persuade her father to withdraw his nomination. The carrot had been the promise his secrets would stay buried. Now too many people knew Lawrence Toomey had been unfaithful to his wife. A big part of his damaging secret was no longer secret.

Amber needed to confess that she'd contacted Ruth. If she didn't, I'd speak up. The Sheriff's Office needed the facts, and Ruth's knowledge of her father's infidelity certainly spoke to motive.

FORTY-FIVE

"Andy, why don't you take Cindy on home," Mom suggested. "Think the excitement's over. As soon as we fill the deputy in, we'll all call it a night."

Andy took Mom's hint: she wanted to thin the audience for this drama's second act. Andy and Cindy—I'd already started thinking of them as a couple—left after a quick round of thanks and goodbyes. And no goodnight kiss for Brie.

Billy also departed. If he'd been planning to sleep over, he didn't let on. Said he had early Sunday morning plans. Gave Eva a peck on the cheek and was out the door.

That left the Hooker clan—Mom, Dad, Eva, me—Ursula and Amber, and, of course, Mollye. Still a sizeable crowd. I doubted Mollye would leave even if someone stuck a stick of dynamite in her ear.

Deputy Danny McCoy arrived less than ten minutes after his fiancé's call. With the absent sheriff out of town, he assumed command. Mollye's baby-faced beau always had an eager puppy-dog look about him. Yet his demeanor tonight made me sense he was quite capable of barking and growling if the need arose. His engagement to Moll seemed to have bolstered his self-confidence.

"Who wants to start?" Danny asked as he hung his jacket on one of the pegs by the door. "What's going on?"

The deputy'd been to Udderly often enough to know his way around, and he was acquainted with all the players. He'd sat in on two interviews with Ursula and Amber. The first followed Harriett's luncheon fatality, the second came after the fire. He'd grilled Amber post-fire, too.

Amber, a fellow law enforcement officer, handed Danny the earring and nodded in my direction. "Brie picked this up on the ground at Summer Place the night of the fire. She didn't mention it then because she thought it belonged to Ursula. It doesn't."

Danny held the golden earring up to the light. "So you're thinking a woman set the fire and lost this earring while running away?"

Amber nodded. "Mollye found a photo of Ruth Toomey wearing these same earrings."

"You're nominating Ruth as arsonist?" Danny looked puzzled.

Amber shrugged. "It's possible. And before you ask, she does have a motive." She offered Danny the same edited rehash of Toomey's slimy history.

The deputy's eyes grew wider as she spoke.

"Sorry but one thing doesn't compute." He looked at Ursula. "If you never shared your story with anyone but Iris Hooker until this week, how could Ruth have gotten wind of the potential scandal? Can't imagine Toomey confessing to his daughter."

Good thinking, Danny. I looked at Amber, willing her to come clean.

The detective folded her arms across her chest. "I've been in contact with Ruth for several months. We've spoken on the phone and texted. She's well aware I'm living proof of her father's infidelity."

"What!" Ursula exploded. "How? I didn't even tell you Lawrence Toomey was your father until a couple days ago."

"Science," Amber answered. She explained how sharing her DNA with a genealogical database that also looked for relatives had identified Ruth as her half-sister.

"Why didn't you tell me?" Ursula's face was scarlet. Tears pooled in her eyes.

"I was afraid your hatred for Ruth's father might cloud your view of her," she answered. "I wanted to meet her. Ruth seemed to share my curiosity. I'm sorry."

Amber turned to me. "Brie, you've met Ruth, talked to her. Do you really think she's capable of setting a fire, trying to burn a half-sister alive? I can't believe it."

"What?" Mom's turn. "Brie, when did you talk with Ruth?"

Deputy Danny stepped in. "I'll ask the questions. Brie, have you met Ruth?"

Okay, my turn in the confessional. I told them everything I remembered about my meeting with Ruth, including my unease at her split personality tendencies—friendly one moment, hostile the next. I ended my story with Ruth's agreement to meet Amber at Jamieson Gorge

Nature Park.

"I still should meet Ruth," Amber spoke up. "If she thinks we're alone, I might get her to talk."

"And maybe get yourself killed," Ursula objected.

"I've worked undercover." Amber looked to Danny for approval. "You can come early, get in position, run to the rescue if things go south. It may be our best chance of discovering the truth."

She glanced my way. "I asked Brie to drop me at the park. Told her I'd call for pick-up when we finished. Gave Brie permission to call for help if thirty minutes passed and she hadn't heard from me. Even if Ruth is a killer, I reasoned she wouldn't try anything with Brie as eyewitness to the meeting. The plan's sound. Even better with deputies nearby."

Almost everyone had objections. But, ultimately, Danny approved, and the naysayers were forced to recognize Amber was a trained law enforcement officer and an adult. She knew how to evaluate risks, and she was entitled to make her own decisions.

Once it was evident the plan would go forward, Danny turned to me. "Brie, you've scouted this park. I'd like you to come with Amber and me tomorrow. You can help us figure out the best way to set up before you drop Amber off."

I agreed.

The only people pleased with my decision were Danny and Amber. Even Mollye was out of sorts. Her fiancé made it plain she wasn't invited.

FORTY-SIX

We drove in two cars. Amber and Danny rode with me in my Prius. A sheriff's cruiser followed in our wake, carrying gear and two deputies. Since the—I guess you'd call it a stakeout—would take place outside Danny's jurisdiction, he'd alerted the Greenville Sheriff's Office, and they were sending a deputy observer.

Our route north took us past the Temple of True Believers about eleven a.m. Times for the Sunday worship services marched by repeatedly on the Temple's gaudy neon sign. Today's service started at ten thirty. The parking lot was packed. No doubt Pastor Nickles was inside, preaching fire and brimstone, hurling verbal fireballs toward Brie Hooker, alleged murderer and devil-goat worshipper.

Was the reverend's granddaughter, Ruth, capable of employing real fire to smite perceived enemies? Would she plot to kill an illegitimate half-sister?

Shop talk dominated the conversation between the two law officers, Amber riding shotgun, Danny in back. Since I didn't care how the Ardon County Sheriff's deputies and the Miami police differed in regard to officer training, equipment, pay, or benefits, I tuned out. That left me ample time to wonder why I was needed to play nature park guide. True, I'd visited before, but I hadn't stayed long.

Except for the deep fissure that gave Jamieson Gorge its name, the nature park's geography was unremarkable. Its rolling hills were covered with dense forests. No marsh areas or sinkholes to avoid. No steep pinnacles to serve as handy lookouts.

We were perhaps fifteen minutes from our destination when I noticed the snow. There'd been enough early morning traffic to make the state blacktop a slushy mess. The snow blanketing the woodlands beside the road looked four-to-six-inches deep. While it would probably melt in forty-eight hours, it wasn't likely to disappear before two o'clock, even if the sun came out. And the sun's appearance seemed iffy. Couldn't spot a single break in the thick gray cloud cover.

February ice storms were more common than snow during South Carolina cold snaps. Yet every few years a system dumped several inches of the white stuff. For kids and employees it was cause for celebration. Even a forecast of snow could prompt preemptive school and plant closings. As an Iowa transplant I snickered at this panic until I'd witnessed inexperienced South Carolinians attempting to drive in wintry conditions. There was also a scarcity of snow ploughs. Hard for authorities to justify their expense.

"Well dang." Danny peered out the windshield. "I didn't count on snow. If the park's as deserted as Brie says, we can't all pull into the parking lot and tramp around. Tire and foot tracks would put Ruth on alert. She'd know something was up."

Recalling my conversation with the Greenville official, I made my first contribution to the conversation. "A trail on private property enters the park from the south. I think my contact called it the Smith farm."

I pictured the rim trail I'd circumnavigated and the less-traveled south-facing offshoot. "Park rangers have occasional trouble with poachers using the farm to sneak inside. If the owner knows hunters use his property to trespass, he might not be keen about giving you access."

Danny pointed at a sign announcing a roadside picnic area ahead. "Pull off up there," he said. "May be muddy but we've got enough muscle to push the car out should we get stuck."

Danny called the deputies on our tail and told them to park behind us. "Brie, wait in the car. Amber and I need to chat with the other deputies. Maybe the Greenville deputy who's meeting us knows the Smiths."

My passengers were gone less than five minutes. In that time my hot breath did a bang-up job fogging the front and side windows. I'd turned off the engine along with the defroster and heater when I parked. Didn't need to run the heater with all the clothes I had on.

Given how cold I got on my last Jamieson Gorge visit, I'd dressed for this outing and was singing the praises of the silky long johns under my jeans and the fur-lined boots keeping my tootsies toasty.

Danny opened the door to the back seat and jumped in. "We have a plan. Take the next left. I have directions to the Smith place. The

Greenville deputy got us permission to visit. He'll meet us there."

The condition of the Smith's drive indicated years had passed since any new gravel had been laid down. I did know how to drive in snow and I skated through muddy slush in more than one spot. I parked when I assumed we'd reached the end of the drive. It was hard to tell. A window shade twitched. After two sheriff's cruisers—one from Ardon County, one from Greenville—bookended my Prius, a gaunt woman appeared on the front porch. Wrapped in a heavy coat, she stared at her visitors.

"Mrs. Smith, thanks for allowing us to walk through your property," the Greenville deputy called to her and tipped his hat. "Much appreciated, ma'am."

The woman turned her back, walked inside, and shut the door. Not a word exchanged. Made me wonder what inducements had convinced her to cooperate. Did she have a son in the county jail?

The hiking party set out on the narrow trail. It only allowed two to walk abreast. Sometimes we had to drop back to single file. Danny took the lead with the observing Greenville deputy and the two remaining Ardon deputies assumed rear guard. Amber and I were sandwiched between the men.

"Thanks for coming, Brie," Amber said. "I feel better having you here."

Why? My only contribution was moral support.

Once we reached the park boundary and the gorge rim loop trail, I suggested the officers turn left. It offered the shortest route to the main trail that bisected the nature park. Our group halted twenty feet short of the parking lot to avoid leaving visible footprints in the pristine field of snow. The white camouflage made it much harder for me to pick out the worn spur trails I'd spotted on my earlier visit, but once I found them the deputies veered off in search of observation spots. The ideal spots would keep them hidden yet allow fast access to the parking lot if Amber got in trouble. Three of the deputies settled in to wait, while Amber, Danny, and I hiked back to the Smith farm and retrieved my Prius.

As I chauffeured Amber to the meeting, Danny hid on the backseat floor under a blanket. Actually under two blankets. One wasn't big enough to cover his not-so-dainty body.

Though I was only along to drive and accompanied by two gun-toting officers, my heartbeat's staccato rhythm could have put a drummer to shame. I was frightened for Amber—and yes for me.

As soon as the park entrance came insight, I realized the entry was blocked. A beefy black Cadillac Escalade was parked smack in the middle of the slender blacktop drive.

I recognized the man in the driver's seat. Jack Ford, Ruth's fiancé. I'd seen his picture in the papers and peeking out of gold frames in Ruth's living room. Ruth glanced our way, then slumped back against the passenger side front door.

I slowed the car to a crawl. "This isn't going to be a private meeting." I spoke loud enough for Danny to hear under the blankets. "Ruth brought her lawyer fiancé, Jack Ford. You know the politician who hopes to be South Carolina's next choice for Senator."

"Drive right up beside them." Amber's voice was dead calm. "I have my gun ready just in case. Let's find out what Jack and Ruth have to say."

"Got it. I'm ready, too." Danny's voice was muffled but understandable.

I pulled the Prius parallel to the Escalade. That put Amber's window a few feet opposite Jack's. The glass dividers in both cars powered down in synch.

I feared I'd wet my pants. Was Jack holding a gun out of sight, too?

"Ruth?" Amber had decided to totally ignore the fiancé, talk over him. "I'm Amber, can we speak in private?"

Ruth didn't respond. Her head was bowed. She didn't look up. Her hair hung forward, hiding even her profile.

"You will leave my fiancé alone," Jack growled. "And you will tell your whore mother she'd better leave Lawrence Toomey alone, too. He's a great man. He'll make an excellent Supreme Court Justice. We thought you people would give it up when your blackmail accomplice died. Harriett was a real bitch. She would have sold you out, too. We fight fire with fire."

"What? Harriett? Blackmail?" Amber shouted. "Ruth, what is he talking about? Say something. He's not making sense."

Ruth slowly raised her head and turned in Amber's direction. She swept her fingers through her lanky hair to get it out of her eyes.

I couldn't believe what I saw.

Winking gold, twin gavels.

Ruth wore a matched set of gavel earrings. Either she hadn't lost an earring or someone had commissioned a chest full of the expensive dangles.

I reached over and sunk my fingernails into Amber's thigh to get her attention. "Look at Ruth's ears," I whispered. "Look at her ears."

Jack revved the Escalade's throaty engine. A second later, they left with a fishtail flourish. Ruth and a hundred unanswered questions disappeared down the road.

Danny popped up from the backseat. "What in blazes?"

Blazes indeed. Had Jack just admitted he or one of the Toomeys had killed Harriett and set the Summer Place fire?

FORTY-SEVEN

I made no attempt to follow Ruth and Jack. Danny, Amber and I sat in dazed silence with the car idling in park.

"You saw the earrings, right?" I asked Amber.

"Yes. Doesn't look like Ruth lost one of hers."

"What are you talking about?" Danny asked. While he'd been able to hear what Ford said, the only thing in his field of vision was the underside of the blankets.

"Ruth was wearing a pair of gavel earrings," I explained. "Unless she found someone to make her a replacement or she's stockpiled duplicates, Ruth isn't the person who lost one at Summer Place."

I paused. "Do you suppose Lawrence Toomey handed those gavels out as keepsakes to all the women in his life? I'd sure like to take a peek in his wife's and his mother-in-law's jewelry boxes."

Amber nodded. "That must be it. The earrings were handcrafted, special occasion gifts marking his Supreme Court nomination. Danny, who could give us a list of area jewelry stores that specialize in custom, high-quality gold pieces?"

The deputy rolled his eyes and looked at me. "Do we have any idea who has the skinny on the area's best custom jewelers?" he asked, his voice dripping with sarcasm.

I practically shouted the answer. "Mollye!"

Danny unfolded himself from his floor hideaway. The blankets covering him had teased cowlick tufts of his hair, making them stick out in multiple directions. I fought the urge to giggle. The deputy looked decidedly less commanding and a lot more cuddly.

"Guess I'd better let the deputies who are freezing their butts off know they can pack it up. No meeting today."

He wasn't the only one who should give folks an update. "Is it okay if

I make some calls? My folks, Eva, and Ursula must be sitting on pins and needles. I'd like to let them know we're all okay, completely out of danger."

Danny leaned forward. "How about I have a deputy make those calls. He can pass the word along that everyone's fine and we're headed back to Ardon County. When people start peppering him with questions, he can honestly say he knows squat. I'm not ready to share what Ford said with anyone yet. In Ardon County a secret shared with one person at breakfast tends to be on the radio by noon."

"What will you tell Mollye?" Amber's tone was teasing. "Are you brave enough to call yourself. Or will you sacrifice a fellow officer?"

Having met Moll, the detective rightly guessed Danny's fiancé would relentlessly pester any caller for details. Then there was a related problem. How could we get Moll to give us the jewelry info we wanted without spilling the beans?

I chuckled. "Here's a thought but you'll have to do the calling. Tell Moll you have an idea for a unique wedding gift and want to run it by a few quality jewelers who work in gold."

Danny shook his head. "I'd pay for that lie, probably with a solid gold trinket. But it's not a bad idea. I can pretend someone at work needs info on jewelers, not me."

While the deputy made the necessary calls to fellow officers, I stared off into space. My brain was working overtime, trying to jam puzzle pieces together. It would be so much easier if I had any notion what the finished puzzle was supposed to look like. I had so many questions. What did Ford mean when he called Harriett an accomplice? Had Harriett been blackmailing Toomey? If so, how did the blogger find out that Amber existed?

Ford had me rethinking my suspicions. Could it be someone in the extended Toomey clan really had intended to poison Harriett at the luncheon? Was his comment about fighting fire with fire an analogy or did he know who torched the Summer Place cottage? Finally, what was Ruth's role? Was she a pawn in this homicidal soap opera or a player?

There were too many questions. Maybe we should start with motive. Was Harriett blackmailing Toomey over a bastard child or had she uncovered some other secret? The answer snuck in my brain's backdoor as I catalogued known victims of Harriett's extortion schemes. Of course, Matt Hill!

He'd been cooperating with police trying to catch Harriett red-handed. Danny could chat with those officers. Surely they'd tell an Ardon County deputy all they knew.

Then again, the subject of the sting was dead. Would the police want to waste time diving back into the case when there was no one to prosecute?

FORTY-EIGHT

I shared my brainstorm about the officers involved in Matt Hill's sting operation with Danny. He asked me to reach out to Matt for the names of his contacts.

I looked up Matt's restaurant and phoned the reservations line. The greeter remembered how Paint and I had helped when they were short staffed and scurried off to find Matt.

I told Matt we needed to determine if Harriett had been blackmailing another prominent Greenville victim. Didn't mention a name. Matt was eager to help. "If she took him for a lot of green, maybe the cops can get some of it back for the poor sap."

I didn't explain my real goal was to put the poor sap—or possibly his kin—in jail for murdering Harriett.

At the Sheriff's Office, I sat down as if I'd been invited while Danny and Amber discussed their next moves.

"I called Sheriff Mason last night," he said. "His niece got hitched in Boston so he's stuck there. That Nor'easter's grounded all flights. Told me I was in charge...to use my best instincts. Hope they're good enough. Can't imagine the stink the Quinns will raise if they find out we're investigating their daughter as blackmailer. Then there's Toomey. He'd crucify us for insinuating his jewelry gifts were somehow linked to an arson attempt. We'd better latch on to hard proof before any hint of our suspicions go public."

"That's a good reason to let Brie and me tackle the jewelers," Amber argued. "That is if you get a list from Mollye. It's Sunday. Most retail shops are closed. Hard for your deputies to make discreet inquiries about gold earrings. But a couple of women determined to get a piece of custom jewelry designed for a special occasion? We can finesse it."

Danny shrugged. "I'll call Mollye."

We sat in amused silence eavesdropping on Danny's half of the conversation. Whenever he fibbed, his cherub cheeks turned pink. Good thing he wasn't Skyping. Mollye'd detect each and every prevarication in an instant.

Danny's need to dissemble about the goings on at Jamieson Gorge gave him the most indigestion. He said Ruth never set foot in the nature park. Technically true. He added it was a shame the hoped-for meeting hadn't succeeded in getting Ruth to disclose new information. Kinda true. The only new disclosures came from Jack Ford.

The deputy also fibbed about my whereabouts, saying he had no idea what I might be up to. Since Amber and I had coached Danny about the jewelry, his request for a list of custom jewelers was slightly more suave. He quickly jotted down three names.

By the time the deputy ended the call, beads of perspiration had popped up all along his hairline. That was despite my conviction the Sheriff's Office had set its thermostat in the sixties. Sweating suspects didn't appear to be part of the winter routine.

Danny tore a sheet from his notebook and handed it to me. "Here's the list of jewelers, names, and phone numbers."

"How about loaning us the earring?" Amber asked. "I understand it's evidence but we may need it."

Danny frowned. "Okay. But, Amber, you need to sign for it. Our chain of evidence already has plenty of room for attack. Any defense attorney can point out we only have Brie's word as to when and where the earring was found. Oh, and I want to take a picture first, just in case anything happens."

Did Danny's "in case anything happens" refer to the earring—or to Amber and me?

The deputy retrieved the earring, laid it alongside a ruler on his desk, and snapped close up shots from several angles. Then he dropped the earring in a little baggie and handed it to Amber.

She turned to me. "First let's see if we can charm some jewelers into meeting with us on a Sunday."

"I've met two of them while tagging along with Moll," I volunteered. "Mollye fires pottery pendants and the jewelers make gold pieces—I think they're called bails—to attach the pendants to chains."

"Great. Why don't you call the ones you've met? I don't think you should tell them you're trying to locate the owner of a lost earring. That could backfire. They could hang up and immediately give our top arson suspect a heads-up that we're on her trail."

I agreed with Amber's analysis. "Here's an option. What if I tell them I have a friend who's in a real bind to quickly arrange a commission for custom jewelry? I can pile it on thick, say you have to leave town in the morning."

"Oooh, I like it." Amber patted her jacket's zipped pocket where she'd stowed the gavel earring.

I was pleasantly surprised when the first jeweler immediately recognized my name. I'd never bought a thing when I'd visited with Mollye, just gawked at the price tags on the out-of-my-price range items locked inside the glass showroom counters. But the owner obviously had that valuable retail talent, the ability to remember people. She invited me to bring my friend by.

"I live over the shop. Not a problem to open up for you."

"Hi, Brie," she greeted me. "Glad to see you. Since you're not with Mollye, maybe I can get a word in edgewise and show you some jewelry. Oh, my, you're not wearing any earrings and I see your ears are pierced. With your elegant neck and short, curly hair, drop earrings would look really stunning."

Okay, the woman had a talent for flattering schmooze as well as name recall.

I turned toward Amber. "Actually my friend here is your best prospect for making a sale. I love your work but I'm low on cash. Amber, why don't you tell her what you're looking for?"

"I want a really special gift for my mother and aunt. They're twins and it's their sixtieth birthday. A biggie. They both love custom gold jewelry. I'd like to give them matching earrings, designed exclusively for them. They're both artists. So I'm thinking something like artist palettes dangling from gold chains. Could you do something that detailed?"

The jeweler cocked her head. "Not anymore, I'm afraid." She stared at her hands and rubbed her slightly curled fingers. "Arthritis. I fight it, but it's hard to do really intricate jobs. I'd hoped you were looking for something more flowing, with less detail."

Amber shook her head. "Sorry, I really am set on charm-type earrings. Do you have any recommendations?"

The woman smiled. "Yes, there's a goldsmith in Clemson who does lots of custom work. Very detailed."

We thanked her. Her recommendation coincided with the third name and number on Mollye's list. I phoned the goldsmith, who agreed to meet us at his store in fifteen minutes.

"In the middle of my spiel, I realized it sucked," Amber admitted as we turned into Clemson's Main Street. "I wanted to prompt her to talk about other charm earrings she'd created. But even if she'd made the gavel earrings, there was no guarantee she'd mention them."

I nodded. "Maybe a more straight-forward approach? Tell the jeweler you were out to dinner recently and saw a woman with lovely gold earrings, an intricately carved gavel dangling from the end of a delicate chain. Might he have created them? You're looking for something similar."

"Worth a try," Amber answered. "No mention of an earring being lost. But we get right to the crux of the matter—did he make the earrings?"

The strategy worked. We'd been standing at the counter less than five minutes when the jeweler responded to Amber's opening salvo by bragging he'd made the earrings for a very important customer, Judge Lawrence Toomey, who'd recently been nominated to the Supreme Court. I guess there's no confidentiality agreement with jewelers.

We were primed to ask follow-up questions. No need. The fellow wasn't done talking.

"I actually made three pairs of gavel earrings and three pairs of gavel cufflinks," he boasted. "The judge wanted to present gifts to the women and men in his family. Said they all deserved special gifts for their unwavering support. What a nice man!"

Yeah, he's a real peach.

Amber made a show of being a real buyer, asking questions about carats, costs, and turnaround time for custom work. To grease our escape, she promised to phone from the road with her decision.

Learning how many earrings Toomey commissioned proved relatively easy. Now came the hard part. Finding out who received those gifts and which of the recipients now had one neckid ear.

FORTY-NINE

Amber and I had just reached the car when my phone vibrated.

"You called me?" a gruff male voice asked. "This is Willard Shuman."

Huh? It took a sec for my brain to un-fart and his name to register. "Uh, yes, yes I did. I need a bid for hauling away an outbuilding that burned to the ground."

I didn't describe the rubble as a one-time cottage since I worried "cottage" implied the job was bigger than it was.

"Am I gonna be dealin' with an insurance company?"

"Uh, no. Sorry."

"Nothin' to be sorry 'bout if you got the dough. I charge less when I don't have to fight a paper blizzard. Where's this outbuilding?"

I gave him the address.

"Can ya meet me there now? I'm close, maybe ten minutes. Know it's a Sunday, but I'm tied up all day tomorrow."

"Just a sec." I turned to Amber. "Do you mind stopping by Summer Place for a few minutes? A salvage guy would like to meet now to look at the cottage rubble."

"Sure," Amber answered. "If you promise we can eat as soon as you finish. My stomach's sending rumbling reminders that we missed lunch in all the excitement."

"Deal. Why don't you call Ursula and invite her and my parents to join us? Figure we've held them at bay as long as we can. Surprised Dad hasn't sent out a search party. We can rendezvous at Summer Place. There are beers and a bottle of wine in the fridge. Everyone can have a drink and relax while the demolition guy and I kick charred boards around."

Amber laughed. "You'd like that, wouldn't you? I get to do all the explaining while you're conveniently absent. Yeah, I'll give Ursula a call."

Amber had plenty of time to chat on the phone during our ride from downtown Clemson to Summer Place. It was usually a five-minute drive, but a car accident slowed Highway 123 traffic to a crawl.

"Ursula will meet us at Summer Place," Amber reported. "In spite of your parent's protests, she found a motel room for the night. With the weekend basketball crowd clearing out, rooms are opening up. Ursula promised to call your folks and share the dinner invite."

Good. A welcome postponement of the interrogation I expected as soon as Mom or Dad spoke to me.

For the moment all I had to worry about was Mr. Demolition Man. Fingers crossed he'd take pity on me and name a price somewhat south of my debt limit.

Willard beat us. He'd parked on the street and stood curbside, bent over a metal storage box in the bed of his truck. I gave Amber a key to the sunporch's new lock. "Go on in, and help yourself to beer or wine. This shouldn't take long."

The demo specialist mumbled as he fished around in his storage box. I walked up behind him. When he didn't turn at my approach I cleared my throat. Finally, I tapped his shoulder.

"Hi," I said when he looked up. "I'm Brie Hooker. Thanks for coming."

The leathery-faced man grunted. He definitely spent lots of time outdoors. "Hey. Didn't hear ya." He pointed at a hearing aid. "Blew up a lot of stuff in the Army. Now a herd of elephants could trample me before I heard 'em. I'm huntin' spare batteries. My laser tape measure's gone dead. Ah ha! There they are."

I pulled my jacket tighter and glanced at the sky as Willard plunked new batteries in his high-tech measuring gizmo. Though the official time of sunset was after six o'clock, leaden clouds, thick and brooding had ushered dusk in ahead of schedule.

Willard wasn't exactly a speed demon, and he wasn't a talker either. He took a variety of measurements to calculate the cubic volume of debris. He also picked up what might have been the cottage's fireplace poker to probe the piles of burnt timbers.

"Not much metal to salvage," he mused. "Saw a toilet seat. You gonna want those fireplace stones hauled off or piled somewhere? Might could use them to edge a garden. They're heavy to cart away."

I shrugged. "If it's cheaper to pile the chimney stones, I'll find a use for them."

Willard spit in the grass. Then he pulled a pencil from behind his ear, jotted down some notes to himself, and gave me a price.

I'm not a spitter, but his number was high enough to make me want to hock one up. I doubted I could do better and Willard promised to start bright and early Tuesday morning.

"Okay. Do you need me to sign something?"

"Nah. I've only been nicked once. I drive by here now and again. I see all the work you've been putting in. You ain't the kind to welsh on me."

I walked him to his truck and we shook hands. Then I headed for Summer Place's sunporch. I was surprised no more cars had pulled into my drive. Hated to admit it, but I was kind of hoping Amber would start the explanations without me. I'd have to find something besides alcohol to tide Amber over until our dinner companions arrived. Maybe hummus and corn chips.

When I opened the sunporch door, I was surprised Amber wasn't sitting on the glider. It was the only comfortable place to kick back. I smiled. The poor girl was starving. Maybe she was in the kitchen scavenging for food.

"Amber, where are you? Don't tell me you've fainted from hunger?"

The detective didn't answer. Huh? Had she got tired of waiting and decided to go for a stroll in the neighborhood?

Just in case she hadn't heard me or had her mouth so stuffed she couldn't answer, I decided to check the kitchen.

"Amber?" I called.

My head exploded in pain. What?

FIFTY

I tried to spit. Couldn't. My tongue wouldn't move, held fast.

Willard spit. I never spit. Why do I want to now? What a stupid dream.

Ouch! Something pinched me. Did I need to cut Cashew's toenails again? I turned my head, sandpaper raked my cheek.

My eyes flew open. *Cursed Colby!* Not a dream.

"About time you came around," Amber whispered. "Wondered how long I'd have to keep pinching you. Left your gag in so you wouldn't scream and bring our new friend running. She should have signed up for that Girl Scouts' knot-tying course. Took me all of a minute to undo the ropes once she left."

I frantically blinked, looked down at my gag, then up at Amber repeatedly. Why wasn't she getting my nonverbal signal? *Shut up and yank the blasted gag out of my mouth!* It was wicking every last molecule of saliva from my mouth.

"Don't make a sound," Amber commanded. "Gotta rip off the duct tape holding the gag. It's gonna hurt."

To distract myself from the anticipated pain, I dug my nails into my palms. Brilliant. Now two areas of my body were aflame. But the duct tape rip won hands down for agony. Yikes! How many layers of my lips and cheeks were flayed? Fleeting thought: not waxing any body part, ever.

Amber extracted the red-checked tea towel that had been crammed between my aching jaws. Then she made a victory sign in front of my nose. "How many fingers?" she asked.

"Two." My mouth—I think there was still cotton in it—was so dry I could barely speak. I swallowed and glared at Amber. "If you don't tell me what the heck is happening, you're gonna see one of my fingers."

Amber offered a fleeting smile. "The woman hid behind the kitchen door, clubbed me soon as I walked in. Tied me, gagged me, and dragged me here. My gun and cell phone are gone. She took your cell, too. I patted you down. Sorry. Gotta give the little lady an A-plus for strength and determination. Neither of us are light weights."

Though scared silly, frustration was making me cranky. "Who is SHE?" My voice sounded like a strangled frog. "Or do I need to start pinching your arm black and blue?"

I rubbed the spot Amber must have pinched repeatedly. No doubt I'd be nicely bruised tomorrow. Just hoped I'd see a tomorrow.

Amber shook her head as she worked to untie my hands. "Can't say. The woman's dressed like a ninja who prefers very loose clothes, all black. She's wearing some sort of do-it-yourself hood with holes punched out for her eyes—like a little kid's ghost get-up."

"Think. Surely you can tell which Tommey it is."

"Sorry, no. Ruth's the only one I've seen. The oversized costume makes it hard to even tell the woman's build. Based on your descriptions, Ruth, Esther, and Jeannie are about the same height."

My head felt as if gremlins trapped inside my skull were tunneling a passage to freedom. I blinked, and tried to focus. I needed to get my bearings. Okay. Even in the twilight, I knew my exact location. A shaft of light from one of the newly created skylights—plastic nailed to seal a hole in the roof—spotlighted the ornate cap on the newel post at the base of Summer Place's grand staircase. The distant post served as an interior North Star. I squeezed my eyes shut and pictured Summer Place's layout. She'd dragged us beyond the dining room. The opening to the refurbished kitchen sat perhaps thirty feet to our left.

"Okay, let's leave the question of 'who' for the moment. Any idea what she's planning?" I asked.

"She hasn't spoken a word. But I have a pretty good idea why we're still breathing. Right after I unlocked the sunporch, Ursula phoned. I answered and sat on the glider to chat. The kitchen door's real close. Our captor had to hear every word I said. Ursula said she wasn't quite ready but she'd come to Summer Place as soon as she could. I said I was starved and I'd get downright surly if she didn't get here in the next half hour."

"So our captor knows they're on their way here—Mom, Dad, Ursula?"

"Your folks aren't coming. Since they were ready, they told Ursula they'd go to the restaurant and put our name in for a table and she could swing by here and prod us to hurry up. Apparently Harvest Café doesn't take reservations for its popular Sunday buffet. Have to show up in person to get wait listed for a table."

Thank heaven. Mom and Dad weren't walking into an ambush. But Ursula would be.

The rope that bound my hands fell away. "Thanks." I rubbed my wrists. Having my hands free didn't slow my pulse. The artery in my neck was doing a shimmy as adrenalin pumped blood faster than a fire hose.

"How long before Ursula gets here? Any guess?"

"A guess is about it. When I came around, you were calling my name. Then I heard you grunt and fall. I pretended I was out when the woman hauled you back here and tied you up. I wasn't out very long."

Amber fiddled with her watch. I saw the digits briefly glow but couldn't read the time. "I checked my watch the second I hung up with Ursula, exactly fourteen minutes ago. I planned to harass Ursula if she failed to meet my half-hour deadline. We have fifteen minutes at most, a few minutes less if Ursula's early, a few more if she's tardy. Let's hope she's tardy."

"We need to get moving." I staggered to my feet.

"Where to?" Amber asked. "It's suicide to rush our kidnapper. She has my gun. She's probably in her favorite hiding spot behind the kitchen door hoping to clobber Ursula. Since there's only the one way for us to enter the kitchen, she'd see us the moment we came for her."

"So we make her come to us," I said. "We set a trap. Lure her deeper inside for our own ambush. If we start making noise, she'll have to come after us. Can't let us warn Ursula to stay out and call the cops."

Amber nodded. "If she didn't have a gun before, she does now. Why didn't she kill us both while we were out cold, helpless? That bothers me."

"That bothers you. I'm pretty thrilled to be alive."

"Me, too, but why bother to tie us up? I don't like my answer—once an arsonist, always an arsonist. As soon as Ursula arrives, I bet she plans to burn the place down with all of us inside. If she hopes to make our deaths look accidental, we need to die from smoke inhalation not bullets."

Amber's words brought back the horror of the cottage fire and how nearly we didn't escape. The choking smoke. The scorching heat on my skin.

"Where can we set a trap?" Her question brought me back from the old nightmare to the new one.

"It's getting really dark," she continued. "How can we even find a place to hide without breaking our necks? Didn't you say this place is lousy with rotten and missing floorboards?"

"We need to be careful. Easier to hide if everything's in shadow. I know where there's a flashlight. I keep two—one on each floor in case the electricity goes while I'm working. Since some windows are boarded up, it can get pretty murky even in broad daylight."

"I'm hoping that a flashlight is close by," Amber said.

"My trusty Eveready is right by the staircase," I answered. "It's a heavy-duty sucker. It'll make a good club once we get the drop on her. I'll be right back."

"What if she comes to check on us? I should come with you."

"No, we can't risk making noise. Don't want to spook her. Then she's bound to check on us. I know my way around. You don't. There's a hall closet right around the corner. You can hide there while I retrieve the flashlight. Put your hand on my shoulder. I'll guide you."

I opened the closet door and whispered, "In you go. Stay put till I come back."

I tiptoed toward the staircase, terrified the creaking boards might give me away. If the woman heard me moving, she'd know we were no longer bound and gagged. My staccato breathing wasn't exactly quiet. But terror had seized control of my heart and lungs. Couldn't be helped. I wrapped my fingers around the flashlight and headed back to Amber.

I was halfway between the stairs and closet when I heard a car in the driveway. Ursula!

I started screaming. "Ursula, don't come inside. Call the cops! I'm headed upstairs. Gonna scream bloody murder from the rooftop."

I kept screaming the same warning over and over as I raced to the staircase, no longer worried about creaking boards. Ursula probably couldn't hear me. Might still be in her car, windows rolled up, heater on. But I was darn sure our lady of the fire could hear my bellows. Of course, so could Amber.

Stay in the closet! I wanted to scream, but didn't dare. Just had to trust the detective had enough smarts to wait until our arsonist started chasing me up the stairs before she came out of hiding. I willed Amber to run outside to Ursula's car. *Call the cops.*

I clutched the banister and stuttered to a stop. One of the stair treads wasn't damaged, it was missing. I flicked on the flashlight, pointed the beam up. Which step? Eighth or ninth? The replacement oak board I'd bought but didn't install leaned against the wall, one step up from the missing tread. I switched off the flashlight and resumed my race up the stairs counting...one, two, three.

At eight, I grabbed the wall rail and the outside banister and swung my body up, over the missing step.

With any luck, my pursuer would break her leg or neck. She'd only have time for one astonished scream when her foot failed to connect with anything but air. I smiled in satisfaction as I pictured a face-first crash. If nothing else, a fall had to slow the witch down. Give me time to find a place I could get the drop on her.

I could hear loud footsteps. And her high-pitched curses. Whoever the woman was, she exercised a vocabulary that would have Temple of True Believers hunkered down expecting lightning bolts from on high.

Amber, did you make it outside yet?

I heard our captor start up the stairs. Knowing she was well past Amber's hiding place, I screamed a new warning. "Ursula, Amber stay outside. Call the cops! She's coming upstairs."

My chest heaved as I reached the second floor. I was winded. Unless my pursuer worked out on a Stairmaster, she'd be huffing and puffing, too.

Okay, where to go? I ran down the hall to the front bedroom. Its windows weren't boarded. Maybe I could see Amber and Ursula. Open a window. Make sure someone outside heard my warning screams.

I glanced over my shoulder. *Moldy Muenster!* A narrow beam of light bounced around the stairwell. I'd assumed my flashlight gave me an edge. Never considered the handy-dandy lights built into smart phones. There went my hope of her leg crashing through a missing tread.

I kept running to the front bedroom even though I knew my footsteps would give my destination away. I was desperate to get to a window.

I raced to the window overlooking the sunporch and driveway. In the darkness, I could just make out Ursula's car, headlights on, and two silhouettes.

I unlocked the double hung window, and braced my palms beneath the meeting rail to push up the lower window. Didn't budge. Painted shut. I tried again. Put every ounce of strength I had into muscling it up, breaking the seal. It groaned and moved. I heaved it up.

"I'm up here," I yelled.

"Get out of the house now," Amber screamed back. "She's poured accelerant all over the place. If she strikes a match, it's all over. You can make it. Just climb out the window. Drop down to the porch roof. You've got to get out!"

No! Please no! I can't.

I couldn't jump out into that black void.

The sound of my pursuer's heavy footfalls changed. The woman wasn't light on her feet, and she made no attempt at stealth. She'd reached the second floor. I'd badly miscalculated. She'd see me if I ran back to the door and tried to set up an ambush. She had a clear line of sight.

Lord, help me. I bent over, heaved my upper body through the window. Hung onto the sash for dear life as I wriggled one leg out. I was straddling the sill when I saw the black demon hurtling toward me gun in hand.

"You've ruined everything!" she screamed. "You're going to die."

I was frightened of heights. More terrified of her. Even more afraid of the bullet that just whizzed past my head. I had one bullet hole scar, wasn't looking for another.

I twisted sideways to free my trailing leg from the window frame's clutch. Screamed bloody hell as I tumbled head first out the window, raking my calf on the splintered sill. My hands scrambled for any purchase. I was headed down. I latched on to a drainpipe and held on for dear life. I skidded to a stop as my tennis shoes fought for traction on the slick shingles.

It felt like I'd fallen thirty feet but, if I made a determined effort, the window was within reach. Not that I wanted to go back inside. Yet I wasn't thrilled with my position—my face aimed at the ground like I was about to sled down a hill. I squirmed around so my feet faced the ground.

Police sirens screamed in the distance, but they sounded too far away.

Apparently the black demon heard them, too. "Where are you?" she yelled. "Don't think they're gonna save you. The fire will get you long before they can. You're going with me."

She leaned out the window, brandishing not the gun but a long lighter, the kind you keep handy for lighting fireplaces or tiki torches.

I was not going to let her burn Summer Place.

I kept hold of the drain pipe with my left hand and swung myself back toward the window. With all the strength in my body and all the reach in my arm, I grabbed the business end of the lighter and yanked.

But the stupid woman didn't let go. I tugged harder.

She wriggled farther out the window, head down. Gravity wasn't her friend. She let go of the lighter to try and stop her fall. Her hands clutched at shingles. One of the shingles pulled free from the roof. Then her hands found only air.

Her scream ended when she hit the ground.

I could barely make out what was happening as two shadows ran toward the crumpled lump on the ground. The woman's black outfit made it nearly impossible to distinguish her body from the shrubbery.

"She's dead," Amber called up. "Now get your butt down before you take a header, too. Or a spark sets the building on fire."

My fear surged back. Just how was I supposed to get down? I clung to the downpipe like a life jacket, but I didn't trust it. It had pulled partially free in my tug of war with the woman and dropped me lower on the roof. No way I could reach the window now to crawl back inside.

My eyes were slowly adjusting to the nighttime light, when I was blinded. Someone had backed Ursula's rental car over the edge of an embankment to tilt the car's headlights up. My high wire act now had a spotlight.

Maybe I should have been thrilled someone was trying to help. Instead I was spitting out meat-and-cheese oaths as fast as my lips—semi-peeled by duct tape—could move. Amber actually laughed as her voice floated up.

"You're okay. We can watch and help you. Just do what I say."

"No," I yelled back. "The firemen have ladders. They can get me."

"The place might catch fire before the firetrucks arrive." Amber said. "You need to do something now."

Fine. I held my tongue. And just as I figured, she began to issue orders. "Shinny down that drain pipe about four feet."

Ten minutes later I was on the ground. I wanted to kiss it. I was willing to forgive Amber my scraped arm, and the two branches I'd snapped off a tree before I found one to hold my weight. I was almost willing to forgive her for being so bossy. She hugged me as Danny bolted from the front seat of a sheriff's cruiser and ran to join us.

He looked at me. "You okay? Got two frantic calls. Where's the woman? Still inside?" Danny had his hand on his gun.

"No." Amber inclined her head toward the crumpled body. "I checked for a pulse. Broke her neck when she fell. She's dead."

"Who?" Danny asked as we approached the still form.

Amber'd pulled the hood away to check her pulse.

"Jeannie Nickles," the detective answered. "I suspected it was her."

For a moment, I peered into Jeannie's dead eyes. Her expression suggested surprise. Even in death, her face looked wholesome, grandmotherly. Right. I let my gaze wander.

Oh, no. Her ears. They weren't pierced.

What the Feta?

Jeannie Nickles had not lost a gavel earring. She hadn't lit the cottage on fire.

FIFTY-ONE

I pointed at Jeannie's virgin earlobes. "Jeannie didn't lose a pierced earring. Someone else set the cottage fire."

I didn't name my candidates. Figured the same names were on everyone's lips. Esther and Ruth. I hadn't ruled Ruth out. What had become of that third set of pierced earrings made for Toomey's loved ones? Maybe Ruth conned someone into lending her a replacement. Explained she didn't want her dad to discover she'd lost half of his special gift.

The firetrucks arrived and Danny gave the fire chief a quick update. Chief MacLeod hurried off to inspect the house and assess the fire danger.

Danny took a call on his handheld. He squeezed his eyes shut, doffed his hat, and massaged the bridge of his nose.

"Pastor Nickles is *en route*. One of our deputies picked him up at the Temple after he called 911. Nickles was hysterical. Kept demanding we find his wife before she committed suicide."

"Suicide?" Ursula's voice vibrated with anger.

"Yeah, suicide," Danny answered. "The deputy hasn't been able to calm him down enough to find out why he thought Jeannie wanted to kill herself."

"Or kill others." I muttered.

Amber nodded. "Maybe Jeannie planned both and intended to die with us. Go out in a blaze of glory. Just not sure why."

Ursula had one of those "ah ha" looks. "To save someone she loved. Trade her life. Perhaps to save her daughter or maybe her granddaughter."

Danny took off his jacket and walked over to the body. He draped his coat over Jeannie's pale face. "Don't want the pastor to see Jeannie like this. Not a sight any loved one should see."

"Did the reverend say anything that could help make sense of this?"

Amber asked.

He frowned. "The call was recorded. I'll get the emergency operator to play it back."

We listened to the call. Again and again the pastor repeated the plea to find his wife, then he cried, "I'm not strong enough to protect Esther. The girl needs her mother. Oh, Jeannie, don't leave me. Please God, why have you abandoned me?"

I'd seen Pastor Nickles' face up close and personal. His hate almost a physical force. On this call his strangled voice communicated a different emotion. The man was inconsolable.

His pain was real. Though I didn't want to, I pitied him.

I noticed the fire chief walking toward us. I held my breath, my mind awhirl with bleak visions. Would he tell the firefighters to light Summer Place ablaze? Do a controlled burn to protect the neighborhood? Ever since I heard the word "accelerant" I'd feared the worst.

"The arsonist used gasoline," Chief MacLeod began. "Only found one empty container. Splashed gas around the structure's ground floor." He paused to glance my way. "None in the portions you've renovated, Brie.

"Gas is volatile and will evaporate rapidly if we encourage it by bringing in big fans and opening every window. We'll monitor the building to make sure there's no ignition source. The danger should pass by morning."

Couldn't help myself. The breath I'd been holding whooshed out as I threw my arms around the fire chief and gave him a fierce hug. "Thank you so much. I was so afraid Summer Place was lost."

My gratitude seemed to embarrass Chief MacLeod. He cleared his throat and I stepped back. "Um, okay then, I need to talk with our men. I'll keep you posted." He hurried off into the night, which now had a Swiss cheese peek-a-boo likeness. Portable lights poked lots of bright white holes in the blackness.

Danny took another call. "The Pastor just arrived." He looked at the ground and kicked at loose gravel with his right shoe. "Sure wish I knew the right thing to do. Maybe we should check the reverend into a hospital before we tell him Jeannie's dead."

Amber touched his sleeve. "I know. You're wondering if there's anything to be gained by questioning him with his dead wife's body in plain view. There's no right answer. But it might be your best chance to get the reverend to spill what he knows."

Danny nodded. "All right. But you three need to get out of sight. The man's been telling his congregation Brie's a murderer." Danny looked at me, then nodded at Ursula and Amber. "Haven't heard if he's denounced you two publicly, but seeing strangers could set him off. Go sit in the cruiser."

"Danny's right," Amber said. "No point arguing."

The deputy's cruiser gave us orchestra seats for the upcoming drama even though we wouldn't have an audio track.

We watched as Danny put his arm around Nickles and spoke to him. The reverend shook the deputy off, ran to the body, and pulled the jacket away from Jeannie's face. Then he fell to the ground, his whole body convulsing with sobs.

Danny and another deputy tore him away from Jeannie and helped him up. Nothing to gain, I thought. Take him to the hospital.

A woman rushed in and cradled the pastor in her arms.

She turned her head. Ruth.

I couldn't hear her words, but felt certain she'd refuse to let anyone talk with her grandfather in his current state.

Danny signaled the paramedics, who quickly escorted the pastor to an ambulance. The only surprise? Ruth didn't go with him. She stayed and spoke to Danny. Whatever she said prompted the deputy to hustle over to the squad car where we huddled. "I'm taking Ruth to the Sheriff's Office," he said. "She says she's ready to make a statement, and she wants all three of you there."

I'd thought the evening couldn't hold more surprises. This was a big one.

What was the woman thinking?

FIFTY-TWO

I called Mom and Dad who'd been waiting impatiently for us at Harvest Café. "What the heck happened to you? We snapped up a large table and people are glaring at us and the empty chairs," Mom began. "I hope you're *en route.*"

I cut off her complaint. "We're not coming." I quickly explained the circumstances. As Mom gasped repeatedly, I could hear Dad's worried voice in the background. "What's wrong, dear?"

I promised Mom that Ursula, Amber and I would come see them no matter what time we left the Sheriff's Office.

"Please have hot coffee and plenty to eat," I added, trying to lighten the mood.

The hind end of Ursula's rental car was stuck in the embankment she'd backed over. Her good deed—aiming the car's headlamps to light my high wire act—meant we'd need a tow truck to free the car. So I drove Amber and Ursula to the Sheriff's Office. Ruth rode in the sheriff's cruiser with Danny. I noticed she sat up front, not in back like a criminal. I stayed on the cruiser's bumper.

However, they ditched us at the Sheriff's Office when Danny dropped Ruth curbside and parked out front. We practically had to park in the adjacent soy bean field. When we trudged in from the cold, the woman at the front desk motioned us down the hall. "Conference room on the left, three doors down." Ruth was already seated. Danny was pouring her coffee. "Cream or sugar?" he asked.

"Neither, thanks, Danny," she answered. "I take it black."

Her use of the deputy's first name reminded me what a small community this was. Of course, Ruth knew Danny McCoy. Though she now lived in Greenville, she'd grown up in Ardon County, went to school here, spent plenty of Sundays parked on a pew at the Temple of True Believers listening to her grandfather, Reverend Nickles, preach.

Toomey's legitimate daughter nodded at the three of us. Her gaze lingered on Amber, her half-sister. "I'm sorry for all you've been through. I told Danny you deserved an explanation. I wanted you to know you're all safe now that my grandmother and mother are dead."

"Your mother's dead? When?" Ursula asked.

"She overdosed tonight. Suicide. Before she killed herself, she posted on Facebook. Said she'd be long dead before the post appeared. The post was a confession." Tears pooled in Ruth's eyes. "I'd hoped to get here in time to save my grandmother."

The tears failed to move me. Ruth had a hand in this. Her fiancé's threat suggested she either suspected or knew what was going on. Yet she'd done nothing to warn anyone or stop the madness.

Danny insisted on reading Ruth her rights and getting her permission to record the conversation. She waved a hand in a don't-bother-me gesture. Given that her father and fiancé were lawyers, I couldn't believe she wanted to proceed without counsel. Did she feel she was blameless? Or did she think refusing a lawyer would make us more inclined to think she was an innocent?

Ruth looked over at Danny. "Recording on? Should I begin?"

He nodded. "Please state your name and address for the record."

Danny's protocol included naming everyone present and getting Ruth on tape waiving her right to legal counsel. Finally, he nodded. "Go ahead, Ruth."

The woman locked eyes with Amber. "After you contacted me, I told my fiancé, Jack Ford, I had a half-sister. Jack was convinced your contact was a prelude to blackmail. I disagreed and begged him not to tell Dad or Mom about you. Mother's always been emotionally unstable. Often so depressed she couldn't sleep and wouldn't eat.

"Jack promised," she continued. "In his mind, he kept that promise. He talked to my grandmother, figuring if there'd been a 'love child' she'd know who the mother was. Too bad Harriett Quinn dropped by the church. When she overheard a snatch of interesting conversation, she hid and eavesdropped. The blackmail started a few days later."

Danny interrupted at this point. "Who did Harriett contact? You or your father?"

"The first letter was mailed to Dad at home," Ruth answered. "Mom opened it. Every so often, Mom would stop taking her prescribed anti-depressants and go on a self-medicating binge. This was one of these times. She became extremely paranoid."

Ursula rapped on the table to get Ruth's attention. Guess she was missing her gavel. "Back up. Did your mother keep the letter or give it to your father?"

Ruth nodded. "She gave it to Dad. He decided to pay off Harriett, who only heard the bastard child's name was Amber. She never learned Ursula was the mother."

I saw Amber flinch at Ruth's use of the term "bastard".

"What did your mother do?" Danny asked.

"She killed Harriett." Ruth answered as calmly as if she'd said her mother'd baked cookies. "Mom may have been psychotic, but she was smart. She tuned into Ardon County gossip, learned Harriett suffered from heartburn and practically bought cimetidine by the case."

Danny interrupted again. "Esther didn't have any medical training. How did she know how to poison Harriett?"

"She'd listened to me rave about drug interactions, so she looked up cimetidine to see if someone taking it might die if they ingested another drug. She found theophylline would do the trick. Brie's tasting provided a perfect opportunity. On her blog, Harriett bragged about when and where she'd be stuffing her face."

Danny's eyebrows practically crossed when he scowled at Ruth. "Theophylline's a prescription drug, right? How did your mother get her hands on it?" he asked.

I silently applauded the question. Working at an urgent care facility, Ruth could easily have forged a scrip.

Ruth shrugged but had a ready answer. "Mom often visited me at work. She could have easily stolen a prescription pad or even palmed a bottle of theophylline when I wasn't looking."

My turn to grill Ruth. "Does your mother own a truck? How did she break into Summer Place? Was she alone?"

Ruth looked peeved by my interruption. Her hazel eyes held no warmth as she focused on me. I was the first to play chicken and blink.

"My mother acted alone," she said. "I have no idea how she broke in.

She did say she borrowed my cousin's truck. Told him reporters knew her car and wouldn't quit pestering her once Dad gained celebrity status."

Ruth finally broke eye contact and stared at her twined fingers. "When Harriett died, Grandmother Jeannie suspected Mom had killed her. To encourage the investigation veering off in a different direction, Grandmother promoted Brie as the killer. The goat incident and Karen's death made Brie a convenient suspect. She wound Grandfather Nickles into a rage. He actually believed Brie killed Karen and Harriett."

What a loving Christian woman. What was her motto? Screw the innocent.

Ursula cleared her throat. "So your mother only intended to poison Harriett?"

Ruth sipped her coffee, and made a face either at its taste or temperature. "Oh, I'm sure Mom would have tried to poison you, too, had she known you were Amber's mother. She didn't learn that tidbit until Dad left for D.C. Mom overheard Jack and me arguing over Amber. That's when she found out you and Amber were staying at the Summer Place cottage."

Ruth held up her hands in a stop motion. "Mom's suicide post only says she watched until she was certain mother and daughter were inside the cottage before she set fire to it."

This admission of guilt stunned us silent. No one said a word. The only sound was Danny's pen scratching paper as he scribbled notes. When he finished writing, he studied Ruth. Frowning, his eyebrows knotted, Danny no longer appeared the gregarious deputy.

We all jumped when a deputy opened the door to the conference room. "Danny I really need to see you," he said.

Danny didn't look pleased by the interruption. "I'll be right back."

We sat in complete silence until Danny returned five minutes later and resumed his questioning. "Earlier you said you drove to Ardon County to try and save your grandmother's life. What made you believe Jeannie needed saving?"

Ruth propped her elbows on the table and dropped her head into her hands. "Granddad Nickles called. Back before Grandmother married him, Granddad suffered a brain injury. Sometimes he gets very confused. Before she left tonight, my grandmother tried to explain she was about to do something dangerous and she might die. Told him if she succeeded, all the family's worries would vanish, and she'd save their daughter from jail.

"I don't know any more than that. I have no details about the arson. I do know Grandmother Jeannie saw that newspaper picture of Brie wearing a gavel earring. She called and asked if I'd lost one. When I said no, she must have figured it belonged to Mom."

"Wait," I said. "Your father commissioned three sets of earrings. You and your mother had two sets. Who had the third? How could Jeannie leap to the conclusion the lost earring belonged to your mother?"

Ruth's dismissive laugh was mocking. "Easy. Dad gave the third set of earrings to his mother. Grandmother Helen is in a wheelchair."

She tapped her finger on the copy of the suicide post that sat on the table in front of Danny. "Mom's confession—it's all there. Though Dad was paying the blackmail, he knew nothing of Mom's or Grandmother's actions. And I only discovered the truth after the fact."

"After the fact?" I piped up. "Then why did your fiancé say Amber and Ursula should have gotten the message after Harriett died?"

Ruth's face flushed as she glared at me. "I'm sure it was just a figure of speech that all blackmailers get their just due."

Yeah, right.

"Grandmother's actions were in a way heroic," Ruth said, changing the subject. "She must have believed if she died with Ursula, Amber, and Brie, everyone would assume she'd set the cottage fire. Who would think to check and see if a charred corpse had pierced ears?"

Ruth looked around the table. "I've told you everything I know. Again, I'm sorry for your pain. But my father and grandfather need me. I have to go."

"I'm afraid not," Danny said. "You're under arrest for attempted murder. Your mother's alive. You set out pills for her to take, told her to take all of them. She felt nauseous, decided to wait and take the pills later. Esther was quite confused when the EMTs arrived. She also denied scheduling a Facebook post to go live hours after it was written. Said she had no idea anyone could even do that."

Ruth swallowed. Tried to look unruffled. "Mother's just confused. Thank heavens she's still alive." Ruth's expression wasn't exactly one of joy.

FIFTY-THREE

I kept my promise and drove directly to my parents' house when we left the Sheriff's Office. Well, not directly. I took a small detour past Summer Place to assure myself it hadn't burned to the ground. Seeing firefighters standing watch boosted my optimism.

Eva opened the door at my parents' house and gave me a crushing hug. I wasn't surprised that Dad had called Aunt Eva and invited her to sit in on the mystery wrap-up.

Mom kept her side of the bargain, pouring hot coffee with liberal additions of spirits, and setting out a cold buffet with something for every diet. I was quite content with peanut butter on toast, an apple, and Oreos—yes they are vegan fare. No animal products. But I do avoid scanning the list of unpronounceable chemicals in the ingredient listing.

"Do you think Ruth will get away with trying to murder her mother?" I asked Ursula and Amber. "Esther may well recant to save her daughter. Claim she contemplated suicide and wrote the Facebook post before she chickened out. Ruth spun a good tale painting herself and her dad as innocent victims. In her version, her father's only offense was failing to report the blackmail."

"She'd hoped all the parties painted as guilty would be conveniently dead," Aunt Eva offered. "Hope there's some way to prove Ruth used her mom's computer to schedule that Facebook post."

"I really wanted to believe her." Amber sighed. "But I'm a cop. Healthy suspicion comes with the territory. It's unclear when Ruth became involved, but even if her mother did poison Harriett and light the cottage fire, she has to share in the guilt. And trying to murder her own mother. Wow."

"I'll urge the Sheriff's Office to check out Ruth's and Ford's alibis for the night the food was poisoned and the cottage torched," Mom said.

"Ruth could be telling the truth about that part of the story or it could be a total fabrication. Maybe Jeannie was trying to protect her granddaughter, not her daughter."

Out of the corner of my eye, I saw Amber bite her lip. Her eyes closed for a minute. She straightened. "Even if we're never able to determine the truth, the guilty will suffer."

Ursula nodded.

Mom squeezed Ursula's hand. "Are you still planning to confront Toomey?"

"No need. The powers that be will politely tell him that he needs to bow out. Too much baggage. His daughter's being tried for attempted murder; his mother-in-law died in the act of attempted murder. The reason one of the Toomeys killed Harriet—blackmail about a 'love child'— can't be kept secret.

Mom patted Ursula's arm. "You're okay with this? Your goal from the start was to stymie Toomey's nomination while protecting Amber's privacy. It looks like you've succeeded, just not how you planned."

Ursula smiled at her daughter. "I just hope the next time Amber and I get together neither of us has to visit a hospital, flee a fire, or outwit a murderer."

"Amen to that," Dad said.

I had my own reason to smile. "Whatever information does or doesn't become public, Danny promised to repeat *ad nauseam* that I, Brie Hooker, an innocent, was callously framed as a food-poisoner and killer."

My aunt, who'd been exceptionally quiet, had the evening's last word. "It's way past time for my niece and me to head home to Udderly. I left Billy in charge, and danged if he didn't just call with the news we have five new baby kids."

FIFTY-FOUR

I called Andy mid-morning and asked if he could drop by Udderly sometime during the day. I didn't mention anything about the evening, though we were supposed to have a standing date since it was Animal Passion week.

My breath caught when I saw him arrive with a dozen roses. How could I tell this sweet man my decision? *You have to do it, Brie. It isn't fair to lead him on.*

Andy bowed slightly from the waist as he presented me with the flowers. He kissed one cheek, then the other like it was a formal occasion.

"I appreciate you wanting to break the news to me in person and in private." He grinned. "I brought the flowers to say I'm happy for you and Paint."

The veterinarian chuckled at my open-mouth astonishment. "Hey, Brie, you're no better than I am at hiding emotions. I've known for weeks how the winds of fate were blowing, and I couldn't help but notice you practically pushed me into Cindy's arms."

"Oh, Andy. You do know I love you, it's just..."

"Say no more." He put two fingers against my lips. "Let's leave it at that. I love you, too, and we'll always be friends. Say, does Paint know yet? He's not as intuitive as me."

"No, I haven't told him."

"Well, make sure you torture him a little. He's my best friend, but he does deserve a bit of torment before he's declared the winner."

I told Paint I knew it wasn't Brewing Trouble week, but hoped he might be free to stop by late afternoon.

When he reached the Udderly cabin, I kissed him.

He wagged a finger at me. "Hey, that's not allowed. While I'm all for breaking the rules, Andy will call foul."

"No, he won't," I answered. "He already knows I planned to give you a surprise Valentine's Day present."

Paint arched an eyebrow and grinned. "Oh, yeah, and what might that be?"

I handed him a Valentine's Day card. He opened it and looked a bit puzzled as he studied the gift certificate inside.

"A certificate for a Couple's Massage at some posh Greenville spa? I've never been to a masseuse."

"Well, let me tell you what happens." I smiled. "When you arrive, you have to take off your clothes...And so do I."

He grinned as recognition dawned. "Ah, you'll be neckid with me on a date?"

I laughed. "You've got the picture."

"So, from now on, every week is Brewing Trouble week?"

"That's exactly what it means."

LINDA LOVELY

Linda Lovely finds writing pure fiction isn't a huge stretch given the years she's spent penning PR and ad copy. Linda writes a blend of mystery and humor, chuckling as she plots to "disappear" the types of characters who most annoy her. Quite satisfying plus there's no need to pester relatives for bail. Her newest series offers good-natured salutes to both her vegan family doctor and her cheese-addicted kin. She's an enthusiastic Sisters in Crime member and helps organize the popular Writers' Police Academy. When not writing or reading, Linda takes long walks with her husband, swims, gardens, and plays tennis.

Henery Press Mystery Books

And finally, before you go...
Here are a few other mysteries
you might enjoy:

I SCREAM, YOU SCREAM
Wendy Lyn Watson

A Mystery A-la-mode (#1)

Tallulah Jones's whole world is melting. Her ice cream parlor, Remember the A-la-mode, is struggling, and she's stooped to catering a party for her sleezeball ex-husband Wayne and his arm candy girlfriend Brittany. Worst of all? Her dreamy high school sweetheart shows up on her front porch, swirling up feelings Tally doesn't have time to deal with.

Things go from ugly to plain old awful when Brittany turns up dead and all eyes turn to Tally as the murderer. With the help of her hell-raising cousin Bree, her precocious niece Alice, and her long-lost-super-confusing love Finn, Tally has to dip into the heart of Dalliance, Texas's most scandalous secrets to catch a murderer before someone puts Tally and her dreams on ice for good.

Available at booksellers nationwide and online

Visit www.henerypress.com for details

THE SEMESTER OF OUR DISCONTENT
Cynthia Kuhn

A Lila Maclean Academic Mystery (#1)

English professor Lila Maclean is thrilled about her new job at prestigious Stonedale University, until she finds one of her colleagues dead. She soon learns that everyone, from the chancellor to the detective working the case, believes Lila—or someone she is protecting—may be responsible for the horrific event, so she assigns herself the task of identifying the killer.

Putting her scholarly skills to the test, Lila gathers evidence, but her search is complicated by an unexpected nemesis, a suspicious investigator, and an ominous secret society. Rather than earning an "A" for effort, she receives a threat featuring the mysterious emblem and must act quickly to avoid failing her assignment...and becoming the next victim.

Available at booksellers nationwide and online

Visit www.henerypress.com for details

NOT A CREATURE WAS STIRRING

Christina Freeburn

A Merry & Bright Handcrafted Mystery (#1)

Empty nester Merry Winters loves three things: Christmas, crafting and her family. To regain purpose and joy, Merry hits the road to a Christmas vendor event with her furry sidekick Ebenezer in her new mobile crafting sleigh, aka an RV.

But it soon turns into the nightmare before Christmas when Merry unwraps her Scrooge of an ex-husband's body in one of the RV's compartments. Add to that his missing winning lottery ticket believed to be stashed somewhere in the RV, leading the homicide detective and Merry's stepdaughter to believe Merry is the one whodunit.

With visions of prison dancing in her head, will Merry be able to solve this Christmas calamity before she's locked away?

Available at booksellers nationwide and online

Visit www.henerypress.com for details

A MUDDIED MURDER

Wendy Tyson

A Greenhouse Mystery (#1)

When Megan Sawyer gives up her big-city law career to care for her grandmother and run the family's organic farm and café, she expects to find peace and tranquility in her scenic hometown of Winsome, Pennsylvania. Instead, her goat goes missing, rain muddies her fields, the town denies her business permits, and her family's Colonial-era farm sucks up the remains of her savings.

Just when she thinks she's reached the bottom of the rain barrel, Megan and the town's hunky veterinarian discover the local zoning commissioner's battered body in her barn. Now Megan's thrust into the middle of a murder investigation—and she's the chief suspect. Can Megan dig through small-town secrets, local politics, and old grievances in time to find a killer before that killer strikes again?

Available at booksellers nationwide and online

Visit www.henerypress.com for details

Made in the USA
Middletown, DE
18 April 2019